ACCLAIM FOR BETH WISEMAN

Hopefully Ever After

"Beth Wiseman has done it again—a story of love, hope, and rising above our circumstances. You don't want to miss this one."

—Vannetta Chapman, *USA TODAY* bestselling author of the Indiana Amish Brides series

The Story of Love

"Beth Wiseman's *The Story of Love* had me turning the pages as quickly as I could read them. Her compelling unpredictable romance between two strong characters with complicated lives plays out beautifully, one unexpected turn after another. Beth has done it again."

—Patricia Davids, *USA TODAY* bestselling author of Amish romance

The Bookseller's Promise

"*The Bookseller's Promise* beautifully illustrates the power of love, family bonds, and the good news of the gospel . . . A captivating story of discovering faith and finding hope in the midst of despair."

—Jennifer Beckstrand, author of The Matchmakers of Huckleberry Hill series

A Season of Change

"A beautiful story about love, forgiveness, and finding family in an unexpected place."

—Kathleen Fuller, *USA TODAY* bestselling author

An Unlikely Match

"With multiple vibrant story lines, Wiseman's excellent tale will have readers anticipating the next. Any fan of Amish romance will love this."

—*Publishers Weekly*

"This was such a sweet story. I cheered on Evelyn and Jayce the whole way. Jayce is having issues with his difficult father, who's brought a Hollywood crew to Amish country to film a scene in a nearby cave. Evelyn has a strong, supportive family, so she feels for Jayce immediately. As they grow closer and help each other overcome fears and phobias, they know this can't last. But God, and two persnickety Amish sisters, Lizzie and Esther, have other plans. Can a Hollywood boy fall for an Amish girl and make it work? Find out. Read this delightful, heartwarming story!"

—Lenora Worth, author of *Their Amish Reunion*

"Beth Wiseman's *An Unlikely Match* will keep you turning the pages as you are pulled into this heartwarming and unpredictable Amish romance story about Evelyn and Jayce, two interesting and compelling characters. Beth doesn't disappoint, keeping you guessing as to how this story will end."

—Molly Jebber, bestselling Amish inspirational historical romance author

A Picture of Love

"This is a warm story of romance and second chances with some great characters that fans of the genre will love."

—*Parkersburg News & Sentinel*

"Beth Wiseman's *A Picture of Love* will delight readers of Amish fiction. Naomi and Amos's romance is a heartfelt story of love, forgiveness, and second chances. This book has everything readers love about a Beth Wiseman story—an authentic portrait of the Amish community, humor, the power of grace and hope, and, above all, faith in God's Word and His promises."

—Amy Clipston, bestselling author of the Amish Legacy series

A Beautiful Arrangement

"*A Beautiful Arrangement* has everything you want in an escape novel."

—*Amish Heartland*

"Wiseman's delightful third installment of the Amish Journey series centers on the struggles and unexpected joys of a marriage of convenience . . . Series devotees and newcomers alike will find this engrossing romance hard to put down."

—*Publishers Weekly*

"*A Beautiful Arrangement* has so much heart, you won't want to put it down until you've read the last page. I love second-chance love stories, and Lydia and Samuel's story is heartbreaking and sweet with unexpected twists and turns that make their journey to love all the more satisfying. Beth's fans will cherish this book."

—Jennifer Beckstrand, author of The Petersheim Brothers series

Listening to Love

"Wiseman is at her best in this surprising tale of love and faith."

—*Publishers Weekly*

"I always find Beth Wiseman's books to be both tenderly romantic and thought provoking. She has a way of setting a scene that makes me feel like I'm part of an Amish community and visiting for supper. I loved the title of this book, the message about faith and God, and the heartfelt romance between Lucas and Natalie. *Listening to Love* has everything I love in a Beth Wiseman novel—a strong faith message, a touching romance, and a beautiful sense of place. Beth is such an incredibly gifted storyteller."

—Shelley Shepard Gray, bestselling author

"*Listening to Love* is vintage Beth Wiseman . . . Clear your calendar because you're going to want to read this one in a single sitting."

—Vannetta Chapman, *USA TODAY* bestselling author of the Indiana Amish Brides series

Hearts in Harmony

"This is a sweet story, not only of romance, but of older generations and younger generations coming together in friendship. It's a tearjerker as well as an uplifting story."

—Parkersburg News & Sentinel

"Beth Wiseman has penned a poignant story of friendship, faith, and love that is sure to touch readers' hearts."

—Kathleen Fuller, *USA TODAY* bestselling author

"Beth Wiseman's *Hearts in Harmony* is a lyrical hymn. Mary and Levi are heartwarming, lovable characters who instantly feel like dear friends. Once readers open this book, they won't put it down until they've reached the last page."

—Amy Clipston, bestselling author of the Amish Legacy series

HOPEFULLY *EVER* AFTER

Other Books by Beth Wiseman

The Amish Bookstore Novels

The Bookseller's Promise

The Story of Love

Hopefully Ever After

The Amish Inn Novels

A Picture of Love

An Unlikely Match

A Season of Change

The Amish Journey Novels

Hearts in Harmony

Listening to Love

A Beautiful Arrangement

The Amish Secrets Novels

Her Brother's Keeper

Love Bears All Things

Home All Along

The Land of Canaan Novels

Seek Me with All Your Heart

The Wonder of Your Love

His Love Endures Forever

The Daughters of the Promise Novels

Plain Perfect

Plain Pursuit

Plain Promise

Plain Paradise

Plain Proposal

Plain Peace

Other Novels

Need You Now

The House that Love Built

The Promise

Story Collections

An Amish Year

Amish Celebrations

Stories

A Choice to Forgive included in *An Amish Christmas*

A Change of Heart included in *An Amish Gathering*

Healing Hearts included in *An Amish Love*

A Perfect Plan included in *An Amish Wedding*

A Recipe for Hope included in *An Amish Kitchen*

Always Beautiful included in *An Amish Miracle*

Rooted in Love included in *An Amish Garden*

When Christmas Comes Again included in *An Amish Second Christmas*

In His Father's Arms included in *An Amish Cradle*

A Cup Half Full included in *An Amish Home*

The Cedar Chest included in *An Amish Heirloom*

When Love Returns included in *An Amish Homecoming*

A Reunion of Hearts included in *An Amish Reunion*

Loaves of Love included in *An Amish Christmas Bakery*

HOPEFULLY *EVER* AFTER

AN AMISH BOOKSTORE NOVEL

BETH WISEMAN

ZONDERVAN

Hopefully Ever After

Requests for information should be addressed to:
Zondervan, *3900 Sparks Dr. SE, Grand Rapids, Michigan 49546*

Library of Congress Cataloging-in-Publication Data

Names: Wiseman, Beth, 1962- author.
Title: Hopefully ever after / Beth Wiseman.
Description: Nashville, Tennessee : Zondervan, [2023] | Series: An Amish bookstore novel ; [3] | Summary: "In the third and final novel of Beth Wiseman's Amish Bookstore series, two young people must find the courage to defy expectations and become who they're meant to be. Sixteen-year-old Eden Hale doesn't want to be defined by her current circumstances. Her mother is in prison, she doesn't know her father, and she's had her own run-ins with the law, but Eden refuses to become what people expect. When she is sent to live with an Amish cousin she's never met in Montgomery, Indiana, she welcomes the chance to become the person she wants to be without the burden of anyone's judgment. Her hopes are confirmed when she meets Samuel, a young Amish man who seems to like her for who she really is.
Samuel Byler has grown up with strict Amish parents, and they aren't happy that their only son is choosing to spend his free time with an outsider. As Eden and Samuel grow closer, assumptions close in around the young couple. It isn't long before Eden starts to doubt herself and wonders if she is doomed to follow in her mother's footsteps, whether she wants to or not. Meanwhile, Samuel finds himself slipping further and further from his faith—to Eden's dismay.
Both Eden and Samuel's futures hang in the balance as they face decisions about who they are-both as individuals and together"--Provided by publisher.
Identifiers: LCCN 2022047474 (print) | LCCN 2022047475 (ebook) | ISBN 9780310365693 (paperback) | ISBN 9780310365723 (library binding) | ISBN 9780310365709 (epub) | ISBN 9780310365716
Subjects: BISAC: FICTION / Romance / Clean & Wholesome | FICTION / Christian / Romance / General | LCGFT: Christian fiction. | Novels.
Classification: LCC PS3623.I83 H67 2023 (print) | LCC PS3623.I83 (ebook) | DDC 813/.6--dc23/eng/20221207
LC record available at https://lccn.loc.gov/2022047474
LC ebook record available at https://lccn.loc.gov/2022047475

Printed in the United States of America

23 24 25 26 27 LBC 5 4 3 2 1

To my street team, Wiseman's Warriors. You gals rock!

GLOSSARY

ab im kopp: crazy (lit: "addled in the head")
ach: [exclamation]
boppli: baby
bruder: brother
daadi: father
daadi haus: parents' small house on property
danki: thanks
Deitsch: Dutch
dochder: daughter
Englisch: non-Amish folk/English language
fraa: wife
Gott: God
grossdaadi: grandfather
gut: good
kaffi: coffee
kinner: children
lieb: love
maedel: girl, young woman
maed: girls, young women
mamm: mom
mei: my

mudder: mother
nee: no
onkel: uncle
Ordnung: the unwritten rules of the Amish
rumschpringe: adolescent rite of passage (lit: "jumping around")
schweeger: brother-in-law
schweschder/schweschdere: sister/sisters
sohn: son
urgrossvadder: great-grandfather
Wie bischt: Hello/how are you
wunderbar: wonderful
ya: yes

PROLOGUE

Yvonne sat beside her husband on the couch with their dog, Blue, curled up by their feet and snoring softly. Abraham rubbed his beard, something he did when he was thinking. Eight months into their marriage, Yvonne was still getting used to his facial hair. She would never see his clean-shaven face again, since once Amish men were married, they never trimmed their beards.

She waited as Abraham reprocessed the information Yvonne had shared with him just now, a repeat from what she'd told him a month ago.

Yvonne had reservations about bringing a troubled teenager into their home, even if the girl was a distant cousin, but Abraham had assured her it would be all right. Selfishly, she had hesitated when asked to welcome the sixteen-year-old guest into their home for four weeks. Yvonne and Abraham were still in the honeymoon phase of their relationship, but it was a huge favor to her aunt, who had raised Yvonne.

"It's only for a month." Her husband shrugged as he glanced her way. "I'm sure it will be fine."

"Like I told you before, Aunt Emma said Eden's mother

went to prison, she never knew her father, and she's had a few minor scrapes with the law. Shoplifting, I think."

"Tell me again how she's related to you?" Abraham looped his thumbs beneath his suspenders as he leaned into the couch cushions and eased his bare feet onto the coffee table. A muscle clenched along his jaw, and Yvonne wondered if he was having second thoughts.

"As I explained before . . ." Yvonne took a deep breath. It was too late to cancel the commitment they'd already made to act as guardians to Eden. "When Aunt Emma went to California for Christmas, she reconnected with some relatives she hadn't seen in a long time. Eden is Aunt Emma's first cousin's child, making her Aunt Emma and my mother's second cousin. And she's my third cousin, I think, since Aunt Emma is my mother's sister."

"So, Eden's mother is in prison for how long?" Abraham turned toward her as he lifted an eyebrow.

"Her name is Jill, and I'm not sure." Yvonne lowered her eyes to her lap as she reached for the string on her prayer covering, wrapping it around her finger. Without looking up, she said, "I feel like you don't want to do this, but it would crush Aunt Emma if she couldn't go with her friends on this trip to Europe that's been planned for so long." Sighing, she kept her eyes down. "I don't know why she agreed to keep Eden when she knew she had this trip planned. And we haven't been married that long, and I probably shouldn't have agreed to—"

"Look at me," Abraham said as he cupped her chin and brought her eyes to his. "It's going to be fine."

She tried to smile. "That's the second time you've said that."

"Because it will be." Abraham kissed her softly. "We are two worldly people compared to the rest of our Amish community. I'm sure we can handle one sixteen-year-old girl for a month."

Yvonne smiled, genuinely this time. Her husband had been born into an Amish family, chosen to become a cop, then returned to his roots. And somewhere in all of that they'd fallen in love, and Yvonne had followed him into the Plain life with no regrets. "You're right. We're not like the others here. We've lived in the outside world." She winked at her husband. "We've got this."

"*Ya*, we do." He kissed her again, and Yvonne relished the heady sensation she still got in the arms of her husband. "So, we better take advantage of these last few days of privacy. And the fact that we both have a day off in the middle of the week." He stood up and held out his hand, which she was happy to accept as he escorted her to their bedroom.

Abraham had worked a double shift the day before, taking inventory at the hardware store, so his boss had given him the day off. Yvonne hadn't taken time off from her job in months, so her friend and owner of the bookstore, Jake, hadn't batted an eye about her request and said tending the store would give him a break from farming out in the heat.

It had been great sleeping in. And now a nap. Maybe today would be the day they conceived. They'd been trying to have a baby since they'd been married.

But even as Abraham pulled her closer, Yvonne couldn't

shed the worry that had built up about Eden coming to stay with them. Things would be very different here in Montgomery, Indiana, than in California, where Eden was coming from . . . this Saturday.

CHAPTER 1

Eden checked her text messages as she slumped into the back seat of the cab, hoping Emma had given her enough cash to pay for this long ride to her new home for a month. She'd already been in the car over an hour, but her cousin certainly couldn't have picked her up at the airport in a horse and buggy.

She felt an air of excitement about visiting a new place, although as the scenery became more and more rural, she wondered what teenagers did for fun here. Farms lined the two-lane road they now drove on, and she hadn't seen a Walmart in at least forty miles.

"Sir, can you tell me how much farther?" She straightened, leaning closer to the front seat.

"Only about five minutes." The older taxi driver cocked his head to one side. "Maybe a little longer. It's been a good while since I've been out this way, but the GPS seems to think it's only five minutes."

Eden took a deep breath as she glanced at the butterfly tattoo on her left hand. It was significant and meant something to her, but she suspected her cousin wouldn't approve.

She'd removed her nose ring at Emma's insistence. And she'd changed out of shorts and a tank top—also at her cousin's recommendation—before she'd left. Now she wore jeans, a short-sleeved red shirt, and flip-flops. It was July. Too hot for jeans, but apparently the Amish were conservative, and Emma wanted her to make a good impression.

She would only be here for a month. Did it really matter what these people thought of her?

Somehow it did, she decided, even if only a little. Eden wondered how much Emma had told Yvonne and her husband about her mother and about Eden's own problems with the law. She'd probably told her everything.

Eden sighed. How cool it would be to go somewhere where no one knew anything about her, a place where her background didn't shadow her like a bad dream she couldn't wake up from.

Her pulse picked up when the driver pulled onto a gravel driveway that led to a farmhouse. She could tell it was old—the way the front porch wrapped around it, the shutters on the windows, the general look of it, like old farms she'd seen in movies. It was beautiful. Sunlight reflected off the plush green grass in the yard, and the flowerbeds were filled with colorful blooms. When she stepped out of the cab, the smell of freshly cut grass wafted up her nose and took her back to a time in her life when she'd been a little girl. And happy.

There were no neighbors that she could see. A big red barn stood off to one side of the white house with shutters the same color as the barn. Eden had never ridden a horse, but she could see a tail swishing back and forth inside the red structure. Two buggies sat parked close to the white picket fence. This might as well have been another planet in comparison to where she was from.

Her cousin and her husband came out of the house wearing the kind of clothes Eden had looked up on the internet—a big, baggy dress for Yvonne with a bonnet on her head and a funky haircut with cropped bangs, along with suspenders, for her husband. Their attire didn't surprise her. But Yvonne's overall appearance did. Even at a distance, and without any makeup, her cousin was pretty for someone older, in her thirties.

Eden paid the driver and tried to ignore his scowl. The ride had been more than Emma had estimated, which left only enough for a two-dollar tip. The guy spun his wheels a little as he backed out of the driveway, sending a whirlwind of dust everywhere. Eden waved her hand in front of her face, picked up her bulky red suitcase, and headed across the yard.

"I've got that." Abraham met her in the yard and eased the luggage from her hand. Eden had been worried more about him than Yvonne, but his blue eyes brimmed with kindness. At least that was Eden's initial impression. Maybe he'd be okay. She believed you could tell a lot by a person's eyes. Max's eyes always blazed with icy contempt when he was angry, which was a lot. His glare grew more brazen when he was in a bad mood. Eden's insides braided into knots each time, just before he smacked her across the face—for back talking, as he called it.

After a slight shiver, she pushed the thought aside, opting to believe that Abraham was a nice guy. *Aren't all Amish good people?*

"Thanks," she said to Abraham as they walked across the yard toward the steps to the porch, where Yvonne stood waiting. "Thank you for having me," she added almost inaudibly to the stranger by her side, and Abraham smiled, nodding. She wasn't shy, but her voice had abandoned her, and she was more nervous than she'd thought she would be, realizing she really did want to make a good impression—more than a little. Maybe this trip could be practice to become the kind of person she wanted people to see. Plus, she didn't need Emma on her case when she got back. They'd had a few run-ins since she'd come to stay with her, mostly because Eden didn't always get home when she was supposed to, and once for sneaking out in Emma's car. But it had been for an important reason the day she did that.

It probably wouldn't be an issue here. There likely wasn't anywhere to go or anything to do. Except maybe ride a horse. That interested her. Maybe she could even go for a drive in one of those buggies.

She extended her hand to Yvonne, but her cousin pulled her into a hug instead, which was nice, kind of like a real hug. Emma tended to barely hug, mostly a light embrace with a pat on the back. But Yvonne squeezed her, almost too much.

"Welcome to our home, Eden. We're thrilled to have you staying with us."

If Yvonne didn't mean it, Eden would never be able to tell. Her cousin's smile looked as real as her hug felt, and she was even prettier up close, with straight white teeth and a flawless complexion. She had a few of those feathery lines by her eyes, but Eden thought that must be because she smiled so broadly. Eden knew from experience that pretty people on the outside didn't mean they were always pretty on the inside. But until Yvonne did something to prove otherwise, she was going to take the same stance as she had with Abraham—nice people. It was part of her "new me" attitude that she'd brought with her for this trip.

I am not my mother. I am not my mother. I am not my mother. She would continue to say it in her mind, and out loud when she could, until she fully believed that she was different.

"Thank you for having me," she said to Yvonne after her cousin released her from the mega bear hug. She felt sweat already pooling at her temples from the short walk across the yard.

"Come in, come in." Yvonne pushed open a screen door, and Eden waited for a burst of cool air to hit her. Then she remembered.

No air conditioning. Or electricity. Or television. Or internet.

She glanced at the phone in her hand. Only one bar of service. But even as she dripped with sweat, an amazing aroma greeted her, causing her to momentarily forget she stood in a furnace. Something smelled awesome, like cookies or bread baking, and maybe something stewing on a burner. She hadn't realized how hungry she was until now.

Inside, a black dog with patches of white lay on a rug in front of the fireplace. Eden loved dogs and squatted down to scratch the animal behind his ears.

"*Ach*, wait!" Yvonne stiffened. "He's not always friendly to strangers."

"I think he's great." Eden continued to love on the dog, who had his paws crossed in front of him. He casually rolled onto his back for some petting on his tummy.

"Wow. His name is Blue, and he sure seems to like you." Yvonne grinned as she rested her hands on her hips. "They say dogs have a sixth sense about people."

"I don't know about that, but he sure likes his tummy rubbed."

Yvonne chuckled. "Indeed, he does. Oh, and I asked Aunt Emma if there was anything you didn't eat, and she said there wasn't." Yvonne chuckled. "So, hopefully she wasn't holding back. We've got a feast in the kitchen to welcome you." She pointed to the hallway. "But first, if you want to get situated, Abraham can carry your suitcase to your bedroom."

"Sure, okay." Eden was starving, but she was eager to see where she'd be staying for the next month as she followed Abraham around the corner.

"It's nothing fancy, and I promise it will cool down in the evening," Abraham said as he set her suitcase down on the wood floor just inside the bedroom door. He pointed over his shoulder. "The bathroom is at the end of the hall, and let us know if you need anything." Then he nodded to a small fan on the bedside table. "That works using batteries, but it puts out a *gut* burst of air." It was blowing at what appeared to be full speed. There was also a lantern on the nightstand.

"That's a pretty quilt on the bed." Eden ran her hand along the pastel colors within the diamond shapes.

Abraham smiled. "*Ya*, glad you like it. *Mei mammi*

made it." He ran a hand through cropped bangs that stood almost straight up after he did so—from sweat, she supposed. "Get settled, and we'll see you shortly for dinner."

"Okay, thank you."

Dinner? It was only one thirty. Then she recalled the little bit of research she'd done about the Plain people. The Amish referred to lunch as *dinner*, and the evening meal was called *supper*. No matter the term, the flavorful smells had followed her to her bedroom, and she couldn't wait to dig in.

After Abraham left, she made a further inspection of her bedroom. Her stomach growled as she eyed the colorful bed covering again. From Abraham's wording, Eden wasn't sure if his mother or grandmother had made the quilt. At Emma's encouragement, she'd tried to familiarize herself with some of the dialect the Amish spoke, but her cousin had also said they spoke fluent English, so Eden hadn't bothered with learning much Pennsylvania Dutch.

There was a plain wooden desk with one drawer against the far wall, along with a small, inornate chair. She gingerly ran her hand along the top of the desk before easing open the drawer. Inside sat a spiral notebook, two pencils, a pen, and a few envelopes. There was even a book of stamps. Eden couldn't think of anyone she wanted to correspond with. Emma had said she would send postcards, but Eden knew how long international mail could take. She'd had a pen pal in Switzerland when she was around ten. It didn't last. Most of Eden's relationships, even domestically, didn't. Her mother either moved them from apartment to apartment, forcing Eden to change schools, or she was cast out among her peers as a mini mold of her mother and not considered good friendship material by their parents.

She'd been placed in foster care when her mother went to jail, before Emma had taken her in. Surprisingly, she'd managed to make a few semi-friends but was yanked from that environment after two months. She had liked her foster parents—they were nice to her—but Emma was family, and it was decided she should live with her, which was mostly okay.

Eden had a few girls she ran around with in the neighborhood where she'd lived with her mother and her mother's boyfriend, Max. But they had stopped returning her calls a long time ago. She was sure word had spread quickly about her mother being sentenced to three years in prison. Max only got six months, which seemed unfair since he was the one who'd gotten her mother involved in their nonlucrative drug business. Eden was sure most of their profit was injected into their arms.

Maybe she would write her mother a letter. Or maybe not. In the beginning, all her mother had done was try to call her collect, knowing Eden didn't have the money to pay for the calls. She took the first few, but when she got a seventy-five-dollar bill, she quit answering. Besides, all her mother did was cry, which caused Eden to cry.

Over the months since she'd been living with Emma, the hurt she'd felt about her situation had morphed into anger. Emma was good to her, but she was old, and they didn't have much in common. Eden didn't even try to make friends at school these days. What was the point? They'd eventually find out her mother was in prison—a fact that seemed to define Eden, whether it was fair or not.

She sat on the queen bed and bounced up and down. It was comfy enough. There was a Bible in the drawer of the nightstand, which Eden had already read, but no novels or other reading material. Eden had learned to bury herself in books a long time ago. She'd been excited when she learned that Yvonne worked at a bookstore. Maybe she could use the little bit of spending money she had to purchase some novels.

She turned the fan toward her until it blew right into her face, and hoped that Abraham was right that it would cool down in the evening.

Her thoughts jumbled as she considered her options. She'd had a month to think about this trip. Emma had been kind when she explained about her planned trip to Europe, and Eden didn't feel like she was being dumped somewhere. Her cousin, Yvonne, and her husband seemed nice based on the brief introduction. They were younger than Emma but old enough that they probably couldn't relate to a sixteen-year-old, and they didn't have any children. Eden doubted they would become close. She would only be here a month, and she wasn't sure how much of her past she was willing to share—things that Emma probably suspected but that Eden had never confirmed. She still shivered when she thought about the way Max always tried to touch her when her mother wasn't around.

She found herself swallowing back sobs in her throat daily. She could either choose to be a victim—life surely hadn't treated her fairly—or let go of the past and commit to being the best person she could be.

Eden chose the latter, but it wasn't without a struggle.

Yvonne twisted her hands in front of her as she stared at the kitchen table. She'd given up her rental property and moved into Abraham's farmhouse when they'd gotten married, but it didn't have a separate dining area. The kitchen was spacious enough for a table that could seat six, and Yvonne had filled it to capacity with food.

"It's just one sixteen-year-old girl," Abraham said as he came up behind her and slipped his arms around her waist. "You've made plenty, if that's what you're looking so worried about."

She spun around to face him, then shrugged. "Who says I'm worried?"

He kissed her on the forehead. "I know that look."

"I just want everything to be perfect."

Yvonne's warped way of thinking had gotten under her own skin. She'd found herself thinking that if Eden liked them and was happy during her stay, she wouldn't get in any trouble while she was here or cause any problems. It was judgmental and wrong to assume there'd be an issue, but Yvonne was proud that she at least recognized it for what it was so she could make a conscious effort not to be this way.

"Wow." Eden walked into the room, and Abraham instantly removed his arms from around Yvonne's waist. "Everything looks awesome."

"I tried to make a variety. A couple of dishes are things I learned to cook when I lived in Texas, and others are recipes Abraham's mother shared with me."

"Yeah, I heard you haven't been Amish for long." She nodded at Abraham. "He has more of an, um . . . Amish accent? Is that what you'd call it?"

"I guess so." Abraham chuckled, then waved an arm over the table. "Pick a seat."

Eden glanced back and forth between them. "Do you have certain places you sit?"

Yvonne chewed her bottom lip for a moment and decided to be honest. "I usually sit there." She pointed to one of the side chairs. "And Abraham usually sits beside me at the head of the table."

"Okay." Eden pulled out the chair right across from where Yvonne always sat. Maybe that was a good sign. She hadn't chosen a chair at the opposite end of the table.

After they were seated, Yvonne folded her hands together, but before she lowered her head, she said, "I know in the *Englisch* world, most people say their prayers aloud. We usually pray silently." She paused, waiting for a reaction from Eden. When there wasn't one, she said, "Do you have a preference?"

Eden tipped her head to one side. "The *Englisch* world?"

Yvonne cringed. "Sorry. That's a term for people who aren't Amish."

"Oh." Eden smiled. "I tried to learn some of your dialect, but I guess I missed that. As for the prayer, it doesn't matter to me either way."

Yvonne glanced at Abraham. Her husband was eyeing the food and probably ready to dive in. "We'll just pray silently." She lowered her head, said her prayers quickly, and raised her head to see if Eden had even lowered hers.

The girl still had her head down. Abraham lifted his eyes to Yvonne's, and Eden still hadn't raised her head. They waited. Yvonne wondered if she had that much to say to God or if she was trying to make a good impression.

Judgmental, she reminded herself.

When Eden lifted her head, she smiled again. She was a beautiful girl with long blonde hair that was pulled back in a ponytail and gorgeous green eyes. Yvonne had noticed earlier that she was about as tall as her, which wasn't saying either of them were very tall at five four. Eden was well proportioned—not too thin, not too heavy. Yvonne could recall her own figure at that age, back when she could eat anything she wanted and not gain weight. Now that she was in her thirties, she tried to watch what she ate to keep off any extra pounds. Pride and vanity weren't something the Amish favored, but some of Yvonne's old mindsets had stuck.

After they'd filled their plates, Yvonne hesitated. She longed to know more about their houseguest, but she didn't want to seem too pushy. "So, you said you did a little research about our dialect. Did you look up Montgomery on the internet and see anything you might like to do? I'm afraid things are different here than what you're used to. Emma has a lovely home, but it's right in the middle of a subdivision." She paused. "Um, is that how your house was in California too? In a neighborhood?"

"We mostly lived in apartments." Eden plunged a heaping forkful of roast into her mouth. After she swallowed, she said, "I knew it would be different in Indiana, but I didn't realize how many farms there are. I saw lots on the way here, once we got out of the city."

"*Ya*, farming is a big way of life here," Abraham chimed in. "But I bet we can find you some fun things to do while you're here."

Eden halted another bite of roast and set her fork down. "There is one thing I'd like to do."

Yvonne smiled. "Sure. Anything." Then she chastised herself for reacting with such excitement. *Calm down.*

"I've never ridden a horse." Eden blushed. "And I'd like to ride in one of those buggies."

"Not at the same time, I hope." Abraham laughed. So did Yvonne after Eden let out a chuckle. "I'm pretty sure we can make both of those things happen."

Eden grinned and sat taller. "Cool. I'd love that."

Yvonne started to wonder if she had worried for nothing. Eden seemed like a good kid, even though she hadn't been with them for an hour yet. Just because the girl had been through a lot, it didn't mean she wasn't a good person.

Yvonne realized she was talking herself into believing what she wanted to believe. She changed tack. "You might already know this, but we only have church service every other Sunday. This is an off weekend, but tomorrow I was planning to deliver some meals to a few shut-ins who live nearby." She dabbed at the sweat on her forehead—mostly from the heat, but possibly her nervousness was in play. "Maybe you would want to go and even learn to drive the buggy?"

Right away, she recalled her aunt telling her that Eden had once snuck out of the house and taken her car. Maybe Yvonne shouldn't have made that offer.

"Really? That would be so fun." Eden took another bite. The girl ate like she hadn't had anything in days, and there didn't seem to be anything on the table she hadn't piled on her plate—roast, potatoes with gravy, carrots, peas, corn on the cob, and buttered bread.

Yvonne glanced at her own plate with a small portion of roast, only a spoonful of peas, and one slice of bread. *Those were the days*, she thought as she watched Eden eat.

"But when it comes to actually riding the horses . . ." Yvonne pointed her fork at Abraham. "There's your teacher. I can ride, but I am not an expert, and I don't go fast."

Abraham snickered. "That's an understatement." He looked directly at Eden. "She rides slower than slow."

"I'd love to be able to ride really fast across an open field, like you see people in the movies doing." Eden used her napkin to clear sweat from her face. It had been dribbling from her temples since she'd sat down. Yvonne remembered how hard it had been for her to get used to no electricity, particularly no air conditioning.

"Abraham is a *gut* teacher." Yvonne smiled at her husband.

"I heard your accent a little just then." Eden smiled. "It's cute."

"Aw, *danki* . . ." Yvonne chuckled. "That means 'thank you.'"

"I actually knew that one!" Eden giggled. "Maybe I'll learn some more while I'm here."

"I'm sure you will," Abraham said as he reached for a slice of bread.

Yvonne's stomach settled as she began to feel more at ease. *I've got this*. Eden was likable and glad to be with them. What could possibly go wrong?

CHAPTER 2

Eden's heart raced as she sat in the driver's seat of an Amish buggy for the first time. Abraham and Yvonne had three buggies. Two of them were enclosed, but Yvonne had chosen the topless one they were in due to the heat inside the other rides. Luckily the sun was behind the clouds. Eden hoped it stayed that way, or this might be hotter than the other buggies. Either way, she was still thrilled to be having her first adventure.

"That's it. Just a gentle tap," Yvonne instructed, pointing to the reins in Eden's trembling hands.

Her cousin had driven them to several houses and delivered baskets of food to elderly people who weren't able to get out much. She'd given Eden driving instructions throughout the journey. Now it was Eden who would get them home, hopefully without any problems.

"Wow. This is so cool." Eden didn't think she could wipe the smile off her face if she tried. She felt like a pioneer woman on the back roads in some foreign land. It was actually an unpaved dirt road that Yvonne had turned onto, saying it would be a good place for Eden to practice.

"There." Yvonne smiled back at her. "Just keep us in a steady trot. You're doing great." Her cousin tucked loose strands of hair beneath her prayer covering, then blotted her face with a handkerchief. It was unbearably hot when they were stopped, but once they were moving, the breeze blew the sweat beads from their faces.

"Uh-oh. There's another buggy coming toward us, and it's going fast." Eden's pulse picked up even more as she glanced at Yvonne before refocusing on the road that was barely wide enough for two buggies to squeeze by each other. Dust blew in plumes around the oncoming buggy, also one without a top.

"It's okay. Don't panic. Just gently pull back on the reins to slow Clyde down a little bit." Yvonne had told her there used to be a horse named Bonnie too—Bonnie and Clyde. It seemed weird to Eden that Amish people would name their horses after criminals, but she hadn't questioned her cousin about it. "Clyde knows what to do. He will naturally move over to the far-right side of the road. And that's probably Leroy, Abraham's *bruder*. He and his family live on this road."

"Okay." Eden relaxed her shoulders and let out the breath she was holding. "I didn't want to have a head-on buggy collision my first time driving."

Clyde moved to the right, like Yvonne said he would, and the horse slowed to a walk, not really even a trot.

"Pull back a little on the reins and tell Clyde to stop. I want you to meet . . . uh . . . Oh, wait. That's not Leroy, but it's his son, Samuel."

Eden was able to get Clyde to halt, and the guy driving the buggy slowed down, then came to a stop beside them.

"*Wie bischt*, Yvonne?" The good-looking Amish guy with sun-kissed blond hair, a beachy tan, and black sunglasses was dressed the way all their people did, but he was working the look. The wind had blown his cropped bangs to the side, and if not for the suspenders and straw hat, he could have passed for a regular guy. He wore a short-sleeved dark-blue shirt and black slacks.

Yvonne leaned forward around Eden. "We're *gut*, Samuel." She nodded to Eden. "This is *mei* cousin, Eden, and she'll be staying with us for a month while *mei* aunt is traveling with some friends in Europe."

"*Ya*, *Daed* mentioned something about that." He flashed Eden a crooked smile, and she noted his dimples. "Nice to meet you, Eden." He scratched his clean-shaven face, still grinning. "As in the garden of Eden?"

If she had a dime for every time someone had said that . . . "Yep, just like the garden. Nice to meet you too."

Samuel chuckled as Clyde began to do his business, and Yvonne and Eden both pinched their nostrils closed. "Ew," Eden said.

"All in God's perfect timing." Samuel laughed again.

"This is Eden's first time to drive a buggy." Yvonne lowered her hand from her nose. "I should have warned her this is an occupational hazard. Next, she wants to learn how to ride one of the horses. I told her Abraham is a *gut* teacher."

"I want to ride fast across an open pasture," Eden said as she pushed back strands of hair that had flown free of her ponytail and were stuck to her sweaty face.

Samuel noticed. "Next month will be worse. August is miserable," he said before rolling his eyes.

At least her first night's sleep had been decent the night before. Abraham had been right that it cooled down. "Can't wait." Eden rolled her eyes back at him, and he smiled again.

"I've got the perfect horse for you." He winked at her, which caught Eden a little off guard, and she swallowed hard. She supposed Amish guys could flirt just as well as regular guys—and winking was flirting in Eden's book.

"Really? How so?" She tipped her head to one side.

"She's an old mare that is gentle as can be, but she's still got it in her to run like the wind." He whistled as his eyes rounded. "If you want to go fast, she's your gal. And I just finished plowing the back pasture, so she's ready for a good run." He caught Yvonne's eye. "If it's okay with you and Abraham, I could easily have her up and riding on Bessie."

Eden wanted to say Bessie sounded like a cow's name, but she turned to Yvonne, who was chewing her bottom lip.

"Um, *ya*, I guess that would be okay," Yvonne said with hesitance.

"Don't worry. I'll keep her safe." Samuel smiled again, and Eden's stomach flip-flopped at the thought of learning to ride a horse—and spending time with her first acquaintance outside of Yvonne and Abraham, who just happened to be a hot Amish guy.

Her cousin nodded, but based on the way she kept gnawing on her bottom lip, Eden didn't think Yvonne was a 100 percent on board.

"I'll be super careful," Eden said as she held up a palm in Yvonne's direction. "I promise not to get hurt on your watch."

Yvonne finally smiled as she pointed a finger at Samuel.

"Actually, it'll be *his* watch. And I'm trusting you, Samuel, to take it slow with her."

He put a hand on his chest as he sat taller. "It'll be *mei* watch, and she'll be fine."

"Well, okay, then." Yvonne sighed, then nodded.

"Wednesday is *mei* day off from work." He took off his sunglasses and blinked the sweat from his eyes, which were a tawny shade of brown. Eden tried to study them to see what they revealed, but he caught her staring and grinned. She felt herself blushing as she looked away.

"Are you still working for Ben Lantz?" Yvonne asked as she put a hand up to block the sun in her eyes.

"*Ya*, *ya*." He looked at Eden. "We build decks, things like that." His eyes shifted to Yvonne. "Do you want me to pick her up, or . . . ?"

"*Nee*, I'll bring her over Wednesday on the way to the bookstore."

They settled on eight in the morning, said their good-byes, and Eden was soon back on the road. She had something to look forward to on Wednesday.

That evening at supper, Eden was bubbly and excited to tell Abraham about driving the buggy. He had been gone all day helping his younger brother, Daniel, repair a broken water line. Sunday was supposed to be a day of rest, but not having water was reason enough to bend the rules.

Eden was animated and fun to watch. Yvonne smiled, and her husband laughed out loud several times when she detailed her time driving the buggy. The girl even had Blue's undivided attention from where he lay on the floor nearby, the dog's eyes wide as he watched Eden.

"I was so nervous at first." Eden shook her head, grinning, before she looked across the table at Yvonne. "But you were a good—*gut*—teacher."

"You might be fluent in Pennsylvania *Deutsch* by the time you go home," Abraham said.

Yvonne was happy the two of them were getting along. And things had gone well between Yvonne and Eden the rest of the day following their buggy ride. Yvonne hadn't learned much about her younger cousin, but she was also trying not to pry. They'd each taken a nap earlier, but something was niggling at Yvonne when she woke up. She wanted to talk to Abraham about it before Eden spilled about her plans for Wednesday, but she doubted the girl would hold back. Yvonne decided it might be better for her to ease into the conversation.

"We ran into Samuel today, and he said he has the perfect horse for Eden to ride. He said he would teach her. We set a date for Wednesday." Yvonne wished she had chosen another word besides *date*. She waited for Abraham to react.

"That's great," he said but kept his eyes cast down. Yvonne knew why, and she wondered if she should have come up with a reason to deny Samuel's kind offer. They all knew Leroy was overly protective with his children, especially his three girls, but also with his only son. He was stricter than most Amish parents when it came to allowing his children to mingle with outsiders. He'd practically denied Samuel, the oldest, a *rumschpringe*. It was considered a given that when a child reached the age of sixteen, they were allowed to venture out on their own and experience the world. Nothing too major. Maybe see a movie, dress like outsiders, even if on the sly. Parents had an unspoken rule that they would look the other way during this time to allow their teenagers to choose baptism on their own. Almost all of them did. It had been almost a year since Samuel had turned sixteen, and Yvonne had heard plenty of stories about Leroy being too strict—that he would run his children off by doing that.

Leroy was good as gold, and Yvonne thought of him like a brother, but she didn't think he was going to approve of Samuel hanging out with Eden. Based on her husband's quiet reaction, Abraham didn't think it was going to go over well either.

"I'm sorry I didn't help you clean the kitchen last night. I was so tired," Eden said after she'd cleaned her plate and finished the last of her tea. "But I will tonight."

"*Nee*, that's not necessary. Really. You're our guest, and Abraham and I do that together. I wash, and he dries." Yvonne stood up and began clearing the table.

Eden slouched in her chair. "But I want to do something to help out while I'm here."

Yvonne continued to be impressed by the girl. She was polite, and so far she seemed quite genuine. A person would have never known what she'd been through with her mother, foster care, and legal issues. Still, Yvonne suspected she didn't have all the facts. Despite outward appearances, there was still a part of Yvonne that had her guard up when it came to Eden, and she could see an explosive situation brewing between Eden and Samuel.

"Well . . ." Yvonne tapped a finger to her chin. "How do you feel about collecting eggs in the morning? And if you want to, you could top off the feed for the horses and make sure they have plenty of water in the trough."

"Sure." Eden's expression brightened. "Anything else?"

Abraham had cut himself a slice of apple pie and was busy adding a scoop of ice cream he'd retrieved from the freezer. Eden had passed on dessert, and so had Yvonne.

"There is one thing. We didn't mention it last night since it was your first night here, but we normally have devotions in the living room after supper each night." Yvonne stood holding a stack of plates as she waited for Eden to bow out. Yvonne doubted Eden's mother or foster parents had introduced her to religion any more than Aunt Emma.

No. That was an unfair assumption since Yvonne didn't know the people from Eden's past. Yvonne chastised herself again for letting judgment slip into her thoughts. But Aunt Emma wasn't a Christian, and she'd raised Yvonne to believe there was no heaven. It was likely she wasn't pushing religion with Eden.

"It's perfectly fine for you to choose not to participate. A person's faith journey is a personal choice." Yvonne said a quick prayer that Eden would open her heart to the opportunity to learn about God while she was staying with them.

Eden sighed dreamily. "Oh, wow. I would love that." She paused, frowning. "I know Emma raised you and that you weren't brought up as a Christian since Emma doesn't believe Jesus died on the cross to save us. She told me that you were called to go on your own spiritual journey later in life, which is super cool. I guess I've had a similar experience." She paused, smiled briefly, then crinkled her nose. "I wish Emma felt differently, but to each his own, and I think we have to respect that."

Yvonne realized her jaw had dropped, so she quickly closed her mouth. This was either the most mature sixteen-year-old she'd ever known—and granted, she hadn't known many on a personal level—or Eden was trying to impress them.

"Um, great." Yvonne set the dishes she'd been holding on the kitchen counter. "If you want to go bathe, Abraham and I will get the kitchen cleaned up and meet you in the living room."

"Sure." Eden stood up. "*Danki* for a *gut* meal." She smiled before she walked away.

"Bravo!" Abraham shouted as Eden hit the stairs, and they heard her giggle on her way up.

Yvonne waited until Eden was out of earshot. "Do you think she's too *gut* to be true? I mean, Emma made it sound like she's been through a lot. Even though I'm sure I don't know everything, it seems like she would have scars, or at the least not be the perfectly sweet girl she appears to be." She squeezed her eyes closed and cringed. "Abraham, I feel bad that I voiced those thoughts out loud."

He shrugged, waited for her to ease the dishes into the sink, then pulled her close and kissed her. "If you can't vent to your husband, then who? Let's give her a chance. She's barely been here a day and a half."

Yvonne pressed her lips into a thin line and thought

about what she was going to say. "And something else is bothering me. I have concerns about Eden spending time with Samuel, but it was his idea to teach her to ride." She paused when her husband flinched a little. "It worries you, too, doesn't it? We both know that Leroy would prefer his children not to hang out with people who aren't Amish. I think Anna might have even stronger feelings about it."

"I did think about that, but it sounds innocent enough." Abraham eased away from her and picked up a kitchen towel.

Yvonne began filling the sink with soapy water. "I don't know about that." She turned to face him. "There was no denying the attraction those kids had for each other. Eden couldn't stop smiling, and Samuel . . . Well, he winked at her."

Abraham grinned. "I remember being that age."

"Me too." Yvonne shook her head but eventually smiled. "I guess we shouldn't borrow trouble. Eden wants to learn how to ride a horse, and hopefully that's all their time together will amount to."

"Agreed. We won't borrow trouble."

After they'd finished the dishes, they heard footsteps coming down the hallway. Yvonne handed Abraham the last dish, and after he dried it and put it in the cabinet, they met Eden in the living room. She was sitting in a rocking chair on the other side of the coffee table. Yvonne and Abraham took a seat next to each other on the couch. Blue lay on his bed near the fireplace snoring lightly.

Eden's long, wet hair fell well past her shoulders,

blowing slightly from the two fans they had near the opened windows. She wore white knee-length tattered shorts—the style for a girl her age—and a pink T-shirt with matching flip-flops.

"I hope it's okay to dress like this while I'm at your house." Eden blushed, and Yvonne realized she must have been staring.

"*Ya*, sure. Of course." Yvonne recalled the way she used to dress before she'd been baptized into the Amish faith. She missed it sometimes, especially in the summer heat.

"So, how does this work?" Eden cupped her chin as she glanced back and forth between Yvonne and Abraham. When neither of them answered right away, Eden said, "We're together, so I'm guessing we don't pray silently?" She grinned as she lowered her hand and looked at each of them again.

Yvonne waited for Abraham to speak, but her husband stayed quiet. "Well . . ." Yvonne cleared her throat. "As you said, Aunt Emma didn't raise me as a Christian, but once I found *mei* way to Him, it's been the most glorious experience. Having a relationship with *Gott* is a beautiful thing. And even though the journey is a personal one, sometimes knowledge of the Lord's Word, combined with educating yourself, can lead you on the path you were meant to be on."

Eden stared at Yvonne as if she'd spoken to her in a language she didn't understand. Yvonne assumed she was going about this the wrong way, but as she glanced at Abraham, her husband merely raised an eyebrow as if he expected her to keep going.

"We'd just like to help you have a relationship with *Gott*. That's all."

Eden fought the sob building in her throat, but she swallowed it back. Didn't Yvonne hear her? Once again, her past was shadowing her. *The poor girl whose mother is in prison, who doesn't have a dad, has been in foster care, and had some legal issues, couldn't possibly be close to God.*

"I know God, and I have a good relationship with Him. I'm never opposed to learning more about God, but I *know* Him," she said firmly as she raised her chin, resentful that Yvonne would assume her faith was stronger than Eden's. "As you said, it's a personal journey and one that I've been on for a while." She paused to take a deep breath, recalling the fun day she'd had and how nice Yvonne and Abraham had been to her. "When I asked how it worked, I meant, do you choose a scripture and discuss it? Or do you say a series of prayers? I guess I wanted to know if there was an agenda for your devotion time."

Yvonne's mouth was opened slightly, and her cousin seemed at a loss for words. Eden hadn't meant to sound snappy, but she'd been looking forward to having people to pray with. Most of her life, she'd had no way to get to church. Emma had taken her a few times, but Emma preferred to sleep late on Sundays and wasn't interested in attending herself, so Eden hadn't pushed the issue since she'd been living there.

"I'm sure Amish families, and non-Amish families, have

their own way of settling into devotions in the evenings." Abraham spoke with tenderness as Yvonne stared at her lap. "Yvonne and I adopted traditions that I grew up with. We usually begin by thanking God for His many blessings. We ask for forgiveness of our sins, and we pray for those who are sick or hurting in some way—specifically naming those people. From there, we take turns choosing a scripture from the Bible, and we discuss it, what it means to us, and how we incorporate it into our lives." He paused, glanced at Yvonne, then reached for his wife's hand. "So, we can follow that line of thinking tonight, if you'd like, and you can choose a scripture if you want to. If not, that's okay too. How does that sound?"

Eden was reactive. She recognized the fault. People were so quick to judge her that she sometimes went on the defensive before it was warranted. Yvonne hadn't meant any harm, and Eden shouldn't have sounded so snippy. "If it's okay, I'd like to choose a scripture when it's time," she said as she attempted to infuse her comment with the tenderness Abraham had voiced so well.

"That would be great." Yvonne glanced briefly at Eden but then gazed at her husband, and Eden saw her squeeze his hand. She loved the way Yvonne and Abraham looked at each other, like they were truly in love. And, just now, Abraham had his wife's back when Yvonne became upset.

Argh. Eden made a mental note not to be so defensive. She would be with Yvonne and Abraham for a month, and she wanted it to be a good experience for all of them.

For the next fifteen minutes, they followed the prayer

schedule Abraham had laid out, and Eden could feel the Holy Spirit in the room. She recalled the first time she'd made what she thought was a real connection with God. She'd been twelve. Her mother was in the hospital from a presumed drug overdose, and Child Protective Services stayed outside the room while Eden stood by her mother's side, watching her trying to breathe. Her face was pale, and she'd had dark circles underneath her eyes. Eden didn't know God at the time, but she had squeezed her eyes closed and begged Him not to let her mother die and to please not send her to foster care. At that point, she'd never been removed from her mother.

When she opened her eyes, there was a man standing next to her. He was dressed in white, had gray hair, and had a stethoscope hanging around his neck. She hadn't heard him enter the room, but when she looked up at him, he told her everything was going to be fine. Her mother had had a reaction to an antibiotic, and they hadn't found any illegal drugs in her system.

Eden could recall how relieved she'd felt. But even more so, she remembered the doctor's eyes, the way he looked at her, and the all-knowing feeling that he was her guardian angel.

Looking back, maybe he had been. Or maybe he was just a nice man Eden had connected with, a person who had delivered good news with kindness.

It wasn't until a year ago that she was introduced to God through a girl who lived in her apartment complex. The friendship hadn't lasted, but her trips to church with the girl's family had set her on a journey toward understanding more about God. She had devoured the Bible, and with every page she had felt a closeness that she relied on above everything else.

Abraham cleared his throat again, snapping her back to the present. "Do you have a scripture in mind that you'd like for us to focus on?" he asked, smiling.

"I do." Eden considered quoting Romans 2:1—"You, therefore, have no excuse, you who pass judgment on someone else, for at whatever point you judge another, you are condemning yourself, because you who pass judgment do the same things"—but it would almost seem like a dig at Yvonne, and Eden didn't want to do that. She chose another one she had memorized and repeated daily, this one from Matthew 6:14: "For if you forgive other people when they sin against you, your heavenly Father will also forgive you," she said barely above a whisper.

Yvonne blinked her eyes a few times, then pressed her lips together. Eden realized that her cousin might be inserting herself into this scenario, but she couldn't be more wrong. There was only one person Eden couldn't forgive. Maybe two, but Max wasn't worth the effort—which wasn't right in the eyes of God, she knew. There was only one person she wanted to truly forgive. Her mother.

Suddenly, it felt too personal to discuss with people she didn't even know.

"Is there someone you are struggling to forgive, Eden?" Yvonne spoke to her with the same tenderness Abraham had voiced earlier. So much so that Eden felt her throat swelling again, and she didn't want to cry.

"No." She tried to smile. Abraham and Yvonne probably

saw through her, and she would apologize to God for the lie later.

From there, a general discussion about forgiveness ensued, and Eden participated in a generic sort of way, not identifying anyone in particular. It wasn't that she simply couldn't forgive her mother—she hated her.

CHAPTER 3

Yvonne sat on the side of the bed brushing out her wet hair, surprised by how much it had grown over the past eight months she'd been married to Abraham. She wondered how long it would get since Amish women never cut their hair. Her husband was reading, and Yvonne kept her back to him for the time being, rubbing Blue's belly with her foot. She wanted to think.

"You're being too hard on yourself," Abraham said, and Yvonne heard him close his book.

Sighing, she turned around. "What?"

"You've been quiet ever since we came to bed. Usually, you're chatty." He reached out to her and laid a gentle hand on her back. "You had no way to know that Eden had a solid faith, if that's what is bothering you."

"That's not true. She was excited about the idea of having devotions with us, and she even said she'd had a similar experience to mine. But I stuck with my assumptions that she probably didn't know *Gott*, and I didn't really listen to what she said. After her reaction, I knew right away that it was wrong of me to presume she didn't have a relationship with *Gott* or to insinuate that I knew *Gott* better than she did. I don't blame her for being defensive." She inched farther onto the bed, wearing one of the white gowns she wore every night, and kept her feet atop the light top sheet. Both fans whirled, and a rain shower earlier had cooled things off a little more than usual.

"She got over it quickly. Don't dwell on it." Abraham rolled onto his side and propped his head up on his hand.

Yvonne groaned. "I have got to let go of any preconceived notions that Eden is hauling around a bunch of baggage from her past. Even if she is, we both know that God can help you get through anything. Eden couldn't be any sweeter, and she seems incredibly smart. I know women in their twenties who don't have the maturity she has."

"Then just be grateful for that. Teenage years are hard, with or without a history like Eden has. She's obviously put her past behind her. Or she doesn't plan to let it ruin her life, anyway. That's admirable. And you're right—a sign of maturity."

"I'm still a little concerned about what Leroy is going to think about Eden and Samuel spending time together on Wednesday." Yvonne fluffed her pillow just as Abraham straightened his arm in time for her to rest her head in the nook of his shoulder.

"It's a horse-riding lesson. That's all. Remember, we're not going to borrow trouble." Abraham kissed her on the forehead.

"I know, but I saw a spark between those two. I didn't imagine it."

Samuel stood from the bed, yawned, then stuffed what he'd been reading between the mattresses. After a couple of seconds, he retrieved the travel magazine, remembering that Monday was wash day. One of his sisters would strip the beds tomorrow, might find it, and possibly rat him out to their mother—or worse, their father. Samuel had written notes in the magazine, marking the places he wanted to visit someday. His parents wouldn't approve of his desire to see the world or, at the least, travel beyond the only life he'd ever known.

He kneeled on the floor and pulled out a box under his bed, then stashed the magazine with the others he didn't necessarily want anyone to find.

After he shoved the box back in place, he stood, lowered the flame on his lantern, then slid back onto the bed and watched the shadows dancing overhead, flickering and swirling like his thoughts. He latched his hands behind his head and fell back on his pillow. He couldn't wait for Wednesday to arrive. Eden was the most beautiful girl he'd ever met. She obviously wasn't girlfriend material, and she'd only be here for four weeks, but he would enjoy getting to know someone from the outside world. Especially someone so easy on the eyes.

He'd overheard his parents talking about Eden, how she would only be here for a month, and how they thought it was a mistake for Abraham and Yvonne to take her in. Samuel's mother and father were stricter than other parents in their district, and they were against too much socialization with the English. He was pretty sure they wouldn't approve of him teaching Eden to ride, but until they forbid him to see her, he planned to spend as much time as he could with her. Unless they didn't click at all. But, based on several looks they had exchanged, Samuel thought she might want to be friends as much as he did.

He extinguished the lantern, but even as he fluffed his pillow and settled in, he couldn't stop thinking about Eden. She probably had a cell phone. He wished he could call her, but his family had only one mobile phone, and it stayed stored in a kitchen drawer for emergencies. Mostly. His mother thought that checking on her sister in Ohio was an emergency sometimes. It mostly sounded like chitchat to him.

Once a week, someone would go into town and charge the phone, and his mother had a portable battery she would charge also. Maybe, if he could get Eden's phone number, he could sneak the phone into his room to talk to her.

He quickly dismissed the idea since he didn't know if the calls would show up on the bill. He closed his eyes, but it was Eden's face he saw before he drifted to sleep. He had so many questions for someone who had experienced a life outside of anything he had known. He would need to play it cool with his parents.

Eden walked into the store with Yvonne Monday morning and breathed in the aroma of books. She was reminded of the one apartment she and her mother had lived in close enough for her to walk to the library. "I love the smell of books."

Yvonne set her purse behind the small counter to the right of the entrance, and a bell jingled as the door closed behind Eden.

"Me too." Yvonne smiled as she began to take money from a small bag and load the cash-register drawer. She glanced at Eden. "So, you mentioned that you liked to read. Any particular genre your favorite?"

"Romance," she said without hesitation, but then felt herself blush. "Not the nasty kind or anything. I just like happily-ever-after stories. And a little adventure is always good."

"Well, you're in luck." Yvonne counted out some one-dollar bills before she looked at Eden. "You won't find any *nasty* books in here. All the romances are sweet and wholesome, and some of the romantic suspense novels might give you that sense of adventure you mentioned." She counted out more money as Eden took in her surroundings.

"Go walk around," Yvonne said. "It's not a huge store, but . . ." She nodded to her right. "Aside from the obvious books to your left, over there are a bunch of gift items."

Eden veered toward the rows of books, perusing the categories until she came to the romance section. Her eyes, then hands, gravitated to a book with a handsome cowboy on the front cover. She thought about Samuel. He wouldn't be wearing traditional cowboy clothes, but on Wednesday he'd be on a horse.

Yvonne moseyed toward her. "That's a really *gut* book.

It's got plenty of romance, a good dose of adventure, and a happy ending."

Eden mentally calculated how much money she had, then eased the book back onto the shelf. "I—I better wait. I probably need to pace myself with the money I brought."

Yvonne folded her hands in front of her. "Listen, I do this job because I love it, not because I make a lot of money. So, I can't really pay you to work. But if you want to help me out around here a little, we can certainly make sure you go home with some books. I can buy them at a huge discount."

"Really?" Eden stared at the book, then sighed. "You're housing me and feeding me. I should work for free."

Yvonne took the book from the shelf. "Nonsense. You're our guest." She smiled. "And *mei* cousin I've never known." She pushed the book toward Eden. "You can help me shelve a shipment of books that came in last Friday. How's that?"

"Sounds great." Eden flipped through the pages of the book, then followed Yvonne back to the counter, where she stowed her purse and new book behind the counter with her cousin's.

Yvonne smiled. "I'm happy you're here. When there aren't a lot of customers, it gets lonely. I like reading, too, but it will be nice to have another person around some of the time." She paused. "But please don't feel like you must come with me every day to the store. I just thought you might want to check it out today."

"I like it here, and I don't mind helping at all." Eden couldn't stifle the smile coming on. "Except Wednesday, I'll be with Samuel and learning to ride a horse. I am so excited about that."

"Samuel's a *gut* kid." Yvonne tucked some loose strands of hair beneath her prayer covering.

Eden stared at her for a few seconds, at her dark-green dress and black apron. "Was it hard for you? I mean, you know . . . becoming an Amish person?" Her cousin's use of Pennsylvania Dutch sounded different from Samuel and even Abraham, both of whom seemed to have an accent.

Yvonne shook her head. "*Nee*, I already felt Amish on the inside, so getting baptized into the faith and changing certain things wasn't that hard." She chuckled. "Okay, to be honest, I really miss air conditioning, especially in August. Next month will be brutal. And it was a little hard to give up *mei* car." Shrugging, she smiled. "But I don't have any regrets."

"That's a big life overhaul." Eden couldn't imagine. "But you look . . . really pretty. Even without any makeup." Eden didn't wear a lot of makeup herself, but she did have on mascara and lip gloss.

Yvonne pointed a playful finger at her. "You're sweet, but if I'm still being honest, I miss makeup sometimes." She touched the corners of her eyes. "I used to be able to cover up these feathery lines."

"My great-grandmother used to say that wrinkles, especially laugh lines, were a sign of a life well lived." She avoided Yvonne's eyes, unsure how much to say about any of her family—which was technically Yvonne's family, too, she supposed. Although she wasn't sure how they all fit together. But she'd loved her great-grandmother.

When she finally looked up at Yvonne, she studied her face. "You're young. I don't really see any wrinkles."

Yvonne batted her eyes and put a hand to her chest. "You are becoming *mei* new best friend. *Danki* for saying that, but I'm thirty-four and just starting to notice things like that." She held up a finger. "However, pride and vanity are looked down upon when you're living an Amish life. So, I get a free pass on wrinkles, I guess." She laughed, and so did Eden.

"We've got coffee and tea in the back," Yvonne said. "And that's where the new books are. Why don't we get something to drink, then we'll bring the shipment up front and get them on the shelves."

"Sure." Eden followed Yvonne to the back of the store, passing the gift section on their left, which consisted of about four rows filled with various knickknacks. On the right was a big door with a deadbolt lock on it. She wanted to ask why it was locked, and she must have slowed her stride enough for Yvonne to notice.

"That door leads to the basement. Jake's grandfather always kept it locked since he caught two kids down there making out one time. And Jake—who owns the bookstore, by the way—also has some personal things down there. It's not much to see."

Eden nodded, then looked down at her feet when a board beneath her groaned. "This is an old building, isn't it?"

"*Ya*, it is," Yvonne said over her shoulder as she walked. "I *lieb* this place, but for all the quaintness, it needs a lot of repairs." She stopped, turned to face Eden, and pointed to the ceiling. "When we have a hard rain, there are several places where the roof leaks. I'm usually running around like a crazy person putting buckets and pots everywhere. It doesn't happen every time it rains, but Jake definitely needs a new roof on this place."

She gently took a few steps to her left and pushed down on a board with her foot. "See how this plank gives way? Be careful of the wood floors near the walls. They give a little, which to me means the building is shifting." She shrugged. "I could be wrong, but it's easy enough to tell that it needs leveling." She waved an arm before she started walking again. "There's more. Plenty more. But the kind of repairs this place needs takes a big chunk of money, and it's just not in Jake's budget."

As they entered the small kitchen area, Eden eyed the small gas oven and tiny refrigerator that had a propane tank next to it. No microwave, of course. There were skylights everywhere, even in the kitchen.

"But this place is also steeped with mystery, which adds to its charm." Yvonne took two cups from the small cabinet above the sink, then looked over her shoulder at Eden and grinned.

"Really? How so?" Eden took a filled cup of coffee from Yvonne. She'd never been much of a coffee drinker, but the few times she had, she'd felt older.

"Sugar is there, and there's milk in the fridge if you need some." Yvonne sat down at the table.

Eden thought the coffee might taste better with something added, but she followed her cousin's lead and sat down across from her without adding anything to the cup.

"Supposedly . . ." Yvonne took a deep breath. "There are old coins hidden somewhere in the building . . . *If* you believe the stories the old man who used to own the building told. He ran a general store here, and the locals say he was a bit off in the head, but he swore that he had hidden a collection of rare coins somewhere in the walls."

Eden sat taller, knowing her eyes had widened. "Wow. That is super cool. Do you think there's any truth to the story?"

Yvonne took a sip of coffee. Eden did the same, trying to hide her reaction to the bitter taste.

"Before I changed *mei* life, I was a book broker of sorts. I tracked down rare books for clients. It's how I met Jake, his wife, Eva, and even Abraham. I was on the hunt for a book that Jake had but refused to sell due to a promise he made to his grandfather." Yvonne paused. "I never did convince him to sell the book, and that's another story, but *mei* point is that old things like that have always interested me. So, when I first heard about the coins, I was intrigued even though Jake and others were sure it was an old man spinning tales." She smiled. "Then I found something."

She got up and went to a kitchen drawer, pulled it out as far as it would go, then took out a small white bag, like something you might put a piece of jewelry in. She sat again, undid the short string holding the bag closed, and turned it upside down. An old coin fell out onto the table.

"I found this in between the floorboards up front."

Eden set her cup down and picked up the coin. "Wow. That kind of thing intrigues me too. When I was little, I loved shows about treasure hunts or discovering anything old and mysterious." She glanced up at her cousin. "Is it worth anything?"

"Apparently so. It has a face value of five cents, but

when I took it to an appraiser, he said it would likely pull in over five hundred dollars at a coin auction."

"Wow," Eden said again as she turned the silver coin over and over between her fingers. "If there were a bunch of these . . ." She raised an eyebrow and looked at Yvonne, who smiled.

"Exactly. Jake could be sitting on a fortune buried somewhere within these walls." She waved her hands around, then chuckled. "If only these walls could talk and point us to where the supposed treasure is. If Jake had enough valuable coins, he could get a lot of the repairs done, but it's just too big a risk to start tearing out walls that he can't afford to replace. Not to mention there are a lot of rules when you own a historical building. You might have seen the plaque out front? Any repairs must be approved to maintain the historical status."

"Yeah, I did see the plaque." Eden set the coin atop the white pouch. "But overall, the Amish don't care about money, right?"

Yvonne sort of laughed, but it was more like a grunt. "*Ach*, *ya*. They care. They aren't materialistic, but money buys wood to build homes, barns, and make repairs. It buys farming equipment. And it buys food essentials that not all Amish grow on their farms. Money buys horses, buggies, and livestock. It buys material to make clothes. See where I'm going? It still takes money to live, even if you're Amish."

"Just not as much money, I guess?"

"Correct. We don't buy expensive cars, have to pay for electricity, or wear ourselves out trying to keep up with or outdo our neighbors."

"There must be a certain freedom in that." Eden thought about all the times she'd been forced to go to school in clothes her mother had picked up at secondhand stores and how self-conscious she'd felt. The popular girls in their designer clothes had looked down on her.

"You're right," Yvonne said softly. "But pride and vanity are still present. Amish people are human. I've seen women competing, especially in the baking arena. But when you consider that no one worries about clothes, dying their hair—things like that—it does make for a simpler life with a lot less stress."

Eden forced another sip of coffee, pondering what her cousin had said. Would those same popular girls have taken her into their circle if she'd dressed the way they did? All the girls here dressed alike, so it wasn't an issue.

After they finished their coffee, Eden helped Yvonne load three boxes onto a dolly, then her cousin pushed the boxes to the front of the store.

"These are all fiction, and they are shelved alphabetically by the author's surname." Yvonne took a utility knife from the pocket of her apron and opened the first box. They were quiet as they sorted the books.

Eden wondered again how much Yvonne knew about her background. Probably a lot. Emma had surely told her that Eden's mother was in prison. Had she told her about the one night she'd snuck out? Or the one time she'd shoplifted? She cringed on the inside. She wanted Yvonne to like her. And so far, Eden liked her cousin. It had hurt her feelings when Yvonne seemed to question her faith, but that was forgivable. Eden probably didn't strike her cousin as the religious type.

What did that mean anyway? "Religious type"? She didn't think there was a certain look that was needed to have a relationship with God.

She glanced down at the butterfly on the top of her hand, surprised that Yvonne or Abraham hadn't questioned her about it. She'd caught them both looking at it at different times since she had arrived. Eden would be happy to tell them why she got it if they asked.

"Someone's here." Yvonne turned an ear. "In a buggy." She smiled at Eden. "I can always tell the way the buggy wheels crunch against the gravel parking lot."

"I can finish this if you want to go help whoever it is." Eden stayed parked on the floor, enjoying the feel and smell of the books.

Yvonne lifted herself from her knees, smoothed the wrinkles from her black apron, and headed to the front of the store just as the bell jingled.

Eden kept alphabetizing the books, but when she heard her name, she stopped and stood up. When she heard it again, she eased her way around the tall shelf until she was in view of Yvonne and an Amish woman who didn't look much older than her cousin.

"Hey, Eden." Yvonne motioned for her to come closer. "This is *mei* sister-in-law, Anna. She's married to Abraham's *bruder*, Leroy."

Eden wasn't sure what proper protocol was. Emma had told her that the Amish weren't openly affectionate, but she held out her hand, and the woman extended hers. "Nice to meet you, Anna."

The woman quickly took back her hand. Eden noticed

it was callused, like maybe she'd been sweeping for a long time or something.

"*Ya*, it is nice to meet you too." Anna smiled. "Welcome to Montgomery. I hear you'll be staying with your cousin for a month." She nodded to Yvonne.

"Yes, ma'am." Eden wanted to make a good impression, for Yvonne to be proud to have her around. "I'm happy to be here."

"I bet things must be quite different here than where you're from, uh . . ." Anna looked at Yvonne. "Did you tell me California?"

Her cousin nodded. "*Ya*."

"It *is* very different here. I love how it's all out in the country, the buggies everywhere . . ." Eden shrugged. "I think it's awesome."

Anna was dressed exactly like Yvonne, except she was wearing a maroon dress, and she had a small black purse hanging from her wrist, almost identical to Yvonne's bag.

"Eden loves to read, and she's helping me out around the store." Yvonne glanced at Eden and smiled. "I'm happy to have the help and company."

Anna nodded. "I always tell the *kinner* that reading sharpens the mind. And the *maed lieb* to read." She chuckled. "I don't think Samuel has opened a book since he graduated from the eighth grade."

Samuel? "Uh . . ." Eden looked at Yvonne. "Is that the same Samuel I met?"

Her cousin cleared her throat. "Um, *ya*." She turned to Anna. "I was teaching Eden how to drive the buggy, and we ran into Samuel."

"He's *mei* oldest." Anna smiled again, and Eden thought she was pretty, too, like Yvonne. "I think *mei* husband—Leroy—wished he had three or four more like him." She laughed. "Not that he doesn't love the *maed*, but I think all men hope for more than one boy to help in the fields."

"I'll be at your house on Wednesday. Samuel is teaching me to ride a horse." Eden grinned. "I've never been on a horse, and I'm so excited to learn how to ride."

Anna's expression fell right away, as if someone had given her some sort of horrible news. Eden glanced at Yvonne. Her cousin was chewing on her bottom lip. Eden wanted to ask if it was some big secret about Samuel giving her lessons, but Anna's bright smile and chipper mood had shifted into . . . something else.

"Anna, is there anything special you need today?" Yvonne plastered on a big smile, but her eyes reflected an emotion other than joy.

Eden wasn't sure what she'd done wrong. But it was obviously a secret that Samuel was planning to teach her to ride a horse.

"Actually . . ." Anna glanced at the clock on the wall behind the counter. "I've lost track of time, and there is somewhere else I need to be. But I'll drop back by when I'm not so rushed."

"*Ya*, sure." Yvonne followed Anna to the door, and for a moment, Eden wondered if she was going to follow her into the parking lot, but she only waved and came back into the store.

There was no place to put this huge elephant, so Eden decided not to try. "Um, I'm sorry. I guess I shouldn't have said anything about Samuel teaching me to ride, but I had no idea that—"

"Don't worry about it." Yvonne waved her off. "Really. Samuel is the one who offered. It's fine."

Eden stood still, not sure what to do and feeling like she might cry, which was lame, but a knot was forming in her throat just the same. "Does she not want me around Samuel because I'm not Amish? I think I read that somewhere, but I didn't really think it would be true."

Yvonne leaned against the counter and put a hand to her forehead. "It doesn't have anything to do with you personally, Eden, so please don't think that it does. Anna and Leroy are super protective of their *kinner* . . . their children."

Eden wondered right away if Anna knew her background. Was Yvonne's sister-in-law judging her based on that or strictly because she wasn't Amish? "I mean, it's not like a date or anything."

"Look, I'm going to be honest with you. I was a little surprised that Samuel made the invitation. He certainly knows how strict his parents are when it comes to outsiders. But there is nothing wrong with making friends while you're here, and Samuel is a *gut* guy."

"You were an outsider before you turned Amish. Did they treat you funny?"

Yvonne half laughed. "First of all, you don't *turn* Amish. And even though my and Abraham's situation wasn't the norm, either way . . . we aren't their children. I think that is the biggest fear that Amish parents have—that their children will grow up and leave one day. And the irony is, hardly any of them do."

Yvonne's hands seemed to find their way to her stomach, and she smiled. "I'll be hoping that *mei* little ones stay around, but I also know that they will have the freedom to make that choice when they are of age."

Eden brought a hand to her mouth as a small gasp escaped. "You're pregnant, aren't you?"

Yvonne covered her face with both hands. "I shouldn't say anything. I haven't even told Abraham." She lowered her hands. "But *ya*, I think so."

Eden didn't know Yvonne at all, but based on the little she'd seen so far, she thought she would be an awesome mom.

"Wow. That is so cool. Congratulations." Eden was warm all over, seeing how Yvonne was so giddy.

Her cousin put a finger to her mouth. "Don't tell anyone. I'm planning to tell Abraham tonight, then we probably won't share the news for a while because that's how it's done here." She blinked back tears. "We've been trying since we got married. I was starting to think it wasn't going to happen."

Yvonne oozed goodness. Eden could recognize badness without any problem, but she believed she had the same gift when it came to seeing the good in people. She went to Yvonne and hugged her, and the way Yvonne squeezed her tightly made her feel safe. It was a strange thought to have, since she barely knew the woman, but the feeling was there just the same. She was more cautious when it came to physical contact with men.

Eden was a little concerned now about her visit with Samuel on Wednesday. Not because she thought there would be any physical contact, but due to Anna's display in the store. She was nervous about her horse-riding adventure and didn't want to cause any problems while she was here.

She pushed the thoughts aside. Right now, she was going to try not to worry about it and just be happy for her cousin.

CHAPTER 4

Anna parked her buggy, then led her horse to its designated area on the north side of the house. Six other horses were happily grazing beneath a cloudless sky. She could see Leroy plowing the field farthest from the house, too far for her to holler for him.

Her chest tightened as she crossed the front yard, briefly admiring her flowerbeds. The girls had done a wonderful job filling the space with colorful blooms. She climbed the porch steps, reached for the whistle on a string that dangled from a nail on the pillar, and blew it. Anna hated the thing, and her ears rang when she was forced to use it, but it was the only way to get Leroy's attention when he was so far away.

She poured herself into one of four rocking chairs on the porch. Her daughters were probably still running the clothes through the wringer and would be out soon to hang the clothes to dry. Anna had plenty of chores she needed to tend to. Buying a birthday present for their elderly neighbor had been on her agenda today, but finding out that Yvonne's cousin would be spending time with Samuel had her unnerved.

"What is it?" Leroy walked across the yard to her, a hand to his forehead as he blocked the sun. "Everything okay?"

Anna should have poured him a glass of iced tea before she blew the whistle, but she was anxious to talk to her husband.

"*Ya*, *ya*. Everything is okay. I think." She stood and walked to him, and they sat down on the porch steps side by side. "Did you know that Samuel has a guest coming Wednesday? Apparently, our *sohn* is planning to teach the *Englisch* girl, Yvonne's cousin, how to ride a horse."

Her husband took off his straw hat, blotted his forehead with a handkerchief he'd pulled from his pocket, then shrugged. "*Nee*, I haven't seen Samuel, so I don't know anything about it."

"I met the *maedel* today." She turned to her husband. "And she is gorgeous. And worldly. And didn't you say that Abraham said she had a tainted background?"

Leroy ran his hand the length of his beard, which was salt and pepper–colored like his hair. Anna and her husband were the oldest in both their families, each nearing forty.

"I don't know if 'tainted' is the right word." Her husband dropped his hand to his lap and faced her. "I know that her *mudder* is in jail for drugs. And I think Abe said the *maedel* had a little trouble with the law." He put a hand on Anna's knee. "She's only going to be here for a month. How much trouble can she and Samuel get into over such a short time?"

Anna frowned. "Plenty." She raised an eyebrow. "Think back. I know it's been a while, but can't you recall us at sixteen? We were making out behind *mei daed*'s toolshed at that age."

Leroy smiled, and Anna nudged him with her elbow.

"It's not funny. It's dangerous for Samuel to be around that *maedel*." She stood and pointed a finger at her husband. "I want you to talk to Samuel and tell him it's not a *gut* idea for him to spend time with Eden. That's her name. Eden."

"If he's already made plans with her, just let it go for now. He was probably just being nice to Yvonne's cousin, and there's no need for us to make a fuss." Leroy stood up, blotted his face with his handkerchief again, and kissed her on the cheek.

"I hope you're right." Anna had a bad feeling in the pit of her stomach.

"*Mei lieb*, he is sixteen. We must give him some freedoms during his *rumschpringe*." Leroy sighed, probably thinking Anna was making too much of this. Maybe she was. "He's our first child to turn sixteen. It's normal to be a little concerned, but I don't think we have to worry about this girl. She'll only be here a short while."

Anna and her husband had worked hard to keep their children shielded from the ways of the outside world and made sure that friendships with outsiders weren't nurtured. Her children needed to be with their own kind, those grounded in their faith. She was sure there were plenty of wonderful English children out there, but they had no way to discern which were the good ones or which could cause their children to stray from the faith.

"I hope you're right," she repeated.

Anna was aware that members of their community thought they were too strict with their children. As recently as three weeks ago, their daughters had been invited to a birthday party an English acquaintance was having. Anna was friendly with the girl's mother. They'd shared a booth at a county fair. The woman—Diana—was very nice, but her children dressed in a way that made them look much older than they were, which was eleven and thirteen. The eldest even wore makeup. Anna hadn't let her daughters attend the party, and the girls pretended to be all right with Anna's decision even though Anna knew they were disappointed. They had to know it was for their own good.

Samuel hadn't tolerated the rules as well over the years, often rebelling when Anna or Leroy refused to let him spend time with outsiders. Clearly, their son was pushing his limits by inviting an English girl to their home without asking.

"Don't worry. Samuel is a smart boy. I'm sure he was just being nice." Leroy kissed her again, on the mouth, and she was once again reminded of their teenage years.

Anna was going to keep a close eye on her son. He was a boy, and Leroy, of all people, should realize there was danger if he spent much time with the beautiful Eden.

Yvonne wanted to wait until she was alone with Abraham before she told him about the baby. Her stomach swirled with anticipation, and she couldn't stop smiling. Neither could Eden. It had been that way all through supper, and now Yvonne couldn't wait to finish devotions.

Forgive me, Lord, for rushing tonight.

She had envisioned Abraham's expression a hundred times throughout the day, every time she thought about telling him she was pregnant. Maybe a person really did glow, since Eden had guessed her news earlier in the day.

"I'm going to go take a shower and probably go straight to bed." Eden beamed at Yvonne from the rocking chair in the living room before she stood up. It was cute the way she seemed excited, especially since she didn't know Yvonne well. Maybe the thought of a new life in the world just did that to people.

After Eden was out of sight, Yvonne stood and held her hand out to Abraham.

"Something is going on with you two," her husband said as he rose and wrapped his arms around her. "I saw you exchanging grins throughout supper."

Yvonne kissed Abraham, then picked up the lantern from the coffee table. "Let's go to bed."

Blue had chosen his bed by the fireplace this evening, but the dog kept one eye open as they passed him on the way to the bedroom. Maybe he could sense something was up. Yvonne smiled. "Night-night, Blue."

Abraham was unbuttoning his shirt before Yvonne had even closed the door, and the passion in his eyes was hard to resist, but she couldn't hold off on her news anymore. She set the lantern on the bedside table.

"Wait." She held him at arm's length as he leaned in to kiss her. "I have something to tell you." Lowering her hands to her stomach, she patted her belly, raised an eyebrow, and grinned.

Abraham's eyes drifted to her stomach, where they paused a moment before recognition seemed to slowly sink in.

His eyes moistened, and he blinked several times before he found any words. "Really?"

Yvonne nodded. "I honestly don't know if pregnancy tests are allowed, and I didn't want to ask anyone. But I've suspected for a few days that I might be with child, so I did a pregnancy test this afternoon, and it's positive."

Abraham put a hand on top of hers. "Wow."

"I know. Finally." Yvonne knew it was way too soon to feel the baby moving, but knowing she was carrying a life inside of her gave her a feeling she'd never had before. "We're going to be parents."

Abraham drew her to him, then smothered her with kisses before stopping abruptly. "Does Eden know?"

Yvonne flinched. "Don't be mad." She raised her shoulders and lowered them slowly. "She guessed. All I did was put my hands on my stomach. I told her I thought I was." She smiled as she batted her eyes playfully at him. "Maybe I'm glowing."

"You definitely are, and I could never be mad at you. Anyway, she is family," he said, kissing her again.

Yvonne eased him away. "As much as I want to bask in this wonderful news, I think I'd better tell you about Anna coming into the store today."

Abraham sat on the bed, and Yvonne sat beside him. "I'd rather bask in the news." He drew her mouth to his, and she returned the kisses but knew if she didn't stop, she might not feel like talking later. She didn't feel like it now, either, but . . .

"Listen. Anna was visibly upset that Samuel is going to teach Eden to ride on Wednesday." She sighed. "Poor Eden didn't know any better when she excitedly said something about it. Anna went cold right away. She made up an excuse to leave. It was obvious."

"That's just Anna being Anna. Sometimes I think she pushes Leroy to enforce such strict rules. Maybe that's not fair of me to say that." He cupped her cheek with his hand. "But remember, we said we weren't going to borrow trouble. Those two might never see each other again after Wednesday. They come from totally different worlds and have nothing in common. I think Eden just wants to ride a horse."

"Maybe. But, like I told you, I saw the way they looked at each other." Yvonne put a hand over her mouth when she yawned.

Abraham seemed to realize he was losing the moment. "Kind of like I'm looking at you now." He gave her an exaggerated sultry expression.

"Stop it." She laughed, but when he pulled her back onto the bed and wrapped his arms around her, she didn't resist.

Maybe Abraham was right. Two teenagers would enjoy a riding lesson and realize they had nothing in common. She was going to adhere to her husband's wise words and not borrow trouble.

Eden only had one bar of service on her cell phone, and that came and went. But she wouldn't have answered her mother's call even if she had full service. She was enjoying her stay so far, and anything her mother said would only upset her.

After silencing her phone, she opened her window as high as it would go and angled the small battery-operated fan so it blew directly on her. Then she lowered the flame on the lantern, climbed into bed, and leaned against her pillow.

A few minutes later, she plugged the phone into an extra battery she'd brought with her, making a mental note that she was going to have to ask Yvonne where she could charge her phone and batteries tomorrow. She planned to go with her cousin to the bookstore again the next day, and Wednesday she'd learn to ride a horse.

Repeatedly, she mentally replayed the scene at the store with Samuel's mother. Any way she spun it, the result was the same. Anna was not happy that Eden would be spending time with her son. It seemed old-fashioned, but if she analyzed the way they lived, maybe it shouldn't be surprising. Samuel was good-looking for sure, with his blond hair, dark tan, and amazing brown eyes. His smile had drawn her in right away. But everyone—or Anna at least—was worrying for nothing. Samuel wouldn't want anything to do with her if he knew her background. Maybe he already did. She disliked having to guess what people knew about her, but she was too embarrassed to bring it up, even with Yvonne. Samuel was just being nice, offering to give her riding lessons. Even if she hadn't misinterpreted the looks they'd exchanged, they were worlds apart. But learning to ride a horse trumped any thoughts of not going on Wednesday. Eden couldn't wait.

Her phone buzzed on the nightstand beside her again, the same number as moments ago. How many times had she told her mother, in the beginning, that she couldn't afford to accept her calls? What she really wanted to tell her was, "Stop calling me. I don't want to talk to you. You made your bed, now you get to sleep in it." But even a short conversation was out of her budget.

She clicked the phone to silence it again, then rolled over and let the fan blow in her face.

Eden had never done drugs. She'd had a few beers in her life, but she didn't care for it. She'd been fighting off boys ever since she started to develop, but she'd held on to her virginity. Dealing with Max had been a constant challenge, but Eden had successfully fended him off—if you called getting slapped across the face in the process a victory. She was never sure how much her mother knew about Max's constant attempts to grope her. Most of the time, it happened when her mother wasn't around, but on a few occasions, her mother had been in the room but was too messed up to know—or even care—what was happening. Her mother had made a string of bad choices. Abusing drugs and alcohol and choosing the wrong men.

I will not be like you, Mom. I won't.

She might not know what she wanted in life, or who she was meant to be, or where God would lead her, but it wasn't going to be on the path her mother had chosen. She'd clung to God before, and she would continue to do so. He would keep her safe.

Closing her eyes, she thanked Him for the good things in her life, determined not to focus on anything bad. She also prayed that Yvonne would have a healthy baby and an uncomplicated pregnancy. Eden asked God to bless her friendship with Yvonne. Emma was great, but she was older. And it wasn't just the age gap between Eden and Emma. There was also an unspoken spiritual gap that seemed to put distance between them. Yvonne was younger and shared Eden's faith. Even though Yvonne was her mother's age, she wasn't anything like her.

She pushed away thoughts of her mother and pictured herself sitting on a horse, giving the animal a gentle kick, then flying across a field as her hair blew in the wind. It was a lovely thought as she drifted off to sleep.

Samuel was sitting up in bed reading by the light of the lantern when there came a knock at his bedroom door. He quickly stowed the travel magazine beneath the sheet. "Come in."

"*Wie bischt, sohn.*"

Samuel glanced at the clock on his wall. It was nearing nine o'clock. His father was usually in bed by now. "Everything is *gut*, *Daed*. Anything wrong?" He straightened and ran a hand through his hair, still wet from his shower.

"*Nee.*" His father sat on the foot of the bed and shrugged. "Nothing's wrong. I was just wondering what your plans were Wednesday. I heard you were going to teach Yvonne's cousin to ride a horse."

Samuel hung his head for a moment, then looked back up at his father. "Word travels fast."

"*Ya*, around here it does."

"Is *Mamm* worrying that I'm planning to spend time with an *Englisch* girl?" He paused, frowning. "Are you? Because I thought you'd be happy that I was being nice to Yvonne's cousin. I mean, she's family now that she's married to Abraham."

"That doesn't change the fact that she's an outsider, and I think the *maedel* has probably lived a"—his father cleared his throat—"colorful life."

"That sounds like judgment about someone we don't know." Samuel regretted the statement right away, and even more so when his father cut his eyes at him in a way that let him know he was on thin ice. Samuel worried he might make him cancel the riding session. "I don't have to spend any time with her. Tell *Mamm* to let Yvonne know not to bring her over."

It was a huge risk to act so nonchalant. Seeing Eden the day after tomorrow had consumed his thoughts. He'd known he was going to hear from his parents about this, but he didn't think it would be until after they saw Eden at their house on Wednesday.

"I didn't say you had to cancel your plans." His father ran his hand the length of his beard. "I'm just reminding you that outsiders can pose a risk, tempt us to do things that don't coincide with our beliefs."

Something about the way his father said "reminding you" felt like a warning.

"*Ya*, I know what you're saying, *Daed*. I won't let anything like that happen." He paused, thinking of ways to put his father at ease, which would ultimately put his mother at ease. "She was so excited about the thought of riding a horse, which seems weird since we grew up on them." He shrugged. "I thought I was doing a nice thing, that's all. But *Mamm* can get me out of it if you're both that worried. I'd do it myself, but I've got work."

He swallowed hard, wishing he hadn't made the offer a second time. But he had faith that his mother would save face and not cancel on his behalf. Both his parents were strict, but his mother wasn't going to embarrass herself by coming up with a lame excuse as to why Samuel couldn't teach a girl to ride a horse.

His father stood and looped his thumbs beneath his suspenders. "*Nee, nee.* You teach the *maedel* to ride." His father turned to go, and Samuel thought he was in the clear until the man turned around and raised an eyebrow. "I was sixteen once. I'm told Eden is a beautiful girl. Just remember that she is not our kind. She doesn't share our beliefs."

Samuel nodded. "*Ya*, I know, *Daed*."

He breathed a sigh of relief when his father left the room, closing the door behind him. He'd heard everything his father said about Eden, how she wasn't of their kind and that she didn't share their beliefs. Eden was pretty, and he had thought about her constantly since he met her. But it was the other things his father mentioned that interested him too. He *wanted* to learn about the outside world. Maybe it would help him decide if he wanted to stay here and be baptized—something that filled him with increasing uncertainty. His lack of freedom had fueled his confusion ever since he'd turned sixteen. How could he be expected to make choices when he wasn't allowed to view his options?

Baptism was a forever commitment, and Samuel wanted to make the right choice. He enjoyed working the land, tilling the soil in preparation for a plentiful harvest. His construction job kept his mind and body sharp. He was the one who measured out the job, then planned it via a blueprint with help from his boss. The hard work kept him physically strong. It wasn't a bad life, and he was wise enough to realize that. He also had the love of his family. But the what-ifs weighed him down, along with the fact that he couldn't see outside the forty-mile radius he'd been allowed to travel.

When he had started feeling this way a few months ago, he began praying about it, because that's the way he'd been brought up. But he hadn't heard the Lord speak to him in a long time. He just wasn't sure this life was for him.

CHAPTER 5

Eden slipped on a pair of black work boots that Yvonne had loaned her. She was tying the laces when her cousin came in from outside.

"The horse and buggy are ready whenever you are." Yvonne picked up her small black purse from the coffee table, rummaged through it, then found a handkerchief and dabbed at her face. "It's only seven thirty, and it's already hot and muggy." She studied Eden's blue jeans and short-sleeved button-up blouse she'd left untucked.

"Am I dressed okay?" Eden was excited about this new adventure but nervous about being around Samuel and getting on a horse. She also didn't want to do anything to upset Samuel's parents, and clothing seemed to be an issue with these people. No shorts, no revealing or tight blouses.

"*Ya*, you're fine." Yvonne waited until Eden finished tying double knots and stood up.

"Ready," she said.

"Do you want to drive the buggy again?" Yvonne wasn't her bubbly self this morning.

"Sure." Outside, Eden climbed into the driver's side

and turned to face her cousin. "Are you okay? You look a little pale."

Yvonne sighed. "I guess I'm having morning sickness." A smile followed. "But I'm not going to complain. We've been wanting a *boppli*—baby—since we got married."

"Well, I'm happy to drive you anywhere you want to go." Eden backed up the horse and buggy the way Yvonne had taught her.

"*Gut* job," Yvonne said when they got onto the road.

"You'll have to show me which road to turn on. I remember it was off the main drag, but I don't remember how far down."

"About half a mile. We'll probably get there a little early." Yvonne dug around in her purse and pulled out her cell phone. "I'll keep this on so you can call me when you're ready for me to come get you. It won't take long for me to get there, and I can hang the Closed sign on the door while I'm gone."

"Okay. And I was going to ask you if there is somewhere to charge my phone and extra batteries." Eden bounced as one of the wagon wheels hit a pothole. "Oops. Sorry."

"Don't be. I hit it every time." Yvonne stowed the phone. "*Ya*, there's a little café not far where we can charge our phones after I close the bookstore this evening. Help me to remember." She pointed ahead of her. "It's going to be the next left, up there a little way."

"So, I didn't want to ask you at breakfast with Abraham there, but was he, like, crazy excited about the baby?" Eden couldn't help but sneak a peek at Yvonne's tummy even though there wasn't anything to see since she wore one of those baggy dresses.

Her cousin chuckled. "*Ya*, he was happy."

"So . . . how far along are you?"

Yvonne put both her hands on her stomach again, something she was doing a lot of. It was cute, Eden thought. "I haven't been to the doctor or a midwife, but I'm pretty sure I'm about eight weeks. But we won't tell anyone for a while."

"Not even your family?" Eden recalled her saying that, but she figured Yvonne surely wanted to shout it to the world.

Yvonne twisted her mouth back and forth. "Well . . . it's customary to wait as long as possible, although I'm not really sure why. And to be honest with you, I don't see how I'm going to keep this from Aunt Emma." She paused, the few tiny lines on her forehead crinkling. "I haven't heard from her. Have you?"

Eden shook her head. "Nope. But she's probably having such a good time that I'm out of sight, out of mind." She smiled. "I'm okay with that. Emma's been good to me, and she deserves a good time." She winced a little. "She's just kind of old, so we don't have much in common."

Yvonne nodded. "I hear you." She pointed. "Oh, slow down a little. That's the turn."

Eden pulled back on the reins, then gently laid them over to the left until the horse turned down the narrow road they'd traveled before. Rows of corn lined both sides and stood about four feet high, green and lush for as far as she could see. "That's a lot of corn," she said.

"*Ya*, it is. Indiana is big on corn, and it's the sweetest you'll ever eat."

Eden glanced at her cousin. "Guess I won't know. I'll be gone before they harvest it."

"Their farm is at the end of this road on the left," Yvonne said, then added, "Who knows. Maybe you'll want to come back and visit."

It warmed Eden's heart to think Yvonne might already be thinking she could come back. "That would be awesome." She liked it here already. Or maybe she just liked herself better here. Either way, it would be nice to have family to visit who weren't in prison or uninterested in her, which was surely the case with her other relatives since Emma was the only one who had stepped up to the plate to take her in.

Eden's heart started pounding when she saw Samuel standing outside a huge white farmhouse surrounded by a white picket fence. Both looked freshly painted, and flowers were planted everywhere. In the distance a huge pond sparkled in the sunlight, and there was a green canoe tied up to a dock that went across the water.

"Wow. What a beautiful place."

The barn was dark red, and the entire place looked pristine. Eden breathed in the aroma of freshly cut grass.

Samuel met them when they got close to the barn, and Eden slowed the horse to a stop.

"You're a natural," he said, smiling, his dimples full force as his brown eyes twinkled. He was cuter than Eden remembered, and her cheeks grew warm.

"Yvonne is a good teacher."

Her cousin stepped out of the buggy and walked around to Eden's side. She rubbed the horse's nose while Eden eased out of the driver's seat.

"Have fun," her cousin said as she scooted into the buggy. "I'm sure Samuel is a *gut* teacher too." She pointed a finger at him. "Remember what I said—it's your watch. Make sure you take *gut* care of her."

He clicked his heels together and saluted, which seemed odd to Eden since he was Amish, no chance of ever becoming a soldier. "*Ya*, she's in *gut* hands," he said before he relaxed his stance.

Eden waved as her cousin headed back down the road.

"I've got two horses saddled up in the barn. I thought I could give you a basic safety rundown before we ride."

She loved the way Samuel's smile crooked up on one side, which made him even cuter, if that was possible.

"Sure." She followed him toward the barn entrance. He pulled open the door, which had a big white *X* across it, and waited for her to go in ahead of him.

"Bessie is the larger horse, but I promise you she's really gentle." He walked over to the solid brown mare, and the horse nodded her head, snorting.

Eden's stomach churned. Her anticipation was quickly turning to nervousness. Bessie was a big girl.

"And this is *mei* ride for the day." He nodded to the black horse tethered next to the mare. "He's a young stallion. I broke him myself, but he's a little moody sometimes."

Eden was already sweating, and she tried to recall her visualizations: on top of the horse, flying through the pasture, her hair blowing in the wind. To keep in line with her dream, she hadn't pulled it back in a ponytail. Now that the time was here, there was a large temptation to back out, but both horses were saddled up and ready to go, as Samuel had said.

"Hey."

Eden pulled her gaze away from the massive animals and turned to Samuel. "Yeah?"

He grinned. "Don't look so nervous. Bessie has never thrown anyone." He chuckled. "Now, the same can't be said for Blackjack."

The horse raised and lowered his head, snorting loudly at the mention of his name.

"Easy, boy." Samuel rubbed the top of the horse's nose as he cut his eyes in Eden's direction. "Do you know CPR or basic first aid?"

Eden's jaw dropped as she eyed the massive black animal. "Uh . . ."

Samuel laughed. "I'm kidding. He hasn't thrown me in months."

Eden tried to smile, then said a silent prayer that no one would get thrown today. She tried to focus as Samuel went through some basic horse terminology, all the while tempted to opt out of this adventure.

"Here." Samuel untied the loose knot keeping Bessie tied to the beam in the barn. "Just hold on to her bridle and start walking her out of the barn. I'll be right behind you with Blackjack."

Eden did as he said, but her feet weren't moving very fast as she stared at the ground and hoped Bessie didn't step on her foot.

Outside the barn, she took a deep breath, hoping the smell of the freshly cut grass and sunshine would put her back in the state of mind she'd envisioned and squash the fear that was building. Eden was always up for a new adventure, so she tried to analyze the apprehension that seemed to have come on rather suddenly. Standing next to Bessie, who seemed much larger up close, was part of it. But she also wanted to look good and do well in Samuel's eyes.

"When you put your foot in the stirrup, hold on to the horn of the saddle, then throw your leg over the other side, but be careful not to kick her in the flank. She might try to take off before you're settled."

Eden felt her eyes widen. "I thought you said she was gentle and would be easy to ride."

Samuel winked at her, which caused her stomach to churn for reasons other than fear. "She is. Just don't kick her in the side when you throw your leg over."

Eden managed to get one foot in the stirrup and her hand on the horn, but she was shaking and felt stuck in that position.

Samuel left Blackjack standing on his own, seemingly confident the horse wouldn't go anywhere. He rubbed Bessie on her nose, then began long strokes down her massive neck. "You'll be fine. Just slowly ease your leg over her back."

She held her breath, grasped tightly to the horn with both hands, heaved herself up, then threw her leg over the horse, barely grazing Bessie's back, which caused her to move a little.

"*Gut, gut.*" Samuel put his hands around her left ankle and eased her foot into the stirrup. "You don't want your feet too snug, on the off chance you got thrown. You don't want to get dragged." He went to the other side and performed the same maneuver with her other foot.

"I—I thought you said she's never thrown anyone," she

repeated and heard the unattractive quiver in her voice. She cleared her throat, determined not to let a little anxiety derail her.

"She hasn't. But it's important to know how your feet should be situated to be safe." He shook his head. "I'd be in a world of trouble if you got hurt."

She let out a nervous chuckle. "Believe me, I don't want to get hurt."

Samuel put a hand on her leg, which sent a shiver the length of her body. "Just relax. I'm not going to let anything happen to you."

She reached her hand out to him and held up her pinky finger. "Pinky swear?" she asked, forcing the shakiness from her voice as she wondered if Samuel knew what the term symbolized.

He attached his finger to hers and looked her right in the eyes. "I'm guessing that's a promise, so yes . . . I pinky swear."

He slowly let go of her hand and went to Blackjack, and he was on the horse and holding the reins within what seemed like a split second. "Hold the reins like this."

Eden did what he said even though she was shaking all over. Didn't animals recognize fear? She didn't want to be the first person thrown from Bessie.

A terrible name for a horse. Bessie sounded more like the name of a cow and unfitting for such a big beast.

"Now, give her a gentle kick with both heels, like this, and follow me." He pointed to his right. "We're going to go to the back pasture behind the house. We can't trample the corn." He smiled and set his horse in motion.

Eden trembled from head to toe as she coaxed her feet to give the horse a gentle tap on both sides, and she jumped a little when Bessie started to move.

"See. No problem, *ya*?" Samuel scooted over, slowed Blackjack, and waited until Bessie sidled up next to the beautiful but slightly scary-looking horse that Samuel was riding. Blackjack bucked his head up and down a lot. The animal's stance was regal, though, and Samuel looked especially handsome in the saddle.

"Are you okay?" Samuel tipped back the rim of his straw hat.

Eden tried to smile, not wanting to appear as nervous as she was. "Um, I think so." She was wishing she'd put her hair in a ponytail, since it was windy enough for long strands to whip across her face, but she still had the vision in her mind of her hair blowing wild and free. Now she wondered if the tousled strands were going to impair her vision.

A wide cattle gate came into view as they went around the house and toward the back of the property, which was as pristine as the rest. It looked like someone had recently used a weed wacker along the fence line. In the distance, the pond gleamed a greenish-blue color. The sun had risen above the horizon, bright and radiant against a blue and cloudless sky, dew still glistening like moist fairy dust on the lush green grass and carried over like twinkling stars across the water. It looked like a postcard. This was what Eden had been waiting for, and her heart pumped wildly with thrilling anticipation and a small dose of terror.

Samuel slowed his horse to a stop, and Eden pulled back gently on the reins until Bessie stopped too.

"When we go through that gate, both these horses will have an instinct to run. It's wide open, and this is where we always ride." He studied her face, surely noticing her pained expression as she nibbled on her lip. "You sure you're okay? Bessie doesn't buck, but she does like to run. If you get nervous, pull back on the reins to slow her down."

I'm already nervous. Eden nodded, and Samuel set his horse in motion again. Bessie started walking even though Eden hadn't given her a tap with her feet.

"Hold on to the saddle horn with one hand and keep the reins in the other hand." Samuel smiled his crooked, dimpled smile, and for a brief few seconds, Eden's pulse slowed. He seemed genuinely concerned about her well-being, so she was going to trust him, trust that he wouldn't let anything happen to her. "You ready?" he asked.

Eden had a death grip on the horn, and her grasp on the reins was causing her fingernails to almost cut into her palm. She nodded. "Ready."

Bessie's and Blackjack's heads were barely over the gate's threshold when the horses briefly faced each other, then looked forward as if they were communicating. Eden squealed when Bessie darted into a full run. No trotting to build up speed—the horse went from a slow walk to a full run. Eden bounced in her seat, held on for dear life, and willed her heart to stop hammering against her chest. Samuel didn't take his eyes off her, and when she finally got comfortable enough to lock eyes with him, he smiled, holding one hand atop his head to keep his hat on.

Eden relaxed into the feel of the running horse, the wind in her face, her hair flying behind her, the warmth of the sun on her cheeks. She didn't think she could stop smiling if she tried. Riding was more than she ever expected, with a certain freedom taking over every part of her being. It was her and the horse, and God had gifted her with a picture-perfect day for this adventure.

More important, she was realizing she wouldn't fall off after all.

"Faster?" Samuel yelled, grinning.

Eden nodded. "Yes!" She'd fallen into sync with Bessie, lifting her rear in intervals to match the horse's gait so that she wasn't bouncing.

Samuel led them around the pond where more land stretched for as far as Eden could see. It was amazing, exhilarating, and the longer she was on Bessie, the more trusting she became, enabling her to enjoy the thrill of the ride.

For another ten or fifteen minutes, Samuel led the way, and Eden's heart was full. It was everything she'd imagined, but she was also surprised by the closeness she felt with God, in His world, such beauty.

Samuel finally pulled back on the reins, and when he did, Blackjack's front feet came off the ground. "Whoa!" he hollered.

Eden hesitated, not eager for Bessie to imitate the other horse, but when she gave the reins a little tug, Bessie slowed to a steady trot right away, and she followed Samuel to the edge of the pond.

"Well, what did you think?" Samuel's tawny brown eyes twinkled, and his smile filled his face, surely a mirror of her own expression.

"It was awesome!" Eden relaxed enough to lean forward

and scratch Bessie's neck, letting go of the saddle horn. "I can't believe you get to do this every day."

He chuckled. "I don't. *Mei* sisters ride for pleasure more than I do, in between their chores. I'm mostly at work. But I try to ride once a week just for the fun of it."

Despite the wind in her face, Eden was drenched in sweat, but not as much as poor Bessie.

Samuel dismounted from his horse, and Blackjack lifted those front legs again. "Whoa," Samuel said as he latched onto the bridle, then rubbed his horse's muzzle.

Eden followed suit and eased her leg around the horse until one leg was on the ground, then dislodged her other foot from the stirrup, but held on to the reins.

"You did great," Samuel said, still smiling. "I'm glad it was fun for you. We can run them back, but they need to rest, and I thought we'd walk them to the pond for a drink."

Eden nodded, breathless. "Sure."

Samuel walked Blackjack to the pier that spilled across the pond for at least thirty feet. It looked more like a small lake to Eden as she briefly eyed the canoe and wondered if that would be part of today's adventure too.

Samuel loosely tied Blackjack's reins to a pole near the pier and then did the same with Bessie. Both horses leaned down and started to drink.

"We can go sit at the end of the pier and dangle our feet in the water to cool off a little if you want." He ran a hand across his damp forehead. "It's *gut* we're riding early. By midday, it will be up in the eighties, and it can be mighty hot on a clear day like this."

"It's beautiful here." Eden took in her surroundings

again, in awe of the simplicity of everything around her that came together like the postcard in her mind.

She followed Samuel when he started walking down the narrow pier that was only a few feet wide, and it swayed gently in the wind. Without any handrails, she kept her eyes on her feet, thinking how embarrassing it would be to fall into the water.

At the end of the pier, Samuel kicked off his black boots, then peeled off his socks, and rolled his black pant legs up to his knees. Eden did the same.

When he sat down, he patted the spot beside him, and when she sat, her leg lay flush against his, which sent a wave of adrenaline up and down her spine. Normally, she avoided physical contact with men—of any age. But this wave of adrenaline felt different and not something to be feared.

She lowered her feet into the cool water, which reached her midcalf. She turned to him and smiled. "Thank you so much for this."

"*Ya*, you're very welcome."

Samuel didn't want to take his eyes off Eden. He longed to tell her that she was the most beautiful girl he'd ever seen, but he didn't want to scare her off. He was also curious about the butterfly tattoo she had on her left hand. He wanted to know everything about her and the life she led that was foreign to him.

Pulling his eyes from hers, his focus moved to her lips.

He took longer than he'd intended, and she looked away first.

He cleared his throat. "Was it as fun as you thought it would be?"

She laughed. "Are you kidding? It was totally amazing, way better than I could have imagined. I was nervous at first, especially when Bessie shot past the gate and started running right away. But after only a couple of minutes, I felt safe and was able to enjoy the ride." She glanced at him. "Thank you again," she said.

"You're welcome." Samuel was aware that their legs were touching. He could have inched over a little and put some space between them, but he liked the feel of her next to him. As she lowered her hand into the water, he took advantage of the opportunity to study her face again. He wondered if she had kissed anyone. Surely she had. Samuel had come close to kissing Sarah King six months ago, but one of his sisters had caught them in each other's arms behind the barn and threatened to tell their parents. Sarah had been terrified and avoided Samuel now. It had bothered him for a while, and he knew it was mostly because of the strict reputation his parents presented to the community, but he would have taken a risk to see her again. However, Sarah had no interest in that scenario, so maybe she hadn't liked him that much after all.

Sitting with Eden like this, kicking their feet in the water on a beautiful summer day, reminded him that God always had a plan. Maybe his destiny was to meet Eden.

"How do you like it here so far?" His foot brushed against hers in the water as he leaned back on his hands.

"I love it. I mean, I haven't been here but a few days, but I like all this . . ." She waved an arm around. "It's so open in the country." She turned to him and smiled. "I like the buggies, there isn't a lot of traffic, and it's quiet."

"*Too* quiet sometimes," he said. "I guess it's a lot different where you live."

She didn't say anything, just smiled. If he was reading her expression, though, it almost looked like a sad smile. "Yeah, it is," she finally said.

He waited for her to elaborate, and when she didn't, he said, "Do you have your own car?"

She shook her head. "No. I'm living with my cousin, Emma, in Texas right now. She said I could take driving lessons when she returns from her trip to Europe. That's why I'm staying with Yvonne and Abraham right now, until she gets back."

Samuel took off his hat and scratched his head. "How old are you?"

"Sixteen." She leaned back on her hands the way he was doing, and they both squinted as the sun took its place higher in the sky.

"*Ya*, me too." Sixteen seemed old enough to stay on your own. "So, that's home? Texas?"

She wagged her head again. "Just for now. I actually live in California."

"How long will you be in Texas?"

She turned to face him, tipped her head to one side, and stared at him. "Um . . . I don't know."

"Mysterious," he said as he gently nudged her with his elbow and grinned.

"Not really." She opened her mouth like she might be getting ready to share but snapped it closed. She eyed the canoe as it gently bumped against the pier.

"Do you want to go for a ride in the canoe?" He wanted to spend as much time with her as possible, and if they got right back on the horses, they'd likely head back to the barn way before he was ready for her to go.

Her eyes lit up. "Sure."

He stood, offered her a hand, surprised how smooth her skin was when she accepted. His mother and sisters didn't have hands like that. Eden probably didn't work in a garden, mow grass, or do other chores that left a woman's hands rough.

"If you want to get in the front, I'll take the stern so I can steer." He offered her a hand again and helped her into the boat before he loosened the tie. As they slowly drifted from the pier, she picked up a paddle and he did the same.

"I bet living here is like being on vacation all the time," she said dreamily.

Samuel laughed. "I have a job, and I help *mei daed* in the fields when I can. *Mei* sisters and *Mamm* take care of the yard, the flowerbeds, the cleaning, the cooking, and the washing. We stay busy. I guess it doesn't really feel like a vacation. But it's all we know."

"I read online that the Amish get to run around a little when they turn sixteen." She glanced over her shoulder. "What do you get to do?"

Samuel hadn't pushed anything with his strict parents. It seemed easier not to rock the boat unless there was a good reason. Eden felt like a good reason. "Anything I want," he said. "It's called *rumschpringe*, the word for our running-around period. We get to do that until we choose to get baptized."

"How long does it last?"

Samuel shrugged when she looked over her shoulder again. "It depends. Some teenagers don't get baptized until they are getting ready to get married. A lot of *Englischers*—that's what we call non-Amish people—think we all get married at seventeen or eighteen, but these days most everyone waits until they're a little older. But sometimes younger people get baptized even before they've chosen a spouse."

"Are you going to get baptized soon?" This time, she twisted in her seat and faced him.

"*Nee*. Not any time soon." *Maybe never.*

She giggled, her eyes still on him. "Is that so you get to play around longer?"

He forced a smile, unwilling to discuss his doubts about his future with someone he didn't know. "I guess you could say that."

The wheels in Samuel's mind spun. He wanted to spend as much time with Eden as he could today, but he also wanted to ensure that he could see her again.

"Would, um . . . you like to go to a movie or something Saturday? I, uh . . . have to work half a day, but I could pick you up after that." He took a deep breath and tried to read her expression.

"I thought I read movies aren't allowed." She smiled. "Oh, but I guess they are since you're in your rum . . . rum . . ."

"*Rumschpringe*," he said as he stared into her worldly

green eyes, not wanting to appear otherwise. "We could get something to eat first."

She faced forward again. "That sounds like a date."

Samuel swallowed hard. He'd never asked a girl to supper and a movie. He'd never even been to a movie. He was already wondering how he would pull it off without his parents finding out. Even though most parents chose to look away when their children took liberties during their running-around period, Samuel was quite sure his parents would forbid going to a movie, especially with an outsider. It was hard not to stay bitter about his parents' rules. Their demands weren't in line with the *Ordnung*—the unwritten rules of the Amish ways. He let that fact justify his actions . . . in his mind, anyway.

"I guess it does sound like a date." He held his breath. If she turned him down, he might have blown his chance to get to know her better, outside of this one day.

She swung around again, laid the paddle across her lap, and smiled. "I think that sounds great."

"There's a shady spot over there." He pointed to a cluster of trees on the bank nearby. "We can park there to get out of the sun for a while if you want to."

"Sure." She put her paddle back in the water, and they made their way to one of Samuel's favorite spots.

His focus had shifted a little. Even though he looked forward to being with her as much as he could today, his mind was already working out a plan for Saturday. The more he thought about it, there was no way he could tell his parents he was taking Eden to supper and a movie. They would absolutely forbid it. He'd never lied to his folks before. A first for everything, he supposed, even though he didn't feel good about it.

Again, he thought about his future and his inability to explore his options if he didn't take some liberties. A movie seemed like a good first step, but there was so much more that he was curious about. Mostly he wanted to know how outsiders lived. What was a normal day like? Did they get up, drive their car to work, maybe meet friends afterward for supper? Despite the socialness in his community, there was still a sense of isolation. The same gatherings with the same people, day after day. The world was vast, with millions of people, and he had only been allowed to see and feel a tiny part of God's glory. Wouldn't God want him to explore his options?

He cringed as he had the thought. It went against everything he had been taught to believe—that staying within one's inner circle was safe and there wasn't a need to discern what those closest to him believed.

Even as he speculated about his feelings, he acknowledged an underlying realization that he was trying to justify his needs. Maybe that's why he wasn't hearing God's voice. Or was he blocking the voice of God, intentionally or subconsciously?

He was only certain of one thing. Something deep within his soul didn't feel right.

CHAPTER 6

Anna peered out the window of the mudroom in the back of the house, the only place she could see the pond from downstairs. What was supposed to be a riding lesson had now turned into a canoe ride, and the two young people were headed to shore on the far side of the pond. Samuel liked the shady spot and went fishing there often. Her son seemed to be needing more and more time to himself, which was to be expected at his age. But the English girl could be trouble. Especially someone as pretty as Eden.

"Mamm?"

Anna startled when Mae came up behind her. Her oldest daughter at fourteen, Mae was like a cat and known to sneak up on a person. "*Ya?*" She pulled her eyes away from the window, but it was too late. Mae was already grinning.

"Samuel has a girlfriend," she said before snickering.

"*Nee*. That's nonsense. Your uncle Abe and aunt Yvonne are hosting Yvonne's cousin for a month. Your *bruder* offered to teach her how to ride a horse."

Mae inched closer to the window, then turned to her

mother and lifted an eyebrow. "It looks like he's teaching her more than riding and canoeing."

Anna gazed across the pond, barely able to see much, except that her son was huddled up on a log with that girl and sitting entirely too close. She cut her eyes in her daughter's direction. "Your *bruder* would never do anything inappropriate, if that's what you're implying."

Mae shrugged. "I'm sure you're right." She smiled before she rounded the corner and went upstairs. Anna wondered if she was going to her sister's room. Grace's room had a better view of the pond and where Samuel and Eden sat.

Anna had worried about this time in her children's lives when they turned sixteen and would expect certain freedoms. But Anna and Leroy were not planning to be lenient and would choose only options they considered safe for their children. Samuel spending time with Eden felt anything but safe. She would have to keep a close eye on this situation. Anna didn't need a worldly and possibly troubled girl tempting Samuel.

She wanted to believe that she and Leroy had instilled a firm foundation for their children. "Boys will be boys," she whispered to herself. Then she silently prayed that Samuel would be wise enough not to get close to this girl.

Eden listened as Samuel told her how Amish kids only went to school through the eighth grade, which she'd read about, but she just nodded. She liked listening to him talk, his accent, the way he punctuated his words.

"I wish we only had to go to school through the eighth grade." Eden rolled her eyes. "I still have two more years of high school."

"Will you go to school in Texas or California?"

Samuel sat on the log next to her, and she wondered if he'd brought other girls here. It was a pretty spot where a breeze blew through the branches of the enormous trees that formed an arch above them.

"Um, I'm not sure. It depends how long I stay with my cousin, Emma." She avoided his inquisitive eyes. A part of her wanted to get it over with and blurt out, *"My mom was sentenced to three years in prison. I have a little blooper on my record for shoplifting. And I got in a little trouble for sneaking out in Emma's car. Oh, and there's Max, my mom's horrible boyfriend who tried to put his hands on me more than once, which he said was my fault. Now you know everything, and you can take me back and never have to see me again."*

But she was enjoying her time with Samuel, and she wanted it to last as long as it could before her past revealed itself. She would see the judgment in his eyes, and her fantasy of being someone else would be over.

Eden tucked her tangled hair behind her ears. "So, what kind of movies do you like?"

Samuel looked at his outstretched feet for what seemed like a long time. "I don't know. I've never been to one."

"Really?" Eden tipped her head to one side. "Are you sure it will be okay with your parents?" She was already on thin ice with his mother. "Because we can do something else or—"

"*Nee, nee.* It'll be fine." He frowned. "But I'm going to get us a driver. There are a couple of movie theaters in neighboring towns, but I think it's too far for *mei* horse from where we live."

"Hire a driver?" Eden raised an eyebrow, grinning. "That's a pretty big deal where I come from, to pay someone to drive you around."

He laughed. "We do it all the time. The horses can only travel about twenty miles before they need a rest." Grinning, he said, "*Mei mamm* and *schweschdere*—sisters—like to go to Walmart, and it's way too far to go by horse. And we need drivers for doctor appointments in town . . . things like that."

"Amish sightings are something you wouldn't see where I live in California or in Texas where I'm staying. I'd never even seen an Amish person until I came here." Eden stretched her legs out in front of her and crossed her ankles. "It's like a totally different world here."

Samuel smiled. "So, tell me about *your* world."

"Not much to tell." Eden swallowed hard and avoided his inquisitive gaze, searching for something that didn't sound horrible. Her living arrangement in California consisted of a small, rundown apartment with a leak in the roof and barely any hot water. It had never felt like home. Usually, they didn't stay anywhere long enough for it to feel that personal. They'd either get evicted for failure to pay the rent, or sometimes Max was on the run from the police and they would pack up in a hurry. Twice, they'd slept in their car for a couple of days until they found a place to lay their heads, and none of those places felt like home.

She searched her mind for anything to make her sound like a normal person. "Emma—my cousin—has a really nice place in Texas, in Houston. I like it there, but I don't really know anyone."

"What do you do for fun?" Samuel stared at her until she looked at him, his eyes still twinkling with interest.

She shrugged, wondering if she was coming off as boring. "I've been to movies," she said as she grinned, not meaning it as an insult and hoping Samuel didn't take it as such. "And there's lots of restaurants, so Emma and I eat out a lot. She actually raised Yvonne. Yvonne's parents were killed when she was young."

Samuel lowered his head. "*Ya*, I heard something about that, and it's terrible."

"Yeah. I think Emma was probably really good to her, but she raised her without any real religious upbringing." Eden smiled. "And look at her now. She's living the Amish lifestyle. I don't know a lot about her spiritual journey, but I'm guessing it must have been amazing. I know that everything changed for me once I found a relationship with God. At first it was like having a new friend, someone I could talk to about anything. And the more I talked, the more I knew God was listening."

She didn't verbalize the last thought in her mind, probably the biggest change in her life since she had found God: she was no longer alone.

Samuel wasn't sure what to say. He wasn't expecting a

conversation about God with his new friend. And he hadn't talked to anyone about his doubts and questions as he struggled to maintain a relationship with God. He felt like he'd slipped, and his footing was off. It wasn't any one thing that had sent him on a path that seemed to be taking him away from God. His feelings had snuck up on him slowly. Embracing God felt like entrapment, like staying here would prevent him from seeing anything outside of this small dot on the map.

But he wasn't ready to have this conversation with anyone.

"You've been to the movies. What kind of shows do you like?" He was dripping in sweat and wanted to take off his hat, but he knew his hair would be flat on his head.

"Don't laugh." She pointed a finger at him but grinned. "I love romances, in books and movies. And I like for everything to have a happily-ever-after ending."

Samuel gave a taut nod of his head. "I like that. It's one of the things I *lieb* about being Amish—that we don't believe in divorce, and couples stay together for life. It's just the other things about our way of life that have—" He stopped, surprised he'd almost shared his true feelings, and wasn't sure how to recover.

"Is it because everything is strict? Or because everyone dresses alike, drives the same kind of buggies? Stuff like that?" She brushed hair from her face and tucked it behind her ears. "But everyone is really religious, right?"

"It's hard to explain." He raised a shoulder and lowered it with a shrug. He was pretty sure God had semi-abandoned him because he was questioning everything he'd been taught instead of accepting it as truth. His parents were never going to allow him to have much of a running-around period to figure things out either. He recalled his early thoughts—that maybe he was the one putting distance between him and God to make it easier for him to get some perspective.

When he glanced at Eden, her eyes were on his, waiting for answers he didn't have.

"It's okay. You don't have to explain. Our faith journey is a personal one. I certainly wasn't raised with any type of religion, and Emma isn't a believer either. But after a friend took me to church with her, I began connecting with God, and I found what I was looking for."

Samuel was surprised. But what had he been expecting? A wilder version of this beautiful girl who had grown up out in the world? Someone who would share her experiences, tell him what it was like to grow up in the city? Still, he wasn't disappointed. She intrigued him and seemed to have a sweet nature. And a year ago he would have been thrilled to befriend an outsider who also had a strong faith in God. Especially someone who looked like Eden. He wanted to know more about the road that had led her to God, but she'd likely ask him about the path that was leading him in another direction.

He looked at her tattoo again, and he must have stared at it for too long. She held her left hand out, the blue and turquoise hues of the butterfly sparkling in the sunlight.

"It's okay to look at it," she said, smiling. "It's symbolic of transformation, change, and hope. I guess it kind of goes hand in hand with my spiritual journey, reminding me to stay on the right path."

"It's really pretty." He was afraid any further conversation about the tattoo would lead them into a heavier conversation about God and faith. He wanted to change the subject. "What kind of food do you like? I mean, there aren't a ton of restaurants nearby, but there are a couple of good cafés not far from the theater. A pizza place, or another place that has really good burgers."

"I'm fine with anything." She smiled, her head tipped slightly to one side, her green eyes gleaming as she stared out across the pond.

"You're so pretty." Samuel didn't think before he spoke, nor did he plan to say it. The words leaped from his mouth with no warning, and he felt his face turning red.

She looked directly at him and smiled. "Thank you."

"*Ya* . . . you're welcome." Their eyes stayed locked, and Samuel was sure God had put Eden on his path for a reason. Maybe it was to get him away from here. Whatever the reason, he liked her and was looking forward to spending as much time as he could with her. Scooting around his parents' watchful eyes would be tricky, though.

Eden was a sweaty mess by the time they took the canoe back to the pier, then got back on the horses, a feat that proved easier this time. She followed Samuel into the barn and dismounted when he did, her legs feeling a little rubbery and sore.

"Are you hungry?" Samuel began pumping water from

a nearby pump into a large pail. "I can get us some snacks or sandwiches."

"That sounds great." She paused and cringed a little as she eyed the outhouse visible from where they stood in the barn.

Samuel chuckled as he led the horses to their stalls. "That old thing has been here for generations. We have an indoor bathroom."

Eden felt herself blushing. "Yeah, I might need to . . ."

"Go on in the *haus*. The bathroom is at the end of the hall on the left." He lifted the pail of water. "I'm going to top off the horses' water, then I'll round us up something to snack on."

Eden hesitated, but she didn't have a choice, so she nodded and started toward the house. She eased open the screen door, then tiptoed when she heard voices upstairs. Maybe she could get in and out without running into Anna.

The place was lovely. Nothing fancy, but it smelled lemony and clean.

When she was done she crossed back through the living room, still trying to be quiet, and picked up the pace once she was out the door. Samuel was brushing the horses when she got back to the barn.

"Sorry the barn is such a mess. I was supposed to clean it this morning, but I'll get to it later." He grinned. "Teaching you to ride was a *gut* way to put off the project." He paused, still smiling. "And a lot more fun."

Eden wasn't ready for the day to end, and she didn't want to be the cause of Samuel's procrastination. "I can help you clean the barn."

Samuel set the brush down. "Really? It's miserably hot in here. I don't want you to have to do that."

"Really, I don't mind. And I don't have anywhere to be." Maybe she'd even score some points with Samuel's mother.

"*Ach*, well . . . if you're sure." His dimples puckered again. "I'm not really ready for you to go."

She felt her face reddening again. "Then let's get to work."

Samuel held up a finger. "Be right back." He jogged out of the barn and returned a few minutes later juggling two large glasses of tea and two sandwiches. "I'd say we could eat in the house, but it's probably just as hot in there, and . . ."

"No, this is fine." Eden relieved him of one of the glasses and took several large gulps of tea, then accepted the sandwich.

"Ham and cheese. I hope that's okay."

"Definitely." She was starving but hadn't wanted to mention it earlier for fear of the day ending too soon.

After they ate, she helped Samuel organize tools into piles atop the workbench, then hung some of them on various racks to the side. After that they tackled a few other projects. She even held one of the wooden shutters on a window while Samuel added some extra screws, after explaining that a big gust of wind had knocked it loose.

They worked on every task together, and even though she was drenched in sweat, Eden couldn't think of anywhere she'd rather be.

Yvonne was totaling up receipts when her friend and boss came into the store.

"*Wie bischt*," Jake said as the door closed behind him, the bell jingling. "How did we do today?"

"Fantastic! One of the best days since I've been working here." She totaled the last two receipts, then stacked them on top of the others.

"The weather." Jake nodded over his shoulder. "It's a gorgeous day. A little hot, but there's a nice breeze. People get out and about more."

"It wasn't just that. A tour bus stopped here, and it was filled with older women, around twenty of them."

Jake raised both eyebrows. "*Ach*, that's great. We're going to put Montgomery on the map after all." He chuckled. "Where's your cousin?" He glanced around the store.

"Samuel, Leroy's son, is teaching her how to ride a horse." Yvonne glanced at the clock on the wall. "Wow. It's four o'clock. They've been together all day." She reached for her purse behind the counter and found her cell phone. "No missed calls. I had figured it would be okay if I closed the shop for a short time to go pick up Eden when she called, but I haven't heard from her."

"What does Leroy think about Samuel spending time with an *Englisch maedel*?"

Yvonne scratched her forehead. "I don't know, but when Anna was in here, the subject came up, and she was visibly unhappy that the two were going to be spending time together."

"Leroy and Anna have always kept a tight rein on their

kinner. But Samuel is sixteen, and he's probably going to test the water, whether they like it or not."

"*Ya*, I'm sure you're right, but I'd rather him not test those waters with Eden. I don't need any bad blood with my *bruder*-in-law and his *fraa*." She glanced at the clock again, chewed her bottom lip.

"There's only an hour left. I can see you're antsy." He waved an arm toward the door. "Go ahead and go. I'll stay this last hour and close it down."

"Are you sure?" She brought a hand to her chest. "I've got to figure out ways to entertain Eden or at least get her some sort of transportation. I'm not comfortable with her driving the buggy on her own." She gasped. "And what if I had left to go pick her up and the tour bus had showed up while I was gone? We would have missed all those sales."

Jake ran a hand the length of his beard. "Do you think she'd ride a bicycle? We've got one at our place. It's been in the barn for as long as I can remember. It might need new tires, but I could get it cleaned up for her if you think she'd ride it. It's a long walk to Samuel's place."

Yvonne grunted. "I'm hoping this isn't going to be a regular thing, her going to see Samuel. It has trouble written all over it, even if they just stay friends. Leroy and Anna won't like it." She thought for a few seconds. "But a bike might be *gut*. She could at least get around town a little."

"I'll get it cleaned up for her." Jake nodded toward the door again. "Go. I've got this."

"*Danki*, Jake."

He laughed. "Sorry. I know you've been here a while,

but sometimes it's still hard to get used to you speaking the *Deutsch*. And you're *gut* at it."

She curtsied. "I try." She scooped up her purse. "Tell Eva I'll be by soon to see that beautiful *boppli*." She wanted to tell her friend about her own pregnancy so badly, but she and Abraham had agreed they would wait.

So much had happened since she'd first met Jake and Eva. Their relationship had started out as professional when Yvonne's job sent her on a quest to find a rare book, but it quickly morphed into a treasured friendship with Eva and Jake. She recalled the budding romance between her friends and the role she'd played to help them discover their love for each other. And all of that had led her to Abraham.

God always has a plan.

Yvonne backed up the buggy quickly, suddenly anxious to see what Eden and Samuel had been up to all day. She'd been so distracted with customers that she hadn't thought about it until now. Her stomach clenched, hoping everything had gone okay.

Eden still wasn't ready for the day to end, but when she heard a buggy coming up the gravel driveway, she peered outside the barn, squinting against the sun's glare, and recognized Yvonne.

"Wow. I wonder what time it is," she said as she wiped her dirty hands on her jeans.

Samuel left the barn, and Eden followed to another water pump near the fence where they both washed their hands. "Probably getting close to five," Samuel said as he looked toward the sky.

Eden shook her hands dry as best she could. Yvonne had gotten out of her buggy, and Eden saw Samuel's mother crossing the front yard toward her.

"What time do you want me to pick you up Saturday?" Samuel asked in a whisper as he stared at his mother and Yvonne just out of earshot.

"Whatever works for you."

"Five o'clock okay?" Samuel stayed focused on the two women talking.

"Sure."

They were quiet as they closed the space between them and Yvonne and Anna.

"Uh . . . maybe don't mention anything about our date in front of *mei mamm*. I'd rather break the news to her privately." He spoke softly again and grimaced before he turned to her. "Is that okay?"

Break the news to her? Had Anna already said something to Samuel about her, voicing her displeasure about him seeing Eden? She didn't say anything, just nodded.

"How did the riding go?" Yvonne asked, holding both hands to her forehead to block the sun. "Must have been a long lesson."

Eden glanced at Anna and was going to smile, but Samuel's mother avoided eye contact—not a good sign. "It was great," she said to Yvonne. "And we took the canoe out, talked for a while, and . . . we even cleaned the barn." Eden again looked at Anna for a reaction, but there wasn't one. "We sort of lost track of time." She flinched. "Sorry."

"It's okay. It was a busy day at the bookstore, and the time got away from me too. I'm just glad you had fun."

"We did." Eden tried not to smile, but when she looked at Samuel and saw he was grinning, too, she couldn't help it.

"I don't remember the last time Samuel missed lunch." Anna folded her hands in front of her. She made the statement in a way that almost sounded irritated.

"I made us a couple of sandwiches around lunchtime." Samuel seemed to force a smile.

"You're both welcome to stay for supper." Anna posed the question to Yvonne with a straight face, so it was hard to tell if it was an obligatory invite.

"*Nee. Danki*, though. I appreciate the offer," Yvonne said. "But we need to run an errand, and Abraham will be getting hungry."

Eden pushed back strands of hair the way she'd been doing all day. Next time—if there was a next time—she'd pull her hair back. "Thank you for a fun day, Samuel," she said, smiling.

"*Ya*, sure. You did *gut* on Bessie. And *danki*—I mean thanks—for helping me in the barn." It took him a while before he pulled his brown eyes away.

She gave a quick wave. "See you . . ." She paused, almost blowing it. "Around," she said, then climbed into the driver's seat of the buggy when Yvonne took the passenger side.

Anna and Samuel waved as Eden backed out of the driveway and began to head down the road.

"So, are you a farm girl now?" Yvonne chuckled. "Because you're sweating enough to look the part."

"It was *so* much fun." She hit the same pothole she'd hit on the way there. "Oops."

Yvonne dug around in her purse, took out a pair of sunglasses, and handed them to Eden. "Here, since you're driving."

"Thanks. I have a pair back at your house. I just forgot to bring them."

She remembered the way home, and successfully stopped the horse before turning on to the main road. She wasn't sure if Yvonne wanted details about her day, but she was anxious to see her reaction about her date on Saturday— and hoped it would be better than what she assumed Anna's reaction would be. "Samuel asked me to go to supper and see a movie on Saturday." She bit her lip. "He wanted to tell his mother in private, and I feel like, based on her attitude at the store, it isn't going to go over well."

Yvonne was quiet, then looked at Eden and smiled. "He must really like you. I'm not sure he's ever been on a date. Probably because his parents are so strict."

"Really?" Eden briefly lowered the sunglasses on her nose and peered at Yvonne. "He's sixteen. You don't think he's ever been out with a girl?"

Yvonne shrugged. "Maybe. But I've never heard Anna or Leroy mention anything about it. I'm just glad he's being upfront with his parents about it."

"Do you think I should have said no?" Eden's chest tightened, fearful of Yvonne's response.

She smiled. "You like him, don't you? I mean, he's a handsome guy."

"We had a lot of fun. And Yvonne . . ." Eden turned to

her. "I know Samuel and I can only be friends, so I don't want you to worry. I'm just glad that I met someone to maybe hang out with some while I'm here."

"I'm not worried," Yvonne said, then winked at Eden. "But I'm not the one you have to be concerned about, apparently."

Eden sighed. "Yeah, I know."

"But I'm not going to bring up the subject. If Anna has a problem with it, I'm sure she or Leroy will say something to me or Abraham."

Eden wondered what that meant. Would she not be allowed to see Samuel?

"Samuel is the one who asked you out, and I doubt he would have done that if he didn't think he would have his parents' approval." Yvonne chuckled. "Even if it might be reluctant approval." She snapped her fingers. "Oh, turn left up here. There's a small café where we can charge our phones. And . . ." She grinned at Eden. "I can hear your stomach growling, so we can get some supper. I'll bring Abraham something to go. He loves the burgers at this place."

"Sounds good." Eden tried to smile, but worry had seeped into her heart. She didn't want to cause any trouble, and going out with Samuel might not be the best start to her visit. She eventually reconciled her thoughts and justified saying yes because Samuel was the one who had asked her to come over today and had asked her out for Saturday. She wasn't the instigator.

But she was looking forward to seeing him Saturday, more than she was willing to admit to Yvonne.

CHAPTER 7

Yvonne filled up Blue's water bowl before she handed Abraham a slice of apple pie, then sat across the table from him with her own helping of dessert. She peered out the window from where she was sitting.

"Eden said she forgot to collect the eggs this morning, and now I see that she's filling up the water troughs." Yvonne savored the flavor of her mother-in-law's pie. "I'm not sure I'll ever be able to bake pies as *gut* as your *mudder*, even though she gave me the recipe."

"I think your pies are great, and *danki* for bringing me a burger." Abraham stared at her stomach sporting a silly grin, so endearing that Yvonne wanted to rush around the table and throw her arms around him.

"My stomach hasn't gotten any bigger since this morning," she said as she winked at him.

Her husband wiped his mouth with his napkin. "I can't stop thinking about how we're growing a *boppli* in there."

"*We?*" Yvonne chuckled. "You might have planted the seed, but I'm pretty sure I'm the one doing the growing, and

I'm reminded about it several times a day when I feel sick to *mei* stomach."

He frowned. "*Ya*, I hate that you're going through that."

She laid her fork on her plate after devouring her dessert. "I'm not going to complain. I'm so excited, and I can't wait to tell people—mostly Aunt Emma and Eva."

"So . . ." Abraham raised an eyebrow. "Not to change the subject, but before Eden comes back in, how do you think things went today? I mean, the little bit she said before she went outside made it sound like she had an enjoyable day with Samuel."

Yvonne sighed. "Yep." She realized she sometimes fell back into her native language. "I mean, *ya*." Abraham grinned before she went on. "There is something brewing between those two. I can tell. And we both know Leroy and Anna aren't going to like it."

Abraham twisted his mouth, his head tilted to one side. "Samuel is their first *kinner* to hit his *rumschpringe*. Maybe they'll surprise everyone and be more lenient than we think."

"I don't know. It seems clear Anna doesn't like Samuel spending time with Eden." She paused. "Do you think that's mostly because she's not Amish? Or do you think she would be that way with anyone her son decides to spend time with?"

"I think Eden might seem like a threat since she's an outsider, but either way, most parents look the other way when their *kinner* begin to run around a little."

Yvonne chuckled. "We both know that Leroy and Anna aren't 'most people' when it comes to their *kinner*. You know how much I *lieb* your *bruder* and Anna, but don't they worry that too tight of a rein might push them away?"

"Leroy hasn't said much about it. I guess we'll see how it plays out, and not—"

"I know . . . not borrow trouble."

Her husband looked over his shoulder out the window. "She seems to like it here so far." He paused, watching Eden. "And I don't mean just because of Samuel. Look at her."

Yvonne smiled as she watched her cousin in the barn. With the door open, she could see her petting the horses. "I agree. It must be hard on her, with her mother being in jail. And she'd only met Emma once before she hauled Eden to Texas. Emma is a wonderful person, if not a bit eccentric at times. The woman can't get her day started without having the same breakfast every single morning—one slice of toast with strawberry jelly, no butter, a half a cup of coffee, and one peanut-butter cookie." Yvonne chuckled. "We ran out of strawberry jelly one morning, and I was promptly instructed, right then, early in the morning, to go get some more." She shook her head, grinning on the inside. "She's got some quirks, but she has a big heart. Eden didn't mention any of that, only their age difference. I sense they aren't super close. I get that."

"I guess I'll get cleaned up before devotions." Abraham slid his chair back just as Yvonne's phone rang on the counter and she stood to see who was calling.

"Speaking of . . . It's Aunt Emma," Yvonne said as she eyed the caller ID. "Finally. I was wondering why I hadn't heard from her."

"I'll let you two chat." Abraham headed down the hall toward the bathroom.

"Well, you must be having such a good time that you forgot about us," Yvonne said jokingly as she toned down her use of Pennsylvania Dutch.

"You are exactly right. I knew that if there was a problem, you would call. This is an amazing trip, but the woman who set up our itinerary is about twenty years younger than me and a few of the other ladies. And she has a lot more energy. But all in all, yes, I'm having a great time. How is Eden doing?"

"She seems fine." Yvonne didn't see the need to bring up Samuel at this point. "She's pleasant to be around, helpful, and even learned to drive the buggy." She decided to dig a little. "I thought you said she was a troubled teenager. Yeah, she's got some baggage that she didn't ask for, the problems with her mother. But overall, she seems levelheaded and like a normal teenager. You said she snuck your car out, but Aunt Emma—" Yvonne laughed—"I snuck your car out more than once when I was growing up."

"Which I did not find out about until you were an adult."

"Okay, so Eden got caught. Her bad luck." Yvonne chuckled again as she watched Eden continuing to love on the horses in the barn. "That doesn't make her troubled."

"All right, maybe that was a bad word to use. She's a normal teenager who pushes the limits. But I'm afraid I have some news for her, and I'm not sure how she's going to take it."

Yvonne put a hand to her suddenly pounding heart. "What's wrong?"

"I'm her legal guardian, as you know, but I didn't feel the need to mention to those in charge of her case that Eden would be staying with you for a month." She cleared her throat.

Yvonne had already expected as much.

"So, of course, they called me to let me know that Eden's mother is sick." She paused for a long while. "According to her caseworker, Jill has tried to call Eden several times since she's been with you, but Eden won't take the calls. She's been denying her mother's calls ever since she began living with me a few months ago. I told her if she was worried about the cost, and if she wanted to talk to her mom, I would cover those expenses. She didn't really say anything one way or the other. But since her mother isn't well, Eden might want to talk to her."

"How sick is she?" Yvonne gnawed her lip as she kept her eyes on Eden, not wanting the girl to come into the house and overhear the conversation.

"Pretty sick." Her aunt sighed. "According to the woman who called, Jill did enough drugs to really mess with her system, mostly her heart. But her other organs appear to be failing too."

"What?" Yvonne's heart rate spiked even more. "Is she dying?"

"Not today or tomorrow," her aunt said coldly. "But I sense it's coming. I have no idea how long she has. And to be honest, I was on a boat when I got the call, so it was hard to hear."

Yvonne swallowed back her emotions. "Do you want to tell her? Or do you want me to talk to her?"

Her aunt was quiet for a few seconds. "I guess I need to tell her."

Yvonne wondered briefly if the news would be easier on Eden if it came from her, in person, but Eden had been living with Emma for a while. Even if the girl thought there was an age gap that made it difficult for her and Emma to be close, Yvonne didn't know her well at all. "Okay. She's in the barn. I'll walk outside and get her."

Yvonne let the screen door slam behind her so she'd get Eden's attention. She held up the phone. "It's Emma!" she hollered. She'd noticed that Eden didn't say "aunt" when referring to Emma, presumably because they were actually cousins.

Eden smiled, picked up a basket of eggs, then left the barn and started across the yard. Yvonne met her halfway and reached for the basket of eggs as she handed her the phone. "I'll be in the *haus* if you need me."

Yvonne walked back to the house slowly enough to hear Eden exchanging pleasantries with Aunt Emma, even telling her about driving the buggy and learning to ride a horse. Mentions about Samuel seemed less important now. She closed the screen door, went to the kitchen, put the eggs on the counter, then sat at the kitchen table where she could see Eden through the window.

"All clean and ready for devotions when you and Eden are." Abraham leaned over and kissed her, and the familiar musky smell of his deodorant filled her senses. "Is your aunt having fun?"

"*Ya*. But right now, she's delivering some bad news to Eden. Her mother is apparently dying." She locked eyes with Abraham as she recalled her former fiancé's death in an airplane crash. At the time, she didn't think she'd ever love another man, and the loss had been unbearable. As she looked at her husband, she was reminded again how God always has a plan. Yvonne would always hold a special place in her heart for Trevor, even though she couldn't love Abraham any more if she tried. Aunt Emma wasn't delivering the same news Yvonne had received when Trevor was killed, but it was still going to be a tremendous blow to Eden to learn her mother might not have long to live. No matter the circumstances, Yvonne had to believe that there was love between Eden and her mother.

Abraham's jaw dropped as he gazed out the window. Eden's back was to them, her head hung.

"I feel like I'm going to say all the wrong things," Yvonne said as a great sadness washed over her.

"Let's let her take the lead, then we'll follow." Abraham put his hands on Yvonne's shoulders.

"You're going to be such a great father," she said as she twisted and looked up at him.

"Here she comes." Abraham eased his hands away and sat down at the kitchen table.

Yvonne did as her husband suggested by waiting until Eden was inside, then giving her an opportunity to say something first.

"Is it time for devotions? Everything is done outside." Eden smiled and handed Yvonne her phone.

Yvonne glanced at Abraham, hoping he would take the lead since Eden had chosen not to and Yvonne didn't know what to say.

"I hear that your *mudder* isn't well," Abraham said tentatively, almost like he wasn't sure, posing it more as a question.

Eden stuffed her hands into the pockets of her blue jeans as she took a deep breath. "Yeah, she isn't doing so hot." There wasn't much emotion emitting from her voice or facial expression. Yvonne wondered if the girl was putting on a brave front for her and Abraham. Yvonne had a strong urge to stand up and hug her, but she stayed where she was and tried to choose her words carefully.

"Aunt Emma told me, Eden, and I'm so sorry. If you don't want to participate in devotions with us, we would certainly understand."

Eden shook her head and even smiled. "Thank you, but I look forward to devotions with you both." She removed her hands from her pockets, spun around, and went to the living room.

Yvonne and Abraham glanced at each other, then Abraham shrugged, and they made their way after her.

Eden was always excited to participate in their devotions, often commenting and questioning certain scriptures. For someone so open about her spirituality, it made Yvonne wonder if she would ever open up about her past, especially with regard to her mother.

Eden held her head high through devotions and withheld the all-consuming sadness that Yvonne and Abraham must have expected. Abraham cut the devotions short, citing a headache, and Yvonne said she was feeling a bit nauseous. The Amish weren't supposed to lie—nor was anyone else, for that matter—but Eden surmised they might be justifying tiny fibs to give her a chance to be alone. And that was fine. She wanted to be by herself, but not for the reasons they assumed. If they suspected that she would go to her room and have a total meltdown, they were wrong.

"Eden?" Yvonne called out to her when she was about halfway down the hallway. She turned around and waited for her cousin to walk closer. "I'm not going to try to get into your head or your heart about your mother. I just want to tell you two things." She paused as if she thought Eden might have something to say. When she didn't, Yvonne went on. "First, I'm here if you want to talk. If not, that's okay too. But I also want you to know that if you would like to speak with your mother, please don't worry about the financial aspect. Aunt Emma said she will cover it, or Abraham and I will be happy to pay for any phone calls too."

A part of Eden wanted to rush into Yvonne's arms and cry her eyes out. But another emotion was fighting for space in her mind and winning. Anger. If she allowed that emotion to surface and creep out of the darkness, it would unleash a flood of rage that had been building for years. Even worse, Eden was sure that if she didn't cling to her anger, a wave of hurt so strong she might not survive it would overpower her. She prayed daily for God to shelter her from those kinds of feelings. It was contradictory. God didn't approve of her hatred and anger toward her mother. She knew that. But allowing herself to lose control due to emotions she couldn't harness felt even worse, almost unrecoverable.

"Thank you," she said. "I appreciate the offer."

Yvonne gazed at her with sympathetic eyes, which only threatened to derail Eden if she said much more and didn't walk away. "Good night." She turned and headed to her bedroom, closing the door gently behind her.

She sat on the edge of her bed, smelling like sweat, hay, and horses—and in need of a shower. But she folded her hands in her lap and stared at the wall. She closed her eyes and wanted to bask in the joyfulness of the day—spending time with Samuel, learning to ride, and even collecting eggs and tending to the horses. Being in this foreign environment made her feel like a different person, but no matter how hard she tried to focus on Samuel and the day, the image of her mother lying in a prison hospital kept pushing toward the forefront of her mind.

Even so, Eden was conditioned to this type of mental feud that often played out like a war in her mind. It was an emotional battle she wasn't going to give in to. Hating her mother—no matter how disappointing it was to God—was the only way she could self-preserve.

She waited long enough to hear Yvonne leaving the only bathroom in the house before she trudged that way to take a shower. If only she could wash the filth from her mind the way she could wash the sweat from her body.

When she returned to her bedroom, her phone was buzzing on the nightstand, and it was a number she didn't recognize. Maybe her mother had been moved to another location due to her health and was calling from another number? She didn't answer, sat on the bed, and began combing her hair, facing the fan only long enough to reduce the dripping from her hair. She liked sleeping with it damp since it was cooler and easier to go to sleep.

It wasn't five minutes later when her phone rang again. Same number. She knew the drill: if it was her mother, she just wouldn't accept the call. If she didn't answer, she feared her mother might be allowed to keep calling her because of her circumstances. Maybe dying gave her additional privileges.

Eden answered but didn't say anything.

"Hello?"

It was a man's voice, and her stomach lurched. Max had never called her. She wanted to talk to him even less than her mother, but there was no familiar recording asking if she wanted to accept the call. Either way, she didn't recognize the voice and was about to hit End when someone spoke again.

"Eden, are you there? It's Samuel." He spoke barely above a whisper.

At the sound of his voice, her heart started to beat like a bass drum. "Uh, hi." She set her comb down and sat taller. "I didn't think you had a phone."

"*Ya*, I didn't. But I got one. A guy from work took me to a place to get one not long after you left today."

"Is that allowed?" She paused, not wanting to come across as accusatory. "I guess so. The running-around thing again, right?"

"*Ya, ya*. Is it okay that I called?" He was still speaking softly.

She scratched her cheek, then leaned back against her pillow. "Yeah, sure, but how did you get my number?"

"Um, well, I hope this is okay, but I, uh . . . texted Yvonne and asked her for it just now." He chuckled. "I figured since she didn't use to be Amish, she probably knew how to text. Lots of our people don't. *Mei* friend who took me to get the phone showed me how. I wasn't sure if Yvonne kept her phone on." He paused. "I was going to text you, but I'm so slow at it, it was taking me forever just to make a sentence. It took me a long time to text Yvonne and ask for your phone number."

Eden wondered how that had gone over with Yvonne, but she quickly realized she was smiling, involuntarily, as a warm feeling settled over her. "I'm glad you called," she said, knowing she was going to have trouble falling asleep and happy to hear his voice. She wondered if this was the first time he'd used a cell phone. It sounded like maybe it was, which led her back to pondering if he'd ever been on a date or kissed a girl. Eden had been kissed by boys, but she couldn't recall any of them taking her to dinner and a movie or anything else that would represent an actual date. Maybe Saturday was her first official date. She doubted Samuel would try to kiss her.

She was so busy speculating that she missed what he said.

"Sorry. What did you just say?" She turned the speed on the fan down so she could hear better since he was talking so quietly.

"I said I had a nice time today, and I'm looking forward to Saturday."

Eden recalled the way he'd told her she was pretty. He seemed to say what was on his mind. She liked that. She wished she could tell him everything on her mind right now, but she'd rather live in this fantasy life for the month she would be here. She selfishly hoped her mother didn't die during her stay. That might cut her visit short. It was a horrible thought to have but present just the same.

"I had a great time today, too, and Saturday will be fun." Eden fluffed her pillow, then settled in, hoping she would get to know Samuel better.

"So, what else can you tell me about your life in California? And is it a lot different in Texas?" Samuel said, beating her to the long list of questions she had for him.

Eden was more interested in Samuel's life, but she quickly calculated a response that would hopefully satisfy him without having to elaborate too much. "California is okay." She thought again about their small apartment with the leaky roof and drug paraphernalia in plain sight most of the time. "But we live in a really populated area, nothing like here. I'm staying with Emma since my mother is sick. It seemed easier this way." She squeezed her eyes closed, sure he wasn't going to understand that last part. "Emma lives in a nice place, but it's in the middle of the city, too, so it's not that much different from where I live in California."

The busyness of each location might be similar, but Emma's home was a palace compared to most of the places she and her mother had lived. She appreciated that part of her situation.

"Have you thought about what kind of movie you might want to see?" She held her breath and hoped he would go along with her shift in the conversation.

"What's wrong with your *mamm*?"

She rubbed her forehead. "Um . . . she has heart problems. She's in the hospital." It wasn't a lie, but she knew Samuel was going to press for more information.

"I hope I'm not being too personal, but why is it easier if you aren't with her?" His voice sounded so caring, but she wasn't even tempted to spill the entire truth. He might cancel their date if he knew everything.

"She just isn't herself, and my relatives thought I'd do better with some distance between us. Emma offered for me to stay with her." It was a lame response and bordered on a lie. "It's hard to talk about."

"*Ya, ya*. Sure. We don't have to talk about it. But I'll pray for a speedy recovery for your *mamm*."

Eden swallowed back a lump in her throat as guilt took hold of her. She hadn't been praying for her mother—for a quick recovery or anything else. Anger versus hurt. It was always there.

"Thank you," she said, desperate to move on as she swirled strands of wet hair around her finger.

"*Mei* friend checked movies playing in the area. I don't have internet set up on *mei* phone. You said you liked romances, and there are a couple playing nearby."

Eden would be embarrassed if they went to a steamy movie, and she was pretty sure Samuel would be, too, but she wasn't sure how to come out and say that. She'd have to trust that he'd choose wisely.

Casting for something else to talk about, she gasped. "Oh! Something happened today. I forgot to mention it to Yvonne and Abraham." It had been on her mind until she spoke to Emma. "There was a snake in the chicken coop earlier. I almost screamed, but thankfully it slithered away and was gone before I totally lost it."

Samuel chuckled. "Chicken snakes. They're harmless, but they like eggs. I see them all the time near our chicken coops."

Eden felt her eyes widening. "How often is 'all the time'?" She wasn't a fan of snakes, harmless or otherwise.

He laughed again. "A couple a month, more in the spring than now, but when it gets cold, you won't see them much at all."

"I guess I'm ready for it to get cold, then." She shivered even though it was far from cold in her room, then remembered that this was temporary. "I'll be gone way before it gets cold here."

He went quiet for a few seconds. "Maybe you'll come back to visit sometimes."

"I hope so." She wondered if that would be a possibility.

"*Ach*, I better go. I just heard *mei* sister go into her room, which is right next to mine. She's a big tattletale. If she hears me on the phone, or even knows I have one, she'll tell *mei* parents. But I'll call you tomorrow evening if that's okay?"

"Sure."

After they ended the call, Eden wondered if Samuel had gotten a phone just so he could talk to her. It almost seemed that way. As much as she would look forward to hearing from him, she also didn't want to be the one causing him to break rules. Then she reminded herself about his running-around time. She googled "Amish running-around time," and the top entry used the word *rumschpringe* and stated "When an Amish teenager turns sixteen, they are given privileges not otherwise allowed. Most parents look the other way during this time in their child's life, giving them a chance to experience the outside world before baptism."

Eden clicked her phone off, placed it on the nightstand, then extinguished her lantern and lay down. It didn't sound like Samuel's parents were going to look the other way if he was worried about his sister telling them he had a phone. Maybe his mother and father would only be accepting about certain things?

She closed her eyes and tried to picture Samuel's handsome face in her mind. But all she could see was her mother.

CHAPTER 8

Yvonne was already awake and sitting up as a hint of sunlight streamed across her and Abraham's bedroom. Her husband yawned as he cuddled up next to her and put his hand on her stomach.

"Good morning, baby," he said through a yawn.

"Which baby?" She put a hand on top of his and smiled.

Leaving his hand on her tummy, he sat up, yawning again. "Both."

Blue verbalized a loud yawn from where he was lying on the floor at the foot of the bed.

"We *lieb* you, too, Blue," Abraham said before he glanced at her hands. "Why are you holding your phone?"

"I was re-reading Samuel's text from last night." She turned to face him. "I'm going to take a wild guess that Anna and Leroy don't know Samuel has a phone. Isn't Samuel afraid I might tell them?"

"Are you? Going to tell them?"

Yvonne shook her head. "*Nee*. Are you?"

"Not unless one of them asks me." Abraham slowly eased his hand from her stomach, swung his legs over the side of the bed, then stood and faced her. "She won't be here that long. Whatever this is—a spark, as you say—it will be over before it has a chance to get started."

Yvonne tugged at her ear. "I don't know. A lot can happen in a month. And remember, he asked her on a date for this Saturday."

"And as of that day, she will have already been here a week." Abraham pulled on his black slacks and slid into his short-sleeved blue shirt. It was a far cry from the police uniform he used to wear, but returning to his old ways had suited him, and Yvonne was overjoyed to be living her life with Abraham. She still felt like a newbie in their Amish community, and she didn't want her cousin to stir up anything with Leroy and Anna that might make it all go sideways.

She stepped out of bed and stretched, reminded of her husband's advice. *Don't borrow trouble.*

After Abraham had headed to the kitchen—coffee was his number one priority in the morning—Yvonne picked up her phone and read Samuel's text again.

> Wie bischt, Yvonne. This is Samuel. Could you please give me Eden's phone number?

She had responded by only sending the phone number. As she stared at his message, there wasn't anything to read into it except that he wanted to talk to Eden.

Eden, Yvonne's beautiful teenage cousin.

Abraham could keep telling them not to borrow trouble, but Yvonne feared trouble was already here.

Anna sent the girls to the market to pick up a few things they were out of, and she gave each of them a few extra dollars to buy something for themselves. This was the first time she'd allowed Hannah to go with them. Her youngest daughter had recently turned eight. Grace was eleven and learning to drive the buggy. Mae had been taking the buggy out for about two years, just after she'd turned twelve. Anna was a little nervous, but Mae was a good driver, and it would give the girls a sense of independence.

As she swept the kitchen floor, her thoughts shifted to Samuel. Anna couldn't shake the way he'd looked at Eden or how cozy they had looked after taking the canoe to Samuel's favorite spot. Anna had tossed and turned with worry during the night about what might be ensuing between her son and Eden. Leroy told her he had spoken with Samuel, warned him to be careful with a beautiful girl who wasn't Amish, but Anna's heart was still heavy.

The screen door closed in the living room, and Anna stopped sweeping when her husband walked into the kitchen. He went straight to the refrigerator and poured himself a glass of iced tea. Sweat trickled from his temples as he chugged until the glass was empty.

"The gate on the fence is repaired. We shouldn't have any more goats escaping." He set the glass on the counter. "Seems hotter than usual for July."

Anna grinned. "It seems hotter each year. Maybe because we're getting older."

"Forty-two isn't that old." Abraham sat down at the kitchen table and reached for a blueberry muffin on a platter Anna had left out after breakfast.

"It feels old some days." She picked up where she'd left off, sweeping the floor, so she could check this chore off her list today.

By the time she was done, her husband was slathering butter on his second muffin. She poured them each a cup of coffee, then sat across from him, strumming her fingers on the table.

"What's on your mind, Anna? I recognize that look." Leroy leaned back in his chair and lifted an eyebrow.

"I know you said you talked to Samuel about Eden, but do you think you should talk to Abraham? He could keep an eye on things from his end, to make sure they aren't sneaking off to meet each other." She shrugged. "It couldn't hurt."

"*Ya*, it could." Leroy frowned. "Samuel spent one day with Yvonne's cousin. One day, Anna. They might not see each other again during her visit here. It would feel judgmental to talk to *mei bruder* about his houseguest. Abraham would let me know if there was anything to be concerned about, and I'm sure there isn't." He paused as his expression relaxed. "Besides, I talked to Samuel. He's a smart boy. He won't let himself get involved with someone outside of our community."

"I hope you're right." Anna took a sip of her coffee, locking eyes with her husband. "She has a tattoo on her hand. It's a butterfly." She shook her head. "I don't like people marking on their body like that. God made us to stay as we are, not cover ourselves with pictures."

Leroy grinned. "Anna, we know lots of *Englisch* who have tattoos, especially the younger ones."

"That doesn't mean I have to like it." She sighed. "I'm not going to worry about it. I know you'll make sure Samuel doesn't do anything inappropriate or make bad choices."

Leroy laughed, which made her smile. "Not going to worry about it, huh?" He stood and walked around the table to kiss her on the forehead. "If you say so." Taking off his straw hat, he blotted his forehead with a napkin, then put it back on again. "I'm going to try to finish painting the backside of the house. What are your plans today?"

Anna slouched down in her chair and raised her chin. "*Ach*, I thought I'd sit around eating ice cream with *mei* feet up. You know, like I always do when everyone is gone."

Leroy chuckled again. "You say things like that, but sometimes I wonder if it's true."

She straightened in the chair. "I assure you it's not." She stood and cleared their cups. After she'd placed them in the sink, she spun around and leaned against the counter. "I have a long list of things I'd like to get done today. I'm planning to make soap, hem those pants I made you that somehow ended up too long, and we're almost out of bathroom cleaner, so I'm planning to prepare a new batch. After that, I'll kick *mei* feet up and eat ice cream."

"You better get started," he said as he winked at her before he left.

Anna had never propped her feet up and privately eaten ice cream when no one was around. She laughed to herself at the thought. Even with the girls helping, there was always a lot to do to keep the household going. But one of these days . . . maybe she would indulge.

Eden tried to look excited and forced a big smile when Jake showed up at the bookstore with a red bicycle for her.

"Thanks so much," she said as she eyed her new mode of transportation to use while she was here. She hadn't expected to drive the buggy on her own, at least not any time soon, but she hadn't ridden a bike since she was nine or ten, and it had been a borrowed ten-speed that she only rode around the parking lot at their apartment complex. This didn't look anything like a ten-speed, and it had a basket on the front.

"There's a lot of places within walking distance from here," Jake said. "But it's mighty hot outside, and I thought this might make it easier for you to get around." He smiled. Eden did her best to mirror his excitement. Back home, she'd die if anyone saw her on a granny bike like this, but she reminded herself she didn't know anyone here. Except Samuel. Did he own a bike like this?

Yvonne thanked Jake for his thoughtfulness, then they talked business for a few minutes before Jake left.

"Okay, so I know it isn't the coolest-looking bike." Yvonne grinned at Eden, then they both stared at the bike. Maybe it was because her cousin hadn't always been Amish, but Yvonne seemed to relate to Eden. "But it will get you around when you get bored hanging out here with me at the bookstore."

"It's fine. Really. That was nice of Jake to think of me." They both stared at the antique bike with its chipped paint but shiny new tires. "Should we move it somewhere?" Eden glanced at Yvonne, who laughed.

"Sure. Let's put it in the back for now."

Eden unlocked the kickstand and wheeled the bike to the back of the shop, where she leaned it against the counter in the kitchen. "Is here okay for now?" There wasn't much room. A small table and four chairs occupied most of the space.

"*Ya*, that's fine." Yvonne took a bottle of water from the small refrigerator. "Do you want one?" She extended the bottle to Eden, who took it and thanked her.

When the bell on the door jingled, Yvonne said, "Can you see if you can help whoever that is?" She pointed to the bathroom. "I'll be in there, then I'll meet you up front."

"Sure."

Eden rounded the corner, then slowed her step until she stood right in front of Samuel. "Hey. What are you doing here?" Her heart raced, the way it had been doing every time she saw him or heard his voice.

He pointed over his shoulder. "We're doing a job right around the corner today and tomorrow, some decking for an *Englisch* couple. I thought I'd come say hi and see if it was okay if I pick you up at four on Saturday? And if so, then I'll hire us a driver." He looped his thumbs beneath his suspenders, and even dressed identical to yesterday, he couldn't have looked more handsome.

"Yeah, four sounds great."

"Um . . ." He leaned to the side and peered around Eden. "Where's Yvonne?" he asked in a whisper.

"Bathroom."

Samuel nodded. "Did she say anything about me texting her to get your phone number?"

Eden shook her head. "No. She didn't mention it."

"Hmm . . ." He rubbed his chin. "What about our date on Saturday? Was she okay with that? And what about Abraham?"

"She seemed to be okay. I don't really know what Abraham thinks. What about your parents?"

He smiled. "*Ach*, *ya*, it was fine with them."

"Okay, good. Then I guess I'll see you at four on Saturday." Eden tucked her hair behind her ears, hoping he didn't see her hands shaking a little. Technically, this would be her first real date, and potentially Samuel's. She hoped everything went perfectly.

"Saturday at four." He gave a quick wave and turned to leave, but at the door, he turned back around. "Do you want me to call you tonight?"

Eden nodded. "That would be great."

Yvonne came around the corner right after Samuel was gone.

"I admit it. I overheard." Yvonne held out both palms as she walked toward Eden, then made her way to the counter and sat on the stool. "I was a little surprised when you said he asked you out for Saturday, but I think I might be even more surprised that he has a phone."

Eden cringed. "I don't think his parents know about the phone."

Yvonne lowered her head and sighed before she looked up at Eden. "I know lots of Amish guys his age who have phones, but I suspect Leroy and Anna wouldn't approve."

Eden bit her lip. "Are you going to tell them? I don't think Anna cares for me as it is."

"It's not that. She doesn't even know you. Her concern is that you're not Amish." Yvonne held her head in her hands. "I'm not going to tell them about the phone. They know about the date, and surely that's weighing heavily on their minds." She paused. "But . . . I'm not going to lie about the phone if they ask me."

"I understand." Eden walked to the counter and faced Yvonne. "I really like it here. I enjoy spending time with you and Abraham. And I like Samuel. But please don't worry, Yvonne. I know we can only be friends. I don't want to start any trouble for anyone."

Yvonne hinted at a smile. "Sweetie, you're not causing trouble for anyone. I just hope Samuel isn't causing trouble for himself. But, since he told his parents about the date, I'm going to assume they realize that they are going to have to give that boy some freedom."

It warmed Eden's heart to hear Yvonne call her "sweetie." She wasn't sure anyone ever had. Then another thought hit her.

"What should I wear Saturday? I mean, he'll be in Amish clothes. Will people look at us funny? Not that I really care, but should I dress Amishy?"

Her cousin chuckled. "Amishy? Not sure I've heard that before. Just wear jeans and a conservative shirt. You'll be fine."

"Okay." She smiled. "And it really was nice of Jake to loan me a bike to ride."

Yvonne held up a hand. "Like I said, I know it's not

what you're used to. Kind of an old-lady bike. But I think you'll appreciate it when you get bored being here and want to get around town."

"I absolutely will." Eden had already thought about how the bike might open opportunities to see more of Montgomery.

Yvonne blew a strand of hair out of her face, then tucked it beneath her prayer covering. "I was thinking . . . If you're planning to hang out here for a while, maybe we can organize that kitchen a little better. There are things in some of those drawers that I know can be thrown away. And we'll find a better place to keep your bike. Jake had it mounted on the back of his buggy, but I'm not sure you and I can get it home that way."

"It's probably not too far for me to ride it home."

"Maybe not too far for *you*." Yvonne stood up. "We'll worry about that later. I brought us some chicken-salad sandwiches, and we can eat lunch and work on that kitchen a little bit."

"Sounds good."

The more time Eden spent with Yvonne, the more she liked her cousin. She was cool and seemed to have a strong faith. Eden liked that combination. Her cousin talked a lot about her spiritual journey during their nightly devotions. It gave Eden hope that her own journey would be as meaningful as Yvonne's.

Facing her uncertain future, she clung to God. He loved her despite her past, and He knew everything about her. Sometimes, she longed to have a human to talk to about her feelings, but putting herself out there felt too scary most of the time. Logic told her that she would have to address the situation with her mother for her to move forward on her journey, but she wasn't ready.

As Samuel walked back to his job, his chest tightened. He didn't feel good about lying to Eden, but twice he'd tried to tell his mother about taking Eden out on Saturday, and he'd chickened out both times. He'd considered talking to his father, but he knew his dad would tell his mother, and they would ultimately forbid him to go, using the excuse that Eden wasn't Amish. He wondered if he would be allowed to go if Eden *were* Amish. Either way, he wasn't going to miss the opportunity to go on a real date with her.

He knew the news would get out. Abraham or Yvonne would eventually say something to his parents. Maybe it wouldn't come out until after Eden was gone. It seemed doubtful that they would keep it quiet that long, but Samuel had more immediate worries. Where was he going to say he was going when a driver showed up at his house?

The day dragged on, and by the time his boss called it a day, Samuel's mind was reeling with challenges about his date on Saturday. He could ask the driver to pick him up down the road. But where would he tell his parents he was going? Maybe he needed to cancel going to a movie and just take Eden somewhere close by in the buggy.

The thought assaulted him with disappointment. He'd been wanting to see a movie for a long time, and seeing it with Eden would be special. There were plenty of boys his age enjoying this time in their life, seeing movies, wearing English clothes, and going to parties outside of town. Samuel respected his parents, yet he equally feared their wrath if he was caught doing things they'd always said they wouldn't allow. But now that Eden was in the picture, he feared not seeing her again more than his parents' wrath.

He pulled his buggy up to the fence and saw his mother standing in the middle of the yard with her arms folded across her chest, shooting daggers at him with her eyes. He stashed his phone under the seat for now, stepped out of the buggy, and tethered his horse.

"*Wie bischt, Mamm*?" he said cautiously, slowing his steps as he got closer to her. She clutched a piece of pink paper in her hand, and Samuel swallowed hard. He knew what she was holding—the receipt he must have left on his nightstand.

His mother held out a trembling hand, palm up, her face as red as the barn. "Give me the phone."

CHAPTER 9

Samuel went back to his buggy, retrieved the phone, and shuffled back to where his mother was standing in the yard, now joined by his father.

He placed the phone into her outstretched hand, then mirrored both their stances by folding his arms across his chest.

"We know you're sixteen, Samuel," his father said in a stern voice. "But you also know that we forbid phones, at any age, except in the case of an emergency."

It was hypocritical, and he wanted to ask if his mother's phone calls to relatives in other states constituted emergencies, but there was no reason to make things worse.

His mother dropped the phone into the pocket of her apron and slid in the receipt also.

"Can I at least return it and see if I can get *mei* money back?" He shifted his weight as he met his mother's fierce glare.

"I'll return it and get your money back." She again folded her arms across her chest as she raised her chin.

Samuel had only communicated with two people on the

phone. He'd gotten Yvonne's phone number from his mother's list on a sheet of paper she kept on the kitchen counter. The other number was Eden's. Samuel's stomach clenched as he wondered if his mother would call one or both of the numbers. She might recognize Yvonne's number and assume the other one was Eden's.

"No mobile phones," his father said. "You're grounded for two weeks."

Samuel could feel his nostrils flair. "Two weeks? *Nee*, that's not fair. That's too long. Lots of *kinner mei* age have phones. Just because it's your rule, that doesn't make it right."

His father took a step closer to Samuel, causing his mother's expression to shift from anger to concern as she put a hand on his *daed*'s arm. His father had never struck him outside of a spanking when he was younger, but Samuel didn't usually disrespect him the way he was doing now.

His father held up two fingers. "Two weeks," he said before he walked away.

Surprisingly, his mother looked down at her bare feet, then sighed before she looked up at him, locking eyes for a few seconds. "Did you get this phone so that you could talk to Eden? I'm sure the *Englisch maedel* has a phone."

Samuel stood rigid, his arms still crossed in front of him as he eyed his mother. "*Ya*, I did. Her *mudder* has heart problems. She's in the hospital and really sick . . . and not herself, Eden said. I thought she might like to have a friend she could talk to while she's here." He wanted to say, *"I suppose that isn't as much of an emergency as you calling Aunt Catherine for a recipe."* But he stashed the thought since he'd already indirectly lied. Again. He hadn't known about Eden's mother until after he'd purchased the phone and called her.

His mother looked down at her toes, wiggling them in the grass. "That's terrible, especially for a *maedel* that age." She looked up at Samuel with sympathetic eyes. "And I am truly sorry for Eden. But, Samuel, rules are rules."

As she walked away, Samuel stood unmoving in the yard. Now he had another problem. Since he was grounded, how was he going to sneak out Saturday for his date with Eden?

Anna walked around to the back of the house to where Leroy stood on a ladder painting.

"The *maedel*—Eden. Samuel said her *mudder* is sick." She held a hand to her forehead to block the sun as she looked up at her husband, his steady hand applying a second coat of white paint. He slowly stepped down the ladder.

"Samuel said the *maedel*'s *mudder* has heart problems, that she's really sick and in the hospital." Anna waited for Leroy to set the paintbrush across the can and put it down. "He thought she could use a friend to talk to while she was here." She chewed her bottom lip. "Does that make us terrible for taking away the phone?"

Her husband frowned. "It's sad for a *maedel* that age to be going through that, but it would be unhealthy for Samuel to get involved with her. Maybe even more so, since I'm sure Eden would like someone her own age to talk to about it, making it easier for them to grow closer."

"I'm sure she has friends back home she can talk to." Anna needed to justify what suddenly felt like a harsh punishment.

Leroy leaned closer and kissed her. "We did the right thing."

"I suppose," Anna said softly as she pictured Eden, probably frightened, far away from her sick mother. But even her sympathy for the girl wasn't going to cause her to bend where her own child was concerned. "Do you think I should say anything to Yvonne?"

"*Nee.*" Leroy ran his hands down the front of his gray coveralls. "Samuel is grounded for two weeks. It's no one's business why. Yvonne and Abraham probably have enough to deal with. The girl's mental state is probably not *gut*. No need to stir up anything. Besides, Eden will be gone in three weeks."

Anna thought Eden's mental state had seemed just fine when she was hanging out with Samuel, which felt like a double-edged sword. Either the girl wasn't that upset about her mother or Samuel was providing her with a much-needed distraction and friendship.

"Maybe we should have grounded him for three weeks." Anna rolled her eyes.

Leroy grinned. "I think two is plenty."

Anna sulked away, not feeling good about upsetting Samuel but trusting her husband that they'd made the right decision.

Eden could sense that Yvonne and Abraham were waiting for a mention of Eden's mother during devotions that evening, but Eden didn't want to unlock that emotional grenade.

After they recited closing prayers, Eden caught Yvonne looking at her butterfly tattoo on her left hand. "I'm surprised you haven't asked me about it sooner," Eden said as she nodded to her hand.

Yvonne reached across the coffee table and gently pulled Eden's hand closer. "I think it's beautiful. Butterflies are thought to be spiritual creatures, that their metamorphosis is a metaphor for rebirth." Her cousin released her hand and smiled.

"And transformation, change, hope, and life." Eden spoke softly as she recalled the fit her mother had thrown when she saw the tattoo, even though her mom was covered in artwork herself. Eight tattoos, if Eden remembered correctly.

She didn't want to bring up her mother. "I didn't think adults really liked tattoos that much." She shrugged. "This is the only one I have, if you were wondering."

Yvonne and Abraham exchanged glances, and Yvonne pressed her lips together as if she were trying not to smile. Her husband put a hand over his mouth as if he was also suppressing laughter.

"Well . . . ," Yvonne finally said, "I guess some adults don't care for tattoos, and I admit, I don't like it when people are covered in them. But, done tastefully, like yours, and with a meaning attached to it, I think some of them are rather nice."

The couple exchanged glances of amusement again.

"I bet Amish people *really* don't like them, being so conservative and all." Eden ran a finger over her butterfly, eyeing the intricacy the artist had created. "I mean, I can't imagine the two of you having tattoos."

Abraham sighed, then stood up.

Yvonne slumped into the couch and covered her mouth with her hand, but her eyes were watering as if she were trying not to burst out laughing.

"What is up with you two? You're acting weird." Eden grinned as Abraham rolled up the edge of his short-sleeved blue shirt, then gasped. "Wow!"

"Remember, I was born into an Amish family, but I spent a lot of years in the outside world as a cop before I was baptized and chose this life." He nodded to the tattoo of an eagle on his upper arm, right below his shoulder.

Eden rose from where she was sitting on the other side of the coffee table from Abraham and Yvonne. She leaned closer to his arm. "That's awesome. Did it have a special meaning for you when you got it?" She gingerly ran her hand over the bird.

"*Ya*, I guess so. When I was at the police academy, another student said an eagle was man's connection to the divine because it could fly higher than any other bird." He raised his tattooed shoulder, then lowered it slowly before he rolled down his shirt sleeve. "Even though I was making big changes in *mei* life at the time by choosing not to be baptized into the Amish faith, I didn't want to ever lose my connection to God, no matter how I chose to live *mei* life."

Eden couldn't hide her surprise or stop smiling. "Totally awesome."

Abraham sat on the couch beside Yvonne and nudged her. Eden's cousin sank farther into the couch cushions. "Your turn," Abraham said.

Eden laughed. "No. Not you too? Really?" Instead of returning to her spot on the other side of the coffee table, she rushed to where Yvonne was sitting and squeezed in beside her cousin and the arm of the couch. "Let's see it." She pressed her hands together and smiled, but Yvonne covered her face with both hands.

"No!" she squealed.

"Aw, what's the matter, *mei lieb*?" Abraham snickered. "I'm sure Eden is eager to see your tattoo and the meaning behind it."

Yvonne lowered her hands, and her face was bright red as she pointed a finger at her husband. "I'm going to get you for this."

Eden held her breath as Yvonne leaned down and peeled off the black sock on her left foot, then buried her face in her hands again and laughed so hard that she had tears in her eyes when she showed her face again. Abraham was about to bust a gut too.

Eden leaned closer to Yvonne's foot. "I don't see anything. Was it done in invisible ink, or what?" She laughed as she held up Yvonne's foot, twisting it from side to side. "There's nothing there."

Abraham pointed, still chuckling. "Go back to where you were sitting."

Eden let go of Yvonne's foot and did as Abraham instructed, plopping down on the other side of the coffee table again. "I'm here." She shrugged, then tipped her head to one side. "You two are weird," she said again through a smile.

Slowly, Yvonne lifted her bare foot onto the coffee table, and Eden saw the tattoo on the bottom of her foot. She slammed both hands to her mouth before she exploded with laughter along with Yvonne and Abraham. "Wow. Oh, wow."

"I was probably your age and young and stupid." Yvonne tried to stifle her laughter. "Not that you're stupid." She waved a hand in front of her face. "You know what I mean."

"Yeah, uh . . ." Eden tilted her head and stared at what appeared to be a smashed bug on the bottom of Yvonne's foot. "I can't wait to hear the symbolism for that thing!" She cringed as she continued to eye what appeared to be a brown spider that had been stepped on. "Is it what it looks like? A spider that's been squashed?"

"That's exactly what it is." Abraham snickered as Yvonne elbowed him.

"Hush." She rolled her eyes at her husband before she turned to Eden. "I went with two girlfriends to a tattoo parlor, much to Aunt Emma's horror when she found out later. Lindsey got a little rose on her ankle, and Gina chose a small rainbow for her own ankle. While they were looking through the books and trying to choose a design, I saw a spider and stepped on it." She threw her hands in the air. "I don't know how it happened, but the next thing I knew, the owner of the shop was showing me a tattoo of a spider that had been stepped on."

"That's hilarious." Eden raised both eyebrows. "I bet the people around here haven't seen your spider."

Yvonne grimaced in a playful manner. "*Nee*, they haven't. So, don't tell anyone, not even Samuel."

Eden's heart warmed at the mention of Samuel's name, but when Abraham cleared his throat and looked away, he appeared a little uncomfortable. He recovered quickly by smiling and offering a hand to Eden and Yvonne, something he hadn't done before. Eden hesitated when Max's face flashed in her mind's eye, but she forced it away. Abraham was nothing like Max. She leaned forward and eased her hand into his and then latched on to Yvonne's. Her heart was full. She felt like part of a real family.

"Let's close with a prayer." Abraham bowed his head and recited a prayer Eden hadn't heard before about choosing to follow God's will above and before our own.

"Amen," they said in unison.

Even if her phone hadn't buzzed on the coffee table, Eden would still have thought of her mother and what God would want her to do. But when she recognized the phone number from the jail, she silenced the call. Abraham and Yvonne glanced at each other.

"You could have gotten that." Her cousin nodded to the phone.

"It's okay." Eden stood up, fidgeting for a couple seconds before she hugged Abraham, then Yvonne, a first for her also. "Good night," she said. When she was almost to the hallway, she decided to leave on a happy note. She spun around and grinned at Yvonne. "Don't step on any spiders."

Yvonne lowered her head and shook it as her shoulders jiggled. "I'll try not to." She lifted her head. "Good night, sweetie."

Eden gave a quick wave, eager to get a shower before Samuel called.

After she had bathed and dressed for bed, she lit her lantern and fluffed her pillows behind her, grateful for the cool cross breeze as the sun set. She stared at her phone, at the number from the prison, and a thought hit her. Exactly how much time did her mother have? Could that have been the prison or someone calling to say that her mother had passed? Panic welled in Eden's throat as a wave of fear swept through her. She didn't want to talk to her mother, or forgive her, but the thought of never seeing her again caused her to choke back a cry. She squeezed her eyes closed.

Please, God, I need help. I know it's Your will for me to forgive her, but I don't know how to stop hating her.

When her phone buzzed on the nightstand, she prayed it was Samuel.

When she saw the screen, her mind congested as her heart pounded in her chest. It wasn't the number her mother always called from, but it was the same area code, and it was a Facebook video call.

Eden was too afraid to answer and too afraid not to. Her hands trembled with uncertainty. Finally, she took the call, and her mother's pale face came into view. "Hi, Mom."

"Hi, baby girl." Her mother spoke in a whisper. Her lips had a bluish tint, and her thinning blonde hair had roots halfway down her head. "One of the nurses here let me borrow her phone. She attempted a smile. "I needed to see your beautiful face."

Eden habitually slipped into her emotional coat of armor, knowing her expression wouldn't give anything away even though her insides quaked with anxiety. "How are you feeling?" It was a dumb thing to say, and probably hateful considering the circumstances. A thread of genuine concern would have been more appropriate.

"I'm okay." Her mother tried to smile again. "How is it going staying with Emma?"

Eden didn't want her mother to know where she was in case being with Yvonne would get Emma in trouble. "Fine," she said before she began gnawing on a fingernail.

"I'm sorry things turned out this way." A tear rolled down her mother's cheek. "I'm sorry I wasn't a better mother. I'm sorry for everything."

The knot in Eden's throat felt like a baseball. This was her chance to do what God would want her to do. *Just say it—that you forgive her.* Maybe if she said it repeatedly, she would eventually mean it. There were so many things for her to reflect on that filled her with miserable memories. The times her mother had left her alone for days at a time when she was only seven or eight. All the men, some worse than Max. And the continual abuse of drugs and alcohol. There was every reason that Eden should have turned out like her mother, but somehow she'd fought off her could-have-been legacy. She owed that to God for staying by her side, guiding her to be a better person.

Did she owe it to God now to forgive her mother?

She opened her mouth, but when tears came on without her permission, she took a deep breath, not wanting her mother to see her crying or to acknowledge to herself or her mother that she might care.

"I gotta go, Mom." Eden's voice cracked as she spoke.

"Wait, Eden."

Her lips trembled, and Eden was sure her mother could see. "What?" she asked.

"Do . . ." Another tear rolled down her mother's cheek. "Do you think I'll go to heaven?"

Eden's mother was aware of Eden's relationship with God and often criticized her for being taken in by all that "bogus religious stuff," as she called it. But the Lord was the only person who decided who went to heaven and who didn't.

"That's not for me to decide."

Her mother offered a weak smile. "I probably don't deserve to go there."

Eden tried to speak, but her voice wavered, and her words sounded inaudible even to her. "I have to go. Bye, Mom."

After the screen on her phone went dark, she rolled onto her side, clutching the phone with both hands, willing Samuel to call. She needed to talk to someone before her head exploded from confusion. If she was brave enough to tell him the truth, maybe Samuel could offer her some guidance. But if he knew everything, would he still want to go out with her, or did she have too much baggage that showed how heavy her burdens were?

At eleven, when Samuel hadn't called, she extinguished the lantern and curled onto her side, pulling her knees to her chest. She didn't try to stop the tears from flowing. She was so far past that.

CHAPTER 10

Yvonne wanted to ask Eden what was wrong. Her eyes were swollen like she'd been crying. Her cousin had been quiet on the way to the bookstore that morning and had even chosen not to drive the buggy. Yvonne had gone over and over in her mind if something she or Abraham had said the night before had upset Eden. She didn't think so. They'd prayed together and laughed a lot. Eden had even hugged them both good night for the first time. It had to be something to do with her mother. Yvonne had thought she heard Eden talking last night, but at the time, she assumed it had been Samuel. Maybe she had spoken to her mother.

By eleven, after praying that she wouldn't overstep and push Eden away, she decided to broach the subject. The girl surely had a lot on her mind, even if she was either hiding her emotions or truly didn't care about her mother. Yvonne didn't think the latter was the case, no matter the circumstances.

She waited until they were sitting in the back room eating ham sandwiches to say anything.

"Eden, are you okay? You've been quiet all morning,

and honestly . . . you look like you've been crying." Yvonne took a sip of tea but kept her eyes on her cousin from across the small table.

Eden avoided her eyes as she set her sandwich on the paper plate. "Um, I'm okay." She smiled. "I had fun last night. Thank you for showing me your tattoo. And if I haven't said so before, thank you for letting me stay with you."

Yvonne studied her for a moment, noticing that Eden seemed to have trouble making eye contact, and she'd completely sidestepped Yvonne's mention of crying. "Abraham and I enjoyed spending time with you too. It feels *gut* to laugh about silly stuff sometimes." She rolled her eyes. "And my spider tattoo is certainly silly."

Eden grinned. "You and Abraham are cute together."

"Aw. *Danki*—thanks. He's a wonderful man." She put a hand on her stomach again. "And he'll be a great *daed*."

Eden lowered her head as she pinched a piece of bread from her sandwich. "You'll be a good mom too."

Yvonne chuckled even though the comment touched her. "I hope so. *Kinner* don't arrive with an instruction manual. I guess every mother wings it and prays she does a *gut* job." She hoped Eden would bring up her mother since the conversation had shifted in a parental direction.

Instead, her cousin took a bite of her sandwich as she nodded at the bicycle still propped up against the counter. "If you don't need help with anything, I thought I would go for a ride after we finished eating."

"I think that's a great idea, and I don't have anything I need help with, but I appreciate the offer." Yvonne searched her mind for nearby places Eden might like to see. "If you keep going down this road, there's a historical marker with a great view of an unusual ravine. I'm not a history buff, and I don't really remember the historical significance, but the view is pretty. And if you go a little farther down the road, there's a dingy white scarf tied to a fence post on your left. It's private property, so you can't go through the gate, but there's a cool cave opening you can see from a distance."

"Oh, wow." Eden's eyes lit up for the first time today. "Have the owners been inside it? I read online before I got here that there were a lot of caves in the area."

Yvonne nodded. "*Ya*, there are. Some are commercial, touristy places. But there are quite a few small ones here and there too. The owners of this one are an older *Englisch* couple. I heard they tied a scarf to the fence a long time ago to keep people from coming to the door and asking where the cave is. This way, people can stop and see it if they know to look for the scarf. But there are also several No Trespassing signs along the property line."

"I wonder how big it is inside."

"Abraham told me that he'd been inside when he was a boy and that he felt like he was inside a bowling ball—that it was rounded out, but with three holes on one side that weren't big enough to crawl through. I think he said it was around twenty feet by twenty feet."

"That's cool." Eden stood and put her paper plate in the trash can, then walked to the bike. "I'll be back in a little while," she said before she began to wheel the bike out of the back room.

"Have fun." Yvonne wished her cousin would talk to

her about her mother. It had to be heavy on her heart. "And be careful."

"I will."

Yvonne smiled when Eden did. Maybe she would open up about her mother soon. At least, for now, she seemed okay.

Eden didn't know exactly where Samuel was working, but it was within walking distance, he'd said. And he'd also told her he would be working there yesterday and today. He hadn't called, and it was eating away at her. Were they still going out tomorrow night?

She didn't have to go far before she heard power saws in the distance. She turned onto a dirt road that led to the noise. There were three buggies tethered to the fence and no power lines in sight. Since Samuel had said they were working for people who weren't Amish, she assumed this must be the place. As she pedaled closer, she spotted Samuel right away, working alongside two Amish guys. One of the men was holding a long piece of lumber while Samuel used the saw to cut, and the third person was stacking the cut wood. There was one man who appeared not to be Amish since he was wearing shorts and sporting a baseball cap. The guy flipped through papers on a clipboard not far from where the power saw was in use.

After parking her bike near the buggies, she started toward the small gate that led to the front yard. No one had noticed her yet or heard her bike tires rolling against the gravel on the driveway. She slowed her steps. What would she say? *"Why didn't you call me like you said you would?"* It wasn't like she was his girlfriend. Maybe he'd fallen asleep early. Or more likely, his phone was dead, and he had no way to charge it.

She took a deep breath and called out his name during a break from the noise.

Samuel pushed back the rim of his straw hat, squinted, then recognized her and waved. After he turned to the other men and said something, he headed toward Eden.

"*Wie bischt?*" Grinning, he shook his head. "Sorry. That means 'How are you?'" He eyed the bike as he raised an eyebrow.

"Jake loaned me this bike to use while I'm here." She bit her lip. "I-I don't mean to bother you at work, but—"

He held up a hand. "*Nee, nee.* You're not bothering me, and I'm glad you came by. *Mei mamm* took *mei* phone away. She found the receipt in *mei* room and said having a phone is against the rules. That's why I couldn't call last night." He winced as he used his hand to wipe sweat from his forehead. "It's not fair, but . . ." He shrugged. "Are we still on for tomorrow at four?"

"Sure." Eden homed in on his tanned arms, the way his muscles filled out his shirt, and she smiled back at him when his slightly crooked smile spread across his face and accentuated his dimples.

He looked over his shoulder. "I better get back to work, but I'm glad you found me. I would have come by the bookstore earlier during *mei* lunch hour, but Mr. Lantz—the owner of the business—wanted to treat us to pizza."

"No problem. You go back to work. Yvonne said there's a cave down the road. I was going to check it out."

"It's where an old scarf is tied to the fence."

"That's what she said. Have you ever been in it?" Eden was intrigued and wished she could have a look inside.

"*Ya*, I have. It's not much to see, just a big hole. But most of us have snuck onto the property to have a look." He chuckled. "When I was a lot younger." He waved. "See you tomorrow."

Eden waved before she got back on her bike and headed toward the cave.

During supper, Samuel's mother directed most of her questions at him. *"How was your day? Why didn't you eat the lunch I sent with you? Do you think it will rain tomorrow? Did you finish the decking job you were working on?"*

Samuel answered respectfully to each question with no elaboration or questions of his own. He wanted to lash out and demand his phone be returned to him, but that wasn't an option. His father had kept an eye on Samuel throughout the meal as if he expected him to bring up the subject. And Samuel had bigger problems than the phone. As much as he hated to ask his nosy younger sister for anything, he was going to need her help.

He participated in devotions and waited until everyone was settled in for the night before he knocked on Mae's door. Since she was the oldest, she had her own room. Grace and Hannah shared a room next to hers.

"What?" his sister said after she eased the door open and frowned.

"Can I come in? I need to talk to you." Samuel loved his sister, but he worked hard to avoid conversations with Mae. She was a smarty-pants who was sure to give his parents more trouble in the future than he ever had.

She turned and shuffled barefoot back into her bedroom, her hands stuffed inside the pockets of her white robe, but she left the door open.

Samuel stepped over the threshold and closed the door. As he stood in the middle of Mae's room, she climbed into bed, leaned against her propped-up pillow, picked up a book she'd obviously been reading, and buried her head in it. "What do you want?" she asked without looking up.

"I need a favor." He sighed as he ran a hand through his hair.

Mae grinned as she slowly closed her book and looked at him. "*Ach*, really?"

Samuel was rethinking his plan. Mae would hold it over his head for the remainder of his *rumschpringe* and most likely all of hers when she turned sixteen. "Tomorrow, I am picking up Eden, Yvonne's cousin, and taking her out to eat." He cringed, not wanting to mention a movie, but the time frame required it. "And to a movie. I hired a driver."

Mae bolted upright, her eyes wide. "Are you *ab im kopp*?"

"I'm not crazy. I'm in *mei rumschpringe*, and I'm allowed certain freedoms."

"*Mamm* and *Daed* don't know, do they?" She clicked her tongue, grinning again.

"*Nee.*" Samuel was sure this was a mistake.

"Um . . . even if *Mamm* and *Daed* turn a blind eye to supper and a movie—and I'm not sure they will—they will never allow you to go on a date with an *Englisch maedel.*" She swung her legs over the side of the bed so fast that the bun on top of her head shifted, loosening until a few strands escaped. She brushed the loose hair from her face and held up a finger. "*Ach*, I see. You need *mei* help in some way with your date."

"Before you say *nee* or threaten to tell, just remember that you'll be sixteen in two years, and you might need me for something." He heard the desperation in his voice, but based on the way Mae was tapping a finger to her chin, she seemed to be considering what he'd said.

She dropped her hand to her lap. "I think you better tell me what you want me to do before I agree to anything."

Samuel swallowed hard. "*Ya*, okay." He paused, hoping Mae would cooperate. "Tomorrow at supper, when *Mamm* or *Daed* ask where I am, I need you to say I told you that I wasn't hungry and wanted to be by myself, that I went for a walk."

Mae grunted. "You're always hungry, so they'll never believe that. And you're asking me to lie." She extended her hands behind her and leaned back, frowning.

Samuel hung his head. He didn't feel good about asking Mae to fib, but he'd already thought about it, and there was a gray area. "You're not really lying. I *will* be going for a walk—to meet the driver at the road so *Mamm* and *Daed* don't see. I'm leaving at three forty-five. And I won't be hungry because around five, I'll be eating with Eden."

His sister scowled. "What time will you be back? *Mamm* will be worried if you aren't home by dark. What do I say if she pushes me about where you are?"

"Just say you don't know." Samuel forced a small smile.

Mae rolled her eyes. "Another lie."

"*Nee*. Not a lie. You won't know where I'm eating or where we're going to a movie."

He had never asked one of his sisters to lie for him. Samuel wasn't sure he'd ever asked *anyone* to lie for him. If his parents were like other parents, he wouldn't be doing this.

"Will you do it? All you have to say is that I went for a walk and that I wasn't hungry. And that I needed some time to myself."

"That last part is definitely not true. You won't be by yourself." She groaned. "*Ya*, okay. Fine. I'll do it, but you better remember this in case I meet a boy and want to sneak out to meet him."

Samuel flinched a little. Mae could be a pain at times, but he wasn't sure he would let her sneak out to meet a boy. At least not one that he hadn't met and approved of.

"*Danki*, Mae." Samuel turned to leave as his sister grunted again.

He went back to his room, wishing he had a phone to call Eden. His mother hadn't wasted any time returning his only means of communication, and she had slipped him the money after supper without saying anything.

For now, all he could do was get into bed, close his eyes, and dream about what it would be like to go on his first date with Eden tomorrow.

Yvonne waved as the blue sedan pulled out of the driveway at four o'clock. "I still can't believe Leroy and Anna are allowing this," she said through a smile from where she and Abraham stood on the porch, Blue lounging at their feet.

With the car out of view, they walked back inside, followed by their dog, and Yvonne slid the meatloaf she'd prepared in the oven as Abraham sat down and picked up the newspaper.

"*Ya*, well . . . I'm still not going to mention it. If they are truly choosing to look the other way and giving Samuel some liberties, they won't necessarily want to talk about it."

"I'm not going to bring it up either." She sat down across from her husband and chewed on her fingernail.

Abraham closed the newspaper and smiled at her. "Don't—"

"I know . . . borrow trouble," she said. "I'm not. I'm wondering if Eden will talk to Samuel about the situation with her mother. I know it must feel so complicated to her. Jill obviously wasn't a very *gut mudder*. Maybe it's not fair of me to judge, but it appears that way. Although the woman is still Eden's *mudder*, and there is bound to be an impending sense of loss. I just hope she doesn't keep things bottled up, then explode."

Abraham scratched his cheek as he frowned. "*Ya*, I know." Then he shed his unpleasant expression, smiled a little. "I'm pleasantly surprised at how much she seems to like it here. And she really is a sweet *maedel*."

"It was lovely the way you held both our hands at the end of devotions last night. It was also the first time Eden hugged us." Yvonne put a hand on her stomach. "Maybe she'll come to visit after the *boppli* is born." She grinned. "Who knows. Teenagers are unpredictable. She might be sick of us by the time she leaves."

Abraham tittered.

"I hope she has a nice time this evening. And Samuel too."

"*Ya*, Samuel is a *gut* boy. Most of the boys in our community are. I wouldn't trust a few out with your cousin, but out of all the teenage boys I know, I trust Samuel the most. I'm biased, I guess, since he's *mei* nephew. The only one old enough to date." He took a deep breath. "The meatloaf smells *gut*."

"*Danki*. I'm eating for two, and I'm starving." She smoothed a wrinkle on the white cloth that covered the antique table in their kitchen. "I'm going to wait up for Eden. If they're going to supper and a movie, it will be after dark when they get home. I wonder if Anna will wait up for Samuel."

Abraham laughed. "*Ya*, I'm quite sure she will. Leroy probably will too. Even if it's just hiding out in their bedroom, halfway pretending he isn't on a date but watching the clock."

Yvonne smiled as she said a quick prayer that Eden and Samuel would have a nice time, but also that God would guide their relationship and not let it progress into more than friendship. That would be a mess for all involved.

Anna glanced at the clock hanging on the wall above the sink as everyone took their seats at the kitchen table. Her son was usually the first one of her children to be seated.

"Where's Samuel?"

Leroy shrugged. "I haven't seen him in a couple of hours."

Grace and Hannah replied in unison that they didn't know. Mae had her head down as she fidgeted with the napkin she'd put in her lap.

"Mae, do you know where Samuel is?" Anna pulled out her chair but didn't sit as she waited for her oldest daughter to look up and respond. "Mae, did you hear me?"

"Uh . . . what? You're looking for Samuel?" Mae slowly lifted her head but stared at her plate. "He went for a walk earlier and said he wanted to be alone."

Anna glanced at Leroy before she slowly eased into her chair and waited for Mae to look at her. "When did he leave?"

"Three forty-five," Mae said louder than necessary, keeping her head down. "And he said he wasn't hungry."

Anna placed her napkin in her lap. "He knew over an hour ago that he wouldn't be hungry?"

"*Ya*, I guess," Mae said as she bit her lip and finally lifted her eyes to Anna's.

Leroy cleared his throat. "Let us pray."

Anna lowered her head with the rest of her family, but instead of praying silently, she pondered Mae's nervousness and wondered where her son was. She waited until everyone had filled their plates before she spoke about it again.

"Mae, did you see Samuel leave at three forty-five?"

It seemed odd that her daughter would remember the exact time.

"*Nee.*" Mae pushed her food around on her plate but hadn't taken a bite yet.

"Then how do you know he left at that time?" Anna spooned mashed potatoes onto her plate, along with a piece of pork tenderloin, some carrots, and a slice of bread. Then she raised an eyebrow and watched Mae twirling her fork in her potatoes.

"I think that was when he left." Mae's bottom lip trembled, and Anna wasn't sure what to make of her daughter's uneasiness, but supper wasn't the time to question Mae any more than she already had. Her oldest daughter was too thin, and Anna didn't want to upset her and cause her not to eat.

Anna stopped herself from twirling her own fork in her potatoes. She realized it was something she did when she was disturbed, a habit Mae must have picked up from her. Something wasn't right. Mother's instinct. And Samuel was always hungry.

CHAPTER 11

Everything had gone according to plan, and Samuel was finally sitting across the table from Eden, who couldn't have looked more beautiful dressed in dark-blue jeans, white sandals, and a button-up blue and white shirt. Her blonde hair cascaded past her shoulders in loose curls, and her green eyes twinkled. He'd already told her on the drive to the restaurant that she looked pretty.

Samuel had chosen a restaurant not far from the movie theater that had a variety of food.

"Have you been here? What's good?" she asked as they each eyed their menus.

"I've never been here, but I heard it's good, especially the burgers." Samuel's friend at work had told him this restaurant had good food, a nice atmosphere, and that it wasn't too expensive. As Samuel eyed the menu, he had to question what Brandon considered expensive. The prices were surely why he and his family had never been here. His parents would consider this too luxurious for their taste, and Samuel was mentally calculating whether he had enough money to pay for the meal.

They both studied the offerings a little longer before Eden closed her menu. "I think I'm going to have a burger and fries."

Samuel snapped his menu closed as relief washed over him that she hadn't chosen a steak. "That sounds great to me too."

After the waitress delivered them each a glass of tea, they placed their order, and Samuel cleared his throat. He didn't want to bring up a sad subject, but he also didn't want to seem insensitive by not asking about Eden's mother. "How is your *mamm*? Is she any better?"

Eden's cheerful expression fell, and Samuel wished he hadn't said anything.

"No. I don't think she has a chance of getting any better." She took a drink from her glass. "But I did FaceTime with her last night."

Samuel gazed across the table, but it was impossible to tell how she felt about the video call. He'd heard the term *poker face* used, and Eden seemed to have it mastered.

"That must have been . . ." He didn't know what to stay. "Hard."

She shrugged and avoided his eyes. "I guess."

"I'll keep praying for her." When Eden flinched, Samuel searched his mind for a way to change the subject. "Did you find the cave yesterday?"

An eagerness shone in her eyes as she sat taller. "Yes, I did, and wow! It took everything I had not to jump the fence and run to see it for myself." She pointed a finger at him. "But I didn't." Pausing, she tipped her head to one side. "Abraham told Yvonne it was like a bowling ball inside with three small holes, but that they weren't big enough for anyone to crawl through. What if there are other unexplored caves within that one?"

"I guess there could be." Samuel shook his head. "But Abraham is right—the holes are too small for a person to climb in. When I was about twelve and some of us snuck onto the property, we went inside the cave, then dared each other to stick our arm in the hole. It's hollow space on the other side. We could extend our arm as far as it would go without hitting anything."

"I wonder why the people living there have never had it explored or excavated by professionals?"

"I'm guessing the older couple probably don't want people messing up their land or to take a chance there might be some huge geological find that could cause some environmental group to get involved."

"I guess that makes sense."

They paused the conversation and thanked the waitress when she arrived with their burgers, which looked fantastic and gigantic—much larger than anything his mother or father would have prepared at home. And the fries were golden brown and plentiful.

"I'll never eat all this." Eden grinned, staring at her plate. "You might have to help me."

Samuel smiled, knowing he could eat his and whatever she couldn't finish. "No problem."

She cut her burger in half. "This looks awesome."

Samuel nodded, already enjoying a mouthful. After he'd swallowed, he said, "Did Yvonne tell you about the bookstore? About the rumor that some rare old coins are hidden in the walls?"

"Yes, she did. She even showed me a coin, one that she found a while back. Apparently, that's the only one that's ever been found. But it seems to lend some credibility to the rumor." Her eyes grew round. "And the one coin is worth around five hundred dollars."

Samuel raised his eyebrows. "That's a lot of money. I didn't know they'd ever found anything."

"Oops. Maybe I'm not supposed to tell." Eden cringed, and Samuel instinctively reached across the table and touched her hand.

"Don't worry. I won't say anything to anyone." He eased his hand away when her eyes traveled to his, and the poker face came back. Had he messed up, or had she welcomed the gesture? He wanted to get closer to her, to learn more about her and the world she lived in, so he made a mental note not to be too forward.

She was about halfway through the first portion of her massive burger when she set it on her plate. "I have to admit, I'm surprised your parents agreed to our date, especially since they took your phone away."

Samuel's stomach twisted in knots. He didn't want to lie to Eden. He recalled the gray areas in his conversation with Mae. There wasn't really a gray area here, but he sorted through his thoughts on how to save face without lying. "It's odd about phones and their usage within our community. I see Amish men who own businesses openly displaying them, but I've heard plenty of people chatting about things that have nothing to do with work. Most of the kids *mei* age have a phone. It irks me that I can't have one too. I'm sure Abraham or Yvonne told you that *mei* parents are very strict, and . . ." Samuel realized he was heading back in the direction of dating again. He cleared his throat. "Anyway, it must be great to have the freedom to do whatever you want where you live."

Eden picked up her burger but held it halfway between her plate and her mouth, unsure how to explain her life to Samuel in a way that wouldn't glorify it but also wouldn't reveal the many secrets and bad memories stored in her mind. Even the simple touch of Samuel's hand had caused her to clam up. Even though she knew Samuel, like Abraham, wasn't like Max or some of the men she had been forced to be around in the past.

"I know the restrictions for teenagers here must seem harsh," she said. "And I admit it's hard for me to imagine some of the rules imposed, but it seems like they are in place to keep you safe." How many times in Eden's life had she felt unsafe? *Too many to count.* "There's a real sense of family here, and not everyone has that. Or not everyone has a great family who cares about them."

He stared at her a long while, his eyes clinging to hers as if deep in thought. She'd said too much.

"I guess your family situation must feel really messed up right now. Are you close to your *daed*?"

Her first instinct was to change the subject. She had planned to keep her private life to herself when it came to Samuel. But for all she knew, he might already know her past, or at least some of it, which could get her caught in a lie. If he knew, he'd still asked her out. If he didn't know and she lied, would he find out later? He obviously didn't know her father wasn't in the picture.

Her thoughts spun around her mind like eggs scrambling. Lying was exhausting, and Eden had given it up a long time ago, for the most part.

She opened her mouth to offer up some version of the truth, but she unwittingly blinked back tears. "I-I . . ."

She longed to talk to someone about the things that scared her, her innermost feelings, and she'd briefly considered talking to Yvonne but decided against it, even though she was pretty sure Yvonne knew everything. Her times with Yvonne and Abraham were some of the happiest she'd had in a long time. She didn't want to spoil any of that with sad tales.

Why ruin her date with the truth now?

Samuel's brown eyes brimmed with tenderness as he reached across the table and put his hand on hers for the second time. She'd read that the Amish weren't openly affectionate. Maybe he was comfortable with the gesture because they were in a booth, protected from view on three sides. Eden's level of comfort had nothing to do with who might be watching. But she didn't pull away from him.

"Eden . . ." He paused, studying her face, which was surely red by now. "We can talk about your *mamm*, your family . . . or not. If you think talking about it will help, I'm here to listen. No matter what, it seems to me that your *mudder* would be the thing mostly on your mind. Getting to know each other means learning what each other's lives are about and what's going on. Please don't think it will mess up our date if you choose to share your personal situation with me. But I'll also respect your choice not to talk about it."

Maybe it was the compassionate way he spoke to her, his hand gently squeezing hers, or the way his eyes gleamed with honesty, maturity, and something pure she'd never seen from a guy her age or any of her mother's male friends. She jerked her hand from beneath his, then covered her face with both her hands.

"Nee, nee." Samuel sounded desperate. "Please don't cry. Please, please, don't cry. I'm such a jerk. I'm so sorry—"

Eden shook her head, then lowered her hands. "Don't apologize. You didn't make me cry for the reasons you think. I do want to talk to someone. I mean, I talk to God, but I . . ." She hung her head, not sure what she hoped to accomplish with all the honesty she was about to spill. "I know that when I tell you about my life, you might regret this date and never want to see me again." She looked up and locked eyes with him. "I considered lying to you, and the only reason I didn't at first was because I wondered if you already knew about my past. But a true friendship should include honesty." A tear slipped down her face. "And I could use a friend."

He leaned back against the booth seat with his mouth slightly open. Had he been surprised that she responded the way she did? Was he regretting the date already? His words had reflected such sincerity, but maybe he didn't really want to know anything bad about her. Maybe he would have been okay only to comfort her at a time when she should be grieving the soon-to-be loss of her mother—not admitting she'd almost lied and hinting that there was much more about herself than he would have expected.

"Eden, I could use a friend too." He gazed into her eyes. "You can tell me anything you want to, and I promise you it won't make me regret our date. Please don't cry."

She sniffled before dabbing her eyes with her napkin. "Samuel, my mom is in prison. She abused drugs for as far back as I can remember, and now it's killing her. She will die in jail or a prison hospital. My cousin, Emma, has temporary custody of me, but she had a trip planned to go to Europe with a bunch of ladies, so I'm staying with Yvonne and Abraham for the month that she will be gone." He opened his mouth to speak, but Eden held up her hand. "Wait. Let me finish or I might not get it all out. I also borrowed Emma's car without her permission. At the time, I was feeling claustrophobic and desperate for some time to myself. It wasn't anything Emma had done, and I shouldn't have taken the car, especially since I don't have a license." She shook her head. "But Emma got pretty upset about it. I shouldn't have done it."

Samuel tried to say something again, but Eden wanted it all out in the open and rushed ahead. "And I went to jail one time for shoplifting when I was living with my mom. It was for snacks because I was hungry, but I still got in trouble." She took a deep breath. "I had to spend a night in jail because my mom was too wasted to come get me."

She paused as her hurt turned to anger, the way it mostly did when she thought about her mother. Even after her emotional video call with her, it was impossible to shed all the bitterness overnight. "I'm pretty sure Emma and Yvonne know about the shoplifting. Who knows what my mom told them, though, or what she said to other people. She probably spun it to make me look bad. That's how she is. Everything was always my fault. I seriously doubt she told them how there was no food in the house and that I hadn't eaten in two days. Even when she was high on drugs, she blamed me, said I drove her to it."

Eden was too young to have a heart attack, but her chest was so tight, she felt like it might happen anyway. "Samuel, I have a bucketful of bad history. I spend every day trying not to be like my mother. My life, the way I was raised—everything is so completely different from your life. And, yes, I do agree that friends should be honest with each other. But after everything I just spilled, I would certainly understand if you don't want to be friends."

Samuel rubbed his jaw, his brown eyes staring into hers, and she feared the worst. "Eden, I appreciate you being honest with me, and I know it was hard for you to do. But it doesn't change the fact that I think you're beautiful . . . inside and out." He lowered his hand and smiled. "And it makes me want to be your friend even more." His eyebrows knitted into a frown, and Eden's stomach churned. "If we're going to be honest, then I guess there is something I should tell you."

She sniffled. "I can't think of a single thing that could be worse than what I just told you." He'd led such a sheltered life, it seemed. "But I'm also here to listen if you want to talk."

Samuel had never told anyone what he was about to tell Eden. It seemed safe with her, like she wouldn't judge him. She'd be gone in three weeks, and he might self-combust if he didn't say how he felt aloud to someone. "I've heard you mention *Gott* several times. You have a strong faith, *ya*?"

She nodded. "Yes, I do. It hasn't always been that way. I didn't know anything about God until I met a girl in our apartment complex about a year ago. I went with her and her family to church and Bible study. It opened my eyes to the fact that it was not my preplanned destiny to be like my mother. I could be different." She waved a hand in the air. "Anyway, just as this girl and I were becoming closer friends, she moved, and we haven't kept in touch. But I'm sure her role in my life was to introduce me to God. And when I began to develop a relationship with God, my life changed. He's been there for me when most of the time I didn't have anyone else. And I know He is with me now and will see me through this with my mother . . . But it's hard."

She paused, tipping her head to one side. "That might be more information than you needed, but why do you ask?"

"I-I guess I'm feeling like you are, about being friends." His heart pounded in his chest. "If I tell you what's heaviest on my heart, I'm afraid you won't want to see me again or be friends. And, trust me, it's worse than anything you told me. Those are circumstances you mostly can't control but that have a direct impact on your emotions."

"There's nothing you can tell me that would cause me to judge you or that would make me not want to be friends." She looked down at her lap before she lifted her green eyes to his again. "And, to repay the compliment, nothing you say will make me think you are any less good-looking, on the outside or on the inside."

Her face took on a pink flush, and Samuel's heart flipped in his chest as he smiled. Then he regrouped, knowing he had to tell her the truth. "I'm going to be as honest with you as it seems you have been with me." He flinched. The first part would be hard to tell her. "I wasn't lying when I said you were beautiful, but I did have a little bit of an alternate reason for wanting to be friends with you. I wanted to know all about your life, how you lived, the things you were allowed to do, and . . ."

Her eyebrows lifted higher and higher until she grinned. "You didn't get what you bargained for, did you?" He was glad she took it with good humor.

"I'm not going to say that those things still don't interest me, but you interest me even more."

"I appreciate your honesty, and I don't fault you for being curious about a world you know nothing about."

Samuel leaned his head back, closed his eyes, then met her eyes across the table. "I wanted to know about the outside world because I don't think I'm going to be baptized. Meaning I am considering leaving the only life I've ever known. I'm not sure I belong here. And . . ." His voice cracked, and now it was his face that was surely turning red. "I'm struggling with *mei* faith, Eden. I've talked to *Gott*. I've prayed about why I have these feelings and might choose to leave. No answers. I don't know if *Gott* is disappointed in me, isn't listening, or doesn't care. Or maybe I've closed off *mei* mind from hearing Him because I don't want to hear Him tell me to stay here." He shook his head. "I don't know."

She was quiet, just staring at him. "Say something," he finally said.

"He hears you, Samuel. God is always listening. I'm no expert, and I'm still learning, but I know He doesn't turn a deaf ear. I do believe that we can turn a deaf ear when we don't want to follow His will and choose our desires over His. Sometimes, when things are going badly for me . . ." She paused as she tilted her head and nibbled her bottom lip. Samuel couldn't help but wonder how bad things had been for her. "Sometimes I question if He is really there. But it doesn't last. In some small way, God lets me know that He will never forsake me. We're human. You may feel like you don't have a good relationship with God right now, but His hand is always outstretched and ready to pick us up every time we fall or slip away from our faith."

Samuel swallowed back an unexpected knot in his throat. "In my mind, I know you're right." He put a hand to his chest. "My heart is a different story."

His stomach rumbled as he briefly glanced at half a burger still on his plate, then at even more food on her plate. "I messed up our meal, didn't I?"

She shook her head, then grinned. "Maybe for you." Nodding at her plate, she said, "I could have never eaten all of that."

Samuel managed to chuckle but sobered when he realized that there was one more thing he had to tell her. "If we're being honest about everything, then I probably need to tell you that *mei* parents don't know I'm here with you. They think I'm out taking a walk."

She let out a small gasp. "Oh no. I don't think your

mother likes me very much. When she finds out about this, there's going to be trouble for you."

"I'll worry about that. This is *mei* burden, not yours. I was the one desperate to spend time with you."

They both sat quietly for a few seconds. "I like you," he said softly.

"You don't know me." She smiled. "But I like you too."

"I vote we get out of here, choose a really funny movie to watch, and load up on popcorn and candy at the theater."

She shook her head and frowned. "Samuel, I don't know how to tell you this, but . . ."

He held his breath.

"The movie theaters no longer sell popcorn or candy. They stopped doing that about a year ago."

He looked at his burger that seemed to be calling his name now. "What? Why?"

She laughed. "I'm just kidding." Then she giggled even more.

"You're a bad girl."

She shrugged. "That's what they tell me."

He chuckled. "It's not true, and I know that because I'm a great judge of character." He stood, dropped some cash on the table, then reached his hand out to her. She hesitated, but when she latched onto his hand, she squeezed his, and he squeezed back. It felt like an unspoken admission that they were going to be good friends, at the very least. Samuel was already hoping for more.

They walked out of the restaurant hand in hand, for all to see, and Samuel couldn't remember feeling this happy. Even though there would be a price to pay when he got home. Until then, he was going to bask in Eden's company and see his first movie.

Yvonne scratched Blue's ears as he lay beside her on the couch. Abraham had gone to bed over an hour ago. Five o'clock would come early in the morning if she didn't get to bed soon, but she wouldn't be able to sleep until Eden was home. She shifted one hand to her stomach and thought about the nights she would wait up for her own child. Rubbing her belly, she couldn't wait to feel her baby move in a couple of months.

By the light of the lantern on the end table, she tried to stay focused on the book she was reading—a light romance with a splash of mystery that might be something Eden would also enjoy—but her thoughts kept winding back to her cousin and Samuel. As much as Yvonne wanted Eden and Samuel to remain friends, this was clearly a date. She wondered how much Eden would share with her about the evening.

She and Blue both startled when they heard a car pulling into the driveway, and she twisted around to face the window, slowly pulling back the curtain in time to see Samuel, then Eden, step out of the car. She clutched the book in her hands as the driver shut off the headlights and Eden and Samuel started across the yard dimly lit by the propane lamp. Blue barked twice, and Yvonne quickly rubbed his head and told him it was okay, hoping the dog hadn't woken up Abraham.

Yvonne kept an eye peeled even though she felt a little bad about spying on the couple. But if Samuel kissed Eden good night, problems were on the horizon. She held her breath and waited, watching the two of them facing each other and talking in the middle of the yard. When Samuel cupped Eden's cheek, Yvonne's book slipped from her hands.

Eden had been kissed by boys before, but no one had ever gazed into her eyes the way Samuel was doing now, and feeling his strong hand gently cupping her cheek was like floating on a cloud of euphoria. She was only vaguely aware of the driver waiting in the car.

"I want to kiss you so badly," he said softly as the lamp in the yard lit his tawny brown eyes twinkling only inches from her face.

She'd never wanted anyone to kiss her the way she wanted Samuel to now. Throughout the evening, she'd grown used to his gentle touch, and even longed for it. Just the feel of his arm around her or his hand holding hers made her feel safe.

"But I'm not." He lowered his hand, and Eden drifted back down where her feet stood firmly planted in the grass. "I like you a lot," he said. "But I don't want to mess with things that might sacrifice our friendship."

In Eden's world, a kiss following a first date wouldn't be unheard of. Or so she'd been told by plenty of girls who went on real dates like the one she'd had with Samuel to-night. She was tempted to make the first move and kiss him, but she considered if he was right. Would moving too quickly mess things up? How much did it matter? She'd be gone in three weeks.

"Okay," she finally said as she forced a smile.

"I can't call you." He rolled his eyes. "Since I don't

have a phone. But I'm taking off work Monday through Wednesday this next week. Do you want to hang out?"

Eden opened her mouth to say she would love that, but reality smacked her in the gut. "What about your parents? They don't know you're with me now. Aren't they going to be mad when they find out? And won't spending time with me next week make things even worse? And you would have to tell them."

"I'll handle all that." He smiled. "So, is that a yes or a no?"

She pointed a finger at him. "It's a yes if you are truthful with your parents."

He hung his head for a couple of seconds, then looked up with the same twinkle in his eyes. "*Ya*, okay."

"I told Yvonne that on Monday I'd help her carry some boxes from the back room to the front. She doesn't need to be carrying them since she's pregnant, and they're super heavy. But we could go do something after that."

Samuel's eyes widened. "Yvonne is having a *boppli*?"

Eden flung her head back and groaned. "Oh no. First, I told you about the coin they found, and now I'm blabbing about Yvonne being pregnant. No one knows yet, not even my cousin Emma or any of your family. You can't say anything."

"*Nee, nee*. I won't say a word." He ran his finger along his mouth like a zipper. "And I can be at the store when you first open and carry the boxes for you. Then we can spend the day together." He edged closer to her, the feel of his breath against her skin as her longing to kiss him grew stronger. "And then we can hang out Tuesday and Wednesday too."

"That sounds awesome." She narrowed her eyes at him. "But you have to promise to tell your parents."

Samuel considered his options. He was already grounded about the phone. There was a strong possibility his mother was waiting up for him and would want to know where he'd been tonight. Had she believed Mae that he'd gone for a walk? He had told Eden he would tell his parents the truth, but the reality was that he was already grounded for two weeks, and if he fessed up, he would be in more trouble and might not see Eden for the duration of her visit. They'd mostly been honest with each other so far, and he knew what lies could do to a relationship of any kind. Eden didn't know about him being grounded, though.

"I can't promise that," he finally said as he looked down and kicked at the grass.

She was quiet, and when he finally lifted his eyes to hers, she was wearing the poker face.

"You're not going to be here that long, and if they say no, I'd probably sneak off to see you anyway. What if I promise not to lie? They'll think I'm going to work, and I won't say anything one way or the other."

A shadow of alarm touched her beautiful face. "You're going to end up getting in trouble. You need to tell your parents."

I'm already in trouble, as in grounded for two weeks.

"I'll get up like I'm going to work, no questions asked, no lies told."

She twisted her mouth, seeming to ponder the situation. "But what about Yvonne? She'll know, and it's bound to come up in conversation when she talks to your parents."

It would be too much to ask Eden not to tell Yvonne about their plans. That would put her in a position of lying, and he didn't want to do that. His own lies were enough. "I'll deal with any fallout." He kissed her on the cheek. "I'll see you Monday."

Then he spun around and walked back to the car, giving her a quick wave before he slid into the front passenger seat. He had never bucked his parents like this before, but Eden was worth it. And if he stayed on his current course, he wouldn't be here that much longer anyway.

Eden didn't want to be caught up in Samuel's deceptions, but her desire to see him was overpowering her will to do what was right. As she tiptoed up the porch steps, she saw a light in the living room, but she still tried to be quiet as she eased the door open in case someone was asleep on the couch.

Yvonne had her head in a book, but closed it when Eden walked in.

"I'm surprised Blue didn't bark when he heard a car pull in," Eden whispered before quietly closing the door behind her.

"He did, but not much." Yvonne shifted her weight and eased Blue's foot off her legs.

Eden set her purse on the coffee table and gave the dog a quick scratch behind the ears. She wondered if Yvonne had seen Samuel kiss her on the cheek, which shouldn't be a big deal—although it felt like a big deal to Eden.

"So? How did it go?" Yvonne's hair was pulled into a knot on top of her head, and she was wearing a blue robe and yawning.

Eden glanced at the clock on the mantel. It was almost nine thirty, but Yvonne and Abraham went to bed around this time since they started their days at the crack of dawn or earlier. Eden had fallen into the routine after a few days. It was nice to eat breakfast together before going to the bookstore with Yvonne. She couldn't recall sharing many meals with her mother, especially not breakfast. Yvonne had left her a plate with breakfast on the counter the first day after Eden arrived, but Eden had started setting an alarm on her phone so she could eat with them, the way families were supposed to do. She hadn't needed an alarm the day she went to Samuel's place. She'd awoke on her own, excited for the adventure and eager to see him again.

"It was fun." Eden told her about the restaurant and the movie they saw. "It was Samuel's first time to see a movie, and he has this cute laugh . . ." She realized her voice had taken on a dreamy tone she hadn't intended. "Anyway, it was a funny movie, and we both loved it."

"That's great." Yvonne smiled briefly before her expression sobered. "I still can't believe Anna and Leroy agreed to this."

Eden was faced with the moment of truth. She could ignore the comment completely or be honest. It was all going to come out eventually. "Um . . . they don't exactly know about our date tonight."

Yvonne dropped her jaw. "Eden, please tell me you're kidding."

She gently slid Blue over and sat down on the other side of the dog. "I didn't find that out until tonight." She squeezed her eyes closed, and when she opened them, Yvonne was frowning.

"Abraham and I had already decided we weren't going to bring up the subject with Anna or Leroy," Yvonne said. "But that was under the assumption that they knew about the date. We figured it might not be appropriate to talk about it. However, we know about the date, and now you and Samuel have put me and Abraham in a bad position."

Eden sighed. "I know, and I'm sorry. But he didn't tell me that they didn't know until we were eating."

"Argh." Yvonne rubbed her eyes as she yawned. "Well, shame on Samuel."

Eden weighed her options. She could tell Yvonne that she was bike riding or doing other things Monday through Wednesday, which would be a lie. Or she could stay true to the person she wanted to be and tell her cousin the truth—which was risky since Yvonne could forbid her to see Samuel unless his parents were made aware they were spending time together.

"He wants me to spend Monday, Tuesday, and Wednesday with him." She cringed when Yvonne did. "He's taking vacation days from work."

"*Ach*, Eden." Yvonne leaned her head back against the couch. "This has trouble written all over it." She jerked her head up. "Is he going to tell his parents?"

"I told him he needed to, but I don't know." Eden nibbled on her lip. "I really like him."

Yvonne moaned. "I gathered that from the kiss on the cheek and the way you were looking at each other." She narrowed her eyes. "*Ya*, I was watching out the window."

"It was just a kiss on the cheek." Eden heard the dreaminess back in her voice, something she needed to work on. "I guess now that you know his parents probably won't know he's off work next week, you won't let me hang out with him."

Yvonne sat still, her expression blank. Sighing again, she put a hand on her forehead. "Eden, I'm not going to forbid you to go. You're a guest in our *haus*, and unless you are doing something that is a danger to yourself or others, I'm going to leave you to use your best judgment." She paused, frowning. "Although, I'm not that old. I remember being sixteen and the lengths I went to when I wanted to see a boy. You could have lied to me. I respect the fact that you didn't. All I'm going to tell you is that I am not going to lie for you—or Samuel—when it comes to Anna and Leroy or anyone else." She groaned. "Abraham might feel differently."

Eden came close to saying "Then don't tell him," but she held her tongue. "So, I can hang out with him next week?"

Yvonne regarded her quizzically. "If that's what you choose to do."

Eden wondered if this was some sort of adult trick. "Okay . . ."

"But I do want to talk to you about something else." Yvonne shifted her weight when Blue did, edging the dog's head off her stomach. "I think we need to talk about your mom."

Eden preferred the other conversation, however hard, over one about her mother. "What about her?"

"If you want to see her, I'll pay for a ticket to California, but I'll have to go with you. I'm willing to do that if you are allowed to visit her." Yvonne's voice had softened. "I'm worried that you are avoiding the subject, for reasons that might not be any of my business, but I'm here for you, whatever you need."

"I saw her last night." Eden's emotions twisted into a knot in her stomach. "A nurse at the hospital loaned Mom her phone and we FaceTimed."

Yvonne's face lit up. "That's great." When Eden frowned, she said, "Isn't it?"

Eden shrugged. "I guess." This was an area she was not prepared to visit this evening. She stood. "I'm sorry for any trouble I'm causing you by being here, with Samuel or otherwise."

Blue stretched to fill the spot Eden had left vacant, and Yvonne tucked a leg underneath her and moved over. "Sweetheart, I want you to have a *gut* time, but also to make wise decisions." She rolled her eyes. "Seeing Samuel without his parents' knowledge probably isn't wise, but I'm going to treat you like an adult. And I'll be praying that Samuel is honest with his parents and doesn't lie."

Eden would be praying for the same thing, even if it meant they didn't get to see each other—a thought that caused a knot to form in her throat. But being the person she wanted to be didn't include lies.

Samuel wasn't surprised to see his mother sitting in a rocking chair on the front porch when he came walking up the driveway. He'd paid the driver and asked him to drop him at the road.

"Where have you been?" His mother crossed one leg over the other and kicked the rocker into motion as she folded her hands in her lap.

"Out for a walk." It sounded like the lie it was, even to Samuel.

"Mae said you left at three forty-five. You've been out for a walk for almost six hours?"

Samuel trudged up the porch steps. "*Mamm*, I *lieb* you, but can I go to bed?" Lying straight to her face was proving harder than he'd thought.

She stared at him long and hard. "*Ya*, okay."

He stood still, unsure why she wasn't pushing the issue. When she didn't say anything else, he walked past her and into the house, feeling like he had dodged a big bullet. But he knew his mother's gun was still loaded.

By the time he had gotten into bed and had time to think about it, he speculated why she hadn't pushed him further. Three options came to mind. She was going to talk to his father before she pulled the trigger on him. Or she was going to wait until she had proof that he'd gone out with Eden—easy enough to get by asking Abraham or Yvonne.

Or there was his most recent speculation—that she was scared he might leave the community if she pushed too hard. Samuel was pretty sure he wanted to live his life in the outside world, but he didn't want it to be on bad terms. At least, not any worse than it would be if he told them he had chosen not to be baptized.

He yawned, his thoughts unresolved, but he flipped a mental switch, closed his eyes, and recalled his date with Eden. He couldn't wait to spend three days with her, and he was willing to risk getting caught, which was likely.

Anna slipped into bed beside her husband, who was lightly snoring. She feared sleep was a long way off if her mind didn't clear the worry accumulating about Samuel. Anna was sure he had been with Eden this evening. The girl was probably tempting her son in ways that made Anna's stomach churn. At the least, she was educating Samuel about a world outside of their community. Anna shared her husband's beliefs that if their children weren't exposed to worldly ways, they wouldn't be enticed to leave.

She could still recall the upset when Leroy's brother, Abraham, had left their way of life to be a police officer. He was gone for years before he returned and chose baptism into the faith not long ago. Anna didn't think she'd recover if one of her children chose to leave their Amish roots behind.

Anna curled onto her side and faced her husband, his face barely visible in the darkness. She wanted to wake him up so they could discuss whatever might be going on with Samuel, but Leroy worked hard, and he needed his sleep. She would talk to him about it tomorrow.

Maybe.

Or would it be wiser to watch and wait, see what Samuel was up to before she said anything to Leroy? There was a fear brewing within her that if Samuel progressed to breaking rules greater than purchasing a phone, Leroy might come down too hard on the boy.

Anna never told her husband when Mae stole a bag of candy from the market. Nor had she confessed to Leroy when Grace was caught cheating on a school test. Leroy detested stealing and cheating, and Anna had worried his wrath would be too harsh, so she had dished out the punishment herself, which was a spanking not hard enough to make either girl cry but enough for them to think twice before they stole anything or cheated.

Hannah wasn't old enough to get into any real trouble, and when Anna thought back, Samuel had never really been in trouble either. There was a level of protection instilled within the role of motherhood, and Anna wasn't immune. There also wasn't anything she wouldn't do to keep her children grounded in their faith where they belonged.

It was a fine line to walk, and Anna planned to tread carefully.

CHAPTER 13

Samuel had thought Monday would never arrive. His mother hadn't questioned him further about Saturday night, but he didn't want to take a chance being cornered this morning. He snatched his lunch pail from the counter, grabbed two pieces of bacon from the plate by the oven, and tiptoed back through the kitchen, having no idea where his mother or anyone else was.

When he had his buggy heading down the driveway, he slowly exhaled the breath he'd been holding, grateful that he had made a clean getaway. He chose the long way to the bookstore since if he went now he would arrive before they opened. His route took him past the store, and as he neared the white scarf on the fence, he pulled back on the reins and slowed to a trot. Recollections took him back to the day that he and some other boys had jumped the fence and gone into the cave. It hadn't been much to see, but Eden was so intrigued by it, he wished she could go inside. She'd have that memory to take home with her.

Home. Hers seemed to be up in the air, and Samuel wondered how that must feel. The thought gave him pause about his plans. How would he feel to be without his family?

As the sun rose above the horizon, he lowered the rim of his hat and peered toward the old farmhouse where the elderly couple lived. The woman was on the front porch and appeared to be holding a coffee cup. Samuel was tempted to take his buggy through the gate and ask for permission to bring Eden to see the cave. But he decided the less people who knew he was spending time with Eden, the better. Samuel didn't know what connections the older couple might have with members of their small community where news traveled fast.

He kept at a slow trot and continued down the road until he had killed enough time to go back to the bookstore. He shuddered inwardly at the thought of having to face Yvonne. He considered pleading with her not to tell his parents that he was seeing Eden, but it wasn't fair to involve her any more than he already had.

Yvonne's buggy was tethered to the hitching post when Samuel pulled his buggy onto the gravel driveway. As eager as he was to see Eden, he moved at a snail's pace to secure his horse and buggy before trudging toward the front door.

He eased open the door, the bell jingling, and quickly scanned the space, expecting Yvonne to verbally assault him right away.

Eden appeared from around the corner and grinned. "She's not here. You look terrified."

Samuel slipped his thumbs beneath his suspenders and tried to shed his nervousness. "*Ya*, a little, I guess. I'm sure you told her about our plans to spend time together. Was she upset?"

"Yep." Eden walked toward him dressed in tan pants that went just below her knees, a short-sleeved pink top, and a pair of tan sandals. Her blonde hair was wavier than usual, like maybe she'd used curlers. His heart thumped in his chest at the sight of her, which made the risk feel worthwhile. He wondered if he would feel differently if he had to confront Yvonne.

"She didn't tell me I couldn't hang out with you, but she also said she wouldn't lie for us if the subject comes up." Eden's eyebrows furrowed. "I'm going to venture a guess that you didn't tell your parents you took off work to be with me."

He shook his head as shame squeezed him. "*Nee*, but I didn't lie about it. I didn't see anyone this morning."

"Avoidance of the truth can still be considered a lie." She walked behind the counter and sat on the stool. "Yvonne forgot that she had a doctor's appointment first thing this morning, but Mondays are slow. She said to lock up if we leave before she's back."

"*Ya*, okay." His nervous stomach began to settle. "Should we get those boxes moved, then we can get on our way?"

"Sure." Eden stood up and motioned for him to follow her.

They walked around the corner into a small room Samuel had been in before. It didn't have a red bicycle propped up against the counter like last time, but he could see why the women would need help relocating the boxes. They were huge and presumably filled with books.

"Normally Jake comes in to do any heavy lifting, but he's at an auction in Bedford this morning." Eden spun around, eyeing the room. "I'm sure there's a dolly somewhere, maybe in the basement."

Samuel went to the top box on a stack of six and lifted it up. "It's not too bad. I got it." It was a chance to flex his muscles in front of her.

"Follow me, then. The boxes are marked by genre, so each one goes on a different row."

Samuel made the trek six times and placed the boxes where Eden instructed.

"Thank you so much," she said as she went back behind the counter and picked up a small white purse with blue stripes. "I have a key to lock up since Yvonne isn't back yet." She chuckled. "Lucky you."

He grinned. "*Ya*, I dodged a bullet."

Eden quirked an eyebrow questioningly. "Do the Amish shoot guns?"

"*Ya*, but only for hunting." He pointed over his shoulder. "Uh . . . I probably need to use your bathroom before we get on the road."

"Do you know where it is? Just walk through the back room and you'll see it."

He returned a few minutes later, and Eden was standing by the door with keys in her hand.

"What would you like to do?" he asked as she turned the key in the lock.

She fell in step with him. "Hmm . . . I don't know. What do you suggest?" She pointed to his buggy. "I'm glad you brought a buggy without a top on it. I love those."

"We call them spring buggies." He gently cupped her elbow to help her step inside. "It might be hot, but you can see the sights better."

"I love it." She fetched a pair of sunglasses out of her purse and slipped them on. Samuel untethered his horse, wound around the buggy, and reached for his black shades on the seat before he sat.

"There are some neat places that most people don't know about down some of these roads that are off the beaten path. I thought I'd show you some of those before it gets too hot. Then we can get some lunch and decide what we want to do this afternoon." He backed up his horse as he turned to her and winked. "If you aren't sick of me by then."

She giggled. "I'll let you know."

Samuel wanted to hold her hand, but he was going to pace himself, maybe even let her take the lead. He was happy just looking at her, the way her hair blew in the wind and her mouth curved upward in contentment.

He was thrilled to have three days to spend with her.

Anna was finishing the breakfast dishes, her hands in soapy water, when Leroy came up behind her. The younger girls were gathering eggs, and Anna could hear Mae running clothes through the wringer in the mudroom.

Her husband wrapped his arms around her middle and nuzzled her neck before planting a kiss on her cheek. "Let's go back to bed," he whispered in her ear.

Anna laughed. "*Nee*, I don't think so. What would the

maed think?" She twisted her neck to face him. "What are you in such a *gut* mood about this morning?"

He inched away from her and moved in the direction of the percolator, then poured himself a cup of coffee. "The sun is shining. It's a beautiful day. *Mei* family is healthy and happy. And I have the loveliest *fraa* in the county, possibly the world."

Anna dried her hands, turned around, and leaned against the counter, smiling. She loved the way Leroy still treated her like a new bride sometimes. *"Danki, mei lieb."*

She had planned to talk to him about Samuel not getting home until late, but she didn't want to ruin his mood. Maybe a milder version of conversation wouldn't cause him to lose the bounce in his step this morning.

"I was surprised Samuel wasn't at breakfast this morning," she said.

Leroy shrugged. "He's mad because we grounded him and took away his phone."

"Did he tell you that?"

"*Nee*. I'm just assuming that's why he is avoiding us. No supper last night. No breakfast this morning."

Anna had noticed a couple of pieces of bacon missing when she returned from the bathroom earlier. "Well, the boy will get hungry eventually. He probably stopped for muffins or a pretzel on the way to work this morning. That little stand the Byler girls are tending to almost always has freshly baked goods, and they open early. Samuel goes right by it."

"The lad won't go hungry. His loss when he misses your cooking." Leroy kissed her on the mouth. "I guess I better get back to work since you don't want to go back to bed."

Anna grinned when he winked at her. "I didn't say I didn't *want* to."

Leroy took his hat from the rack by the kitchen door. "Today should be *mei* last day painting the backside of the *haus*. I'll be glad to have that project behind me." He blew her a kiss before he left.

Anna ran through her list of chores for the day. She had some mending to take care of, all the lanterns needed refilling, and she had six potted plants on the porch that had outgrown their containers. If she didn't get them into the ground, they were going to die.

Her girls were lined out for the day. Now, if she could only keep her thoughts from straying to Samuel. She and Leroy had agreed that he could get a job, at least for the summer. They'd thought the sense of independence from having a job might satisfy any longings to experience the outside world. There was at least one boy he worked with who wasn't Amish. Anna wondered how much influence the fellow might have on him. And what had Samuel done last night? Had he seen Eden? Anna was almost sure of it.

Speculations were exhausting, she thought, as she slipped on her gardening gloves, deciding to get her plants in the flowerbeds before the heat set in.

But despite her attempts to distract her thoughts, her son stayed on her mind.

Yvonne unpacked the last box of books, then leaned against the wall at the end of the aisle. She'd had four people come into the bookstore, and every time the bell jingled, she had quickly said a prayer that it wasn't Anna. Maybe her sister-in-law wouldn't come into the store for fear of running into Eden—something that wouldn't be happening for at least three days.

"Ugh," Yvonne said aloud. She wished she didn't know that Samuel and Eden were together without the consent of his parents. And, maybe worse, she hadn't said anything to Abraham about Anna and Leroy not knowing about the date or the three days they were spending together.

Maybe she should give Samuel the benefit of the doubt. Perhaps he had told his parents about his plans.

She doubted that was the case.

As her chest tightened with worry, she put a hand on her stomach and tried to focus on the life inside of her, which always made her smile. After a few minutes of envisioning how she planned to decorate the nursery—which wouldn't be anything fancy—she stood and began collecting the empty boxes from each aisle.

She wondered what Eden and Samuel were doing. Samuel had grown up in a super-conservative environment. Yvonne didn't know Eden well, nor did she know much about her background, except what Aunt Emma had told her. Her cousin appeared to be a sweet girl with a solid faith. Even so, it was hard not to worry. Yvonne remembered being sixteen—the transition between girl and woman, and the temptations that accompanied that age. She couldn't help but wonder if Eden might lure him, physically or otherwise, to a place Samuel had no business going. Neither did Eden, for that matter.

But no, she was going to choose to trust both the teenagers.

Yvonne chastised herself for being judgmental, then chose a book to read. As she got comfortable on her stool behind the counter, she dove in. Or tried to. Eden and Samuel kept creeping into her thoughts. Yvonne felt a sense of responsibility for her cousin and her husband's nephew. She didn't want things to get out of control on her watch, and with each passing second, she wished she had talked to Abraham about the situation.

Eden eyed the lush green cornfields that met with a cloudless blue sky at the horizon, then closed her eyes behind her sunglasses and basked in the warm sunlight combined with a gentle breeze. Breathing in the sweet aroma of wildflowers lining both sides of the road reminded her that she was a long way from home.

"I promise we have a destination. I know you must be wondering where we're going since we've been on this back road for a while." Samuel flicked the reins and picked up a little speed.

Eden shook her head. "I'm in no rush to get anywhere. I could ride around like this all day." She opened her eyes and glanced his way. "It's beautiful here. I can't imagine why you would want to leave."

He was quiet, and she knew his motivations ran deeper than geography. "I know you are confused about your faith too," she said. "But if I lived here, I would never leave."

"That's easy for you to say because you're on vacation. But this is all I've seen for *mei* entire life. There's no excitement here like I'm sure there is in the city. I'm not saying I would leave Indiana." He motioned with his hand. "And it is pretty. I can't deny that. But in cities or larger towns, there is a lot to do and to see too."

Eden pushed her sunglasses up on her head and waited for him to look at her. "Yes, there is a lot to do and see. And there is a lot of excitement . . . like cars honking all the time, sirens blaring in the distance, televisions continuously reporting bad news, people rushing around like they're late for a funeral—" She stopped when her mother's face came into mind at the use of the word. "It's not everything it's cracked up to be. Trust me."

"You would get bored if you lived here."

"No. I wouldn't."

He chuckled. "I'll ask you again in about three weeks when you're heading home."

Eden felt like she'd taken a punch to her gut. Where was home? Emma's house? Back in California with another fostering relative, or worse, a stranger? She wanted to believe that Emma would let her stay as long as she needed to, at least until she had a job and could afford to live out on her own. She swallowed back a small lump that had taken up permanent residence in her throat as if waiting for her to fall apart at any moment. The uncertainty of her future kept her on edge.

"I think if you experienced all the things you dream about, you would want to come back here." She lowered her sunglasses again. "But faith doesn't have geographic boundaries. I know you're having some trouble in that area, but I believe that if you keep praying about it, God will show you what His will is for you."

"I've prayed about it a lot, Eden." He sounded defeated, as if he'd given up, and she searched her mind to say something that might mean something to him.

"I fit the perfect mold for someone who should be mad at God or who shouldn't believe in Him at all. I could blame Him for the bad things that happened to me, but if everything hadn't happened exactly as it did, I wouldn't be here enjoying this beautiful ride." She bit her lip but decided to throw caution to the wind. "And I wouldn't have met you."

He reached for her hand and held it. "*Ya*, and that would have been awful."

Eden held tightly to Samuel's grasp. He felt like a lifeline for a better life, a better version of herself. She wondered if he felt the same about her, that she was his lifeline to another type of life. Eden's mind was like mush a lot of the time with thoughts about her mother and her future. Right now, though, she was certain she and Samuel were going to be more than friends.

When Eden hadn't returned by five o'clock, Yvonne locked up the bookstore. She dreaded going home since she needed to have a hard conversation with her husband. Abraham needed to know that they were unwilling participants in whatever was going on with Eden and Samuel.

After she got supper in the oven, she poured two glasses

of tea and carried them to the front porch. Abraham was always home from work at five fifteen.

When he pulled his buggy into the driveway, he waved and smiled before he led his horse to the barn. A few minutes later, carting what she knew to be an empty lunch pail, her husband came across the front yard.

Yvonne wanted to get the conversation over with right away. Maybe they'd have time to decide how to handle things before Eden got home.

Abraham leaned down and kissed her before he sat in the other rocking chair and gulped several sips of tea as sweat pooled on his forehead.

"I made your favorite for supper."

His face split into a wide grin, and she considered skipping the conversation about Eden and Samuel, but she knew she couldn't. She'd never kept anything from Abraham.

"Chicken and dumplings or meat pies? They're both *mei* favorites."

"Meat pies." She folded her hands across her stomach.

"How's our *boppli* today? Moving around yet?"

Yvonne shook her head. "*Nee*, not yet. But I didn't get sick this morning, so I'm grateful for that. And the doctor said everything looked fine." She paused, tried to think of a good way to explain the situation to him. There wasn't one, she decided. "Um . . . I need to talk to you about something before Eden gets home."

His eyes shifted in her direction as the lines on his forehead deepened. "Is she still with Samuel?"

"*Ya*. He picked her up this morning while I was at the doctor. She left me a note that Samuel had carried the boxes to the right aisles, and I was able to get them all on the shelves today."

Abraham smiled. "He's a *gut* boy." Pride shone in her husband's eyes, the lines on his forehead softening.

"*Ya*, he is," she said before she cleared her throat. "But Abraham . . . Leroy and Anna don't know about their date Saturday night, and I don't think they know that Samuel took off three days of work to spend time with Eden."

"Eden lied to us about Saturday night?" Abraham asked in a tone that was coolly disapproving, as Yvonne had expected.

"Not exactly. When they left on their date, Eden thought Anna and Leroy knew about it. When she got home, she told me Samuel confessed he hadn't told his parents about the date. She also said that she didn't know if he told Leroy and Anna about taking off work." Yvonne cringed when Abraham's face reddened. "But Eden was hoping he'd tell them, and she said she encouraged him to do so."

"*Ach*, well . . . We weren't going to borrow trouble, but it seems it found us." There was an edge to his voice. "Do you believe her? That she really is trying to get him to fess up to Leroy and Anna?"

"I do." Yvonne didn't hesitate because it was true. "And maybe Leroy and Anna know everything by now. I wasn't there when Samuel got to the bookstore, or I would have asked him directly if he'd told them."

Abraham slouched into the rocker as he stroked his beard. "If Leroy and Anna don't know about his time with Eden, and they find out, they will hold us accountable. But that's not the worst of it. Samuel is lying to his parents, and that's not like him."

"We don't know for sure that he hasn't told them." Yvonne heard the accusation in her husband's voice—that this wasn't like Samuel, so it must be Eden's fault. Part of her wanted to jump to Eden's defense, but she didn't want to bring on more trouble.

"Guess we will know soon enough." Yvonne pointed to the approaching buggy as her stomach clenched.

Both teenagers were laughing and smiling until they saw Yvonne and Abraham sitting on the porch. Their expressions sobered right away.

Abraham and Yvonne stayed seated as Eden and Samuel shuffled across the yard and toward the porch like they were on their way to a court sentencing.

"Samuel, I'm told your parents don't know about your date Saturday night. Do they know that you are off work and spending your time with Eden?" Abraham spoke in a firm and parental tone that Yvonne hadn't heard before as he glared at his nephew.

"*Nee.*" Samuel lowered his head, shaking it.

Abraham took off his hat, set it in his lap, and ran a hand through his hair. "You've put me and Yvonne in a bad spot."

Samuel lifted pleading eyes to Abraham. "*Onkel* Abraham, you know how strict they are. I'm sixteen. I should be allowed some freedoms, and they—"

"Stop." Abraham shook his head, his eyes still fused with Samuel's. "They are your parents, and you must respect their wishes."

"It's not fair." Samuel folded his arms across his chest as his chin rose in defiance.

Abraham shrugged as the lines in his forehead deepened again. "Life isn't fair, *sohn*, but it doesn't excuse you defying your parents. You're also dragging Eden into your deceptions, which she's not comfortable with." He glanced at Eden, whose head was down, then back at Samuel. "You either tell them the truth, or you don't see Eden again."

Yvonne had grown up in the outside world and spent most of her life there. She agreed that Samuel's parents were too strict, but Abraham was right that Samuel shouldn't disrespect them.

Eden and Samuel glanced at each other in a way that led Yvonne to think they might have expected this.

"I better go." Samuel snuck a quick glance at Eden and almost smiled as Eden bit back a grin too. These were not heartbroken kids who would never see each other again. They'd probably already prepared for this and had a meeting place picked out for tomorrow. That's what Yvonne would have done at their age. Even though Abraham hadn't said so, Samuel would be taking a big risk by trusting that Abraham and Yvonne wouldn't tell his parents. Eden would be in trouble with them, too, if she defied Abraham by seeing Samuel under the current circumstances.

Samuel put the horse into a gallop as soon as he was in the buggy again, and he didn't turn around.

Eden stood perfectly still as if she assumed she was the next one to get grilled.

"You can't see him if he doesn't come clean with his parents. You understand, *ya*?" Abraham said to Eden firmly.

Yvonne wondered if Abraham would be as strict with their child as his brother was with his children. She didn't think so, but it might be a conversation they would have to have down the line.

"I'm sorry." Eden hung her head and walked slowly to the front door. She pulled the screen door open, but then she shut it and walked back to where Yvonne and Abraham were still sitting. "You know . . . He wants to leave here."

Abraham and Yvonne exchanged glances before Abraham cut his eyes at Eden. "And are you encouraging this?"

Yvonne opened her mouth to tell Abraham that he wasn't being fair. He had no proof of that. But she wanted to hear Eden's response.

After tears filled her cousin's eyes, Yvonne regretted not speaking up. "No!" Her voice was loud and filled with emotion. "I understand that it's natural to blame the bad city girl with a history, that I'm luring him away, but you have no idea what's going on with him."

"Eden, that's not what we—" Yvonne wanted to temper this conversation before it got out of hand, but Abraham interrupted her.

"Then enlighten us," he said much too condescendingly for Yvonne's liking. Her husband was reacting to a potential fallout with his brother, but this attitude toward Eden wasn't helping.

Eden swiped at tears that had begun to spill down her cheeks. "His parents are too strict. He wants to see the outside world. And, worse than that, he is having trouble with his faith, questioning it. I'm trying to talk him out of leaving. I would never leave here. Never! What I wouldn't do to have a family like this. So, go ahead and blame me all you want to, but you and his parents are pushing him further away!" She spun on her heels and rushed inside.

After Yvonne and Abraham both lifted their jaws from the ground, Yvonne scowled at her husband. "Her mother is dying. She went out with a boy believing it was okay with his parents, and she's trying to talk him out of leaving our community." Yvonne's voice cracked as she stood up. "She's just a kid, and she has a whole lot going on. And what you said wasn't fair. I'm going to go talk to her."

"*Nee.*" Abraham clasped the hat in his lap, then stood slowly. "I should be the one to talk to her."

Yvonne heard regret in his voice. "We'll both go," she said in a shaky voice.

CHAPTER 14

Eden slammed the door to her temporary bedroom, threw herself facedown on the bed, and buried her face in her pillow as she sobbed. If Yvonne and Abraham wanted to make her out to be the bad girl, then maybe she'd act like the bad girl. She and Samuel had planned for this, and they already had a meeting place picked out for the next day. Eden had fought hard against Samuel lying to his parents and her fibbing to Yvonne and Abraham, but maybe she would never escape the person people assumed her to be. Even if she chose not to meet Samuel tomorrow, she'd already been cast as the villain by her family, and Samuel's parents would place her in the same role—if they hadn't already. She thought about devotion times with Yvonne and Abraham, how they'd laughed about their tattoos, and the overall feeling that she was part of a normal family, even if only temporarily. She didn't want to mess that up, but she also didn't want to stop seeing Samuel.

"I don't want to talk right now," she said in a muffled voice when she heard the knock at the door.

She rolled over on her back, sat up, and didn't even try

to clear the tears from her eyes as the door opened. "Can we please not talk right now?" she said to Yvonne and Abraham.

"Sweetheart, we need to talk." Yvonne walked to the bed and sat beside her. Abraham stayed just inside the doorway.

Hearing Yvonne's use of the endearing term caused her to cry harder. She wanted Yvonne to love her, and she hadn't realized how much that was true until now.

Eden found her mask—the imaginary one she wore to hide behind, leaving her expressionless when she didn't want anyone to see her true feelings.

"First of all," Yvonne said as she put a hand on Eden's knee, "you aren't a 'bad girl.' We don't see you that way, and you shouldn't place that label on yourself either."

Eden's mask was slipping. She blinked back more tears. "I've made some mistakes, and I think I've owned up to them." She looked directly into Yvonne's caring eyes. "I want to be a good person. I love God. I pray all the time. I know I am a victim of my circumstances, but I don't want that to define me." Her voice cracked. "But it seems like other people judge me because of my background."

Yvonne found Eden's hand and held tightly. "We weren't judging you." She glanced at Abraham, who was staring at the wood floor. "Were we, Abraham?"

He cringed a little. "*Ya*, I guess I was being judgmental at first, Eden, and I'm sorry. I reacted emotionally because I don't want to end up getting sideways with *mei bruder*. I owe you an apology, and I'm sorry."

Eden respected men who could apologize. In her past

experiences, it hadn't happened very often. She nodded but kept her eyes cast down.

Abraham sat down in the chair near the far wall, propped his elbows on his knees, then held his chin. "Is Samuel really thinking about leaving here?"

Eden waited for Abraham to lock eyes with her. "Yes. And I'm probably breaking a confidence by saying anything to you. If you tell his parents—"

He waved her off with one hand. "*Nee, nee*. I won't. I need to think this through." He tipped his head. "Did he say if it's more a faith issue, or is it the lure of the outside world that has him enticed?"

"I think it's a little of both." Eden sniffled. "Maybe he needs to leave to find himself, but I promise you that I have not encouraged him at all. He seems to think the bigger cities offer excitement and fun. I told him that was far from true and that I'd never leave here." She lowered her head. "And I mean that."

Yvonne's heart was undergoing an emotional tug-of-war. She wanted to do the right thing by Samuel and her in-laws, but she also wanted to do right by Eden. It touched her that Eden felt the way she did about staying here. She opened her mouth to say something, but words wouldn't come, and ultimately, Abraham needed to be the one to take the reins since it was his family. Her husband had experience with this since he'd left when he wasn't much older than Samuel.

"Are you having any luck?" Abraham straightened in the chair and scratched his bearded jaw.

"Luck?" Eden frowned. "What do you mean?"

"You obviously talk about his faith and his longing to leave here. Have you had any luck getting him to believe that the outside world isn't all it's cracked up to be?" He shook his head. "Leroy and Anna would be devastated if he left."

Eden shrugged, still clasping Yvonne's hand. "I don't know."

Abraham stood. "I am sorry for *mei* attitude and the way I spoke to you, Eden. Like I said, I was reacting emotionally to a situation that I don't want to see get out of hand. Having said that, I must ask you not to see Samuel if he is lying to his parents about it."

Eden nodded, but Yvonne wondered if her cousin could stay true to that commitment. Again, she remembered being a teenager and the extreme measures she'd taken when it came to boys.

Abraham excused himself. Yvonne cupped Eden's cheek, then pulled her into her arms. "We really are happy to have you here."

After they'd eased away, Eden offered a weak smile. "I like being here, and I like you and Abraham."

Yvonne put a hand to her chest. "It warms my heart to hear that, and I appreciate you being so agreeable about not seeing Samuel unless he tells his parents." She paused, nudged her a little. "I know you like him. I've seen the way you look at each other. Even though it came to a crummy end this afternoon, did you have a fun day?"

Eden took on the dreamy look, and Yvonne reconsidered whether she should have asked, but she wanted to cheer her up.

"We did. We talked a lot, and he drove us around and showed me some cool places. Did you know that there is a house that's built almost completely underground? From the road, you wouldn't be able to see it unless you knew it was there. All you can see are the skylights. And he showed me a tree—which required a hike in the woods—where a bunch of people who believe they saw a Sasquatch carved their names, and—"

Yvonne gasped. "Wow. Jake took me to that tree on *mei* first trip here. It is kind of neat how so many people think they saw a real Bigfoot."

"And we ate pretzels and cheese sauce at a little stand run by some Amish girls. I am sure they were the best pretzels I've ever had. And he shared his lunch with me." She looked at her lap, took a deep breath, then cringed. "The one his mother made since she thought he was at work."

"Well, for what it's worth, I'm glad you had a *gut* day today. But Eden, maybe this happened for the best. It's clear you two like each other, and if you continued to get closer, it would just cause heartbreak in the end."

"I know. And . . . since we're being honest, we did pick a place to secretly meet tomorrow if things blew up."

"I figured that." Yvonne frowned.

"I want you to know that I'm not going. I want to, but I don't want to get you and Abraham in trouble, and I don't want you to not trust me."

"I appreciate that very much, Eden." Yvonne stood up.

"Does that mean you're coming with me to the bookstore tomorrow? I missed you today." She smiled.

"Sure. I'll go with you."

"Okay, I'm going to go check on supper. Just join us when you're ready. It should be about done."

"Thanks, Yvonne."

"You're welcome, sweetheart."

Samuel had no plans to tell his parents about spending time with Eden. He wished Yvonne and Abraham didn't know. But he didn't think Yvonne or Abraham would be visiting tonight to rat him out. He would meet Eden tomorrow at the place they'd picked out, in front of the library. It was close enough that she could ride her bike. This was all going to blow up in his face, but he would have another good day with Eden before it did. Maybe two days if he was lucky.

He stayed an extra-long time in the barn brushing his horse after he got home. He dreaded facing his mother, but he was hungry and not planning to miss supper. His mother had a superpower way of knowing things, and he'd have to be careful what he said. His stomach churned from knowing he'd have to lie when she asked him how work had gone today.

By the time Samuel washed his hands at the pump outside, then slowly made his way to the kitchen, everyone was seated. Mae had told him that she'd done exactly as he asked Saturday night by telling his parents he had gone for a walk, but Samuel was sure his mother didn't believe him when he returned that night, and she'd been looking at him funny since then.

He slid into a chair, and everyone lowered their head for prayer, then Samuel reached for a slice of bread before spooning a generous helping of pinto beans onto his plate. No one made beans like his mother.

His father was in a good mood, happy to have finished painting the house and rattling off details. "And next on *mei* list of projects is to repair the plumbing that leads to the cow troughs." He turned to Samuel. "*Sohn*, maybe you can take off a day or two of work to help me with that?"

Samuel stopped chewing. Did his father know something, that he'd taken off work three days this week? "Uh . . ."

"You can't ask him to do that, Leroy. He has a real job." His mother frowned before she looked at Samuel. "I don't think your boss would like that."

Samuel swallowed the bite in his mouth. "Uh . . . I guess if I gave enough notice, it might be okay."

"*Ach*, I can probably handle it myself." He pointed his fork at Samuel. "But I will need help with the harvest in a few months."

"*Ya, ya.*" Samuel's roiling stomach began to calm. His parents didn't seem to know about his current vacation.

His sisters starting bickering about whose turn it was to do the dishes this evening, but his mother settled it quickly before turning to Samuel and asking, "Speaking of work, how was your day on the job?"

Samuel's stomach started acting up again. He had managed to get through most of his life without telling bold, intentional lies. Maybe a little white lie here and there, but nothing like he was about to do. “It was fine.” With his head down, he cut his eyes in his mother’s direction. Her lips were set in a straight line, a certain expression she took on when she wasn’t happy.

Samuel kept his eyes diverted from hers for the rest of the meal, and he went directly to his room after the devotions that followed supper to wait his turn for the shower. There was a rotating schedule for the one bathroom upstairs that he had to share with his sisters, who took forever. He was last on the list tonight.

As he sat on his bed waiting, he looked back on the day. Facing off with his uncle Abraham and aunt Yvonne had been unpleasant, but the rest of the day had been wonderful. He couldn’t wait to see Eden again tomorrow. They would meet outside the library as planned. Eden would tell Yvonne she was going for a bike ride, which wouldn’t be a lie. It would be a challenge for Eden’s bike ride to last all day, so they’d already agreed that they might have to cut the day short. At least he would get to spend some time with her.

Eden went with Yvonne to the bookstore Tuesday morning. She wondered how long Samuel would wait outside the small library before he figured out that she wasn’t coming. As much as she wanted to see him, she’d promised Yvonne she wouldn’t, and it was a promise she planned to keep. Today, she was going to man the counter while Yvonne did paperwork on the table in the back room.

She looked at the time on her phone. Nine o'clock, the time she was supposed to meet Samuel. Her heart was heavy, and she wondered if he'd go to work when she didn't show up. She was doing the right thing, but she wished she could at least explain to Samuel why she'd chosen not to go, how she didn't want to get caught up in a web of lies or disappoint Yvonne and Abraham. Yvonne was right about her and Samuel growing closer. It would only cause heartache in the end. It sounded like Samuel wanted to leave as much as Eden wished she could stay here forever. Life with Yvonne and Abraham was like a normal family, complete with their first squabble last night. But no one had slapped anyone, hit each other, cursed, or threatened to throw her out of the house.

There was still a huge disappointment filling her senses about not being able to see Samuel. She closed her eyes and pictured his sun-kissed blond hair with the cropped bangs, his tanned and well-defined arms, and that smile of his with the cute dimples. Sighing, she wondered if she would find anything else to do while she was here. She enjoyed being at the bookstore, and Yvonne had given her several more books to read, but she would like to spend more time outside. She wondered if she would have another opportunity to ride a horse again.

Probably not with Samuel.

She opened her eyes when she heard footsteps. Yvonne had her hands folded across her stomach and her expression was tight with strain.

"Are you okay?" Eden stood from where she was sitting. Her chest tightened as she wondered if something was wrong with the baby.

Yvonne shook her head and dropped her arms to her side as she walked to the counter. "I can't find that coin I showed you, the old one that was in the little white pouch. When we were cleaning back there, did you maybe put it somewhere else?"

"No. I took everything out of the drawer, wiped it down, then threw away the things you told me to before I put the stuff back, including the coin." Eden paused, remembering the day. "I'm sure I put it back in the drawer."

Yvonne blew out a long breath of frustration. "Well, it isn't there. I'm going to owe Jake five hundred dollars if it doesn't show up." She groaned, then sighed again. "It didn't just sprout legs and walk away."

Eden found her invisible mask and put it on. Was Yvonne accusing her of stealing it? "You know how sometimes drawers come off the track, or sometimes things fall behind the drawer and land below the—"

"I looked. I dumped the contents on the table, then searched the drawer below it, and then on the floor." She threw up her hands. "I don't understand. It was there the day I showed it to you, and now it's gone. The only reason I noticed was that the calculator I was using kept locking up, and I remembered there was a small one in that drawer." She groaned again. "And I can't get the checkbook to balance, so I'm frustrated."

Yvonne paced a few steps, her mouth set in annoyance, then they both turned their attention to a buggy pulling in the parking lot. "Great." Yvonne rolled her eyes. "I sure hope Samuel came clean with his parents."

Eden's face tightened behind her mask. She wasn't sure what to say or do.

Yvonne stuffed her hands into the pockets of her black apron. "And I hope that coin shows up."

Eden's bottom lip began to quiver just as the bell on the door jingled and Samuel cautiously crossed over the threshold, glancing back and forth between Yvonne and Eden. She knew he wouldn't speak openly in front of Yvonne and question why she wasn't at the library to meet him earlier.

"Samuel, please tell me your parents know that you're here and not at work." Yvonne's voice was clipped with irritation, and she was acting totally out of character. Or so it seemed.

"They don't know," he said as he rubbed his chin.

"Well, I know about you and Eden's little plan to meet. She chose not to go because we asked her not to. As we told you yesterday, you can't see each other without your parents knowing." She thrust her hands to her hips.

Samuel glanced at Eden with a sunken expression, presumably for telling Yvonne about their plans. But he walked to the counter and locked eyes with her. "Are you okay? You look like you're about to cry."

It was so sweet that Eden almost let a tear escape. "I'm fine," she said softly as she tried to force a smile.

"Nobody is fine!" Yvonne was practically yelling now, and Eden's jaw dropped. "You shouldn't be here, Samuel. And Eden needs to help me find something that is lost. Something she saw last."

Eden's head started to spin with anxiety, and it reminded her of the fights she had witnessed at home. Yvonne was overreacting. She slowly picked up her purse, slung it over her shoulder, then went around the counter and grabbed Samuel's hand.

"Come on, let's go." Even though her hurt far outweighed her anger, Eden shot Yvonne the meanest look she could. "I didn't steal your stupid coin, and I know that's what you think!"

She dragged Samuel out of the bookstore, and she didn't stop when Yvonne repeatedly called her name.

Surprisingly, Yvonne didn't follow them out to the parking lot or even leave the bookstore as Samuel pulled the buggy out of the parking lot.

She never cared about me.

Yvonne bent at the waist and put her hands on her knees as she wept. Maybe she should have stopped Samuel from leaving and had him give her a ride to the clinic, but getting to the local clinic by buggy would take longer than getting to the hospital by car. Abraham had called a driver and should be there any second. She'd called him the moment she saw blood.

Grasping her cramping stomach, she found her purse behind the counter, then locked up.

Please, dear Gott, *don't let me lose this baby.*

CHAPTER 15

Samuel didn't have a lot of experience with crying women, and he could only grasp bits and pieces of what Eden was telling him. "It's like she was possessed or something," she said through her tears. "She's never acted like that. How could she think that I stole that coin?" She shook her head. "No, I know why. She knows about my past and that I got in trouble for shoplifting and spent the night in jail." She covered her face with her hands and mumbled, "I was so hungry, Samuel. That's the only reason I did it."

Samuel hadn't been hungry a day in his life, and he wondered how many times Eden had missed a meal. "I doubt she thinks you stole anything. She's probably just mad at me about this whole situation."

Eden shook her head and uncovered her tear-streaked face. "No. She was fine this morning. It wasn't until she couldn't find that coin. Then she went all crazy."

Samuel was quiet, unsure what to say to make her feel better. He tried to push past his hurt but was having trouble. "When you didn't show up at the library, I thought you didn't want to see me anymore. I just wanted to come talk to you. I'm sorry that happened with Yvonne."

She sniffled. "It wasn't that I didn't want to see you. I was trying to do the right thing and not disrespect Yvonne and Abraham's wishes since I am staying at their house." She rolled her eyes. "Or I *was* staying at their house. I don't know how I'm going to go back with her acting like that."

"I'm sure she's going to tell *mei* parents about our date and me taking off work this week. And I guarantee they'll extend me being grounded for a lot longer than two weeks."

Eden's jaw dropped. "You're grounded? You didn't tell me that."

Samuel frowned. "*Ach*. I thought I did." She knew about his phone and that his parents didn't know they were seeing each other. He had forgotten that he'd chosen not to mention being grounded. This was a good example of one lie leading to another, and it was hard to keep everything straight. He wasn't feeling very good about himself.

"If I had any money, I'd get on a bus and go somewhere . . . anywhere." Eden covered her face with her hands again, sobbing.

Samuel had money he could give her, but the last thing he wanted was for her to leave. He considered his words carefully before he spoke. "We could go somewhere together, just the two of us." They weren't in love. It was way too soon for that, he assumed, even though he'd never been in love and could only rely on hearsay. On the other hand, was there such a thing as love at first sight? He didn't know, but he'd never wanted to be with anyone the way he did Eden.

She snapped her head in his direction. "No. Absolutely

not. No. I will not be the bad girl who dragged you away from your family."

Her face looked like it was set in stone, and Samuel couldn't help but grin. It was better than her crying. "I was thinking about leaving before I met you."

Eden blushed. "Um, yeah, a bit presumptuous of me to think you would leave to be with me."

"In a way . . . I would be." He smiled, and she did too.

Yvonne held tightly to Abraham's hand as they sat in the emergency-room cubicle. She jumped when the nurse rubbed cold jelly on her stomach.

"Breathe," the nurse said in a soothing voice as she ran the ultrasound wand across her stomach.

Yvonne released the breath she'd been holding and found her husband's eyes. Stark and vivid fear shone in his expression as sheer fright swept through Yvonne. She'd prayed constantly since she saw the first trace of blood, and she'd prayed even harder when her stomach began to cramp. So far, the nurse hadn't mentioned a heartbeat, and Yvonne hadn't heard one.

"Abraham . . ." She bit her bottom lip when her voice cracked, and her husband squeezed her hand tighter.

"There we go," the nurse said as she smiled. "Listen. It's your baby's heartbeat."

Yvonne burst into tears. "*Danki, Gott*," she whispered. Abraham's eyes watered with relief.

"First baby?" The nurse left the ultrasound wand in

place as Yvonne and Abraham listened to their child's heart beating.

Yvonne nodded. "*Ya*, it is."

The older nurse, maybe the age of Aunt Emma, removed the wand and gave Yvonne a handful of tissues to clear the gel from her stomach. "Sometimes a little blood is normal. And different things can cause cramping, including gas. And then your anxiety could have made it worse. Everything sounds and looks fine to me, but I'm going to have a doctor come do an exam to make sure everything is all right." She helped Yvonne lower her maroon dress and black apron. "He should be here shortly."

After the nurse left, Yvonne and Abraham both closed their eyes, and she knew her husband was thanking God in prayer the same way she was. Then she gasped.

"*Ach*, Abraham . . ." She let go of his fingers and covered her face with both hands, then dropped them to her stomach. "I was awful to Eden." It had been such a panicky ride to the hospital, she hadn't told him about Eden leaving with Samuel. "I can't find the coin that we found that day—the one we think came from whatever coin collection might be hidden somewhere in the bookstore. I was so upset and scared, and Eden thought I was accusing her of stealing the coin. Maybe I was. She was the last one to see it."

She reached for his hand again and clung to it. "But she wouldn't do that, Abraham. I know she wouldn't. There must be another explanation for why it isn't in the drawer. But when I think back to the way I spoke to her . . ." She shook her head. "I was so scared at the time, worried I might be losing the *boppli*. But I hurt her feelings so badly that she left with Samuel. He had just come into the bookstore. I guess when Eden didn't show up at their meeting spot, he came looking for her. Abraham, I need to call her."

She let go of his hand again and held her palm up. "Can I please use your phone? Mine is at the bookstore. And we need to call Jake and let him know I had to close the store."

"I already called Jake in the car on the way to pick you up. He said he would head to the bookstore and said he'd be praying everything was okay. Of course, I had to tell him you were pregnant. He said he wouldn't tell anyone, except Eva." He eased his hand from hers, stood, then reached into his front pocket for his phone. Sitting again, he stared at the device. "I don't have Eden's number in *mei* phone."

"Call Jake. Hopefully he will have his phone on. Tell him *mei* phone is in the back room. I was in such a panic that I grabbed *mei* purse from behind the counter and forgot *mei* phone. Ask him to text you or tell you Eden's phone number."

Abraham did as she instructed.

After Jake answered and after a short wait, Abraham's phone dinged with a text. "Got it. *Danki*, Jake."

"Wait." Yvonne held out her hand. "I need to talk to him before you hang up."

He handed her the phone.

"Jake, I'm so sorry—"

He interrupted her and began telling her that she had nothing to be sorry about, that her health and the baby's was all that mattered.

"*Danki*, Jake, but that's not what I meant. The coin is gone—the one we found in between the cracks in the floor.

Remember how we put it in that little white pouch and placed it in the drawer?" Her voice was shaky. She knew this wasn't a top priority since she was lying in a hospital bed, but she wanted him to know. "It's gone. I can't find it anywhere."

Then she listened with a combination of relief and horror as Jake told her he'd gone to the bookstore on Sunday and taken the coin.

"I ran into a man who said he knew someone who could give me a second opinion about how much it was worth," he said. "And this appraiser will be able to tell us more about the authenticity of the coin."

Yvonne draped a hand across her forehead and chose not to elaborate about how she'd treated Eden. She was ashamed enough without having to explain it to anyone else.

"Thank *Gott*," she said. "I thought we'd lost it."

After he told her to take it easy, and to give herself a few days off if she needed to, they ended the call. Hopefully the doctor would be in soon to tell her everything was fine, and she wouldn't need to miss work.

She gave the phone to Abraham. "Can you please call Eden, then hand me the phone if she answers?"

Abraham made the call but ended it quickly. "It rang twice and went to voice mail. Do you want me to call back and leave a voice mail?"

"*Nee*. I'll do it."

Yvonne was getting ready to dial when the doctor walked in. "I'll call after we know everything is okay."

Following an exam, and with assurance from the doctor that everything was fine, Yvonne found Eden's number.

This time the call went straight to voice mail. In a shaky voice, she left her young cousin a message.

"Eden, I am so sorry for the way I spoke to you." She paused, sniffling. "Jake has the coin, and I didn't know it. I'm so sorry," she said again. "Abraham and I are at the hospital. I thought I was losing the *boppli* at the bookstore because I started bleeding. I was scared and worried, but that's still no excuse for the way I talked to you. I'm fine. The *boppli* is fine too. Please call me as soon as you get this message. I'm calling from Abraham's phone because mine is at the bookstore. I'll be going home from the hospital shortly, but I won't be going back to work today." She chewed her lip, feeling like there should be more to say. "Please call me."

Eden stared at the phone number on her screen before she powered the device off.

"Who was it?" Samuel bit into a breakfast taco at the small café they'd been to before. She didn't know how he could eat. Eden had ordered, too, at his insistence, but she'd only taken one small bite.

"I don't know. I don't recognize the number. I thought it might be Yvonne, but apparently, she doesn't care enough to even check on me."

Samuel finished his taco. "I'm sure she cares." He wiped his mouth with his napkin, and now that he had a full stomach, she saw the worry creep into his expression.

"We can't just run away together." Eden raised an eyebrow. "You know that, right?"

They'd chosen to eat at an outside table, and Samuel still had his hat on. He pushed back the rim and rubbed his forehead. "*Ya*, I guess. But I'm going to be in a heap of trouble when this all comes out. And I'm sure it will."

"Me too." They were both quiet for a few moments, but she saw Samuel eyeing her taco. "You can have that if you want."

"*Nee*. You need to eat." His gaze drifted to somewhere over her shoulder, and he looked like he was deep in thought.

"Should we face the music now or later?" Eden took a small bite of her taco, then put it on Samuel's plate.

"Are you sure that's all you want?"

Eden nodded, and Samuel picked it up and took a bite. "I think we should face the music later," he said after he swallowed. "We're already in trouble. We'll be in trouble if we go home now or later."

"True." Although Eden wasn't sure she'd have a good time with everything up in the air like this.

"We could go to that cave where the white scarf is. I can leave the horse and buggy tethered here. It's close enough to walk."

Eden pondered the idea. She really wanted to see inside that cave, and it would be a nice distraction. "But it's private property. We're not allowed."

Samuel shrugged. "If we're not going to run away together, I'll probably be grounded for the rest of *mei* life. I might as well have one last adventure." He grinned, but it didn't last. "I'll be forced to stay with *mei* parents and stay grounded. I need to save more money before I can actually leave for good."

Even though the thought of doing something adventuresome sounded enticing, she didn't want to stray from this conversation just yet. "I think you're making a mistake if you decide to do that." She held up a hand when he opened his mouth to say something. "I'm just saying. I keep telling you, you don't realize how good you have it here. Trust me about that. I can't think of a more peaceful environment to work on the elements of your faith that you're questioning." She peered across the table. "What exactly are you questioning, by the way? You've said you're confused about your faith, but how so? You've told me a little bit about your reasoning, but I'm not super clear about your motives."

He leaned back against his chair, sweat forming on his forehead as the sun came from behind the clouds. Maybe it was the heat, maybe sheer worry about their situation. Or was he thinking how to explain about his faith? He took a long time to respond.

"I *lieb*—love—*Gott.*"

Eden loved how he said it with such conviction. "I know you do."

"But I don't understand why I feel so conflicted. On one hand, I really do realize what a *gut* place this is. I *lieb mei* family too. But if I get baptized into the faith, it's a lifelong commitment, one I can't break. And it seems to me that I should be able to see what's out there. That's the whole point of having a *rumschpringe*, which I'm being denied. My faith feels confused because I've prayed about it a lot, and I'm not getting any answers. This might sound dumb, but I feel like if I leave, that *Gott* will be disappointed in me.

But if I stay, I feel like *Gott* will still be disappointed in me because *mei* heart isn't in it."

"It's not dumb. I get it. Your parents are making a mistake by not giving you an opportunity to see what's out there. I guarantee that once you do, you'll hightail it back here and be eternally grateful for your family and the peacefulness here."

He tipped his head to one side and stared into her eyes. "You really believe that, don't you?"

"One hundred percent."

Samuel stared across the table at Eden. The wind kept catching her hair and lightly fanning loose strands across her face, which she was constantly brushing away. Her green eyes glistened in the midday sunlight, but her expression always seemed to reveal an unspoken pain.

"Since we're talking about faith . . ." He wanted to tread lightly and not mess up their day any more than it had been, but something was niggling her just below the surface, and Samuel suspected there was more to Eden than she was letting on. "I know yours is strong, but you haven't said much about your *mudder.* I don't want to bring up a sad subject for you, but her illness and prognosis must be taking a toll on you. I've spilled *mei* guts to you. Is there anything you want to share with me? It might make you feel better about that situation."

A look of withdrawal came over her face right away, and Samuel wished he hadn't brought up the subject. She had a way of shutting down her emotions, at least on the outside.

She stared at her empty plate, then started shredding her napkin into tiny pieces. "I didn't grow up like you, Samuel." Her eyes stayed cast downward.

"I know."

"My mom has done drugs for as long as I can remember. I can count on one hand the times that she was straight and sober." She lifted her eyes to his. "That's no way to raise a kid."

Samuel couldn't imagine what her life must have been like. "If you don't want to talk about it, we don't have to. I just want to know you better."

She shook her head. "I'd rather you know the person I am now without me dumping all my dirty laundry on you." She shrugged, followed by a sigh. "My mom represents everything I don't want to be, and I can't forgive her for some of the things she did or the times she left me alone and hungry." Her stony expression tightened with strain. "And, yes, I know that the Christian thing to do is to forgive her. But I can't."

"You have to." He spoke without thinking, but it was an honest answer. "Otherwise, you'll never be free. If she dies before you forgive her, you'll regret it the rest of your life."

She lowered her head again. "Forgiveness doesn't come that easily when it comes to my mom."

"At least consider giving *yourself* that gift of forgiveness."

She eyed him with a critical squint that wasn't from the sun in her eyes. A frown set into her features. "I know it's the right thing to do, to forgive my mom so she can pass peacefully into the next world. But I don't see how it's a gift for me. If you're going to tell me how it will set me free, etcetera . . . I've thought about all that. Letting her off the hook for a lifetime of what most people would call abuse feels like a gift to her, not me."

Samuel homed in on her trembling bottom lip, not wanting to make her start crying again but feeling like the subject was too important to just drop. "You're right about it being a gift to her, an unselfish act of love that maybe she doesn't deserve. But if you don't forgive her, the burden stays with you to carry forever. It will only get heavier and heavier over time."

She stared at him long and hard. "Are you speaking from experience?" She raised an eyebrow, but there was a pained tolerance in her expression.

"*Ya*, I am. Maybe not to the extent that you are facing, but I've had to forgive people lots of times."

She shook her head. "It's not the same, Samuel. You've led a sheltered life. I can tell. I'm not doubting that you've been hurt or that someone has done you wrong and that you chose to forgive that person. But this is my mother." She held on to her stony expression. "I wish my mom would have grounded me. At least she would have cared. I know you think your parents are being totally unreasonable, and in some ways, I think so too. It's part of the reason you want to leave. But to look my mom in the face, even if it's via a video call, and tell her I forgive her . . . I can't do that."

Samuel heard the pain in her voice, and he also heard the conviction in her statement, which tugged at his heart.

"Well, if it's okay with you, I'm going to pray that you'll change your mind."

A muscle quivered at her jaw, and he hoped she wasn't going to cry. But she nodded. "And if it's okay with you, I'm going to pray that you won't take the life you've been gifted for granted, that you'll take a hard look at your life and choose to stay here. God is everywhere—in the big cities, here, and all over the world. You don't have to leave here to get right with God. He won't be disappointed in you, no matter what choice you make, because every action we take can lead to Him in some way or another. Maybe you do need to go and see for yourself what's out there. But I'm telling you, Samuel . . . it's not what you've dreamed of."

He almost said, "*Maybe not for you,*" but he bit back his words since they seemed cruel. "Then I guess I need to see for myself."

"Maybe so. But don't close a door here that you can't reopen."

"I'm not baptized, so I wouldn't be shunned. At least that's the way it's supposed to work. When I leave, I'm pretty sure *mei* parents will practice their own version of a shunning." He forced a smile. "Do we really want to keep talking about this right now, or do you want to go see that cave?"

Her mouth curled into a small smile. "I vote we table this topic and go see the cave." She paused, still grinning. "Are we going to hop the fence? We could get caught." She raised her eyebrows up and down a few times as her tears dried up and her smile broadened.

Maybe that's what they both needed—a little adventure to get their minds off everything else. "I guess we could go up to the door and ask permission. You know, say you're only here for a short while and so on."

Her expression fell, and he didn't want her to think he didn't have an adventurous side. "Or we can just jump the fence and take our chances." He winked at her. "You up for it?"

She nodded enthusiastically. "Yep. Let's do it."

He stood and offered her his hand, which she accepted, and they left the outdoor table of the café hand in hand.

"I hope you can run fast." He nudged her gently with his elbow.

She laughed. "I hope you can keep up with me."

He grinned. Perhaps a portion of this day could be salvaged after all.

Anna returned home with fits of rage burning her insides. She tethered her horse near the water trough, then pounded her way across the front yard to where Leroy was sitting on the porch sipping tea.

He held up a hand on her approach. "I'm only taking a break, *mei lieb*. I'll be back to work shortly." He winked at her and grinned until she got close enough for him to see her expression. "Uh-oh," he mumbled.

"You will not be returning to your project right now." She pointed to the house. "Get cleaned up. We are going to go see Abraham."

"He's at work. Can it wait? Do we have to bother him at his job?"

Anna was trembling. "He isn't at work. I borrowed a phone while I was at your son's place of employment. Abraham is at home right now. I don't know why, and I don't care. He answered. I asked him where he was. He said at home, and I said we'd be over shortly, then I hung up."

"Why were you at Samuel's work? Do you mean at the main office?"

"*Ya*, the main office." She thrust her shaky hands to her hips. "I had this niggling feeling, and after I dropped off the cookbooks for the upcoming auction, I stopped at his work. Ben Lantz said that Samuel took vacation days yesterday, today, and tomorrow. That means"—she pointed a finger at him—"your *sohn* lied to us about going to work yesterday and today, and apparently he would have lied again about tomorrow." She stomped a foot. "When did he become so disobedient, Leroy?"

"When he met a *maedel* he likes," her husband said almost under his breath as he stood from the chair. "I'll get cleaned up."

"He's with the *Englisch maedel*. I'm sure of it. And Abraham needs to put a stop to this."

Her husband shuffled into the house. Anna sat in the rocking chair and finished off his tea, wishing for the first time in years that it was more potent than the meadow tea she prepared daily.

CHAPTER 16

It was nearing one o'clock when Abraham received what sounded like a frantic call from Anna. Yvonne didn't need to speculate. Anna and Leroy were on their way here because they had figured out Samuel was with Eden.

"How mad did she sound?" She cringed from her spot on the couch. Abraham was standing nearby staring out the window.

"Pretty mad," he said matter-of-factly. "And they're coming down the driveway now."

It had only been about twenty minutes since the phone call. "That was fast." Yvonne had brewed a fresh pitcher of tea, but she didn't see them all sitting down and casually chatting over cookies. She joined her husband by the window.

"Should we go outside? It's cooler out there." She held her hands over her stomach and thanked God for the hundredth time that everything was okay with her baby.

Abraham didn't say anything, but he walked out onto the porch and Yvonne followed.

Leroy had a habitual way of raising an arm and saying

"Gut *to see you*" no matter if he'd seen you the day before or three hours earlier. Yvonne had liked Leroy from the start. He was a cheerful man. But not today. He followed his wife with his eyes cast down. Anna looked like she was about to spit nails, her face set in a vicious grimace. Yvonne had never seen her this way, and her stomach roiled since she knew what was coming.

"We know Samuel is with Eden. Where are they?" Anna stopped at the foot of the porch steps and didn't venture up. Leroy stood beside her looking up at them and waiting for an answer. There was no "Gut *to see you*" from him, only a congested expression set into his features.

"We don't know," Abraham said as he removed his hat and ran a hand through his damp hair. Yvonne was sweating, too, more than usual, and she was glad Abraham was going to take control of this situation. "They took off earlier this morning from the bookstore, and we haven't seen or heard from them."

"Eden and I had words, and I think she's mad at me. She isn't calling me back." Yvonne didn't see the need to mention the coin or what they'd squabbled about.

Anna's face was as red as the barn. "Did you know about this?" She directed the question to Yvonne, her piercing glare causing a shiver to run the length of Yvonne's spine.

Yvonne glanced at Abraham, but she'd been wrong about him handling things. He looked at her briefly before lowering his head.

"We thought you knew about the date," Yvonne said. "That's the only reason we allowed it. As for the three days off work, when we learned about that, we told them both that Samuel must be truthful with you and Leroy or they couldn't see each other."

"But yet they are together!" Anna hollered.

"Stop." Abraham took a step closer to Yvonne and put an arm around her. "I know this is important, and we are worried about Eden too," he said. Yvonne wanted to smack Anna when she rolled her eyes as if Eden didn't deserve worry. "But this has been a hard day for Yvonne, and I'm not going to have you upsetting her. I *lieb* you, Anna, but I won't have this yelling." He glanced at his brother, who turned to his wife.

"He's right. Let's all stay calm." Leroy stayed put by his wife, but he also put a protective arm around her.

"What's wrong, Yvonne?" It was like flipping a switch as Anna's maternal instincts apparently kicked in. "What's wrong?" she asked again as she walked up the stairs until she was standing right in front of Yvonne.

Yvonne loved her sister-in-law, too, and the concern in her voice, especially considering what was going on, was touching. She fought tears before she gathered herself and explained how the day had gone.

"You poor thing." Anna lowered her less hostile gaze. The caring, sweet woman Yvonne knew was slowly returning. Was this what it was like to be a parent? She recalled her teenage years again and reminded herself that someday she would find herself in Anna's shoes.

Leroy came up the steps until all four of them stood in a circle. "Yvonne, praise *Gott* that you and the *boppli* are okay." He glanced at each of them. "I'd love a glass of tea if you have some, Yvonne, then we can sit and calmly discuss this."

Anna nodded. "When were you going to tell us you are with child?"

"Soon," Yvonne said as Anna followed her into the house. "Aside from Abraham, only Eden knows." She looked over her shoulder in time to catch the disappointment on her sister-in-law's face. "She guessed, more or less. Oh, and I guess after what happened today, now Jake and Eva know. We had to let Jake know I'd left the store."

Yvonne poured four glasses of tea, and they each took two and went back onto the porch. The men had settled into two of the four rocking chairs that sat side by side.

"I'm happy for you and Abraham," Anna said as she handed her husband a glass before sitting down by Yvonne in the last available chair. "Congratulations to you both."

Leroy echoed her sentiments, and they were quiet for a few moments, squelching the heat with long gulps of tea.

"What are we going to do about our *kinner*?" Leroy addressed the question to Abraham. Despite Anna's rare outburst, Yvonne had gotten used to the men making decisions, as they were considered the heads of the household. Abraham always included her in important conversations, though, even if it was to ask her advice later when no one was around. Now, he turned directly to her. The ball appeared to be in her court.

"For what it's worth . . ." Yvonne began. "Eden loves it here, and she can't see why Samuel would ever want to leave. And I truly believe that she tells him so, probably frequently."

Anna blinked back tears. "Has he actually said he wants to leave?"

"It's just a phase." Leroy spoke with authority, but then they all turned to Abraham.

"*Ya*, well, it happens, doesn't it?" He grinned wryly. "And Leroy—and Anna—if I'm speaking out of turn, I apologize. However, if you don't give the boy some freedoms during this time in his life, he's going to take them on his own, I fear. You're not allowing him a *rumschpringe*."

"We let him get a job out in the public. He is around outsiders all the time," Anna said.

Yvonne cringed before she spoke. "Maybe that's not enough?" No one said anything. "Eden seems to have a strong faith. She joins us in devotions nightly. If Samuel is having any problems in that area, I think that Eden would only help him in that regard, the same way I think she encourages him to stay here in our community."

"She's not Amish," Leroy was quick to say.

"And she's leaving in two and a half weeks." Yvonne crossed one leg over the other, kicking her bare foot. "It has heartache written all over it, I know. But is it worth it to forbid them to see each other? I mean, we were all sneaky growing up when it came to this kind of thing."

Anna stiffened. "*Nee*, we weren't. I know you didn't grow up here, Yvonne, but our parents kept a thumb on us, and we did not abuse any privileges or seek out adventures we knew were forbidden."

Abraham cleared his throat as he raised his eyebrows at Leroy. "Not sure that's completely true."

All eyes swung to Abraham's brother. Leroy stammered a bit before his words became audible. "*Ya*, okay. I admit, we did a few things we probably shouldn't have."

"We snuck out of the *haus* every time we got a chance, and it started when we were younger than Samuel. And, Leroy, we never got into any real trouble," Abraham said.

"You left when you weren't much older than Samuel." Leroy stroked his beard. "And you were gone for years."

Anna shook her head. "I couldn't bear that."

"My circumstances were different," Abraham said. "And you know that. I felt like a friend had been wronged, and I wanted to go into law enforcement because I thought I could make a difference." He paused. "And I think I did until *Gott* called me back to *mei* original roots."

Yvonne startled when the phone rang from inside the house. "I need to get that. It might be Eden." She scurried inside, picked up her phone, and saw that it was Emma calling, not Eden. Unwilling to worry Emma on her trip, she briefly considered how much she should tell her.

"Aunt Emma. Hi. Are you having fun?" Yvonne pulled a paper towel from the roll and blotted her damp forehead.

"Yes, we're having a lovely time, but I have some news about Jill. Is Eden nearby?"

"*Nee*. I mean, no. What's wrong?" Yvonne squeezed her eyes closed. Would she have to tell Eden that her mother had died?

"Jill isn't expected to make it through the night. She's still vaguely coherent. I don't know if Eden will want to video call her, go see her, or go to the funeral. Obviously, I can't get her to see her mother. I might be able to cut my trip short and get back for the funeral. What a mess."

Yvonne thought for a few moments. "Aunt Emma, don't cut your trip short. You didn't even really know Jill. If Eden wants to go home to California for the funeral, I'll fly there with her. If anyone asks questions, I'll tell them you are out of town, which isn't a lie."

"Honey, Eden is my responsibility. I hate that you have to deal with this, and you shouldn't have to take her to her mother's funeral. I honestly don't know if she'll even want to go."

"But she should have the opportunity to go if she wants to." Yvonne gnawed on a fingernail. "She's not here right now. Maybe it's best if I talk to her in person as opposed to you telling her over the phone."

"I'll have to agree with that since I can't be there to break the news. Just call me after you've talked to her, and we'll go from there."

After the call ended, Yvonne walked back to the porch to join the others.

"Was it Eden? Are they all right?" Anna stood. "*Ach, nee*. You're so pale. What's wrong?" Anna's voice was shaky.

"It wasn't Eden." Yvonne sat, leaned her head against the back of the rocking chair, and closed her eyes for a couple of seconds before she looked at Abraham. "It was Aunt Emma. Jill isn't expected to make it through the night."

Her husband lowered his head.

"Who is Jill?" Anna asked.

"Eden's *mudder*." Yvonne blinked back tears. "There is some turbulence between Eden and her *mudder*. But no matter what, this will be a blow, whether Eden realizes it or not." She covered her face with her hands. "I dread telling Eden about this, and what if her *mamm* passes before I find her and she has a chance to say goodbye?"

Anna was quickly kneeling beside Yvonne. She reached for her hand and squeezed. "We will find her."

It was another three-sixty for Anna. Her concern had shifted from her son to a girl she barely knew, someone who was about to lose her mother. Had she softened since the first mention of Eden's mother dying, or had the reality set in just now? Was this part of having maternal instincts no matter whose child was in peril?

"We will find them both," Leroy said firmly.

Samuel stood nervously beside Eden, shifting his weight from one foot to the other, both of them staring at the forbidden cave from the other side of the fence.

"The scarf is there for a reason," he said. "Locals know to tell people they can view the cave from the street, but they're not to go on the property or knock on the door."

"Are you having second thoughts?" Eden raised her eyebrows again, but she wasn't smiling like she was before.

"I don't know. Are you?" Even though he wanted her to see that he could be adventuresome, he didn't want to make her feel bad about doing something they weren't supposed to do. They'd done enough of that.

She sighed, put her hands on the fencepost, then rested her chin there as she gazed at the cave. "I'm not perfect, for sure, but I try to play by the rules. I'm terrified of turning into my mother."

"I don't see that ever happening." He decided to leave it up to her.

They were quiet for a few moments, and Samuel could feel the sun almost burning his already tanned skin. Sweat was trailing down both of their faces just from the walk here.

"Well . . . I guess we are already in trouble." She shrugged as she turned to him and grinned.

Samuel remembered when the fence had been a three-tier wooden type, easy to jump over. Years ago, it had been replaced with a barbwire fence mostly used to keep cattle in. Here it was meant to be a deterrence for people wanting to sneak onto the property. Luckily, no one had mowed in a while. If they crouched down, they might not get caught.

He walked a few feet to his left and found a spot in the barbwire that was looser than where they'd been, then pushed the bottom two strings down with his shoe and raised the top two enough for her to carefully squeeze between them.

"Bend lower," he said when her shirt almost caught on a barb.

After she'd cleared the fence, she held it in place so he could crawl to the other side.

Eden put a hand to her forehead. "Are there cows out here anywhere?"

"I've seen some before, but they are all probably in a shady spot somewhere out of sight."

She turned to him and smiled.

He pushed his straw hat farther down on his head. "I'll keep you safe." This time it was Samuel who held out his pinky finger, and she curled her finger in his. "Pinky swear." He smiled. "You ready?"

Eden nodded. "Yep."

"Try to keep bent at the waist so the weeds will hide us." He grabbed her hand, and they raced toward the cave, keeping their bodies as low to the ground as they could across the overgrown field. Eden laughed, which was nice to hear, especially under the circumstances.

When they reached the entrance to the cave, Eden's eyes grew round. "That's it?" She fought to catch her breath. They'd run full speed, and Samuel was winded too. "From the road, the entrance looked bigger," she said as she rested her hands on her hips.

Samuel laughed. "Are you chickening out?"

"No way." She held out her hand, and he gave her the flashlight he'd found in his buggy before they started the trek here. After shining it inside the dark space, she looked over her shoulder and almost bumped noses with him. "I bet there are bugs in here. What about snakes?"

"I'd be more worried about the turkey mites in this field we just ran through." He shrugged. "But *ya*, I guess there are probably bugs. Maybe snakes would come in here. I don't know."

She straightened, handed him the flashlight, then took a step back. "I don't care for bugs or snakes."

"City girl," he said, grinning as he edged past her and shined the light inside. The opening was large enough for him to bend at the waist and duck inside. "You coming?"

"Once you clear it for bugs and snakes."

Samuel straightened once he was inside. The rock ceiling spanned only a few inches above his head. He cast the light in every direction. "If there are any bugs in here, they aren't big enough to see with this flashlight."

"Reassuring. What about snakes?"

He poked his head out. "If there had been a snake in here, you'd have seen me sprint out quick. I'm not a big fan of those slithery creatures either." He motioned with his hand. "Come on."

She latched on to the back of his shirt as they stepped into the cave, then he shined the light around again. "It seemed bigger when we were little." He chuckled. "At ten or eleven, it was a big deal."

"I still think it's awesome." She reached into her back pocket. "I brought my phone so I can take a picture. But wait . . . you can't be in a picture, right?"

"I'm supposed to be in *mei rumschpringe*, so *ya*, I can." He hoped she would remember him after she left. Maybe he could have a copy of the photo printed, something to remember her by too.

"Okay, if you're sure." She shrugged, and Samuel held the flashlight pointed out to the side as she pulled him toward her. "Let's see how good of a selfie I can get in here."

She held the phone out in front of them with one arm. He'd seen outsiders taking pictures like this plenty of times. Then she groaned and brought her arm toward her. "I guess it would help if I turned it on. We'll have to wait a few seconds for it to power up."

Her phone dinged, and she studied the screen. "It's a voice mail. I'll listen to it in a minute."

She repositioned the phone until they were cheek to cheek, then snapped several pictures, a bright light almost blinding him each time.

"Hopefully one of these will come out good." She

pressed a couple more buttons and put the phone to her ear before she held it out to look at it again. "I lost service. I'll try again on the walk back to the buggy." She briefly wondered if the call might be about her mother, but she didn't want to consider that right now. She scowled. "Maybe it's from Yvonne. I hope she's apologizing so I have a place to sleep tonight. Otherwise, it would feel weird. Although I don't know where else I'd sleep."

"I guess you'd have to stay here in the cave." He smiled at her, but his eyes were on her lips. Taking pictures together had given him a new awareness of what it was like to be close to her. Samuel had never wanted to kiss a girl as much as Eden.

"I'd sleep on a sidewalk before I slept in here with bugs." She shivered even though sweat was rolling down both sides of her face. "I thought caves were cold."

"Not little ones like this in July."

She locked eyes with him as they stood facing each other. "I'm sorry this isn't as exciting as when you were a kid."

It was now or never for Samuel. By the time his parents and aunt and uncle got through with him and Eden, they might never see each other again. At least not without sneaking around, and Eden didn't like doing that. He was sure his aunt Yvonne and uncle Abraham had told his parents how they had run off together this morning.

He cupped one of her cheeks in his hand while he held the flashlight with the other. "I really want to kiss you, but I'm not sure if I should ask or—"

Her lips met his in one swift motion as she stood on her tippy toes, then pulled back.

"I'll take that as a yes," he said, weak in the knees.

Samuel knew he could do better than the welcomed peck she'd so sweetly planted at the edge of his mouth. He drew her to him and slowly lowered his head until their lips met again. Kissing her was like breathing, something he knew he wouldn't be able to live without on a regular basis.

Eden was sure Samuel Byler was going to unintentionally break her heart. She breathed lightly between parted lips, only to have him kiss her again, then again. Everything else in her mind faded away as she savored the sweet tenderness of his mouth on hers, the heady sensation that overtook her when he kissed her. It seemed to last forever—or until they were both so hot and sweaty that getting out of the cave became the priority.

"I've wanted to do that since the day I met you." Samuel pointed the light toward the exit and nudged her to go ahead of him.

"Was that more exciting than when you came to the cave with your friends when you were little?" she asked after they'd both cleared the opening.

He laughed. It was a sound she'd miss if his parents locked him in the basement or something, never to be seen again.

"Uh, that was definitely more exciting."

Eden leaned down to scratch her leg. "I think something bit me."

Samuel frowned. "Turkey mites are the worst. I think

we better jog to the road. Less chance of getting bitten. I should have thought about that. *Mamm* makes a spray, and we cover ourselves this time of year if we're going to be somewhere the bugs might be."

They started to jog toward the road. "What are turkey mites? Are they like chiggers? Emma said they have those out in the country in Texas but not where she lives."

Samuel picked up the pace. "I guess they're kind of like chiggers. I don't really know."

"In that case, I'll race you."

He was yards ahead of her and casually waiting by the road when she arrived breathless. "Show-off," she said, grinning as she wiggled through the opening he made in the fence. Once safely on the other side, though, her mood fell. "I gotta listen to that voice mail. I've only got one bar on my phone, but let me try."

Apprehensively, she punched Play on her phone and listened as Yvonne's voice came through the speaker.

"Eden, I am so sorry for the way I spoke to you."

There was a pause and sniffling.

"Jake has the coin, and I didn't know it. I'm so sorry."

More sniffling, and she was crying.

"Abraham and I are at the hospital. I thought I was losing the boppli *at the bookstore because I started bleeding. I was scared and worried, but that's still no excuse for the way I talked to you. I'm fine. The* boppli *is fine. Please call me as soon as you get this message. I'm calling from Abraham's phone because mine is at the bookstore. I'll be going home from the hospital shortly, but I won't be going back to work today. Please call me."*

"Oh no," Eden said, her voice cracking as she pulled her phone away from her ear. "It sounds like she's okay, but Yvonne was at the hospital."

"What?" The alarm in Samuel's voice was genuine. Yvonne was his aunt, even if by marriage for only a short time. "What happened?"

Eden swiped at her teary eyes before she replayed the message on speaker.

"I want to go home," she said after the voice mail ended.

He nodded, and they took off in a slow jog again back to the café, where they'd left the horse and buggy in a shaded area with a bucket of water. As they traveled, Eden reminded herself that Yvonne and Abraham's house wasn't her home.

Oh, how I wish it was.

CHAPTER 17

Anna stayed on the porch when her son pulled his buggy in at Yvonne and Abraham's house. Abraham and Leroy also remained, but Yvonne walked slowly down the steps. When Eden stepped out of the buggy, she ran across the front yard and into Yvonne's open arms. The girl was sobbing.

"I'm sorry! Are you okay? Are you sure the baby is all right?"

Yvonne cupped the girl's face and kissed her on the cheek. Both were openly crying now. "*Nee*, don't be sorry. I'm sorry. Eden, I'm so sorry. I spoke so horribly to you, but I was terrified I was losing the *boppli*. Sweetheart, it's still no excuse." She held her at arm's length. "Are you okay?"

Eden nodded, her face streaked with tears.

Anna put a hand to her heart. It was impossible not to be touched by the connection Yvonne seemed to have with this girl she'd known for such a short time.

Samuel hung back, but he eventually shuffled across the yard looking a mess. His hair was sweaty and flat on top, and he had a smudge of dirt on his face. He held his hat clutched to his chest as he walked toward the heap of trouble he knew he was in.

Leroy's face was bright red, and Anna wasn't sure whether it was from anger or heat from sitting outside for so long. Yvonne had made snacks, and there was a lot of tea, but they were still sweating profusely.

Yvonne held Eden close to her side as they walked across the yard, both sniffling as they came up the porch steps. Anna didn't envy Yvonne having to deliver bad news to Eden. Her sister-in-law had decided she would wait until Eden got home before she told her about her mother.

"*Sohn*, you have some explaining to do." Leroy looked down at Samuel, who was still standing in the yard. "You have disrespected your *mamm* and me, and there will be consequences!"

Anna swallowed back an unexpected knot in her throat. Yvonne swooshed by her, still clinging to Eden, as if she was trying to rush her into the house to avoid what was coming. But Eden turned around before they went inside. Her face was as red as Leroy's, but it was from crying, and the worst was yet to come for that girl. Even though Eden knew her mother was dying, the reality of the situation would surely settle around her like a dark, heavy fog, whether they were close or not.

"*Ya*. Yes, sir. I know." Samuel hung his head.

"Look at me!" Leroy stormed toward the porch steps, but Anna put her arm in front of him, blocking his way.

"*Nee*, Leroy." She glanced at Eden, who didn't seem to see anyone but Samuel. He gazed back at her in a way she recognized. Leroy used to look at her like that. He still did sometimes. "Let's go," she said to her husband, firm enough that he took a deep breath. "Now is not the time," she whispered.

As an adult, she wanted to say that these kids couldn't have any sort of real feelings for each other. They barely knew each other. But she recalled her first kiss with Leroy. They were promised to each other the following week. Anna had been Eden's age.

Leroy glanced at Eden, looked back at his son, then nodded before Eden and Yvonne entered the house.

Samuel started back to his buggy with his head down. Leroy motioned to Anna for them to leave, but she told her husband to give her a minute. She went into the house and through the living room to the kitchen. Yvonne was sitting at the kitchen table holding her head in her hands. She lifted her head when Anna came into the room.

"Eden went to take a shower."

Anna didn't sit. Leroy would be ready to go, and she dreaded their talk with Samuel when they got home. But she suspected Yvonne's talk with Eden would be worse.

"I hope your conversation with Eden goes as well as can be expected." Anna's emotions spun like a tornado. Since she'd viewed her as a threat, she wanted to continue disliking Eden. But if what Yvonne said was true about Samuel wanting to leave and Eden encouraging him to stay, maybe she'd been wrong.

"Danki." Yvonne offered up a weak smile.

Anna needed to tread lightly, especially since Yvonne had already had such an awful day, but she felt like there was more to say. "You and the *maedel* have gotten close in the short time she's been here."

"*Ya*, we have. I don't know much about dealing with teenagers from a parental point of view. I've been trying to plan out how I'm going to tell her about her mother. I need to do it soon, but I thought maybe a shower would make her feel better. She knows her mother is dying, and I honestly don't know the details about their relationship, but I think that knowing it is really happening is going to hurt her more than she realizes."

"I agree." Anna pursed her lips, then peered out the kitchen window. Samuel had walked back to his buggy, and Leroy and Abraham were talking on the porch. "I will pray for you and Eden."

"And I will pray that all goes well when you talk to Samuel." Yvonne looked at her with eyes still glistening with tears. "Be careful, Anna," she said. "If you push him too hard, he's going to leave." She held up a hand to signal she wasn't done speaking. "I know it's not *mei* business, that he's your *sohn* to raise as you see fit, but I know that the thought of him leaving terrifies you."

"It does." Anna was quiet as her thoughts swirled with confusion. "I should go. I'm sure Leroy is ready." She tried to smile, but it wasn't much of an effort. "And I'm sure Samuel is scared to death. He's never lied to us before, that we are aware of."

"Maybe keep that in mind when you talk to him."

Anna's first instinct was to fire back at her sister-in-law, since the comment sounded a bit snippy, but Yvonne had enough on her plate. She nodded and left as her stomach churned with worry.

After Samuel and his parents were gone, Abraham came into the house and sat by Yvonne on the couch. "Do you want me to stay while you talk to Eden, or do you think it should just be the two of you?"

Yvonne was worried she was going to mess up and not handle this correctly. "I'd like for you to stay, if you don't mind."

He put a hand on her leg. "Of course I don't mind."

They both looked toward the hall when they heard footsteps.

Eden walked into the room barefoot and wearing a black T-shirt and jeans. Her long blonde hair was wet and tucked behind her ears.

She sat in the rocking chair across from them. "I'm sorry again for the way I left this morning."

"Eden, I'm the one who is sorry. But . . ." She took a breath. "We need to talk to you, but it's not about you and Samuel. It's about your *mudder*."

The girl's expression went blank. "What about her?"

"You know how sick she is, right?" Yvonne could feel a lump forming in her throat.

"Yes." Eden remained stoic, her lips pinched together, her eyes revealing nothing.

"Aunt Emma called today. Someone at the hospital where your *mudder* is said that it was likely she would pass during the night or soon after." She glanced at Abraham, but his head was hung. Yvonne shifted her gaze back to Eden. "I don't think we have time to fly to California, or I would make that happen. But I'm sure you want to video call her, *ya*?"

"I already knew she was dying," Eden said as if she were stating a fact about the weather or some other mundane issue. "I don't need to talk to her or see her. I accepted a video call with her recently. She wanted me to forgive her." Her bottom lip trembled. "And I can't, so I don't see the point in having another conversation with her."

Yvonne had expected more of a reaction from Eden, but it was possible she was carrying a lot of heavy burdens where her mother was concerned and hiding them behind the hurt and anger she must feel. She decided to take another route.

"Eden, do you think your *mudder* knows Jesus?"

"I doubt it." Eden began fidgeting with her hands in her lap.

Abraham finally looked up. Maybe he would say what was on the tip of Yvonne's tongue, although she didn't know how to say it.

"As a Christian, do you think you have a responsibility to show her to Jesus, even if it's in a video call?" Abraham spoke the words Yvonne had been looking for.

"'Responsibility'?" The question had invoked an emotional response from Eden. Her face reddened as she glared at Abraham. "Where was her responsibility when she left me for days at a time with no food or supervision? Was she responsible when she was doing drugs in front of me for most of my life? I'm stuck living with a stranger in a totally foreign place because of her." She paused as her chin trembled even more. "And Emma is super nice. You know that's not what I mean when I say that. But my mother obviously didn't factor me into any of her choices."

Abraham put his elbows on his knees and leaned forward. "You're right. It doesn't sound like she did right by you. But your inability to forgive her is going to hurt you in the end more than her, whether you think so now or not. And doesn't everyone deserve an opportunity to meet the Lord, no matter where they are in their life?"

Eden stood up. "I appreciate what you're saying, but with all due respect, she made her bed, and now she's lying in it, dying. And she put herself there by doing all those drugs. If God wants her to find Him, He will see that she does. Can I go now?" She crossed her arms across her chest in a show of defiance, but her lip still trembled. Sometimes Eden acted with the maturity of a young adult. But now, in some ways, she looked like a little girl to Yvonne. Yvonne remembered being sixteen. It was a tricky age.

"Of course you can." Yvonne searched her mind for something else to say, but nothing came to her before Eden went around the corner and down the hallway.

"These have to be her decisions," Abraham said after they heard her bedroom door close.

Yvonne thought back. "I grew up not knowing *Gott*. You know that. And without Jake and Eva—and that book I read—I might not have found Him." She looked at her husband. "The fact that I stumbled upon that book wasn't just a coincidence. The author had lost his faith. *Gott* found me at just the right time in *mei* life, and part of His plan was for me to read that man's story."

"I agree, but . . ." Her husband shrugged. "I don't know. I think all we can do is pray that Eden will make the best decisions for her and her *mudder*."

"I hope she does. But I'm telling you, there is a lot of hurt bottled up beneath that anger with nowhere to go."

They were quiet for a while, then Yvonne decided to redirect the topic of conversation.

"What did Leroy have to say while you two talked on the porch?"

Abraham raised a shoulder and lowered it with a shrug. "He is fit to be tied that Samuel lied to them, and it worries me that they are going to be too hard on the boy." He paused, seemingly lost in thought as he gazed across the room. "I can see me in Samuel, searching for answers to the questions he doesn't know how to articulate. Even though I felt I was on a mission to defend a friend when I chose to be a cop, there were a lot of other emotions going on as well. Looking back, I think I tried to justify my actions because I also wanted to see what else was out there. The teenage years are tough, confusing. And we don't admit it at the time, but we don't like to be told what to do. I hope Leroy thinks about what the repercussions could be if he's not careful."

Yvonne reached for her husband's hand and squeezed. "I cautioned Anna, too, about not being too hard on Samuel. It might have fallen on deaf ears. I don't know." She paused. "Maybe you should have been the one to talk to Samuel."

"That's his *daed*'s job." He shook his head. "I'll be praying he doesn't push Samuel away."

Yvonne recalled the tormented expression on Anna's face whenever someone mentioned Samuel leaving. "Me too," she said.

Samuel sat at the kitchen table across from his parents. His mother had laid out two platters of cookies, as if that would defuse what was coming. His father had sent his sisters upstairs.

He reminded himself that he wasn't in the habit of lying or being disrespectful to his parents, but when they forbid him to see Eden, as they certainly would, he couldn't be sure that he wouldn't betray them again.

"Samuel, your *daed* and I talked about this on our way home." His mother spoke in a calm voice, her hands folded in front of her atop the table.

Samuel had also thought about it plenty as he followed them in his buggy.

"We want to have a calm conversation about how you're feeling and why you did what you did," she said.

"*Nee*, your *mudder* wants to have a calm conversation. If it were up to me, you would be grounded for a month, and—"

"Leroy . . ." His mom cut her eyes at his father. He was the man of the house most of the time, but Samuel knew that at the end of the day, his mother called most of the shots, even if it was behind closed doors. At least about the important stuff.

"Fine." His father frowned, but he didn't say anything else.

"You know how we feel about *rumschpringe*—that it's dangerous. It can lead to temptations and other worldly situations that don't fit in with our beliefs." She took a deep breath. "Having said that, we want you to be baptized into our faith, but we know that it must be your choice. We don't want to do anything that hinders that."

"But you are." Samuel regretted the comment right away, especially when he caught the taut expression on his father's face.

"This is all about that *maedel*. And it proves your *mudder*'s point. She's an outsider, and you never disrespected us until you met her." His father leaned back in his chair and looped his thumbs beneath his suspenders, maintaining his sour expression.

"*Daed*, I was thinking about leaving before I ever met Eden. And believe it or not, she gave me plenty of *gut* reasons why I should stay." He glanced back and forth between his parents. "But how am I going to walk *mei* own journey if you won't let me? *Mei* faith is suffering because I'm confused." He shook his head. "You're wrong about Eden. She's given me lots to think about, so I don't make any rash decisions. And you'll be making a mistake if you don't let me spend time with her while she's here, because she is the only one making any sense to me."

Anna needed to speak up quickly before Leroy countered and the conversation got messy, even though Samuel was answering the question Anna asked.

"We grounded you, Samuel," she said. "But in light of the circumstances surrounding Eden's *mudder*, and the fact that you already took time off from work, your father and I will allow you to spend the day with Eden tomorrow." She glanced at Leroy, who was recoiling even though they had agreed on this earlier in the buggy. "But then you will continue to be grounded."

"*Nee*, I don't agree to that." Samuel's face turned red. "She's not going to be here that long. Why can't I be grounded after she leaves in a couple of weeks?"

Leroy stood from the table. "That's not how it works, and I'm done with this conversation." He stomped off, crossed through the living room, and went into their bedroom, slamming the door behind him.

"*Mamm*, you've got to get him to change his mind." Samuel's eyes pleaded with her, and a part of her wanted to give in, but that would only anger Leroy and make things worse.

"You heard what your *daed* said." She stood, went to the bedroom, and gently closed the door.

Samuel reconsidered what he'd always thought to be true—that his mother ran the show. He could see in her eyes that she wanted to come to his defense, but she didn't.

He headed for the stairs. After he was in his room, he glanced around at his belongings and tried to decide how much he could take with him. This was happening way too soon. He didn't have enough money to get a place, nor did he know where he would go. If only they would have let him see Eden, maybe she would have changed his mind about leaving. They had to realize they were pushing him to do this.

Samuel pulled his suitcase from underneath the bed and wiped off the dust with his hand. Maybe he'd sleep in someone's barn. He hadn't thought things through. He had considered that this might happen, but in the back of his mind, he'd expected a little leniency despite everything.

One day with Eden was not going to be enough. And no one was going to stop him from seeing her.

CHAPTER 18

Eden had opted out of supper and devotions this evening. Even though her stomach growled, she worried she'd vomit if she tried to eat. She felt badly about declining, but neither Abraham nor Yvonne gave her a hard time about it. Yvonne's eyes reflected sadness, and that had tugged at Eden's heart, but if she talked about her mother much more, she feared everything would spill out of her. She wasn't prepared for that any more than having to see her mother one last time on another video call. She struggled with one thing Abraham had said: If she didn't show her mother the way to Jesus, would she feel guilty for the rest of her life? She'd been praying about it ever since she came to her room.

As it got later, Eden became more anxious. Would her mother be dead by morning? By the time it was dark, she'd chewed down most of her fingernails, paced the room, then sat on the bed, then paced more. Was God nudging her to call?

Glancing at the clock, she assumed it was too late to call the number stored on her phone from the last video call.

She gasped when she saw a face peering at her through

the window screen. As the person came into focus from the dim light of the lantern, she rushed across the room.

"Samuel, what are you doing here? It's almost eleven o'clock." She looked over his shoulder to see if a buggy was visible beneath the propane light outside. Surely, she would have heard him pull in. "Are you on foot?"

"*Ya*. I left."

"I appreciate the fact that you snuck out to see me, but your parents will go nuts if they wake up and find you gone." Eden tried to pull the screen out to let him in. "I don't know how to get this thing out to let you in."

"Uh . . . do you think you could come out here instead? I-I don't think I should be in your bedroom."

Eden smiled on the inside. "Sure. But it will take me a few minutes." She was wearing pajamas, and while not revealing, she wanted to put on some real clothes.

"I'll be in the barn," he whispered before he left.

She scurried into a pair of worn jeans, then pulled the same black T-shirt she'd worn earlier over her head. She tiptoed down the hallway, glad she didn't see a light coming from underneath the door to Yvonne and Abraham's bedroom.

After unlocking the deadbolt, she eased the door open, cringing when it squeaked. She tiptoed down the porch steps before sprinting to the barn. Samuel was sitting on top of Abraham's workbench with a flashlight shining at his feet, which were propped up on a suitcase.

"What's that?" She pointed to the piece of luggage as her stomach lurched.

"I didn't just sneak out to see you. I'm leaving. *Mei* parents were going to let me spend the day with you tomorrow, but then I'd be grounded for two weeks, and you'll be leaving then. I'm not doing that." He shook his head as he sighed. "I admit, I haven't thought things through. I just needed to get out of there, at least for a while."

Eden's stomach clenched even more. "Samuel, where are you going to stay? I think you should have waited and not left on an impulse." She walked closer to him, and he pulled her into his arms, kissing her softly.

"*Nee*. I need to be here." He kissed her again, more passionately, and she fought the heady sensation she'd felt before, knowing this was a bad situation. She was about to ease out of his embrace, but he did so first.

"Did you talk to your *mamm*? I overheard *mei* parents talking about her on the porch, that she was, um . . . maybe not expected to make it through the night. Eden, I'm so sorry. I'm here if you want to talk about it, or I'm here if you don't. I just wanted to be with you."

Eden began pacing again, the dry hay rough between her toes. "I thought I was okay about not calling my mom. Abraham and Yvonne talked to me about it, but I didn't want to do it." She recalled her snappy responses and regretted speaking to them that way. "I've been awake thinking about something Abraham said, and I can't help but wonder if it's my job to lead my mother to Jesus. But what if she's already gone?"

A river of tears threatened to break a dam she'd built a long time ago, but if she let go, the flood of emotion would drown her.

Samuel jumped down from the workbench and gently took both her shoulders. "Eden, forget about everything that has happened in the past. Push it from your mind along with anything negative bouncing around in that beautiful head of yours. Go with your instinct. Right now. What do you want to do?"

She buried her face in his chest, and the dam broke. She couldn't remember crying that hard, gasping for breath. "I want to call her," she said, sobbing. "I didn't think I could or wanted to, but I want to call her, Samuel."

He held her while she cried, drenching his shirt with her tears.

"Abraham, wake up." Yvonne shoved her husband, probably harder than she should have.

"Ow."

"There's someone in the barn. I see a light." She climbed out of bed and hurried to Eden's room. Without the lantern on, she couldn't see. "Eden?" She felt around on the bed. "Eden, are you in here?" Next, she looked in the bathroom before she bumped into Abraham in the hallway. "She's not in her room or the bathroom."

"Stay here," he said.

"*Nee*. I'm coming too."

"*Nee*."

"Yes."

He shook his head. "Okay, but stay behind me."

She did as he asked until she heard crying, more like wailing. "Eden," she said as she sprinted past Abraham, flinging the barn door open ahead of her husband.

Abraham was beside her almost instantly.

"Samuel, what are you doing here, *sohn*?"

Eden rushed into Yvonne's arms.

"Sweetheart, you're okay. You're okay." Yvonne stroked her hair. "Honey, what is it?"

"I want to call my mom. It's late. What if she already . . ."

Yvonne wrapped Eden in her arms as the poor girl trembled. "I'll let you handle him." She pointed to Samuel. "I'm taking Eden inside." She kept her arm around her cousin as she cried. Yvonne struggled not to cry along with her. Then she prayed that Jill was still alive.

Samuel stood tall and raised his chin, prepared for the verbal lashing he was about to get from his uncle.

"What's that?" His uncle Abraham pointed to the suitcase.

"I left."

His uncle wore a pair of gray drawstring pajama bottoms, a white undershirt, and bare feet. Mostly he was wearing a disgusted expression. "I see that. Where were you planning to go?"

Samuel shrugged. "I don't know for sure."

"Well, you didn't get very far, did you?" Abraham ran a hand through hair that was already sticking almost straight up. "I'm guessing your parents don't know about this, that you just snuck out?"

He nodded as a dose of shame slapped him.

"So . . . you wanted to see Eden, and then were you

going to sleep in *mei* barn? But no plans past that?" He took two steps closer to Samuel until he was in his face. "Please tell me that you weren't having impure thoughts about—"

"*Nee, nee*! I would never disrespect Eden." Samuel was surprised his uncle had even said such a thing. He had known him his whole life.

"*Ach*, well, it sounds like you disrespected your parents."

"*Onkel* Abraham, you know they are unreasonable and not being fair. I should be allowed to experience *mei rumschpringe*."

"It's not up to me, Samuel." Abraham yawned, then motioned for Samuel to follow him. "I know your parents don't keep their cell phone on, so I'm going to leave them a message. Hopefully, when they see you are missing in the morning, they will check their phone. For now, you can take the couch." He stopped and turned around. "And there will be no canoodling."

"Yes, sir." Samuel got into step with Abraham. "But I'm not going back."

His uncle stopped and faced him. "Then you tell them like a man that you're leaving. Don't be a coward and sneak out in the middle of the night."

Samuel didn't move as his uncle walked toward the house. Earlier, he thought he'd felt a slap of shame. His uncle's statement was a punch in the gut and inflicted a lot more pain.

Eden sat alone in her bedroom. She'd heard Abraham come

into the house with Samuel earlier, and Yvonne had gone to join them in the living room. Yvonne had first sat on Eden's bed with her almost an hour just holding her and letting her cry. They'd tried to call the number stored in her phone as soon as they came into the house, but the call had gone straight to voice mail. She'd tried two more times with the same result. Her mother had probably died. She'd waited too long.

The dam had broken and freed all the feelings she'd kept inside, stabbing her like a knife, slicing her open and releasing her pent-up emotions. Yvonne's soothing words had helped keep her somewhat calm, but alone now, and with each passing minute, she became more tortured that she hadn't told her mother goodbye. She tried to call again, and this time a woman answered on the first ring, and Eden tearfully told her who she was.

"Let me take my phone to your mom." She paused. "Hon, she doesn't have long, and I hope she . . ."

Her voice trailed off, and Eden's heart pumped so fast she hoped she didn't pass out. She heard footsteps, machines beeping in the background, and voices. She wondered if her mother was in a hospital within the prison or at a regular hospital.

A woman's face appeared on her screen—an older woman with short gray hair. "Turn on your camera, and I'm going to hold the phone so you can see your mother and she can see you."

Eden swallowed hard, hoping she could form words and praying she would say the right things. She held an arm across her stomach. It was tied in knots and cramping.

Her mother's pale face appeared on the screen with cheeks so sunken she was almost unrecognizable. She had declined so much in such a short time that Eden's jaw dropped.

"Hello, baby girl." Her mother's voice was barely above a whisper, even though Eden had her volume turned up all the way. Her eyes were barely open.

Tears streamed down Eden's face. After the dam had opened, she'd only been able to temporarily patch it before she was flooded with emotion again.

"I love you, Eden. I've always loved you." Her mom took a labored breath. "I know you can't forgive me, and I understand that." Another long and even more laborious breath. "But thank you for calling me so that I could see your beautiful face and be able to tell you that I love you. I'll be able to go now. Don't cry, baby."

Eden's insides were shredding as she sobbed. Somewhere, buried beneath the anger and the hurt, pooled an emotion she hadn't expected to explode from within her. "Momma, I love you. And I forgive you!" She was shouting, but nothing had ever seemed so important to her in her short life. "And I want you to accept Jesus as your Lord and Savior. Can you please do that for me?"

The corners of her mother's mouth curled upward slightly. Eden hoped she was considering it.

"Momma, Jesus loves you. God loves you." She heard the hysteria in her voice. "Ask Him to forgive your sins and tell Him you accept Him into your heart."

"I already did," her mom said, still smiling slightly, but her words were followed with another deep and long breath.

Suddenly, the older woman's face came into view. "It's difficult for her to talk, but I want you to know that a member of clergy came in earlier and gave your mother her last rites, and he also led her to God through His Son, Jesus." The woman smiled, but her eyes were filled with tears. Her mother must mean something to this woman, she thought, before her mother's face came back into view.

Eden hadn't helped to save her mother's soul. Someone else already had. If Abraham hadn't brought that up, would she have made this call? Or would she have always regretted not giving her mother the forgiveness she sought—something Eden apparently needed also? If things hadn't played out exactly this way, would Eden have found that love had been buried beneath the rubble of emotions she'd been carrying?

"Thank you for forgiving me," her mother said even softer than before. "And for your love, even though I don't deserve it." She attempted another smile. "Have a good life, Eden. I have comfort knowing I will see you again. I will be a better parent in the next life."

Her mother closed her eyes. "Momma!" Eden screamed. The older woman dropped the phone, and there was a flurry of activity. "Momma!" she yelled again.

Yvonne burst into the room followed by Abraham and Samuel. Eden couldn't breathe, as if her throat was closing. It was several moments before the same woman picked up the phone. Eden knew what she was going to say by her expression and tears.

"She's gone, hon. I'm sorry for your loss. Despite the hard life Jill lived, and the mistakes she made, she was a kind person. I must go now, dear."

Eden dropped the phone from where she was sitting on the bed, and it bounced twice on the floor, but no one made a move to pick it up. Samuel gazed into her eyes as he blinked back tears. Yvonne was openly crying. Abraham had his head down.

"I don't have a mom." Eden's voice cracked as she spoke. She had always thought not having a mother might be a good thing. Now she wondered if the sting would ever go away.

Yvonne sat beside her and pulled her into her arms. "But you have us, and we are your family too."

Eden just cried harder.

"Abraham, come back to bed." Yvonne patted the empty spot beside her. "They aren't going to do anything they shouldn't. They are comforting each other."

Her husband closed their bedroom door, which he had cracked barely an inch as he peered to where Eden and Samuel sat on the couch.

"He's a boy. I don't want him comforting her too much." Abraham climbed in beside her and pulled her into his arms.

"I wouldn't want to be sixteen again." Yvonne shivered at the thought.

"Not unless I knew everything I know now." Abraham winced. "I can already see Anna and Leroy getting my message in the morning, telling them Samuel is safe, but they will also be hit with the reality that their son ran away from home. I hope they think to check their phone when they realize Samuel isn't there."

"I feel badly for them, but I also sympathize with Samuel." She draped an arm across his chest and snuggled closer. "And seeing Eden the way she was tonight, seeing her mother die while being so far away . . . The whole thing just broke *mei* heart."

"*Ya*, that was tough to watch." Abraham kissed her on the forehead. "You're always there for Eden. You're going to be a *gut mamm*."

Yvonne smiled. "I hope so." Her thoughts drifted. "I'm going to need to fly with Eden to California for the funeral if she wants to go. I know it's allowed for emergencies."

"*Ya*, flying is okay for funerals and emergencies, but I hope you don't have to do that. I'm not saying that I hope Eden chooses not to attend her mother's service, just that I'd worry about you and our *boppli* flying and being so far away."

"The doctor said everything is fine. Let's see how Eden feels, what she wants to do, and we'll go from there."

Abraham shifted his weight, then lifted his head and looked toward their closed bedroom door. Yvonne pressed her arm down on his stomach. "*Nee*, you don't need to check on them. They aren't going to do anything they shouldn't," she told him again. "Especially since they aren't far from our bedroom. Besides, Eden is upset, and Samuel was raised with high morals."

Abraham gave a half shrug. "I hope you're right. It's late. I guess we better get some sleep before everything breaks loose in the morning."

Yawning, Yvonne agreed. But before she let herself drift off to sleep, she said prayers for Eden, Samuel, Leroy, and Anna. They were going to have a hard day tomorrow.

Anna placed the last of the breakfast offerings on the table. Everyone was seated except for Samuel. She walked to the window to see if his buggy was there, and it was. Her son had skipped supper the night before, and that might have been for the best. Anna worried Samuel and Leroy might have more words. But surely Samuel would want breakfast this morning and would take them up on his one day off from being grounded. Anna was nervous about him spending another day with Eden, but she was going to trust that each of them would keep a level head and not stray into a forbidden arena. She doubted they would do anything sinful right now. Eden would need consoling after such tragic news. As she recalled Samuel saying Eden had been encouraging him to stay in the community, maybe good things might come from that.

"Mae, go tell your *bruder* he's late for breakfast." Anna took a seat and looked across the table at her husband. Leroy was generally a cheerful man, but she could tell by the scowl permanently etched into his expression that last night's conversation was still wearing on him.

Mae huffed. "He didn't want supper last night. He'll come down if he wants breakfast."

Leroy cleared his throat and glared at Mae.

Their eldest daughter pushed back her chair and stomped out of the room.

"Let's go ahead with the blessing." Anna lowered her head along with those left at the table. She was reaching for a biscuit when Mae returned.

"He's not in his room. His bed doesn't even look slept in." Mae sat down and accepted a bowl of eggs from Hannah.

Panic welled in Anna's throat as she fought to steady her erratic pulse. "What?"

Mae shrugged. "Maybe he went for another walk."

A tense silence enveloped the room, and no one spoke for a few moments.

Anna rose and headed for the stairs, her heart fiercely pounding against her chest. She opened the closed door. As Mae had said, the bed hadn't been slept in. Anna crept closer, and on shaky legs, she kneeled and looked under the bed. Anxiety spurted through her. His suitcase was gone. After standing on legs even less stable, her eyes drifted around the room. There weren't any clothes on the rack or shoes lined up against the wall.

"Leroy!" she belted out as she flew down the stairs, breathless by the time she reached the kitchen. "Samuel is gone. His suitcase isn't under the bed, there aren't any clothes on the rack, and two pairs of shoes are missing."

"Did Samuel run away?" Hannah asked in a shaky voice, her lip quivering.

She ignored her youngest daughter. "Leroy, what do we do?" Her worst fear was playing out. She needed to remain calm in front of her girls, but worry knotted inside her. "Would he have gone to see Eden?"

"*Mei maed*, keep your minds on your meal. Samuel is fine. Eat your breakfast," Leroy said as he stood up and went to the drawer where they kept the phone. "I'll call Abraham."

She waited while her husband powered up the mobile phone.

"Someone left a message. A voice-mail message, I think." He handed the phone to Anna. "I don't know how to listen to them."

Voice mails were supposed to be for business use only, but if there was ever an emergency with relatives they had living out of state, Anna wanted to know. She'd set up the voice mail for that purpose. Her hand shook as she put the phone to her ear.

"It's Abraham. Samuel is at our haus, *and he is fine. Please visit in the morning."*

"He's at Abe and Yvonne's *haus*." Anna hit End before she rushed upstairs to put on shoes and socks. From her bedroom window, she could see Leroy readying the horse and buggy.

When she got downstairs, she pointed to her oldest daughter. "Mae is in charge. Hannah and Grace, don't give your *schweschder* any problems, and you can all share in the breakfast cleanup. We will be back as soon as we can."

Anna jogged out to the buggy, her fear turning to anger. "Leroy, I can't have *mei sohn* leaving us. You were too hard on him!"

"We will get things right," he said, although he sounded defeated before they even knew the full situation.

"I hope so."

CHAPTER 19

Now you're the one spying," Abraham said through a yawn from their bed the next morning as he stretched his arms above his head. Yvonne stood by the door, having opened it just enough to see into the living room.

"Come look," she said in a whisper as she gazed at Samuel asleep on the floor next to the couch where Eden lay.

Abraham peered over her shoulder.

"Look how sweet that is. He has his hand up on the couch, holding hers." Yvonne couldn't help but smile. Things were going to explode soon. She wanted to savor the moment.

"*Ya*, take it all in, because that sweetness is about to blow up when Anna and Leroy get here. In addition to Samuel being missing, they aren't going to be thrilled that Samuel slept under the same roof as Eden."

Yvonne closed the door as quietly as she could. "Samuel is safe, and I'm sure nothing physical happened. But *ya* . . . I'm sure it was very upsetting when Anna and Leroy realized their *sohn* was gone and heard your message."

"If they even heard *mei* message. If they don't show up soon, I'll go to their *haus*."

Yvonne tapped a finger to her chin. "What if they hear your message and choose not to come?"

Abraham grinned. "What would *you* do?"

"I'd get here as soon as possible."

He kissed her tenderly. "Exactly."

"I guess I'll start breakfast. I'm a little surprised they aren't here yet since we slept later than usual." Yvonne slipped out of her nightgown and pulled a dark-green dress over her head.

"I think I hear horse hooves. You might want to wait to start breakfast." Abraham shuffled to the window. "*Ya*, it's them."

Eden awoke to the sun streaming in from the living-room window, and it took her a few seconds to realize where she was.

Samuel was sitting on the floor next to the couch where he'd fallen asleep the night before. They hadn't talked much before they fell asleep from mental exhaustion.

"*Gut* morning," he said when she sat up. "I didn't want to wake you."

Yvonne walked into the room. "*Gut* morning, you two. I was getting ready to start breakfast, but your parents are getting ready to pull in, Samuel."

He hung his head before he looked up at Yvonne. "*Ya*,

I might not feel like eating breakfast after they get here and try to drag me home by my ear."

"Maybe it won't be so bad," Abraham said as he came into the living room fully dressed.

Eden looked down at her wrinkled T-shirt. She was sure she had mascara under her eyes from crying, or at the least dark circles. After she looked over her shoulder and saw Samuel's parents coming across the front yard, she tried to smooth her hair with her hands, then ran a finger under each eye.

Samuel stood up. "*Onkel* Abraham, you've gotta help me."

"I told you last night that it's not *mei* place to interfere."

Eden was still reeling from the night before, and every time she envisioned her mother's face, tears welled in her eyes. She wasn't sure she could handle any more drama, but it was too late to leave the room without being rude.

"Samuel, can we see you outside?" Leroy said through the screen.

"At least come with me," Samuel pleaded with Abraham, who shrugged, then followed him out the door.

Eden could hear them through the screen of the opened window.

"Let's go home," Samuel's father said in a stern voice.

If Samuel responded, Eden didn't hear him, but she heard what sounded like whimpering.

Yvonne sat beside her. "Anna's crying, isn't she?"

Eden leaned closer to the screen. "I think so."

"Are you going to be okay? I think I'll step outside and at least offer a shoulder to cry on."

Eden nodded with the knowledge that she would be okay eventually, but it would take a while. She was grateful God had blessed her with the opportunity to tell her mother goodbye and that she loved her. All this time, she'd thought it was just anger she'd kept bottled up for so long. Buried beneath it all, though, she'd managed to find love for her mother, despite everything. There was a certain comfort in knowing she had the capacity to love deeply against the odds.

"I'm not going home."

It was the last thing Eden heard out the window before Abraham asked Leroy if the four adults could speak privately. Samuel walked in the door just as the grownups moved out of earshot to the middle of the yard.

He slumped into the rocking chair across from the couch. "I guess the four of them are going to try to choose my fate, but I'm not going home."

Eden took a deep breath. "Samuel, how much of this is because of me?"

"Some of it, but you know I had thoughts of leaving before."

"Not like this, though." Eden tucked stringy slept-on strands of hair behind her ears. "You were still thinking about it, and if you'd chosen to leave, you would have planned it out."

He stared at her for a long while. "Let's not worry about me right now. How are you? I think that's a dumb question, but I'm asking it anyway. I don't want you worrying about me or my fate when I'm sure you have things to decide. Will you go to the funeral?"

Eden hadn't gotten that far in her thought process. "I don't know."

"It's a lot to think about. And whatever you choose is the right choice."

"Is it?" Eden didn't know. Wasn't there some unspoken rule that you must attend a parent's funeral, no matter the circumstances?

"*Ya*, it is." Samuel stood and walked to the couch but didn't sit down. He stared out the window. "It doesn't matter what they come up with. If they try to force me to stay because I'm only sixteen, I'll leave anyway. I'm not waiting until I'm a legal adult, which is eighteen. If they would just give me the freedom to find out who I am and the right path for me, I wouldn't feel so trapped and bitter. Holding me hostage isn't helping me or them."

Eden couldn't help but wonder how much of Samuel's convictions were the frustrations of a rebellious teenager—an odd thing for her to think since she was the same age—or driven by his desire to see the outside world or his confusion about not hearing God's plan for him—and how much of it was because of her.

She wanted to tell him that they barely knew each other, and that she shouldn't be a consideration when he chose his future, but the thought of not seeing him again ripped at her insides. She stayed quiet.

"I wish I could hear what they're saying," he said, his eyes glued to the foursome outside.

They stayed perfectly still and quiet, but Eden couldn't hear a thing.

CHAPTER 20

Yvonne remained close to Anna while Leroy and Abraham argued.

"He disrespected us," Leroy said. "He lied to us about his whereabouts and about seeing Eden, and—"

"I know all of that. We've covered it. But if you push him too hard right now, at this moment, you run the risk of losing him for good. You can try to legally make him stay since he's not eighteen, but it won't stop him from running away again." Abraham stood face-to-face with his brother. "I had an idea earlier. I haven't even mentioned it to Yvonne. It might be a way for everyone to take a breather and calm down."

Leroy's face turned red. "He is not staying here. I will not have him staying under the same roof as an unmarried *Englisch maedel.*"

"First of all, she'll be gone in a couple of weeks, but Leroy, I wouldn't allow that either."

Yvonne tried to guess what kind of idea Abraham had come up with, but she couldn't think of anything.

"I ran into Esther and Lizzie not too long ago. They are

looking for a renter for Gus's old cottage on their property. Esther said their renter moved out last month. Two people were interested in it, but both were *Englisch* and decided not to take it when they found out it didn't have electricity. Maybe Samuel could rent the place."

"*Nee, nee.*" Leroy shook his head. "That's giving in to a teenager's whim. He will live at home."

"But he left home." It was the first time Anna had spoken up since Yvonne went out there. "Like Abraham said, if we make him come back, he'll likely run away again."

"Leroy . . ." Abraham paused. "Just consider it for a minute. It would keep Samuel close by, right down the road. It would give him a level of responsibility by paying rent. And, I think, most important, it will give him time to really think about his life and what he wants out of it. It also keeps him in the Amish community where his roots are." He smiled. "Look at me. I never really left."

"You left, Abe, even if it wasn't in the physical sense by moving far away. You left our way of life." Leroy folded his arms across his chest, glowering at his brother.

Abraham glanced at Anna, who wasn't crying anymore.

"He probably doesn't have enough money to go very far anyway." Leroy shook his head, frowning.

"We don't know that, Leroy." Anna inched closer to her husband and put a hand on his arm. "What if he does have enough money saved? He might find a better job far from home and move there."

Leroy stroked his beard. Yvonne thought Abraham's idea was a great one, but she stayed quiet as her husband made his case and Anna seemed to be considering it.

"I don't think Lizzie and Esther charged their last renter much at all. It's something to think about. And Leroy . . . Either way, you can't force him to be baptized. He might need to find his own way in the outside world before he decides his future, and why not keep him close to home while he's doing it?"

Anna lowered her arm, pinched her lips together, and gave a taut nod of her head. "That's what we should propose to Samuel."

Leroy glared at her, but Anna returned the stare tenfold and squinted her eyes at her husband. Yvonne wanted to say, *"You go, girl"*—something she might have said in her old life—but it wouldn't be wise now.

"Maybe if you give him the chance to choose, which is what the *rumschpringe* is supposed to be about, then he'll choose to be baptized. Right now, he's confused." Abraham shrugged. "But it's up to you and Anna."

"He's letting a *maedel* influence him." Leroy dropped his arms to his side, then looked at Anna.

"I still think that's what we need to propose to Samuel," Anna said, her eyes softening.

Leroy was quiet, then said, "We are not paying his rent. If he wants to be out on his own, then he's out on his own."

It sounded like Leroy might be coming around, but Yvonne realized no one had told them about Jill. "Um, I hate to interrupt this discussion, and I know how important this situation is to you." She glanced back and forth between Anna and Leroy. "But I have a young *maedel* inside whose *mudder* passed last night. She died while Eden was having a video call with her to say goodbye, and it was traumatic for her. I respectfully ask that everyone practice calm if this conversation is going to take place in our home or within earshot. I'm not sure Eden can handle any more upset."

Leroy rubbed the back of his neck. "We will let the boy rent Gus's cottage, and there will be no arguing in front of Eden."

Anna sidled up to her husband and rubbed his arm. "I knew you'd handle things the best way."

Yvonne was pretty sure Leroy wouldn't have chosen Abraham's suggestion if Anna hadn't been there to stroke his ego. It was smart of her to give her husband credit for making the best decision. Still, Yvonne was a bit disheartened that Anna and Leroy hadn't offered condolences about Jill's death.

"They're coming back." Samuel's stomach clenched as his parents, Yvonne, and Abraham headed back to the house. He shook his head.

"Keep an open mind," Eden said as she stood up. "I wonder if I should go to my room. This is a private family matter."

"*Nee*, just stay." He wanted Eden in his life. She should hear the outcome. Samuel reminded himself to be respectful, no matter what happened. He owed his parents that, and he didn't want Eden to see him be confrontational with them.

He sat on the couch beside Eden as the foursome came into the house. No one was smiling, but no one was crying either.

Yvonne and Abraham hung back and stood close to the fireplace near their dog, who had slept through most everything. Samuel's parents walked right up to the coffee table and stared at Eden sitting next to Samuel on the couch. He wouldn't be able to maintain calm and not react in a negative way if they said anything hurtful to Eden, especially now.

"We are very sorry for your loss, Eden," his mother said, echoed by his father, who also offered condolences.

"It is a time in your life that must present much hurt and confusion." Leroy glanced over his shoulder at Samuel's aunt and uncle. "Abraham is a smart man, and Yvonne is a compassionate woman. Together, they will help you to heal. We will be praying for peace and comfort for you."

Samuel gazed at his parents, reminded of the good things about his family. Eden might not know it, but his father hadn't just offered words. His parents *would* pray for her. As much as he longed to be out in the world to clear his head, he wouldn't forget the loving foundation he'd been brought up on.

"Thank you," Eden said as she stood. "I will go to my room so that you all can talk."

Samuel had told her he wanted her to stay, but maybe she wasn't comfortable with the idea. Or she didn't want anyone to see her cry. Samuel saw her blink back tears.

When no one argued about her leaving, she rounded the corner as his mother and Yvonne sat in the rocking chairs. Abraham stayed by the fireplace. His father remained standing, and he was apparently the one who was going to deliver Samuel his head on a platter.

"We have an option to offer you, one that might be suitable for everyone." His father took a deep breath, and Samuel couldn't imagine what they'd come up with that would make everyone happy. "Gus's old cottage on Lizzie and Esther's property is vacant and in need of a renter. If this interests you, your *mamm* and I won't fight you on it."

Samuel's jaw dropped. Could this really be happening?

"If you choose to lease the cottage and go out on your own, then you would be"—his father narrowed his eyebrows—"truly out on your own."

This was too good to be true, even if it was his parents' own version of shunning. Would they even want to see him? The thought of not seeing them stung more than he would have expected, but it would give him the freedom he had been searching for.

"You would need to pay rent and buy and prepare your own food. You would be adhering to the Amish way of life by living in a place without luxury and no air conditioning. As for the choices you make concerning your future, it will be up to you to decide how much you will cross the lines we have established for our way of life. We will not control what you do or your choices but only pray that you make *gut* decisions. If you decide to visit other religious denominations, we ask that you still come to worship service and to keep the option of baptism into our faith open. If you choose to dress like the *Englisch* . . ." His father scowled. "We ask that you not wear such clothes to church or visits to our *haus*."

Not only did this sound way too good, it sounded perfect. Not like a shunning at all. He would still be able to go to worship and be welcome in his parents' home, but he would also have full control of his life. He envisioned Eden coming over for supper, them watching movies on television—the first rule he would break in this form of *rumschpringe* he was being offered—then kissing on the couch. He was struggling not to jump for joy, but he was also waiting for the catch.

"Samuel, does this sound acceptable to you?" his mother asked, her hands clasped together in front of her and hope in her eyes. They must have thought he was planning to venture far from home. Maybe he would have when he had enough money.

Money. He didn't have enough to pay a deposit on the cottage and first month's rent. He wondered if Lizzie and Esther would require a deposit. Maybe he could work off some of that and the rent by helping around their property. He would figure it out. Right now, he needed to jump on this proposal while he could.

"*Danki,*" he said. "I like this idea."

His father turned to his mother. "Anna, I will be outside."

Abraham followed his brother to the door, and Samuel heard him whisper, "I'm proud of you."

Samuel suspected his uncle had something to do with this wonderful outcome. He couldn't wait to tell Eden that as soon as he could, he would move into Gus's cottage, which he knew was furnished. They'd have a little over two weeks to spend together when Samuel wasn't working. If she didn't leave early to go to her mother's funeral. If so, would he ever see her again? The thought brought his high-on-life feeling down a few notches. He also wondered if his parents would be giving him a horse and buggy to get around. That was an important fact that he needed to know.

After Yvonne told Anna bye, she excused herself to go check on Eden.

"*Mamm*?" Samuel said.

She locked eyes with him, and his heart ached because of the moisture around her eyes and the dark circles under them. She'd obviously been crying.

"*Ya*?" she said softly.

Maybe he should have considered more how this would affect his parents, especially his mother.

"Am I going to be able to take *mei* horse and one of the buggies?"

"I'll have to confirm with your *daed*, but your horse is yours, so *mei* thoughts are that you should take the animal. But you know we share the buggies, and if you take one, it will leave Mae without a ride to run errands." She shook her head. "I'm sorry. You will have to save your money and buy a buggy."

Samuel had seen the price tags for a decent buggy. "How am I going to get to work?"

"Perhaps an *Englisch* coworker can pick you up? Otherwise, it's only a couple of miles, so it isn't impossible to walk."

"In August?" he said. "I'll be drenched by the time I get there."

"Leave early, before the sun rises." His mother smiled, but it wasn't the kind of genuine endearment that usually showed on her face. "I better go. Just assume you can take your horse if you don't hear otherwise from me." She eyed him long and hard. "Bye, *sohn*."

Samuel rubbed his chin as he weighed this new living arrangement. He'd need a cell phone, too, so he could talk to Eden after she left. The thought caused his stomach to roil, but he moved on to other plans swirling around in his mind. What about food? He didn't know how to cook.

He recalled the way his mother had told him goodbye, with such finality that it stung. But this truly was the best thing for all involved. He couldn't wait to tell Eden. Unless Yvonne already had.

On the way home, Anna told her husband about Samuel wanting to take the horse and buggy when he left.

"*Ya*, the horse is fine. The buggy, *nee*. We need that, and I don't see any reason to make this easy for him. If he wants to be a man at sixteen, then he will need to learn to take care of himself."

"He's getting close to seventeen."

Leroy shrugged. "Sixteen, seventeen . . . He's still a boy."

"There are boys and girls here who get married at that age. Not as many wed so young anymore, but this is different. Samuel is leaving us because he isn't sure if he wants to grow up the way you and I did, along with generations before us." She twisted the string of her prayer covering.

"I know how much this upsets you," Leroy said, sounding equally disturbed.

Anna pointed in front of her to the pothole that her husband managed to hit every time they made this trek.

"*Ya, danki*. I see it." He guided the horse around the dip in the pavement.

"I'm upset, *ya*, but I also don't think Samuel has thought this through. It was easy enough to see his elation when we mentioned living in the cottage, but I wonder if he's thought about a few things, like having to wash his own clothes. That boy has never run a piece of clothing through the wringer, and the only time I can recall him hanging clothes on the line or taking them down was when Grace and Mae both had the flu. Hannah was too little to help at the time, and I couldn't do it all."

She paused with more worrisome thoughts. "I wondered at first if Eden would ever spend the night there, but after thinking about it, I trust that Abraham and Yvonne would never allow that. I'm sure she will visit him at the cottage, though." She jerked her head in his direction. "If Lizzie and Esther see her visiting him, what will they think? Word will get around in the community."

"Those thoughts crossed *mei* mind at first, too, but I agree that Abraham and Yvonne will keep *gut* tabs on Eden. This is the lesser of all the evils, Anna. He stays close by, learns what it's like to really be a man out on his own, and the boy feels like he won. Hopefully he will see it as a triumph but still choose baptism. And we must keep in mind that Eden will be gone soon, probably sooner than planned. I would think the *maedel* will go home to attend her *mudder*'s funeral. If not, she'll only be here a couple more weeks."

Anna sighed. "Maybe he will decide to come back home after she leaves. This move might not be everything he perceives it to be. The newness will wear off. When he goes home to the cottage and doesn't have supper on the table or anyone to pack his lunch or wash his clothes . . ." Her voice became shaky. "He might reconsider."

"I'm not happy about this, either, but I guess Abe is right. It's better than him traveling far away."

Anna supposed her husband was right. "I wonder how much money Samuel has saved, if he even has enough to get settled."

"I guess we will see."

A part of Anna hoped he didn't, that this would be hard on him and that he would move back home where he belonged. Another part of her—the maternal part—would worry constantly if he was getting enough to eat.

She prayed the rest of the way home that she would be able to accept God's will, but that He would also guide Samuel's steps and not let him get too far off the path he was meant to be on.

Eden listened as Samuel detailed his plans to her. There was excitement in his voice when he first began talking, but she could see it dwindling by the time he'd talked through moving.

"It's a lot to think about," he said as he scratched his head.

"Yes, it is."

They were sitting on the couch when Yvonne came into the room. Abraham had left earlier to go to work.

"Jake called. He asked if I was well enough to come to the bookstore. I had already told him I was fine and could go in today, but he insisted I take the day off." She twisted her mouth. "It's probably just as well that I didn't go, considering recent events." Holding up a finger, she went on. "Anyway, he said he has something important to tell me, but I'm not leaving you two under this roof unsupervised. I know you would behave yourselves, but certain people would get on me for leaving you here alone. So, two choices—you can go with me to the bookstore or go on a walk or something."

"We can go to that little park not far away," Samuel said, and Eden nodded.

Yvonne put a hand on her hip. "While you're walking, you might consider where you're going to stay tonight, Samuel. Certain people would also be unhappy if we let you spend the night here again."

"Certain people meaning *mei* parents." Samuel stood. "I know, and I don't want to put you and *Onkel* Abe in a bad spot."

Yvonne looked at Eden. "Sweetheart, later today we probably need to talk about what you want to do about your mother's funeral. Do you want me to find out from Aunt Emma if she's heard any details?"

Eden didn't want to talk about this later today or ever. "Okay, thanks." She got up and the three of them left the house.

"Do you want me to drop you at the park?" Yvonne asked as she untethered her horse from the fencepost.

"No, thanks. We can walk. Okay with you?" she said, turning to Samuel.

"*Ya*, walking is *gut*."

Yvonne waved as she rode by in the buggy.

"I wish I could stay here forever." Eden had never felt more at home than she did with Abraham and Yvonne.

Samuel reached for her hand. "Then stay forever."

"I can't."

"Why?"

Eden thought about the reasons she couldn't remain in Indiana. "I have two more years of school, and Emma technically has custody of me. I'm probably expected to go to my mom's funeral in California. Is it terrible that I don't want to?"

"*Nee*. I think that's a personal choice. And like I said, there's no wrong answer." He paused. "I think *Englisch* funerals are different from ours. We celebrate the life that was lived more than we express grief over the loss, even though folks are still sad. We don't have flowers or decorative caskets. It's plain and simple."

They walked quietly hand in hand until the park came into view. Eden eyed the swings, the slide, and the merry-go-round. "I wish I could be five again and play on the playground. Those are the last happy memories I have of my mom before the drugs started."

When they reached the small park, they each sat in a swing. Eden grasped the chains on either side of her, lowered her head, and fought another onslaught of tears.

When she looked up, Samuel had a faraway look in his eyes.

Eden decided to refocus on his situation. She pulled a twisty from her wrist and tied her hair in a loose bun on top of her head. "Are you sure you want to move out on your own?"

"*Ya*. I'm nervous about it, but it's the only way for me to see what's out there, outside of our community. I don't mean distance but the way everyone who isn't Amish lives."

"If I go to my mom's funeral, I'm guessing I'll be leaving soon." Eden blinked back tears. "I know it's probably the right thing to do, but I wish I didn't have to go."

"Can you talk to Yvonne about it? She's a wise woman. I guess her and *Onkel* Abe are more worldly since they spent time living an *Englisch* life. I've talked to her about stuff before. Nothing big, but she's easy to confide in."

"And she's gentle and kind. She's going to be a great mom." Eden wished Yvonne was her mother—a terrible thought considering her mom had died only the night before.

Eden pushed with her feet until the swing got going, then she shut her eyes and let the breeze dry the tears forming in the corners of her eyes. "Yeah, I think I'll talk to Yvonne. She wants to talk later anyway. But maybe she can help me work through some things too."

Samuel nodded, set his swing into motion, and Eden pictured herself at five years old, even managing a slight smile. They swung in silence for a while. They both had a lot to think about.

CHAPTER 21

Jake was sitting behind the counter when Yvonne walked into the bookstore, the bell jingling behind her. "Hey, that's *mei* spot." She winked at her good friend. "Do you want me to take over from here?"

"*Nee*, I had planned to be here all day, and I'm sorry I asked you to come in, but like I said on the phone, I have something to tell you."

She knew Jake pretty well, but his expression wasn't giving away much.

He continued. "Eva wanted to come so badly since she hadn't seen you in a while, but she had a quilting party to go to."

Yvonne had opted out of the event just this morning since Samuel was there. At the mention of Eva, she put a hand to her chest, deciding the news must be good. "Aw, Eva's pregnant again? We will be expecting at the same time."

Jake shook his head. "*Nee, nee*. As much as we'd like that to be true, we aren't expecting another child."

Yvonne laid her purse on the counter. "So, then . . . What's going on?"

Jake glanced around the bookstore. "This place has needed an overhaul for years. The slab needs to be leveled, it needs a new roof, and I think there's mold growing in the basement. And that's just to name a few things in need of repair."

Yvonne stuffed her hands into the pockets of her black apron, still wondering what was so important that he insisted on talking to her in person. "I thought you didn't have the money to do those repairs."

"I don't. We're going to gut this place, find those coins, and make all the repairs."

Yvonne's mouth dropped open. "You said you would never do that, even after we found the one coin from whatever collection is supposedly buried in the walls or beneath the floor. What if the one we found stuck in the floorboard is the only coin we ever find?"

Jake held up the little white bag and dumped the coin Yvonne and Abraham had found in the floorboards. "I got a second opinion. Remember, I told you?"

"Yeah, I remember." She rolled her eyes. "When I thought Eden misplaced that one."

"The appraiser who gave the second opinion verified that the coin is worth around five hundred dollars."

"Jake, it would thrill me to no end to be able to go on a hunt for that collection. But you said it was a rumor, that there was no way to know if the old man who ran the general store in this building was telling the truth. You, and others, said he was *ab im kopp*." She paused, tipped her head to one side. "Not to state the obvious, but what if you tear this place apart and never find the coins? What if there are no more and it was a fluke that Abraham and I found that one lone piece?"

He stood up and reached under the counter to the shelf where Yvonne always stowed her purse. When he pulled his hand back, he dropped three more coins beside the white bag.

Yvonne gasped and brought a hand to her mouth. "That's four now." She gingerly picked up one. "Are these worth five hundred dollars like the other ones?"

"*Ya*, they're dated around the same time, so they must be." He shrugged.

Money had never been important to Jake, only his lack thereof because he couldn't make the repairs on the building. He was fearful he wouldn't be able to keep his grandfather's memory alive if he had to close the bookstore that had been left to him. Now that the possibility was upon them, Yvonne was fearful they'd tear out all the walls, not find any coins, and there wouldn't be a bookstore to keep his grandfather's legacy.

Yvonne thought for a few moments. "I don't want to kill your excitement, but back to *mei* original concern. What if you don't find the rest of the coins? If those are worth five hundred each, that's two thousand dollars. That won't rebuild the floor, put a roof on the place, or get the mold out of walls you'd have to tear down."

"The appraiser did some investigating. Apparently, those in the business of rare coins have heard the rumor for decades—that a coin collection of significant value was hidden somewhere in this area—but they'd never heard that it might be here. So, it doesn't sound like the ramblings of an *ab im kopp* man after all. Especially since we now have four coins."

Yvonne's should-be excitement was being gobbled up by worry. "I've always been intrigued about those coins and the story. I used to be a book broker, remember? I love searching for old and rare objects. But this just sounds so . . . risky." It wasn't like Jake to make such a huge decision based on a possibility. He was usually more calculated than that. "Where did you find these other three?" Yvonne picked up another one of the coins and brought it as close as she could to her face without losing focus. "The markings are similar. Wow."

"In the basement when I dug into one of the walls checking for mold. I assumed if the rumor was true, the coins would be in a box somewhere, not spread out all over the place. So, it might be a treasure hunt, but the treasure might be everywhere." He frowned, which confused Yvonne even more.

She glanced around the beloved bookstore that had become a second home to her. She pictured it with walls torn down, a big mess, and no money to make the repairs. "I don't know, Jake . . ." Glancing around again, she noticed that something didn't feel right.

"I don't have a choice." Jake took off his straw hat and set it on the counter, then ran a hand through his hair. "I knew we had some mold in the basement, in addition to the other repairs needed. But I also saw some bugs that looked like flying ants in several places too."

"Oh, *nee*. Termites?" Yvonne bit her bottom lip. She knew how expensive it could be to treat termites.

Jake nodded. "*Ya*. And between the mold, the termites, and the other things that need to be fixed, we could lose our historical plaque they awarded us. And, even worse, they could eventually condemn this place."

Yvonne loved the way Jake always said "us" when referring to the bookstore. If she had the money to help him, she would hand it over. "So, you treat the termites and get rid of the mold. Then slowly make the other repairs."

He was shaking his head before she even finished talking. "I had a couple of inspectors come out after hours. I didn't want to worry you until I knew for sure what was going to happen. The termites are bad, worse than I thought. And if it was just that, we could probably treat them. But the mold is in a lot more places than the basement, and it's unhealthy for us and customers." He smiled a little. "These walls have to come down. And I'll be praying like crazy that *Gott* sees fit to show us this treasure trove of coins to pay for the reconstruction."

"He will. I know it." Yvonne didn't hesitate. Even though the risk scared her, she would choose to be optimistic. "We will look at it like a big adventure." She smiled broadly, hoping to cheer up her friend.

He chuckled. "I guess it might be exciting in a scary sort of way." He rolled his eyes, but at least his demeanor seemed a little lighter.

Her phone rang in her purse. When she retrieved it and looked at the screen, she said, "I need to take this. It's *mei* aunt."

"You do that, and I'm going to gather up the trash in the back so I can haul it off today."

"How's Eden?" Aunt Emma asked when Yvonne answered.

"I'm not sure, to be honest. I think she's okay, but Jill died right in front of her while they were on a video call. At first, she didn't want to see or talk to her mother, but I think it wore on her for hours, and she made the call late last night. It was awful."

"Well, I wish I had better news. It appears that her immediate family—if you want to call them that—either don't have or aren't willing to cough up the money for a funeral. I think Jill probably hurt or angered just about everyone who loved her at one time or another."

"What happens in a situation like that?"

"I'm not going to let a member of my family, however distant and messed up she was, have a pauper's funeral. I'm going to pay to have her cremated. Apparently, that's what she wanted. As for any type of a life celebration, I don't think there's going to be one."

"That's sad for anyone to leave this world without a proper send-off." Yvonne knew better than to take the conversation any further. She loved her aunt, but their religious views were miles apart.

"Can you let Eden know, or do you want me to do it?"

"*Nee*—I mean, no—I'll do it. We've gotten kind of close since she's been here."

"I knew you'd be a good influence on her. You will be a wonderful mother someday, and I can't wait to smother a little one with love."

Yvonne was quiet but decided she couldn't hold her tongue any longer. "Well, you're not going to have to wait too long." She broke out in a smile. "Only around seven more months."

There was a gasp on the other end of the phone. "Are you really . . . ?"

"Yes, I'm pregnant."

"Oh, darling! Wonderful news. I can't wait to share it with my traveling companions. That's okay, isn't it?"

"Of course." Yvonne didn't know any of the women. Soon word would get out that she was expecting, and she was excited to share her joy with others in their community.

"I better go. My friends are waiting for me nearby, but I wanted to check on Eden. Please keep me posted. And congratulations, Yvonne! I'm so happy for you and Abraham."

"Thank you."

Jake came around the corner just as Yvonne and her aunt ended the call.

"You can get back to your family," Jake said as he went behind the counter and put the coins in his pocket. "I just wanted to tell you *mei* plans in person and show you what I'd found."

"It's all going to work out." Yvonne was tempted to tell Jake that Samuel would be moving into the cottage on Lizzie and Esther's property, but it probably wasn't her place to spread that news. "Is it a secret? I mean, should I not say anything to anyone?"

"Maybe keep it between me and Eva and you and Abraham for now." He shrugged. "I know you're close to Leroy and Anna, so it's okay if they know. How much longer is Eden here for?"

Yvonne hoped Eden and Samuel were having a decent

time. They both had a lot on their plates. "A little over two more weeks. Her *mudder* died last night while Eden was on a video call with her."

"What?" Jake shook his head. "That's terrible."

"*Ya*, I know. She and her mother weren't close at all, but she still took it hard. I don't think there is going to be any type of funeral or celebration of life, either, which is also terrible, in *mei* opinion." She waved a dismissive hand. "Anyway, you're right. I should probably get back to Eden. I think she'll probably come into the store with me tomorrow."

"Eva and I are just glad you and the *boppli* are okay."

Yvonne laid a hand across her stomach. "We are both fine, and *danki*." Smiling, she said, "Give Eva *mei lieb*." She started toward the door but turned around and pointed a finger at Jake. "It's all going to be fine, Jake."

He barely smiled.

Eden's lips were swollen from all the kissing she and Samuel had done throughout the day. She loved how she didn't have to worry about roaming hands with Samuel. It wasn't his style to cross any boundaries, and even though they hadn't verbally set any, he seemed to understand lines were in place.

The undertone was that Eden could be leaving anytime to attend her mother's funeral, if she chose to do so. Fear of guilt was pushing her to attend, and that would mean goodbye soon.

By the time they had walked back to Yvonne and

Abraham's house, they were both sweaty and tired from lack of sleep the night before. Samuel had started yawning on the way home. Yvonne's buggy was in the driveway. In case she could see them, they shared only a quick peck.

"I'm back at work tomorrow, but I'll find a way to stop by the bookstore or meet you somewhere when I get off. I need to talk to Lizzie and Esther, make sure the cottage is still available, and find out how much the rent is."

Eden leaned down and clawed at her legs. She'd been fighting the urge to scratch most of the day, but it was becoming unbearable. "I think I have bites or something."

Samuel's expression turned solemn. "Turkey mites. I think I have them too. It's from when we went to the cave yesterday. It takes a day or so before they really start to itch. I saw some bumps this morning, and I put a salve *mei mamm* makes on them. I was hoping maybe you didn't get any bites. Tell Yvonne. Everyone around here makes something that helps with the itch."

"Ick. Just the name—turkey mites—makes me itch."

"I better go." He brushed his lips softly against hers one last time. "Remember, whatever decision you make about going to your *mamm*'s funeral is the right one. Follow your heart."

"I will."

Eden trudged toward the house, reaching down to claw at her legs along the way. She always looked forward to being around Yvonne—her cousin had a calming effect on her—but she dreaded the conversation they were going to have. If Yvonne pushed her to go to the funeral, Eden would probably go if for no other reason than guilt.

She found Yvonne in the kitchen.

"How was the park?" Yvonne slid a loaf of bread into the oven.

Eden would miss homemade bread fresh from the oven, best with butter slathered on it. "It was okay. Samuel has a lot on his mind, about moving and everything."

"I'm sure you have a lot on your mind too."

Eden pulled out a kitchen chair and sat. "Yeah, I do." She leaned back in the chair, her mind swirling with confusion and, surprisingly, a fair amount of grief. It was weird not to have a mother. "I guess I need to go to my mom's funeral, don't I? To be honest, I really don't want to, and I think that makes me a terrible person."

Yvonne sat across from her at the small kitchen table that Eden would miss when she left. "One thing I've learned since I've gotten to know you in the short time you've been here is that you are not a terrible person. I see a loving young woman who beat the odds and chose to live differently than the way she was raised. As for your mother's funeral, there isn't going to be one."

Eden stared across the table at her. "I thought everyone had a funeral or a celebration of life." Then it hit her. "Is it because there's no money for that?"

"Maybe partly, but I talked to Aunt Emma today, and she is going to pay for your mom's cremation. That's what Jill wanted."

"So, I don't have to go to a funeral?" Eden was relieved she didn't have to make a choice whether to go or not, but then her heart sank a little. "Shouldn't everyone have some sort of funeral?"

Yvonne shrugged. "Not everyone does. Sometimes people share the ashes and pay their respects in different ways. Maybe you and Aunt Emma can discuss it when you get home—how you might want to honor your mother."

"Then I don't have to leave yet, right?"

"*Nee.*" Yvonne smiled. "You're stuck with us a bit longer."

Eden once again wished she was stuck with them forever.

"I have some news that might take your mind off of things." Yvonne remembered she was going to stay optimistic about the bookstore renovations. "Jake found three more of those old coins, and he semiconfirmed the rumor that there are more hidden somewhere in the bookstore. He's decided to make some long-overdue repairs based on the assumption that during the renovations he'll find more coins to be able to pay for the repairs."

"What if he doesn't find any more?"

"That's what I said. And it is a huge risk, but it has become a necessary one." Yvonne detailed the other repairs and the news about the mold and termites. "It's crazy how he randomly found the other coins in a basement wall. It makes you wonder if the old man just stashed them here and there throughout the building. All we can do is hope and pray that he finds enough of them to cover the renovations."

"Wow." Eden shook her head. "That's exciting. And scary, I guess. I wish I could be involved in that search, though."

"Jake said he's going to start working on the teardown soon. I'm not sure what 'soon' means, exactly, but you might get to do a little treasure hunting with us."

"That would be so cool." Eden allowed herself to picture everyone ripping out walls like a real treasure hunt. "But I'll be praying, too, that Jake finds enough coins."

"On another note, how's Samuel?" Yvonne reached for a cookie on a platter. "I bought these at Walmart. Don't tell anyone."

Eden grinned. "I won't."

Yvonne's past life as a non-Amish person shone through sometimes. Eden thought it was the perfect mix of lifestyle and personality. Her cousin had seen the world and chosen her life, unlike Eden, whose life had been chosen for her.

"I think Samuel is happy to be moving out but also having mixed feelings. He hasn't been at his job for very long. I don't think he's saved much money."

"It will be a big adjustment for him. Maybe when he has a taste of non-Amish living, he will choose his religious roots. Abraham has always thought Leroy and Anna were too strict with their children, long before I came along and noticed it too. I think him renting the cottage is a good compromise for all of them."

Eden wasn't sure about that. Samuel's excitement had seemed to cloud as the day went on. "Maybe so," she said as she reached for a Walmart cookie and took a bite. "Yours are better."

"*Ya*, they are, aren't they?"

They both chuckled. At least Eden had two and a half more weeks to relish in this lifestyle, sharing her time with Yvonne and Abraham. And Samuel.

Samuel walked into the cottage after work. He was soaked in sweat, tired, and had no idea what he would eat for supper. As he had expected, walking to and from work was exhausting, and the August heat had arrived. Over the past week, he'd only seen Eden twice. He'd thought that when he had the cottage, they could spend more time together. But as he eyed dirty dishes in the sink and stepped over a pile of dirty clothes in the living room, he wondered how he was going to keep up with things. He intentionally hadn't invited Eden over and had made an excuse every time she suggested riding her bike to visit him. Instead, he had met her somewhere else.

It was a small cottage—just a space that included the living room with a bar separating it from the kitchen, a small bathroom, and one tiny bedroom. That was all okay. He didn't need anything fancy. But he couldn't keep up with the chores that went with living on his own, especially since he worked all day. People did it all the time, though. Surely, he'd fall in sync with his new lifestyle.

Then he remembered he needed to mow the lawn around the cottage, the other guesthouse, and the Peony Inn before dark. As he'd feared, he hadn't had enough money for the first month's rent—not even half of the amount needed. The mowing, along with a few repairs to the fence surrounding the bed-and-breakfast, was to make up for the shortage.

He hadn't seen his parents since he moved out, nor had he taken advantage of any of the freedoms he'd dreamed of. His horse was still at home. He couldn't afford to go to a movie or even take Eden out to eat. As badly as he wanted a cell phone to communicate with her, that expense was far down on his list of necessities, way below food.

His mouth watered when he thought about his mother's meatloaf, chicken and dumplings, and the baked goods that were always out on the counter. Samuel had chosen foods that came in a box, things he could easily heat up in the propane oven, meals blander than anything he'd ever had and with a funky aftertaste.

He was trying to stay optimistic that things would come together, and he was trying to keep fear and worry out of his mind since he knew it blocked the voice of God. Despite his prayers, he wasn't sure if he had done the right thing. This wasn't how he'd envisioned life on his own. There was no time for Eden. He didn't have any money to speak of. And he was exhausted.

Where are you, Gott?

Anna eyed the empty chair at the kitchen table with a heavy heart. Was her son getting enough to eat? Would he remember to drink lots of water when he walked back and forth to work? Did he have clean clothes? How serious was he getting with Eden, and did it matter since she would be leaving soon?

"Maybe I should pay Samuel a visit," she said to Leroy as

she cleaned the supper dishes, having excused the girls from helping so she could talk to her husband. "I'm surprised he hasn't stopped by or come to get his horse. It's close enough to come get the animal and ride to the cottage. Lizzie and Esther have a pasture on the other side of their pond."

"*Ach*, he's probably living it up, doing all the things we wouldn't allow him to do under our roof." Leroy frowned before he took his hat from the rack, then kissed her. "I'm sure he is fine. I'm going to feed the cows and check their water. I repaired the leak in the trough. It wasn't as bad as I thought it would be. Hopefully it held."

Anna dried her hands and leaned against the kitchen counter, alone with her thoughts. A mother knew when something wasn't right with her child, and the feeling that something was wrong niggled at her to the point she hadn't been able to eat much of her supper.

Maybe Leroy was right that Samuel didn't miss them and was busy with his new life. Anna wished they had given their son more freedom. Now that he was on his own, they had no idea what he was doing, and Anna stayed in a state of worry. She wished they hadn't agreed to this move, but at the time it had seemed like the lesser of the evils, as her husband had pointed out. Otherwise, Samuel might have moved far away, maybe even to Texas so he could be close to Eden.

By the time she went to bed, she had envisioned every worst-case scenario possible. She couldn't fathom Samuel spending the night with Eden since he wasn't married. Leroy was right about that. But were they spending intimate time together alone at the cottage? Were they making plans to see each other after she left? Would he consider going to Texas?

Leroy was snoring, but Anna lay awake for a long time worrying about her son.

Eden walked into the kitchen Saturday morning much later than usual. She'd tossed and turned all night long.

"I saved you a plate." Yvonne pointed to a covered dish on the counter filled with eggs, bacon, biscuits, and fruit. "You must have been tired since you slept so late."

"I couldn't get to sleep. It was after midnight before I finally dozed off." She uncovered the plate and took it to the table. "Thank you for saving me some breakfast."

"*Ya*, sure. You're welcome." Yvonne joined her at the kitchen table. "So, what kept you up last night?"

Eden wasn't sure how much to say to Yvonne, but she didn't have anyone else to talk to. "I was thinking about my mom, and I was wondering about Samuel. He only came into the bookstore once, and another time I met him at that little café not far from here. I thought he would want to spend more time with me now that he's out on his own. I thought he would have bought a phone, but I don't think he can afford it."

"I wonder what's going on. Maybe he realizes that you'll be leaving in a week and he's putting some distance between you so the sting of you going back to Texas doesn't hurt so much."

Eden finished nibbling on the piece of bacon in her

hand. "Maybe." She didn't buy it. "I was thinking I might ride the bike to the cottage to see what's up. Sometimes he works part of the day on Saturday, so I'll go later."

Yvonne nodded. "I can't believe you only have a week left before you head home. The time has flown by."

"I'm probably going to miss the bookstore renovation since Jake hasn't started it yet. That's going to be so exciting, like searching for buried treasure. But I know there is also a lot at stake."

"*Ya*, there is. Keep those prayers flowing after you've gone. I'll keep you posted." Yvonne paused, smiling. "We've really enjoyed having you here. Maybe you'll come back to visit?"

"I hope so. I love it here. And there's been so much going on, I only got to ride a horse once."

"I know. We'll make sure you have more horse time on your next visit." Yvonne stood, then motioned with her hand. "Follow me. I want to show you something."

Eden walked down the hall behind Yvonne, past her bedroom and to a third room Eden had never been in since the door had always been shut. When Yvonne opened it, she had to give an extra push, like the door was hitting something behind it.

"It's a horrible mess in here. Someday, I hope to convince Abraham that some of this stuff needs to go." She pointed to the back of the room. "He hasn't used that workout bench for as long as I've known him. You can't even get to it because of all the boxes everywhere. I know some of this stuff is important to him, but hopefully we can eventually relocate some of it to the basement."

There was a narrow pathway into the small room. Boxes lined the wall and were even stacked on top of the workout bench. Yvonne went to the left of the room, and Eden saw what Yvonne wanted to show her.

"I know it's too early to be buying things for the *boppli*'s room, but when I saw this on sale, I couldn't resist." She stepped all the way to the side so Eden could have a better look at the picture of the crib on the outside of the box.

"It's nothing fancy." Yvonne smiled, then winked at Eden. "Since we don't do fancy. I always envisioned a white crib, but since we painted all the walls white—kind of standard in Amish households—a white crib and furniture would have made the room look too sterile, I think. I love this dark mahogany." She picked up a colored printout that sat on top of the box. "And this is the changing table I'd like to get, along with that matching dresser. A lot of homes don't have dressers, but it was my concession for not having white furniture." She handed the paper to Eden and moved to her right, then reached into a plastic storage container and lifted a beautiful baby blanket with delicate yellow flowers and white lace trim. "What do you think? I'm not very far into the process, and like I said, it's probably too soon to be planning all this."

She lowered the blanket onto the nearest pile of boxes and put a hand on her stomach. Eden thought she was probably thinking about the scare she'd had recently.

"I think everything you have chosen is beautiful." She eyed the massive mess in the room. "This is a lot to clean up, and you can't lift all these boxes and get them to the basement. Abraham will have to relocate these things."

Yvonne shook her head. "It won't happen anytime soon, and I'm not going to push him on it. He needs to go through a lot of these boxes and hopefully get rid of some things. But I am going to have him move the furniture in your bedroom to the basement. I'll set up the nursery in there."

Eden's heart sank as she wondered where she would sleep when she came to visit. Yvonne was all wrapped up in baby stuff and must not have thought about that. She'd said she hoped Eden would visit.

"But don't worry," Yvonne said as she made her way back along the narrow path and out to the hallway. She waited until Eden had crossed the threshold before she closed the door. "If you come to visit—and you better—I'll have a twin bed put in the nursery for you to sleep on if Abraham hasn't cleaned out the back room yet."

Eden felt a small level of relief, but she was losing what she'd considered to be her bedroom—although it would be cool to get to sleep in the baby's room when she did come to visit. She had two more years of school and no money, so she wasn't sure when that would happen. Maybe during the summers. She couldn't ask Emma to fly her back and forth because she loved it here so much. She'd get a job and save her money. Whatever it took to be a part of the only place that had ever felt like home.

Eden waited until after lunch before she told Yvonne that she was going to ride her bike to Samuel's cottage.

"Take a bottle of water. It's hot outside." Yvonne

walked to the refrigerator that they powered with propane and handed Eden a bottle.

"Thanks." She opened it and took a big gulp.

"I hope your visit goes well. You only have a week left here. I'm sure that must be weighing on both your minds since you've become friends."

It was weighing on Eden's mind, but she wasn't sure how much her leaving was on Samuel's mind since he'd made little effort to spend time with her.

"Yeah, goodbyes are hard." She thought about having to say bye to Yvonne and Abraham too. "But I have this last week." Her heart ached, and she wanted to make the best of her time here, but she had to know what was going on with Samuel. "I'll see you later."

"Have fun. Be careful."

You're going to be such a great mom, Eden thought as she walked through the living room, then made her way to the bike. She placed her water in the big basket on the front of the bike, then headed toward the Peony Inn Bed-and-Breakfast with a nervous stomach.

She had no way to know if Samuel was there since he wouldn't have a buggy parked outside the cottage. He'd told her he was walking back and forth to work. She'd asked him during their last visit if he wanted to use her bike, but he had declined, probably embarrassed to ride a bicycle that looked like it belonged to a twelve-year-old girl.

After she parked the bike, she tiptoed up the porch steps and saw movement inside through the window. She knocked on the door, and after heavy footsteps came closer, Samuel opened the door.

His mouth fell open as his eyes widened. "Eden. What are you doing here?" He stepped onto the porch and hurriedly closed the door behind him.

She wasn't sure whether to be hurt, angry, or both. "Do you have company?"

"*Nee*," he said as he shook his head. His blond hair was tousled, like maybe he'd just gotten up even though it was early afternoon. But she'd seen movement, which meant he hadn't been sleeping. He wore his usual black slacks and a dark-blue short-sleeved shirt that was untucked, and he was barefoot.

She put a hand on her hip. "Did I do something wrong?"

"*Nee.*" His forehead crinkled. "Why would you ask that?"

She had one week left and nothing to lose—but Samuel—if she wasn't honest. "I feel like you've been avoiding me, and we've only seen each other twice the past week. Samuel, I know I'm not your girlfriend, but we've sort of fallen into some sort of relationship that surpasses just friends."

He looked down at his bare feet and didn't say anything.

"I just don't understand why you haven't invited me over to see your new place and why it seems like you aren't eager to spend time with me. I leave in a week. If you're not comfortable being alone with me in the cottage, just tell me that, and we can sit on the porch, take a walk, or whatever." Her voice began to crack.

"*Nee, nee.*" He stepped closer and pulled her into a hug. "I'm sorry."

She eased away, her bottom lip trembling. "Then what is it?"

There were two small chairs on either side of a little table on the porch.

"Let's sit down." He sat and waited for her to do so as she wondered why he wasn't inviting her in. She'd been right that he wasn't comfortable being alone with her in his little house.

"It's okay if you don't want us to be alone. I know that's how you were raised, and I respect that. But I can't help but wonder if there's more."

He put his elbows on his knees, folded his hands together, and rested his head there. After he inhaled deeply and blew out a long breath, he said, "Eden, all I've thought about is sitting on *mei* couch and hanging out with you. I'd never take things further because you're right—I believe a person should be married for that type of intimacy." He grinned a little. "Even though I think about it." He shrugged. "I'm a guy. But I'd never disrespect you that way. And you have no idea how much I've missed you, how much I want to spend time with you, and how much I'm aware that you leave in a week. Honestly, that thought rips at *mei* insides. I care about you a lot, in case you haven't figured that out."

Even though she was relieved, she raised her shoulders at the same time she lifted her palms. "Then what is it? Why haven't you tried to spend more time with me? I know you wouldn't try to take things further. I just don't understand." She sounded whiny, and that hadn't been her intent.

"I considered lying to you and telling you that I was giving you time to grieve your *mudder*, but I don't ever feel *gut* about lying, and I definitely don't want to lie to you." He raised his arms from his knees, then slumped into the chair, rubbing a hand through his messy hair, which only made it stand on end and look worse. Although it did nothing to deter from his amazing good looks. He locked eyes with her. "The truth is I don't have any money. I can't take you to a movie or out to eat or—"

"I don't care about that, Samuel. I just want to be with you."

"I didn't have enough money for rent, so I'm doing some work for Lizzie and Esther to make up for being short. They've been great about it, but it hasn't left me much time. And the reason I don't want you coming in the cottage is because I'm embarrassed. By the time I walk home from work, I'm stinky and need a shower. I don't have any way to wash *mei* clothes, nor do I know how to. I've watched *mei mamm* and *schweschdere* using the wringer, but it's still foreign to me. Laundry isn't something *mei daed* or me have ever done."

He pointed over his shoulder. "The sink is filled with dishes because I haven't had time to clean them. I don't want you to see how I'm living right now." He grinned when she did. "And I'm starving. You can get just about any kind of food in a box, and it's all bad."

Eden's heart warmed as she began to shed her worries. She walked to him, squatted down in front of him, and reached for his hand. "Samuel, you don't have to be embarrassed about anything. I know we haven't known each other that long, but I care about you too. I hope we can stay in touch after I leave and that I'll be able to come back and visit." She thought about losing her bedroom she'd grown to love, despite the heat, but she was happy Yvonne had mentioned her visiting and making a place for her. "Now let's get your new home cleaned up."

"Really?" He raised his eyebrows. "But I don't want you to do that. It's not how I pictured it in *mei* mind. I wanted everything to be clean, to cook for you, and make it nice."

"Well . . ." She grinned. "That hasn't really worked out, has it? Let's move on to plan B."

"*Ach* . . ." Shaking his head, he slowly lifted himself from the chair.

He waited until they were inside before he kissed her the way she'd been longing for. She couldn't imagine them staying just friends, but geography was going to make it impossible to be anything else.

After they'd made up for lost time, Eden looked around the cottage. She could see the kitchen and living room from where she stood. "Oh, my." There were dishes on the counter and piled in the sink, glasses on the coffee table, a large pile of clothes near what she assumed must be the bedroom, and the heat was stifling.

"I told you." Samuel hung his head.

"Do you even have all the windows open?" She looked around and quickly walked to one window that she could see was closed. After she lifted it up, she turned to him and playfully scowled. "You have no idea what you're doing, do you? But I would have thought you knew plenty about creating cross breezes."

He shrugged. "It's a *gut* thing you showed up."

"It really is."

They both laughed but found time for another embrace and a quick kiss.

It was two o'clock on Saturday when Anna decided she couldn't stand it any longer. "I'm going to go check on Samuel." She lifted her chin, her black purse dangling from her arm, almost daring Leroy to argue.

He eyed her curiously for a moment. "Do you want me to go with you?"

She wagged her head. "*Nee*. But I'm not getting much sleep since I worry if our *sohn* is getting enough to eat and doing all right."

"He's not a *boppli*, Anna. I'm sure he is okay."

"You don't know that." She picked up a pair of sunglasses from the end table. "I will be back soon."

After she blew him a kiss, she rushed down the porch steps before he could say anything else to deter her visit.

When she arrived at the Peony Inn, she decided to go say hello to Esther and Lizzie and thank them for renting the cottage to her son.

"*Wie bischt*, Anna." Esther pushed the screen door open and stepped aside.

"I can't stay. I'm on *mei* way to visit Samuel, but I wanted to thank you for renting him the cottage. I know he's a bit young to be a tenant, but he was craving some independence, and we agreed to this as part of his *rumschpringe*. I hope he is behaving himself." Smiling, she wasn't expecting the frown that filled Esther's face.

"I feel terrible for the boy. When he didn't have enough money for the rent and deposit, we waived the deposit, but he was still short. We told him that was all right, that he could pay us what he could afford. He was insistent that he work off the difference." She looked past Anna toward the cottage. "He walks to work and walks home, then he does chores around here until almost dark. I don't know when he finds time to cook and eat."

Anna had always prided herself on being a good mother, but she could feel humiliation creeping up her neck and causing her cheeks to turn pink. She didn't think Esther meant to sound accusatory about her role as a mother, but even to Anna, it sounded like bad parenting—allowing her son to rent a cottage that he didn't have money for at his age. Esther was probably wondering why Anna hadn't been by sooner.

"Lizzie took him a pie about an hour ago. There was a young *maedel* there scrubbing his floor when Lizzie arrived. She saw her through the window before she knocked. Normally, we would be suspicious of an outsider visiting a young man his age, but Lizzie said the girl was a relative of Yvonne's." Esther paused, grinning. "Lizzie said the *maedel* was delightful and that it was easy to tell that the two young people are smitten with each other"—she paused again when Anna's jaw dropped—"even though there was nothing affectionate going on. Just cleaning."

Anna wanted to beg Esther not to encourage anything between Samuel and Eden. Everyone in the community knew that the two elderly sisters tried to play matchmaker anytime they saw the hint of a spark between two people.

"*Ya*, they are friends. How nice of her to help him. I'm wondering . . ." She cleared her throat. "Does she visit often?"

"*Nee*. We haven't seen her there before. But, of course, we aren't home all the time."

"I best go and visit him. Nice to see you, Esther." She pointed over her shoulder. "I'll just leave *mei* horse and buggy tethered to your fence while I walk over there, if that's okay?"

"*Ya, ya*. Of course."

Anna crossed the field between the Peony Inn and the cottage. There was another house on the property, but Anna didn't see any activity. The only activity going on was between her son and Eden, who was supposedly there to help Samuel clean the house—clearly an excuse for them to spend time together.

She tried to let that fact overshadow her guilt for not knowing what a hard time her son was having in his new home. Tough love and insisting Samuel be a man and make it on his own had been a mistake. It wasn't going to make him come home. All they'd done was provide a little love shack for him and Eden, even if only temporarily until the girl went back to Texas.

Anna picked up the pace, but when she reached the house, she didn't go up the porch steps. She tiptoed around the side of the house to where she heard voices. Voices coming from the bedroom. Her heart raced as she planted her back flat against the siding and listened.

"No, not like that," she heard Eden say. "Haven't you ever made a bed? You tuck the corners in like this."

"*Ya*, I've made a bed before." Samuel chuckled.

Anna stiffened and wanted to put her face to the screen and say, *"Samuel, when have you ever made a bed in your life?"* but she stayed quiet. Guilt wasn't going to pry her from this spot. She'd just caught her unmarried son with an English girl in his bedroom. If there was any hanky-panky going on, Anna was sure she couldn't stop herself from storming the place.

"I don't know why you don't just go home," Eden said. "I know you want to be independent and do things outside of your community, but I've told you before, the outside world isn't what it's cracked up to be. You have a loving family, wonderful parents, and your mother cooks for you, cleans your clothes, and takes care of her family. That's the way a family unit is supposed to work. Or so I'm told. I haven't ever had that until my visit here. Emma is great, but she has her own friends and a life. And, as I told you, she's older. We just don't have a lot in common. With Yvonne and Abraham, it feels like a real family. They kind of treat me like an adult, but they also keep me grounded too. It makes me not want to do anything to disappoint them. I'd do anything to stay here forever."

"Then stay," Samuel said in a smooth voice that raised Anna's antenna.

"I can't. I'll go back to school soon. And I've thought a lot about my mom. No matter how awful she was at being a parent, I want to get at least some of her ashes and, in my own way, do something for her. I have no idea what, but I feel like something should be done. She lived a life, and if I think back really far, there was a time when she cared for me the way a mother should."

"I wish you could stay, but I understand. Part of me wants to go home, but *mei* parents are just too strict. I'd end up running away or something eventually."

Anna cringed, thinking again about the parenting mistakes they'd made all around.

"Then I'll trade places with you," Eden said. "You go to Texas and deal with all the chaos, and I'll move in with your family, work at the bookstore, and pretend your parents are mine. Although . . ." She paused. "There is a flaw in that plan because your mother doesn't like me."

"*Nee*, it's not that. She just sees you as a threat, the wild *Englisch maedel* who is going to whisk me away into a life of sin."

Anna was taking mental notes of all the changes she would make when her girls each turned sixteen. Maybe you were expected to mess up with your oldest child, then learn and do better with the others.

"What I want is for you to be happy. I'm leaving in a week. Are you going to be happy here when I'm gone? I know you envisioned us spending time together here, but it really doesn't look good for you to have an unmarried girl at your house. What will those two older ladies who run the inn think? What would other people think? Believe me, people make judgments based on rumors or without really knowing a person. I believe you and respect you for not wanting things to get physical with us, for believing stuff like that should be reserved for marriage. I feel the same way. But other people won't know that. And they won't know that when I saw the state of this cottage on my very first visit today, I knew you needed some help." She laughed. "Not only can't you cook or wash clothes, but I'm also not sure you would have ever gotten this bed made correctly."

"*Gut* thing Lizzie brought me that pie." Samuel chuckled. "It might be *mei* supper tonight."

Anna bolted around the corner and up the porch steps as adrenaline flushed out her tainted system. Surely there was a better mother inside her somewhere.

"Samuel, it's *Mamm*," she said through the screen as she rapped.

Both teenagers came out of the bedroom together with stricken expressions on their faces.

"*Mamm*, this isn't what you think," Samuel said with wide eyes.

Anna pointed to the cleaning bucket filled with supplies and the sweeper nearby. "What it looks like to me is that Eden is helping you tidy up this place." She smiled at her. "Hello, Eden."

The poor girl looked as scared as her son and sounded even worse when she barely squeaked out a hello.

"It looks like you could use another hand." Anna walked to the sweeper and picked it up. "If it's all right, I'd like to help, then take you out to supper." Smiling wider, she said, "Both of you."

The children exchanged glances, confusion on their faces.

"I thought maybe we could enjoy a meal together, then

discuss a few things, ways we can make this situation work and run more smoothly for all of us."

Samuel frowned as if Anna had underlying intentions. But Anna was going to make things right. For all of them.

CHAPTER 23

Yvonne had their driver stop at the bookstore on the way to take Eden to the airport. Her young cousin wanted to tell Jake goodbye, and Jake had already planned to meet an architect there to discuss renovations on the building. Since it was a historic building, he wanted to use care when they started the teardown, especially since he'd be doing it himself, along with Yvonne's help, and probably some others in the community. Word would spread.

Jake appeared to excuse himself when the bell jingled and Eden and Yvonne walked in, leaving two men near the gift aisle.

He hugged Eden. "I can't believe a month is already up. Thank you for all the help you gave Yvonne around here. I hope she at least rewarded you with great meals and a little bit of fun."

"She did. And some really good books." After the hug, she looked at Yvonne. "She's been great, and I'm going to miss everyone here."

Yvonne had a huge lump in her throat that she'd had since she woke up this morning. She was going to miss Eden like crazy, and she'd chosen to ride to the airport because she didn't want Eden making the long trip by herself.

"I guess I better go," Eden said. "I have one more goodbye before we head for the airport."

Yvonne was sure that saying goodbye to Samuel would be the hardest of all for her cousin. They had agreed to meet at the cottage after Samuel got off work at noon.

Samuel sat in the chair on the front porch of the cottage. He hadn't slept much knowing Eden was leaving today. They'd spent as much time as they could together this last week, but they had avoided being alone in the cottage for fear of rumors spreading. With all Samuel's chores, work, and obligations, it hadn't been enough time.

After his mother had taken them to supper the week before, the climate had changed all around. She seemed to accept—and even respect—Samuel's choice to explore his feelings as related to God and his future. She'd also been kind to Eden and sympathetic about the loss of her mother.

Now that he had all this freedom, some support from his family, and an opportunity to explore the outside world, it didn't hold the allure it did before. It only made things worse that he wouldn't have Eden to talk to. He hoped to get a mobile phone soon, but it wouldn't be the same as seeing her in person. She tried to explain to him that they could video chat, but Samuel was skeptical that he could afford a phone that allowed for that.

He stood up when a blue van pulled into his driveway,

willing himself not to cry and feeling more lost than ever. He hadn't left home for Eden, but it had been a bonus to have her around even though things hadn't panned out the way he had hoped.

His heart flipped in his chest when she stepped out of the van and started toward the cottage. He would want to kiss her goodbye, but Yvonne was in the car. Eden looked beautiful in a bright-pink blouse and white pants that hit just above her ankles. Her blonde hair was wavy as if freshly curled, and her pink toenails matched her shirt.

"You look so pretty," he said as she walked up the porch steps.

Her eyes watered. "Remember, we said this isn't 'Goodbye,' only 'See you later.'"

He nodded but wondered if that was true. Even if he got a phone, they might talk for a while, but distance would likely cause things to dwindle. Eden would meet someone else. Samuel didn't think he would ever find someone to fill her void.

"*Ya*, I know." He tried to smile, failing miserably. "We'll see each other later."

Were they just two star-crossed teenagers from two totally different worlds who were experiencing love for the first time? At least, it was love for Samuel, even though he'd never told her.

"I'm coming back. I don't know when, but I am."

She spoke with such conviction that Samuel wanted to believe her. "I hope so," he managed to say.

"I don't have long, or I'll miss my plane." She shrugged. "I guess that wouldn't be so bad."

Samuel pulled her into a hug. "I'm going to miss you so much."

"Believe me, I'll be missing you too." She inched out of his arms and pointed a finger at him. "Get a phone, mister."

He tried again to feign a smile. "I will." Then he cupped her cheeks in his hands and decided he wasn't going to miss this opportunity. "Eden, I *lieb* you. I know it hasn't been that long, but I do, and I'm sure of it."

A tear escaped and rolled down her cheek, and Samuel gently brushed it away with his thumb.

"I love you, too, and I'm sure also." She leaned up and kissed him on the cheek.

Samuel was filled with joy and torture all rolled into uncertainty, but he wasn't going to let that be their goodbye kiss, whether Yvonne was watching or not. He pressed his mouth to hers, hoping she could feel the way he felt about her.

As they forced themselves to separate, she tearfully said, "See you later."

All Samuel managed to get out was, "Later."

Yvonne's heart sat in her throat as she watched Samuel and Eden say goodbye. This was probably puppy love or some version of it, but whatever it was, she could tell by their expressions that they were both hurting.

When Eden slid into the back seat of the van, she fell into Yvonne's arms and cried.

"You can head to the airport now," Yvonne said to

the driver as she held Eden in her arms, stroking her hair. "Sweetheart, I'm so sorry. I know how much this hurts."

"I don't want to go, Yvonne." Eden struggled to catch her breath. "It's not just Samuel." She lifted herself up and swiped at her tears. "It's you, it's Abraham, and even Jake. It's the bookstore, the peacefulness here . . . Mostly it's you." She buried her head into Yvonne's chest, crushing her heart that was breaking as full-on tears came on for Yvonne as well.

"Eden, you are so special," she said, sniffling. "And you are welcome back any time." She eased her away, dabbed at her eyes, then cupped Eden's cheeks. "And don't stay gone too long."

"I won't." She snuggled back into Yvonne's embrace and stayed there until they arrived at the airport.

Yvonne stepped out of the van when the driver did. As he made his way to the back to get Eden's luggage, her cousin slowly stepped out of the van. Face-to-face now, Eden's bottom lip trembled, as did Yvonne's.

"Call me when you land. I'll keep *mei* phone on," Yvonne said, sniffling. "And call me a lot," she said as she pulled her into a hug. "I'll check *mei* phone often, and if I miss a call from you, I'll call you back as soon as I can."

"I will." Eden walked to the back of the van, and Yvonne followed. Eden picked up her red suitcase and another small bag Yvonne had given her to use for trinkets she'd purchased as well as some books Yvonne had bought her to take back with her. "Yvonne?" Eden said.

Yvonne waited.

"You're going to be an awesome mom."

"Thank you, sweetheart. I hope so." Yvonne put a hand on her heart.

Eden began to sob. "I love you. I love you so much." She dropped her suitcase and bag and rushed into Yvonne's arms.

"Oh, *mei* sweet *maedel*, I *lieb* you too. So much." Yvonne was sure there was a hole in her heart, a place that only Eden could fill. Their relationship had been unexpected, but it was something Yvonne treasured now.

Eden finally picked up her suitcase and bag, then gazed into Yvonne's eyes. "Always call your kid 'sweetheart.' He or she will remember that kind of stuff."

Yvonne put a hand over her mouth, but all she could do was nod as Eden walked toward the terminal. It took everything she had not to call out to her and tell her to just stay. But life and legalities didn't always work that way.

The weeks passed for Eden, and she kept waiting to feel better, to not miss Samuel, Yvonne, Abraham, and the community. She talked to Yvonne often, even though it was a breach of the Amish rules to use telephones other than for business or emergencies. Yvonne joked that if that was the worst thing she ever did, God would forgive her.

Samuel still didn't have a phone, but his mother allowed him a short call every other day from the one cell phone they kept at their house, and he found other ways to call her, usually borrowing a coworker's phone.

He had moved back in with his folks a month after he'd taken possession of the cottage. Eden had seen that coming, but she was glad he was back home, and she hoped he never took his family for granted again. Maybe they had been too strict, but it was obvious that there was an abundance of love, and Eden believed that love really could conquer all.

As she sat in her history class, she tried to focus on the teacher, but as they often did, her thoughts kept drifting back to Indiana. Maybe enough time hadn't gone by for the hurt to stop.

Emma had told her not to worry about her living arrangements, that she could stay for as long as she wanted, and she'd told Eden she would buy her a car for her seventeenth birthday, even though her birthday wasn't quite here yet. Emma knew Eden wasn't happy, and her cousin did her best to brighten her days, so she faked it as best she could for Emma's sake.

Friday had rolled around, and a couple of girls Eden had been having lunch with asked her to hang out with them. She should have been thrilled to be included, especially since these girls were part of the "in crowd," a place Eden had always thought she wanted to be. But Samuel called on Friday nights, so she declined, knowing she wasn't going to make any close friends if she didn't accept some of their invitations.

"*Wie bischt*," he said when he called that evening. "I miss you."

It was the first thing he always said when he called. She crossed her legs beneath her where she was sitting on her bed—in her thermostat-controlled bedroom filled with cool air. Going without air conditioning was the only thing about Amish living that she didn't care for. Samuel said a person eventually got used to it. If she had stayed longer, like forever, maybe she would have gotten used to it also. "I miss you too."

They were barely into the conversation when Emma knocked on her bedroom door but didn't wait to come in. "I need to talk to you," she said. "It's important."

"Samuel, can I call you back? Or can you call me back in a little while? Emma needs to talk to me and says it's important."

After the call ended, Emma sat on Eden's bed, then handed her an envelope. Emma was a hard person to read in general, but right now, she was almost scaring Eden with her blank expression.

What could be so important about this envelope?

Yvonne looked around the bookstore with sheet rock torn from the walls, two-by-fours in full view, and a cloud of dust that hung in the air. They'd sectioned off one portion of the bookstore for patrons, but the bulk of it was under construction. The effort had been worth the reward. She glanced at the thirty-six coins laid out on the counter, all found randomly within the walls. It was crazy and thrilling and just plain fun since they would be able to pay for the repairs.

Eva and Abraham had joined her and Jake every chance they got, and Yvonne wished Eden could be here for all the fun. Samuel had stopped by a few times, but it seemed hard for him, like it reminded him of Eden.

Eden and Yvonne spoke often, and sometimes it was heartbreaking to hear her talking about how much she missed Indiana and that she still struggled with the loss of her mother. She was in possession of her mother's ashes, but she hadn't decided what to do with them yet. Emma said she hadn't made any close friends this year in school either. Yvonne wondered if her continuing long-distance relationship with Samuel was more than the puppy love she had thought it might be. Their feelings weren't waning on either end.

"Okay, that's thirty-six times five hundred dollars," Yvonne said as she punched the numbers into the battery-operated calculator they kept on the counter. "That's eighteen thousand dollars." She laughed. "Wow. Unbelievable." She glanced around at the mess. "Your *grossdaadi* would be so proud that you are using these coins to renovate the bookstore. He'd be even prouder that you've gone to a lot of extra effort to keep things as original as you can."

"*Ya*, I don't want to lose that historic marker they presented to us, remember?" Jake scooped all the coins into a plastic bag. "I thank the Lord every day that we found these coins."

Yvonne thought back to the day she'd accepted the historic plaque on Jake's behalf since she wasn't Amish yet and could be photographed. "That seems so long ago."

Yvonne was lost in recollections when Esther and Lizzie walked into the bookstore. The elder of the widows, Esther, carried a large picnic basket.

"We're too old to help." Lizzie shuffled her dentures around in her mouth, something that had become as much a part of Lizzie as her limbs. Yvonne didn't think Lizzie would ever be able to keep those teeth still in her mouth. "But we brought lots of goodies for the workers."

Yvonne laughed. "*Ach*, well . . . at the moment it's just me and Jake. Our other halves are busy. Eva took the *boppli* for her regular checkup, and Abraham is at work."

"More for us," Jake said, smiling as Esther set the basket on the counter.

"Lizzie needs more books." Esther's eyes darted to the left where the filled bookshelves had been.

Yvonne pointed toward the gift section. "The books are over there. It's crowded with the gift items and books all sharing the same space. Let me know if you need help with anything."

"How's the treasure hunt going?" Lizzie raised her eyebrows up and down. "Find more coins since we were here last time?"

Yvonne couldn't recall the widows' last visit. One day seemed to run into the next as she and Jake worked long but exciting hours. They had started yelling "Ding, ding!" every time they found one of the coins. Word had gotten out about what they were doing. Yvonne didn't think anyone would ever steal from Jake—at least no one who knew about the coins—but he had been hiding them in the basement in a fireproof box that didn't look like it would survive the heat. Yvonne wasn't sure that was the best plan in case a fire did break out, but they'd never had a fire at the bookstore, Jake had told her.

"We're up to thirty-six."

"That's *gut*." Lizzie grinned. She turned to Yvonne. "How is your young cousin doing back in Texas?"

"I think okay, but she misses Samuel. They were *gut* friends, and it's been hard on them both." Yvonne didn't want to make it sound as bad as it was. Anna had told her that Samuel moped around even though she and Leroy had compromised, agreeing he could enjoy some privileges during his running-around period.

Opportunities that Samuel hadn't taken them up on.

"Maybe the *maedel* needs to come back. People talk, and I think we all know those *kinner* were more than just *gut* friends." Lizzie clicked her tongue as she shook her head. "Sad when an opportunity for *lieb* doesn't have a chance to flourish."

Yvonne stifled a grin. It was a typical response for Lizzie, always the optimist when it came to love. The woman read more romance novels than anyone she'd known. "*Gott* will direct their paths, but Eden is still in school, and she has another year too. I'm sure she will visit. Maybe over the holidays, spring break, and hopefully over the summer."

Esther glanced at Yvonne's stomach, and Yvonne folded her hands across her growing belly. "He or she is very active," she said. "I'm about four and a half months along." She and Abraham had gone public with their news once the doctor felt they had reached a point where Yvonne could expect to carry full term without foreseeable complications.

Jake cleared his throat. "I'm going to the appraiser to see exactly where we're at." He had put the plastic bag of coins inside a brown paper bag. On his way to the door, he nodded at Esther and Lizzie, then pointed outside. "*Mei* driver is here."

Both women smiled as he walked by, but Lizzie turned

her attention back to Yvonne. "I always knew those coins were buried here somewhere. *Gott* was just waiting for the perfect opportunity to reveal them so Jake could make the repairs to this place."

Lizzie and Esther were old enough to remember the old man who had run a general store in the building, but Lizzie was one of the few who had actually believed the coins were hidden within the walls.

"*Ach*, well, it's been crazy the way they are randomly hidden here and there. I'm thrilled for Jake too. He loves this place, and it's his *grossdaadi*'s legacy." She glanced around. "We haven't found any more coins in a few days, and all the wood is exposed. If there are any left, they will likely stay buried. Jake has enough to make all the repairs. He met with an architect a while back, and he has contractors scheduled to start soon."

"I'm sure members of the community would have helped him even if it is getting close to harvest season," Esther said.

"*Ya*, I think so, too, but Jake didn't want to burden anyone, especially this time of year."

"I need books." Lizzie raised her chin and eyed the mess on the other side of the room before she turned to her sister. "I'll be over there." She pointed to the books, some on shelves, some in boxes.

After she'd walked away, Esther frowned. "I don't know how healthy it is for Lizzie to read so many romance books at her age."

"At least they are all clean books." Yvonne grinned. "And we all like a happily-ever-after ending."

"True." Esther chuckled. "Maybe I'll find myself a nice *lieb* story."

Yvonne nodded to where Lizzie was thumbing through a book. "Go have a look."

Two men arrived in a car in the parking lot. Yvonne recognized them to be the roofers, and Jake had left a deposit check for them. She couldn't wait to see Jake's vision become a reality. They'd agreed to expand the back room to include a propane oven so it would be easier to heat lunches and baked goods, as opposed to the heating plate they were using. He was also going to add more storage space.

It's going to be great, Yvonne thought as she waited for the men to enter.

CHAPTER 24

Eden read through the paperwork Emma had given her with her jaw dropped the entire time.

Emma put an arm around her. "It's a lot to take in, I know."

It was more than hard to take in. Eden was gobsmacked. "When did my mom have the time"—she swiped at her eyes—"or the inclination to get a life-insurance policy with me as the beneficiary?"

Emma eased her arm away and sighed. "Jill had problems. No one will dispute that. And based on what I've heard, she wasn't the greatest mom. But at the end of the day, I know she loved you, and I'm sure she was filled with regret." She crossed one leg over the other and twisted until she was facing Eden. "This opens a lot of possibilities for you. Even though the school year has barely started, and you've got another year after this one, it's never too soon to start thinking about where you might want to go to college."

"College?" Eden blinked her eyes a few times at the realization that she could afford to further her education with the life-insurance money. "I never even considered college before. I just assumed that my grades and lack of money would prevent me from going."

"Well, that's all changed." Emma patted her on the leg. "It's nothing you must decide right this minute. And, as I told you before, you are welcome to stay here as long as you'd like."

Eden could barely find her voice. "Thank you."

"I'm off to shower and get ready for bed." Emma kissed her on the forehead. "Sleep well."

Eden didn't think she'd sleep at all. She reread the insurance policy with her as the sole beneficiary, and she thanked God that she had been able to tell her mother goodbye and that she loved her. She dialed Samuel's number right away and hoped he was still near the family cell phone.

He answered on the first ring.

"You're never going to believe this," she said in a shaky voice. "My mom had an insurance policy, and she left me some money. Well, not just *some* money, but a considerable amount of money. I can go to college, or a trade school, or whatever I want to do."

Samuel was quiet.

"Are you there?"

Samuel wanted to be happy for Eden. She deserved to go to college, to do and be whatever she wanted. But her choices would take her even farther away from him, both figuratively and geographically.

"That's great," he said as he tried to muster up as much enthusiasm as he could.

"I'm in shock." She paused. "I never thought of myself as college material, but maybe that's because I never saw that option in the cards. I just figured I would finish high school, get a job, and get a small apartment I could afford."

Samuel could already feel her slipping away before she'd even received the money. "Now you can do whatever you want."

She let out a nervous laugh. "What I want to do is buy a plane ticket and go back to Indiana, to you, to that peacefulness I feared I would never find again. I miss you so much that it physically hurts sometimes."

"I know that feeling," he said as elation began to build. "So, come back."

"I can't. Not now, anyway. I need to finish school. My mom never did, and I've always promised myself that I would get my high-school diploma." She paused. "Ugh. And I have two years left."

"We have schools here," he said, trying to keep the comment light. Two years felt like an eternity.

His heart sank again when she seemed to ignore the comment and continue on about where she might want to go to college.

"*Ya*, I understand," he said. "You should have everything you want in life."

"I guess I just need some time to let this soak in. I don't care about what the money can buy me, so to speak, but it does give me some options that I didn't ever think I would have." She was quiet. He knew it was a lot to think about. "How's it going at home?"

"*Gut. Mei mamm* and *daed* have kept their promise—that if I moved back, I could have a real *rumschpringe* if I let them know when and where I was going so they don't worry. I still haven't really done anything. My heart is somewhere else."

"Mine too. I love you, Samuel, and I miss you so much."

He closed his eyes and tried to picture her beautiful face smiling back at him. The family cell phone didn't have video capabilities, and he still hadn't been able to afford to get his own phone, much less one that would allow for video calls. Technically, smartphones weren't permitted, but if his parents didn't see him using it, they'd let it slide based on all the things they had come to agree upon. "I *lieb* you, too, Eden. I'm sure of it." He lay back on his bed and draped an arm across his forehead. He pictured her finishing high school, then going off to college. She would meet someone else.

"I'm sure too."

They were both quiet. "Maybe you could come here, to Texas? I think you'd like Texas more than where I lived in California. I have enough money to pay for you to get here."

Samuel sat up. Was she asking him to move there? "You mean, like for a visit?"

"Yeah. Don't you get any vacation from your job?"

The thought of seeing her caused his pulse to spike. "*Ya,* I get a vacation." He was still trying to figure out exactly what she was saying, but it sounded like a visit and another goodbye. It was better than nothing, he supposed. Or maybe . . . "You could come here to visit?"

"I can't think of anything I would like more, but I have school."

"*Ya*, you're right." He swallowed back a huge lump forming in his throat. "I guess I better go before *mei mamm* comes in and tells me my time is up." His mother was downstairs chatting with two women in her quilting group about their next project. He doubted she knew he was on the phone, but he didn't want Eden to hear his voice crack.

"Don't do that, Samuel. Don't close up like that. You know I love you, and we will work something out to be together."

Even if that was true, would Eden be giving up these new opportunities and regret it later? He didn't think he could live in Texas, that far away from his family. At one time, when it wasn't anything more than a fantasy, it seemed like he could. But Eden had been right—he had a loving family, and he couldn't see his life without them in it. Even if he chose not to be baptized, his family would still be close by.

He wondered if breaking things off would be the unselfish thing to do so that she would choose her life without factoring him into it.

"Samuel, talk to me," she said.

"I'm just thinking, that's all."

"Don't overthink it. I just found out about this life-insurance money. It's still soaking in for me. I'm aware that money can't buy love, but it can buy plane and train tickets so we can see each other."

Samuel didn't like the idea of her paying for things like that. He'd grown up where the man was the head of the household. Yes, his mother assumed the role fairly often, but his father took care of the family financially. He wasn't comfortable taking money from Eden, and he didn't see that changing.

"Let's talk tomorrow, okay?" Eden said.

"*Ya*, okay."

After they said goodbye, Samuel lay back down on the bed. The kindest thing he could do for Eden was to let her go.

Anna hadn't seen Samuel since supper, and he hadn't eaten much, always a sign that something was bothering him. She knocked on his door.

"Samuel, is everything all right?"

"*Ya.*"

"Can I come in?"

"*Ya.*"

He was lying on the bed. It wasn't dark yet, and she could see by his sober expression that he wasn't all right. Her son had moped around since Eden left six weeks ago. Anna had thought he would be better by now. They'd given him permission to mingle in the outside world, but to her knowledge, he hadn't taken advantage of his new privileges.

"You don't look all right," she said as she sat in the rocking chair by his small desk.

"I'm okay, *Mamm*."

She tried to think before she spoke, but there was only one thing to say. "I know you miss Eden. I can see it in your eyes, the way you don't seem to have that twinkle anymore."

"*Ya*, I miss her, but . . ." He sat up, dangled his feet over the bed. "I think I need to cut things off with her."

Anna took a deep breath. This should have been good news. Even though Eden was a nice girl, she was still a threat. Anna worried constantly that Samuel would save enough money, then go to Texas to be with her. "Cut things off?"

He nodded. "She got some life-insurance money from her mother. She can go to college now or do anything she wants. Things she'd never considered before." He shrugged. "It seems best to break up so she can pursue those things without having to worry about my feelings."

It was such a grown-up, unselfish way of thinking, and Anna was proud of her son for coming to that conclusion, but it left her feeling terrible. Despite it all, seeing her child in pain trumped everything else. "Samuel, this is your first *lieb*, and you're young. I know you'll find a nice girl in our community, someone Amish who will be a much better fit. It doesn't seem that way right now, but—"

Her son bolted from the bed, a mixture of hurt and anger springing to life in his eyes. "I'm not ever going to *lieb* anyone the way I *lieb* Eden. *Ya*, we're young, but so were you and *Daed*." He shook his head. "You got your wish. Eden will be out of *mei* life soon, and you'll be happy." He brushed past her, left his bedroom, and closed the door behind him, leaving Anna in the rocking chair alone with her thoughts.

He had no idea how very wrong he was. It had never been Anna's wish for her son to have a broken heart.

What if this really is true love?

Yvonne, Abraham, Jake, and Eva sat at the kitchen table in the back room. It was after ten o'clock, and they'd all been sitting there for almost two hours. Eva had left the baby with her parents for the night. They'd missed supper, and darkness had set in over an hour ago. Three lanterns lit the small room.

"We've talked this through over and over again." Jake gently pounded both fists on the table in front of him. "Stupid, stupid, stupid."

Her friend and boss had been beating himself up since he'd returned from the coin appraiser—two of them, actually—only to discover that the coins they'd found weren't worth even close to what they had assumed. All but three of the silver dollars weren't worth more than fifty dollars each. Jake had three thousand two hundred and fifty dollars' worth of coins and three thousand in the bank that could go toward the project without bankrupting the bookstore. In total he had six thousand two hundred and fifty dollars to go toward a project bid of seventeen thousand.

"Jake, I assumed, just the same way you did, that all of the coins would be roughly valued the same since they were within a few years from each other." Yvonne had learned, along with Jake, that a coin's value was dependent on the number of coins minted that year. Back when the old man who owned the general store had stashed the coins in the wall, he probably thought he was sitting on a fortune. In today's world, it wasn't a fortune at all.

"All I have is enough money to buy the supplies. Most of the bids were for labor." Jake sighed and shook his head.

"All isn't lost," Abraham said. "We will figure this out."

Yvonne's mind had been on overdrive since Jake shared the bad news with them. "I think I know how we can do this, but we would need to close the store for a few days."

Jake glared at her—a first since she'd been working for him. "If anything, I need to keep the store open longer, not close it. I'll go bankrupt for sure."

Yvonne knew he only spoke to her harshly because he was understandably upset. "Just hear me out."

Before she even finished detailing her plan, Jake was shaking his head. "It's too close to harvest. I'm not asking for help."

"She's right, Jake." Eva had sat quietly for most of the informal meeting. "It's the only way to save the bookstore."

Samuel hadn't spoken to Eden in two weeks. He had no way to know if she had called since his mother kept their cell phone turned off. Yvonne had caught up to him and told him that Eden was trying to reach him. He had confided in her and told her that he thought it would be best to let Eden go so she could finish school in a big city and pursue her education anywhere she wanted. He'd gotten teary when he told Yvonne that it seemed better not to say goodbye. Yvonne highly disagreed, but when he almost broke down in front of her, she'd hugged him and said that everything would be okay.

Samuel disagreed. He didn't think he'd ever feel okay again. But today was a big day, and he needed to keep himself together.

He arrived in his buggy at the bookstore at the designated time of daybreak. Buggies were everywhere. The parking lot was full, and buggies lined the side of the road, with families filing out and walking to the bookstore. Trucks filled with lumber, tar, roofing supplies, and various equipment sat in a field across the street. It was a barn-raising of sorts, but today's project was the bookstore. Despite Jake's objections, Yvonne had rallied the community to come to her boss's aid, and folks were happy to participate. Even Samuel couldn't imagine not having the bookstore in their community.

Inside, people scurried around. Jake looked scattered, scared, and elated as he personally thanked everyone who walked in.

"Where do you want me?" Samuel asked Jake when he finally pinned him down.

"Can you believe Yvonne did this?" Jake glanced around at the people bustling about. "It's harvest time, but everyone made the time to help me keep the bookstore."

Samuel smiled, which felt good. He'd been wrapped in sadness the past couple of weeks. "Why do you look so surprised? It's what we do. How is this any different from a barn-raising?"

"I am a blessed man." Jake hung his head, then quickly lifted it. "*Ach*, Lizzie was looking for you. She's in the back with Esther. They brought a lot of food, baked goods, and tea."

On the way to see Lizzie, he passed his mother and Yvonne talking. He couldn't help but wonder how much Yvonne had told his mother about him breaking things off with Eden—the cowardly way. His mother had tried to talk to him about it, but he'd brushed her off. The less he talked about it, the better. Every time he thought about Eden, his stomach twisted in knots, then his heart felt like it was breaking.

"You're late," Lizzie said when he walked into the small kitchen area in the back. It looked like preparation for a wedding with food spread everywhere and several ladies bumping elbows as they maneuvered around in the small space. "I need you to go to the inn and get a paper bag full of plastic plates and silverware. I forgot it, and I need it. People can't eat with their hands." She shuffled her teeth around and looked up at him.

Samuel opened his mouth to say, "Why me?"

"And before you say, 'Why me?' you need to stop at the cottage too. You left two pair of black slacks when you moved out, and the new renter found them."

She was right. He was short two pair of pants. "*Ya*, okay."

He wound his way through the crowd, went back to his buggy, and left for the Peony Inn. The bag was where Lizzie said. He put it in his buggy, then drove across the field to the cottage. There was a car parked out front. His mother had mentioned that Lizzie had rented out his former home, but he didn't realize the new person had occupied it already.

He knocked on the door. His jaw dropped when Eden opened the door. His heart flipped in his chest as he struggled to find words to describe the joy bubbling up inside him.

Is she really here?

He blinked his eyes, then refocused to make sure he wasn't dreaming. He'd dreamed of her so much since she'd been gone.

She slammed her hands to her hips and glowered at him. "I should smack you for not calling me."

"Uh . . . what are you doing here?" He asked the question knowing he was smiling ear to ear.

"It's a good thing for you that Yvonne told me you were as miserable as me. Otherwise that smack would be coming your way. You don't abandon people you love."

After another moment of shocked silence, Samuel grabbed her in his arms and smothered her with kisses. "What are you doing here?" he asked again as he held her, reassuring himself she was really in his arms. He had missed this feeling more than he could put into words.

"I live here." She pulled away and waved a hand around the room as he stepped over the threshold. "I arrived two days ago. Look around. This is how it's done. Nice and clean." She sniffed the air. "Smell that candle I have burning? Very homey, wouldn't you say?"

Samuel stood with his mouth open, trying to make his brain compute what she was saying. "You've been here two days? Why didn't you call me? And . . . why? What about school?" He shook his head vigorously to make sure he wasn't dreaming.

"I had a few things to take care of before I talked to you. I needed to feel like this move was as much about me as it was about you. Meaning I couldn't move here just for you. I had to be sure that my intentions were lined up."

Sometimes Eden seemed a lot older than she was. "Okay . . ." He tipped his head to one side, still confused—and perhaps the happiest he'd been in his life.

"I want to finish school. It's important to me. Yvonne was granted guardianship of me, and she is going to homeschool me. I'll go to her house for two or three hours per day. Not to toot my own horn, but I am way ahead in my classes compared to the school here. That's why I chose homeschooling, and Yvonne was all for it. I'll graduate earlier this way."

She glanced around the space again and shrugged. "I decided not to live with them, even though she offered repeatedly, because I need a place of my own to grow into my own person. We got permission from the court for that too." She smiled. "Besides, they have a baby on the way, and it would be crowded. They need that time as a family together. And even if you don't want to be with me, I'm staying here anyway because I love it here, and it's my number one choice of places to be."

Samuel burst out laughing. "If you can't tell how much I want to be with you, let me show you again." He pulled her into his arms and kissed her the way he'd been dreaming about. "I love you. I want to always be with you. Forever."

After making up for more lost time, Eden said, "Samuel, I don't know if I can convert. I mean, live an Amish lifestyle. But it's something I'm considering, which complicates things because I know you are thinking about not living the Amish way."

He shook his head. "I decided not long ago that I don't

want to leave. Everything I have is here. Everything but you, and now that has changed. I'm just glad you're here, and we'll figure everything out."

She walked to the couch and returned with two folded pair of slacks, then handed them to him, shaking her head. "I found them under the bed."

"*Danki.*" Samuel was still reeling with surprise and elation. "I'm glad Lizzie forgot that bag and told me about *mei* pants."

Eden laughed aloud. "Lizzie didn't *forget* the bag. It was her idea to send you to get it, then to find me at the cottage." She tapped a finger to her chin. "I'm not sure who was more excited about me being here, me or Lizzie. Yvonne said Lizzie and her sister, Esther, are known matchmakers. Lizzie practically salivated to be involved somehow when Yvonne told her I was moving here to surprise you."

Samuel chuckled. "*Ya*, Lizzie and Esther are known for that."

"And . . . I feel like I'm following in Yvonne's footsteps in a way. We've talked a lot about her spiritual journey, how she wasn't brought up Christian but searched until she found her way to a life with Abraham as an Amish wife. I found God on my own, with a little help from a friend, but I want to continue to learn about other religions, including the Amish. I want to choose what's best for me. I'd be lying if I said I wasn't taking you into consideration, but I'm not going to convert just to be with you. We're young. I feel like our relationship needs time to grow."

"I hope it's okay if I secretly pray that we will end up

together in the end." Samuel stared into her beautiful—and wise—eyes.

She offered him her pinky, and he gave her his, and they locked their fingers together. "Pinky swear, and here's to 'hopefully ever after.' I believe in 'happily ever after,' but for now, let's be hopeful." She lowered her hand. "I love you."

"I *lieb* you too."

She held up a finger. "One more thing I forgot to mention. I spoke with the bishop about my intentions. What a nice man."

"Did you just go up to his door, or . . . ?" Samuel couldn't imagine her doing that.

"No, I didn't go by myself. I wouldn't have even known where he lived."

"That's *gut* that Yvonne went with you."

She tilted her head to one side. "I didn't say Yvonne took me."

Samuel scratched his cheek. "Who, then?"

Eden smiled. "Your mother."

His eyes widened.

"We had lunch the day after I arrived—yesterday. It wasn't really planned or anything. I ran into her at that little café we used to go to. She had stopped in for coffee and asked if she could join me. We talked, and when I told her about my plans, she offered to take me to see the bishop. We went straight from the café. I asked her not to tell you I was here so I could surprise you."

Samuel's love for his mother filled him in an unexpected way. She'd gone the extra mile, and he would remember to thank her later.

She motioned toward the door, then walked that way, Samuel following. After they were on the porch, she locked the deadbolt. "You're also my ride to the bookstore."

Samuel took a bow. "At your service."

Before they got into the buggy, Eden stopped and latched on to both of his hands. "I'm happy to be here."

Samuel had that knot in his throat again as he swallowed. "And I'm happy you're here." He kissed her with all the passion he'd stored up just for her. "Here's to hopefully ever after."

"To hopefully ever after," she said.

EPILOGUE

One year later . . .

Eden stood with Samuel on the Williams Covered Bridge, built in 1884 and closed to traffic in 2010. They had hired a driver to take them from Montgomery to Williams, about a forty-minute drive by car and too far for the buggies.

As their driver waited in the car, Eden and Samuel had made the short trek to the red tunnel-like structure that spanned the East Fork of the White River. Eden had the urn with her mother's ashes clutched to her chest. There were a few broken boards on the side of the bridge that provided a makeshift window.

They were quiet for a while, and Eden silently prayed for peace for her mother now that she was in the arms of Jesus.

"I can't believe it's been a year." She pushed her sunglasses up on her head and peered out over the rushing river, overflowing from the recent rains. "I don't know if I'm supposed to say something aloud before I release her ashes." She turned to Samuel with tears in her eyes.

"I think that anything you choose to do will be perfect." He put an arm around her, and they stood silently.

Eden took the lid from the urn as a tear rolled down her cheek. With both hands, she held it over the water. It had been a year since her mother died, and Eden tried to focus on that last video communication with her as opposed to all the years before. She remained grateful that she'd had the opportunity to forgive her mother and tell her she loved her prior to her death.

Samuel moved behind her and put his arms around her waist as Eden released her mother's remains into the water, picturing her running free in heaven the way the water below them flowed freely underneath the bridge.

"Bye, Mom." She dabbed at her eyes as she watched the breeze catching the ashes and carrying them to the water below. "Be at peace."

She turned to Samuel. "*Danki* for coming with me."

He brushed back loose hair that had fallen from beneath her prayer covering. Eden had been baptized into the Amish faith two months ago, and she still couldn't get her long blonde hair to stay beneath the white head covering. Yvonne had homeschooled Eden, and they'd managed to cover two years of work in only one. Eden had been dedicated to getting her high-school diploma even though the Amish only completed their education through the eighth grade. Finishing high school had been a promise Eden had made to herself long before she'd met Samuel or her wonderful family in Indiana. Her decision to become Amish and marry Samuel didn't include college, but Eden loved learning new things, and the world was a place of wonder, with or without college. And growing her faith was a top priority. She was also almost completely fluent in the Pennsylvania dialect.

Eden and Samuel were secretly engaged, but it was customary that the Amish didn't publish the news until a wedding was drawing near. Their families were aware and supportive of their intentions, and most of the community expected a wedding soon, but they remained tight-lipped about their plans. Eden still lived in the cottage and worked at the bookstore. She'd slowly taken on more hours in the beautifully renovated structure so that Yvonne could spend more time taking care of her husband and baby, whom they'd named Bethany.

Samuel still lived with his parents and had recently bought himself and Eden a five-acre tract of land where they would build their home. Eden had bought her own horse that she kept in the back pasture of the Peony Inn. She rode as often as she could, sometimes with Samuel and sometimes alone. She didn't think she'd ever tire of the freedom she felt while riding. God had blessed her far more than she could have imagined.

"We should go. Yvonne and Abraham are expecting us by four. It's date night for them." She grinned. "Yvonne's idea, but maybe it's something we should incorporate into our relationship when we're married, especially after we have *kinner*."

Yvonne was a wonderful mother, as Eden had known she would be, and Abraham had stepped easily into the role of father. Eden and Samuel spent a lot of time with them. Eden had also become close to Anna and Samuel's sisters.

She'd finally found the family she'd always wanted and the peacefulness that had eluded her for such a long time.

They had taken their pinky-swear toward a hopefully ever after and turned it into their own happily ever after. Eden planned never to take God's blessings for granted, and she looked forward to the family she and Samuel would have. A home filled with faith, hope, love, and happily-ever-afters.

ACKNOWLEDGMENTS

Thanks and praise to God for continuing to trust me to do His work, books that I hope entertain readers and glorify Him.

To my family and friends, thank you for always supporting me, especially my husband, Patrick.

Natasha Kern, my fabulous agent, your continued support and friendship means so much to me, and I thank you from the bottom of my heart for your wisdom and spiritual guidance.

To the entire team at HarperCollins Christian Fiction, your grace, kindness, and willingness to work with me on deadlines and personal hurdles is always appreciated. What a wonderful journey this has been. I'm blessed to have you all in my corner.

Wiseman's Warriors, it's an honor to dedicate this story

to you, my faithful street team who continues to help me spread the word about my books. You ladies are awesome.

I love and appreciate you, Janet Murphy, for your friendship, knowledge about the industry, and your additional role as my continued voice of reason (not always an easy job, lol).

Thank you to my readers for believing in me and my stories.

DISCUSSION QUESTIONS

1. In the beginning of the story, Yvonne is struggling not to judge Eden based on her background and circumstances. Have you ever been guilty of presumptions about a person that turned out not to be true? If so, how did you handle the situation?
2. People often make comparisons between Amish and non-Amish people. In this story, there are many similarities that are relatable to parents, no matter their religious denomination, when it comes to teenagers. What are some examples of this in the book?
3. Which character in the story could you relate to the most, and why?
4. Several early readers said they cried while reading certain parts of the story. Did you? And, if so, what scene or scenes did you find so emotional that it brought you to tears?

5. Do you think Eden would have always regretted not being able to tell her mother goodbye? In what ways might it have affected her down the line?
6. Many of my readers tell me that they only read Amish fiction books. Whether you are one of those people or not, why do you think some folks are drawn to this type of Christian fiction book? Escapism? Longing for a more peaceful way of life?
7. If you could alter the story and have a character take a different path, who would it be and how do you see their journey unfolding?
8. Were you intrigued by the mysterious coin collection? Have you ever been a collector? Did you suspect that the coins might not all be the same in value, despite having dates that were close together?
9. As readers, most of us love bookstores. How do you envision Jake's store based on the descriptions in the series? Discuss, and see if everyone has the same general idea about what the bookstore looks like.
10. Eden was thrilled to be able to ride a horse for the first time. Is there anyone in your group who hasn't ridden a horse? If so, is there a reason, or just a lack of opportunity?

From the Publisher

GREAT BOOKS

ARE EVEN BETTER WHEN THEY'RE SHARED!

Help other readers find this one:

- Post a review at your favorite online bookseller
- Post a picture on a social media account and share why you enjoyed it
- Send a note to a friend who would also love it—or better yet, give them a copy

Thanks for reading!

The Amish Bookstore Series

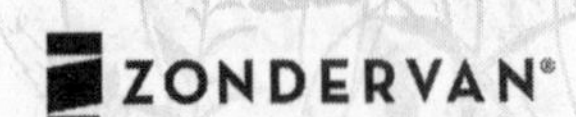

AVAILABLE IN PRINT, E-BOOK, AND AUDIO

The Amish Inn Series

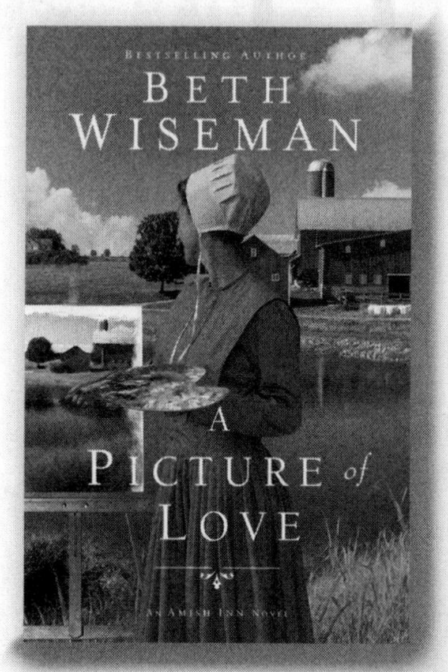

ABOUT THE AUTHOR

Photo by Emilie Hendryx

Bestselling and award-winning author Beth Wiseman has sold over two million books. She is the recipient of the coveted Holt Medallion, is a two-time Carol Award winner, and has won the Inspirational Reader's Choice Award three times. Her books have been on various bestseller lists, including CBA, ECPA, Christianbook, and *Publishers Weekly*. Beth and her husband are empty nesters enjoying country life in south-central Texas.

Visit her online at BethWiseman.com
Facebook: @AuthorBethWiseman
Twitter: @BethWiseman
Instagram: @bethwisemanauthor